OUT OF TIME

Martin Blake

Published by New Generation Publishing in 2015

Copyright © Martin Blake 2015

First Edition

www.newgeneration-publishing.com

 New Generation Publishing

1

She lies in an open stone coffin, the lid propped behind on its edge. The description on the plinth states that this was a well-to-do woman in what we would term middle age who lived and died in the fourth century. Her resting place was unearthed, literally, when a new housing estate was built in Arbury in the 1950s.

The jaw-bones have been set wide apart, as if frozen in a scream of horror at her violent awakening. The skull whose orbits once held her eyes is turned, slightly but disturbingly, towards the viewer. Her fingers curl inwards, giving gesture to her impotent fury. The skeletons of a mouse and a shrew remain within the coffin, the tiny creatures entombed as innocent victims of a more momentous death, rodent collateral. Were they mourned by their families? What terrors did they suffer as they struggled for life in total darkness until the air ran out? One of the dead woman's ankles has been gnawed.

Rosemary is by no means the first to be struck by the poignancy of the drama played out by this exhibit. The description indicates that Sylvia Plath observed this same scene while studying at Cambridge in the 1950s, and was inspired by it to write a poem entitled *All the Dead Dears*. Rosemary makes a note to look it up on the internet.

'We're closing in five minutes, Dr Torrance.'

She turns around to see a short, thin man with kindly brown eyes, dressed in a navy blue uniform surmounted by a peaked cap a size too large for his head. He smiles as he holds out his arm towards the exit.

'I'm sorry,' she says. 'I must have lost track of time.'

Outside the museum, she screws up her eyes against the harsh light of early summer. Traffic queues impatiently along Downing Street towards the St Andrew's Street junction, car horns sounding to no purpose as the rising wail from the siren of an approaching ambulance carves through the air. She walks in the opposite direction and crosses King's Parade heading towards the river, trying to filter out the rush-hour cacophony, only then realising that she has no idea how the museum custodian knows her name. Perhaps on one of her previous visits she was still wearing her library name-tag. Clenching and unclenching her fists, she veers away from the main road and makes her way along narrow passageways, past college gardens aflame with rudbeckias and dahlias and red-hot pokers, observes all the 'Keep to the path' signs and finally subsides onto the freshly-mown bank beneath the comforting embrace of a mature willow which is cooling its fingers in the sluggish waters of the River Cam. High above, a few clouds are starting to drift across the sky, but not in sufficient density to reduce the temperature. One of them has formed itself into the shape of a picture-book fairy, complete with wand and gossamer wings.

Not caring that the grass will stain her dress, Rosemary lies back and closes her eyes. The air is still and humid, and the white noise created by the drone of bees and hover-flies is on an unending loop. She hears, increasingly distantly, the cries and laughter of the young men and women on the flotilla of punts clogging the river, the commentaries of the boatered and waistcoated chauffeurs as they relate the arcane, legendary or downright fictional history of each college. At length she passes the seductive point at which these sounds begin to fade into another world, finally arriving at a place just this side of sleep, still controlling her senses but not her imagination.

'I thought I'd find you here.'

The voice is a familiar one, a warm, deep baritone which conjures up the vision of a hillside of heather and gorse and thistles. Rosemary ignores it.

'Wandering round the museum is no way to spend your afternoon off, especially on a hot summer day. You should get more fresh air.'

Still she makes no response, does not open her eyes.

'What's up, tongue worn out with—'

'What are you doing here, Adam? I want some time by

myself.'

'But now I've arrived, you don't mind me being here, do you?'

'Yes. Now please piss off and leave me alone.'

'I'll take that as an invitation to stay, then. You know, you're losing too much weight. It doesn't suit you. You should try and have regular meals.'

'I do. Mostly marmite sandwiches and yogurt.'

'Rosie, I'm only saying this because I care about you. You'll regret it if you don't look after yourself. I try to keep an eye on you, you know.'

'There's no need, I can look after myself. Anyway, why are you here?'

'I like to revisit familiar haunts. Did I ever tell you about the Anchor's main claim to fame? It was—'

'I already know. Syd Barrett used to drink there with Roger Waters.'

'Oh. Have I already mentioned that? Well, did you also know that—'

'Sylvia Plath and Ted Hughes used to meet up there. Adam, you're boring me.'

'No need to be like that. It's a piece of history.'

'Yes, well now so are you. Goodbye.'

'Do you really want me to go?'

'At this precise moment, yes. As someone once said, I vahnt to be alone. Come and see me tonight.'

It is a long street of renovated Victorian terraced houses, the narrow frontages adorned with hanging baskets and replacement windows with small, circular, Arts-and-Crafts stained glass panels. Rosemary is in no hurry to negotiate it. She suppresses a shudder as she approaches a house devoid of these decorative touches, but which is nonetheless impossible to ignore as its red-brick facade has been concealed behind beige mock-Cotswold stone cladding. Taking a deep breath, gripping her bottle of sauvignon blanc and thinking that perhaps she should have brought flowers as well, she walks up to the front door and rings the bell. From within, the ancient chimes distort the tune of 'Land of Hope and Glory' as if playing an old, stretched cassette tape. The door is opened by a thin woman in her fifties with short greying hair, sweating slightly and wearing a heavily soiled kitchen apron. Even as she stands in the doorway, every muscle in her body seems to be in motion. Her eyes protrude as if the skull around them has shrunk.

'Hi mum.'

'Rosemary dear, come on in, better late than never. Good God, whatever's happened to your dress? Have you been taking part in a gang bang on a compost heap?'

'Yes, I have, mum. You should have been there, you'd have loved it. You need new batteries in the front door bell, by the way.'

Her voice fades as she sweeps past the drawing room (a term her mother stubbornly refuses to part with), cluttered as always with coffee tables, standard lamps and glass equine ornaments, and makes for the kitchen where she knows she will find alcohol and company nearer her own age. A tall young man with light brown hair is waiting, leaning back against the sink, wine glass in hand. On the formica surface of the table in front of him is a vase containing chrysanthemums. He smiles readily.

'Rosie, you look like shit, as usual. You obviously need a drink.'

'Thanks, Jamie, make it a big one. And none of mum's drain clearer. That tight stripy shirt makes you look like a rent boy, by the way.'

'I know.' He lowers his voice. 'I'm only wearing it because mum hates it. I keep telling her I really am a rent boy, and I just go out with women for the sake of appearances. I think she's half-tempted to believe it.'

'Be careful what you wish for. She might stop seeing you as her blue-eyed boy.'

'Never. She needs one man in her life. Though I'm sure she's got a soft spot for you too. Somewhere. Deep down.'

'Don't be ridiculous,' Rosemary says. 'As far as mum's

4

concerned, I've been ploughing my own wanton furrow for years.'

'Your words, not mine. Hang on, I spy strangers.'

They fall silent as mum enters the kitchen. Rosemary makes a pretence of re-arranging the chrysanthemums.

'What plot are you two cooking up now?' mum says. 'Come on, out with it.'

Rosemary clears her throat, leaving her hand in front of her mouth to disguise her smile. 'Jamie was telling me that you've got a new stud.'

Jamie turns around and looks out of the kitchen window.

'Was he indeed?' mum says, staring at his back. 'Your father was enough to put up with for one lifetime, I can tell you, and he was no stud, not with me anyway. If Benedict Cumberbatch becomes available I may reconsider, but until then I'll keep my powder dry, thank you. Now, I hope you're both happy with lasagne. You've always said you like it.' A puff of smoke escapes as she opens the oven door. 'Oh dear, I hope it's not overdone. We can always scrape off the burnt bits.'

The burnt bits, it transpires, constitute a significant proportion of the whole. They eat furtively, forks delving deep for the edible fragments, to the backdrop of a silence interrupted only by the ringing of the telephone. Mum picks up her napkin as if to leave the table to answer it, sees her daughter and son frowning and replaces it. Whoever is calling does not leave a message. Long after the phone has ceased to ring, she continues to glance towards the hallway as if she can still somehow retrieve the call.

'Probably just a recorded message from some ambulance-chaser,' Jamie says at length. 'We get them all the time, they drive me mad.'

No-one picks up this potential thread of conversation. Rosemary notes that it has taken the best part of a bottle of wine for her to force down half of her plate of lasagne. After two more mouthfuls, she places her fork on the plate and pushes it away. She knows that she should compliment her mother and thank her for the effort she has put in, but the words refuse to form themselves.

The edible portion of the dinner consumed, the triad lean back in their chairs. Mum looks from Rosemary to Jamie and then back again. They avoid her gaze, and each other's.

'You know, I worry about you two, I really do.'

Rosemary rolls her eyes, knowing from previous experience the direction in which this opening gambit will lead. Jamie smirks.

'Neither of you seems to have any idea of getting a proper job.'

'Oh, I don't know,' Jamie says. 'I make good money, and there's plenty of variety. No two clients are ever the same.'

Mum's face screws up like a pug's. 'Don't be disgusting, James. I'm trying to be serious. I do worry so how you're going to end up. And I won't be around for ever to keep an eye on you.'

Rosemary empties her glass and replaces it on the table with a little more force than she intended, then makes a show of trying to replenish it from the empty bottle in front of her. Her mother's eyes narrow.

'I don't think there's any left. Look, Rosemary, I know things have been difficult for you, but I do think you've—'

'Rosie's brought another bottle,' Jamie says. 'It's in the fridge. I'll go and fetch it.'

He breezes out of the dining room, and without his mediating presence Rosemary feels the air stretch taut. She looks out of the window, hoping that some addition to the garden will offer a new topic of conversation, but sees only the usual tangle of honeysuckle, hydrangea and hybrid tea. Her eyes return to her mother who, to her alarm, is staring at her. At that moment Jamie returns with an open bottle and tops up her glass, then goes to do the same to mum's but she places her hand over the top, so he shrugs and refills his own.

'Now, who's for lemon meringue pie?' mum asks.

'I don't need a career,' Jamie says, 'I'm working on being a kept man. And when you think about it, Rosie has got a good job.'

Rosemary scowls at him for continuing the theme.

'In a library,' mum replies. 'It's not exactly glamorous.'

Rosemary takes a swig from her glass and breathes deeply, but her patience is already drawing close to breaking point.

'You worked most of your life as a dentist's receptionist, mum.'

'I was limited by what I could fit in between bringing up you two. You were always my first priority, not that I expect any thanks. Or have ever had any, for that matter.'

Rosemary continues to glare at her brother, demanding that he accept responsibility for re-igniting the controversy.

'Come on mum, be fair,' Jamie says. 'Rosie works in one of the top libraries in the country.'

'That's as may be. But I remember what your father always used to say.'

Rosemary's patience is being tested to destruction. 'Dad said lots of things, but he's been a bit quiet the last few years, hasn't he?'

'Now don't start, Rosemary. I know it's the wine talking.'

'No, it's me talking. Daddy's baby girl. Remember those days? I wonder where they went.'

Mum's lips form angry but voiceless words. Jamie sips from his glass, eyes fixed on a sauce stain on the tablecloth. Mum slaps her napkin down and strides out of the room. They see her moments later, striding up and down among the roses, drawing on a cigarette fit to burst her lungs.

'Bit harsh,' Jamie says.

'She asked for it.'

'That doesn't mean you have to oblige. Anyway, sorry to leave you with the washing up. Duty calls elsewhere.'

'Don't think of going anywhere. You can stay and take your share of responsibility for this disaster.'

'Sadly, I seem to have double-booked. And I don't like

to let people down.'

'Apart from your own family.'

'A bit below the belt. Anyway, she'll be all right when she's calmed down.'

Rosemary hears Jamie call goodbye to mum from the back door, then leave via the side gate to avoid returning through the house. She drains her glass.

'She must be an easy lay if she's waiting for you,' she says under her breath, even though no-one is in earshot.

The curtains are open, allowing the pale sodium glow of street lights to filter into the bedroom. She shifts onto her left side and sees a familiar clump of red hair sprawling across the pillow, wide shoulders moving in time with each intake of breath. She slides closer.

'Adam. Are you asleep?'

Adam's reply is muffled by his pillow. 'I never sleep. You know that.'

'I can't settle either,' she says.

'In your case it must be the sign of a guilty conscience. Are you still fretting about this evening?'

'It seems to get worse every time I see her. I end up saying things just to be hurtful.'

'The truth often hurts.'

'I expect more than platitudes from you, Adam.'

He turns towards her, his gaze rising slowly from her breasts to her face. Have his eyes lost a little of their old sparkle?

'Mothers and daughters always fight like pit-bulls,' he says. 'It doesn't mean they don't love each other, but they've spent years being rivals for the same man's affection. It's just nature, don't beat yourself up about it.'

'Ah, how could I have been so stupid? The scales have just fallen from my eyes. The reason I can't get on with mum is that deep down I'm jealous that she got to fuck dad and I didn't.'

'Come on Rosie, that's not—'

'I reminded her in no uncertain terms tonight that dad

8

walked out on her.'

'Ouch. But dare I suggest that your mum might actually bear some responsibility for that?'

'I'm sure she does, but I still wish I hadn't said it.'

'Just remember Adam's first Principle of Life.'

'Don't expect East Fife to win?'

'No, that's number six. The first is, Never apologise, someone else may already have got the blame.'

Rosemary lies on her back and stares at the ceiling. Adam's hand drifts across to her breast, and she places her own hand on top. She feels herself sliding into sleep, knowing that she has more to say.

The next morning, with daylight in her eyes, the hum of traffic in the street below and a sour taste in her mouth, she turns to confirm what she already knows, that Adam has gone. She places her hand on his pillow and feels that it is cold. She buries her face in it.

2

A large sign on the office door, white lettering on black perspex, reads: 'Roger Thomas, Head of Manuscripts'. A smaller one beneath it says: 'Rosemary Torrance, Research Assistant'. Rosemary opens the door and sees Roger hunched over his keyboard, typing laboriously with two long fingers. Beside him is a box containing a loosely-bound sheaf of yellowing papers. His dark hair is beginning to show tinges of grey at the temples, but he still somehow manages to look ageless. Perhaps sensing her attention, he looks up.

'Morning, Rosemary.'

'Morning, Roger.' She nods towards the papers. 'What have you got there?'

'A couple of hundred years' worth of estate records from a minor stately home in Norfolk.'

'Wow. Sounds riveting.'

'I'm having to breathe deeply to calm my racing pulse. You look a bit peaky by the way, if you don't mind me saying so.'

'Not sleeping too well recently. Still, I'm sure it'll pass.'

She sits at her desk and switches on her own computer. While it boots up, she stares at her reflection in the still-black screen; for a moment the face she sees looks unfamiliar, out of focus. At length the screen brightens and the library's home page bursts into view. She opens her e-mail, reads the first entry and groans.

'Sorry Roger, I've got to go on a treasure hunt. Another lost item. Allegedly.'

Turning the spring-loaded switch brings basement room 3 into time-limited illumination. The haze back-lit by the flickering lights represents the disturbed accumulation of dust on long-untouched volumes, the slow disintegration of the medium on which once-fêted human beings poured

10

out their soul and their spleen, a testament to centuries of futile and unregarded endeavour. What might be the effect on the lungs of years of inhaling this intellectual detritus? Case 38 is situated beneath a vent directing hypercooled air from the library's newly-installed filtration and climate control system. Rosemary shivers as she reflects, not for the first time, that the new system does not appear to perform either of its principal objectives with any efficiency. Doubtless the manufacturer and installer have given assurances that it needs time to settle in.

The box containing volume 13 of the Kellett papers resides in exactly the spot where the library's finding list says it should be. Rosemary withdraws it and begins to leaf through the faded contents for item 30, finding it in the correct place, in numerical order. Anyone who can count that far would have had no difficulty in locating it if they had bothered to look, which they clearly did not. She snatches the offending sheets from the box, replaces the lid and thrusts it roughly back into the space from which it came. She gasps when, as if from nowhere, a slim figure in white materialises a few feet away.

'Sorry Rosie, I didn't mean to startle you.'

She pats her heart as if to still it. 'It's okay Kerry, I didn't realise there was anyone else here.'

'You're becoming a bit of a regular down in these parts.'

'I seem to be the finder of last resort. It pisses me off. The assistants claimed they couldn't find these papers, but they were exactly where the list says they should be. They hadn't even bothered to look.'

'To be honest, our assistants don't like coming down here these days. At first I thought it was just the cold, but they say it's creepy now. Strange noises and all that.'

'Well perhaps they should remember what they're paid for. Frankly, I've got better things to do.'

Emerging at ground level, Rosemary breathes a sigh of relief. Outside, in contrast to the arctic chill of the basement, the heat of the day is building up once more, as she can see through the window from the prevalence of shorts and t-shirts. Stepping into the corridors of the library, however, is like entering a sealed chamber where conditions for life are at someone else's whim. Kafka's imagination would have run riot: a whole dimension of meta-reality within four massive walls (a lot more if you count all the added wings and annexes), impenetrable to all but those with the necessary security clearance. Once inside, whether eminent professor or humble undergraduate, you play by the same rules. Somehow, though, it doesn't feel like an egalitarian, non-hierarchical community.

She opens the heavy swing doors and inhales the silent reverence of the Manuscripts Reading Room. A thin, auburn-haired man, dressed fashionably for about 1995, looks up expectantly from behind the counter. Rosemary sidles up to him and speaks in a whisper.

'Here they are, Donald. Has Quasimodo arrived?'

'Not yet. And he'll hear you calling him that one day.'

'No he won't, he's as deaf as a toilet wall.'

'Walls have ears, even in toilets.'

'Touché. Anyway, it was exactly where it was supposed to be. I'm afraid your assistants didn't even look for it. Yet again.'

'They seem strangely reluctant to spend much time in the West Court basement.'

'Don't tell me they're seeing ghosts.'

'Oh, you know about those?' Donald grins. 'Did I ever tell you the tale of the haunted box of correspondence between members of the Bloomsbury Set? Whoever tries to read their letters completely loses the will to live.'

That evening at 7.55, six members of a poetry group sit around a table in a bare room above a pub in Mill Road. Rosemary has bought a decent-sized glass of wine, 175 millilitres, getting on for a quarter of a bottle, in the hope that it will last for the duration, but notes with dismay that only a mouthful remains even though the meeting has not yet started. The other five are occasional drinkers, and can somehow make half a pint last for two hours. Sally, a brusque retired academic who chairs the group and gives every impression of having spent her life keeping people in their place, looks to be on the point of calling them to order. Rosemary panics, drains her glass and hurries to the stairs, sensing five pairs of eyes boring into her back.

When she returns, sheepishly cradling her replenished glass, George, short, rotund and with comb-over, has a sheet of paper in his hand, impatient to stun the rest of the group with his offering for this month. George believes that real poetry died with Tennyson, so composes in the style of revered poets from the distant past. Rosemary is often tempted to ask him if he is familiar with the word 'pastiche', and wonders why Eliot and Auden bothered. He launches into a neo-Elizabethan sonnet, but he is no Shakespeare. She cringes at the stilted archaisms, 'thou' and 'wilt' and 'gaiety', but George is a ship in full sail. His fourteen lines of doggerel seem to last an eternity but eventually, after a dramatic pause, he pronounces the final word, 'tarry', which he has contrived to rhyme with 'Harry', then closes his eyes and slumps back in his chair as if exhausted by the creative effort involved, at the same time allowing a slight smile to stretch his lips.

His audience is divided. The other two traditionalists cry 'Bravo, George' and 'Splendid effort'; the three modernists remain silent but nod to ensure that they can't be accused of being unsupportive. Next up is Polly, who in the past dabbled in gestalt therapy, not to mention, it seems, just about every other kind. Rosemary suspects that her poems are created by the time-honoured method of opening a dictionary and sticking a pin into words at random. Like a fly-half preparing to kick a penalty, Polly places her palms together to channel her chi, inhales and exhales noisily, then launches into her contribution.

I open my soul
to spear and dart and
lucid anger and
deadly horn of conscience.

I parade my body,
offer it to flash of light
and pain and prick
and cancerous lust.

Penetrate me, violate
my secret longings
till I scream for silence.
I will not be lost.

More in hope than expectation, Rosemary waits for a further stanza to bring together this random assemblage of words and images, but after some moments it becomes clear that none will be forthcoming. Polly's energies are spent, a month of cerebral activity focused into twelve short, incoherent lines. The murmurs and warm smiles of some of her hearers perhaps convey a concern that the poem was cleverer than it seemed. Rosemary sits with her arms folded. Sally has noticed this.

'Well, we've had two contrasting pieces of work so far. With Rosie we never know what to expect. Would you like to go next, Rosie?'

Unless she is very much mistaken, there is a malevolent glint in Sally's eye. She takes a drink, removes a scrappy piece of paper from her jacket, opens it and then puts it away again. She knows the poem by heart.

You swept up all my scattered parts,
reformed me in your image.
I drank your beauty from a glass.

I saw reflections in your eyes
of oceans, deserts, Xanadu,
a waiting world within your dreams.

Grains of pollen on the breeze,
petals spinning in a stream,
fossils in a crumbling cliff,

fragile fragments of my life
that once you held secure. Now
they're free to fall apart.

Through the silence which follows, she keeps her eyes on the table. She neither knows nor cares what the rest of the group have made of her offering because she wrote it for her own benefit, not theirs. Sally moves without comment to the next contribution. When Rosemary can bring herself to look up, the other members of the group pretend they cannot see her.

It has started to rain as she unlocks her bicycle from a drainpipe outside the pub. She stares up at the drops falling in the light of the street lamp above, like a shower of arrows. By the time she arrives home she is soaked, and cold water drips from her hair onto her neck as she fumbles with the door key. Inside, a glimpse of herself in the hall mirror conjures up a picture of Medusa from a childhood book of Greek myths. Avoiding the bag of recyclable refuse in the hall which she forgot to put out earlier, she towels the worst of the water from her hair, and is about to take off her sodden jeans when the phone rings. On the other end is Jamie.

– Hi Rosie. Haven't woken you up, have I?

'No. If you talk too long I may get pneumonia, though.'

– Should I ring back another time?

'No, only try to make it quick.'

– I will. I just wanted to make a suggestion. Mum phoned earlier, and she's still a bit upset about what happened last night.

'You walking out like that, you mean?'

– No, apparently she's only too happy to see evidence that I'm a normal red-blooded male with needs. It's more what you said. About dad.

Rosemary waits.

– Okay, sore point, but I think she'd really like to smooth things over with you. She mentioned she's going into town tomorrow, and I thought you could suggest meeting her for lunch or something. I'm sure she'd jump at the chance.

'Well, I'll bear that in mind. Anything else, before I freeze to death?'

– Just one thing. I'll mention it because mum's sure to. I'd better forewarn you.

'Tell me why I have negative feelings about the turn this conversation's just taken.'

– I may as well come out and say it.

'Well get on with it then.'

– Mum's concerned about the amount you're drinking.

She grips the receiver more tightly. 'I see. And is that what you think too?'

– I'm not in a position to judge, am I? I mean, I'm hardly guiltless on that front.

'So you do think the same as mum.'

– Rosie, I didn't say that.

'Come on, Jamie, we wouldn't be having this conversation if you thought she was wrong.'

– Look, mum's from a generation where women generally left drinking to the men. She wouldn't dream of going into a pub on her own, would she?

'Whereas sluts like me think nothing of it.'

She holds the receiver away from her ear and takes several deep breaths. Jamie has fallen silent. She wants to put the phone down, but instead says: 'Look, I'd just like everyone to—'

– Rosie, listen to me. You've had a lot to put up with.

'Now this really is mum talking.'

– Sis, no-one's blaming you, no-one's criticising. Just

let me know if there's anything I can do to help. Promise me.

Rosemary is torn between sobbing and falling asleep on her feet. She is about to put the receiver down when Jamie's voice comes through one more time.

– Keep the faith, sis.

He pre-empts her decision to end the call. She fulfils her original intention to take her jeans off, abandons them where they land, walks into the living room, falls onto the settee, grabbing a cushion to place under her head, and closes her eyes.

3

The bright, airy restaurant in the department store seems as safe a place as any to attempt a rapprochement with mum. Rosemary looks around and sees no sign of her, despite having made it clear that her time would be limited before having to get back to work. Realising that she cuts a forlorn figure who appears to have been stood up, she sits at a small vacant table strewn with dirty plates. She can see an assistant working in her direction, clearing away debris onto a trolley and wiping tables, but she is still some distance away. In the end, Rosemary piles everything onto a tray and dumps it on a neighbouring, equally squalid table, wrinkling her nose as she wipes her fingers on a paper serviette. Apart from bored children, she seems to be the youngest person there.

After ten minutes her mother sweeps into view, struggling with as many large carrier bags as her hands can physically contain. As if guided by radar, she turns and makes straight for the table which Rosemary has commandeered and hurls her bags to the floor with a flourish.

'Shopping, shopping, what a chore, still what's one to do? Sorry to keep you waiting, you should have seen the queue in Top Shop. You never seem to have any nice clothes so I bought you something, hope you like it.'

Mum picks up one of the bags which clearly contains a number of items, rummages inside and picks one out. She holds it up for half the restaurant's customers to see. It is a pink chiffon jumper.

'I thought it's about time you started wearing something more feminine, Rosemary. Do you like it?'

'It's a very kind thought, mum. Anyway, sit down, let's sort out something to eat.'

'Oh, I had something earlier, I couldn't hang on any longer, but don't let me stop you.'

'I thought we'd arranged to meet for lunch.'

'Really? I thought you said coffee. Never mind, you carry on. I'll have a cappuccino.'

Still gritting her teeth, Rosemary drags her tray past the chilled cabinet containing small bottles of wine and beer silently begging to be put out of their misery. A minute later, she returns to the table with two cappuccinos and a ploughman's sandwich whose ancestry, she knows, has nothing to do with the eating habits of pre-industrial farm workers. Mum is systematically checking the receipts from her purchases.

'Is that all you're having, Rosemary? It's not much to keep you going through a working day. My mother always used to tell me, breakfast like a king, lunch like a lord—'

'And dine like a pauper. Yes, I know, mum. Anyway, what else did you buy?'

'Stuff for the house mainly. Including some new batteries for the front door bell. Oh, and I bought this for Jamie. Do you think he'll like it?'

She flourishes a shirt, light blue with white collar as worn by 1980s estate agents, still wrapped in its cardboard and foil. The price sticker indicates that it cost £55.

'That's a lot of money to spend on a shirt. You can't really afford that, mum.'

'My children are all I've got, and after all you can't take it with you. Anyway, you get what you pay for. Your father used to buy cheap shirts which looked fine until I'd scrubbed the collars a few times, then they started to fray and look awful. But he never listened to me.'

Rosemary takes a bite out of her sandwich, then replaces it in its container.

'Don't you want a plate, dear? I'll go and get you a plate.'

She swallows hurriedly. 'It's fine, mum. I'll use this, it'll save washing-up.'

Mum sips her coffee and looks around restlessly. The din of random conversation and cutlery on earthenware starts to cut through the proximal silence. Rosemary looks down at her sandwich and decides she will donate it to any passing ploughman.

'Thanks for inviting us round the other night, mum. It's a pity Jamie had to leave early.'

'Off with one of his fancy women, I suppose. He seems to take after his father. I just hope he finds someone he really wants to settle down with.'

Unlike dad, apparently. How much of this behaviour does transmit itself down the generations via some form of emotional DNA? Are daughters doomed to end up like their mothers?

'Do you ever feel you'd like to see dad again?' Rosemary asks.

'Not for a moment. He can rot in hell for all I care.'

'But suppose something happened to me or Jamie. Would you know how to get in touch with him?'

'Nope. He made his bed, he can lie in it.'

Rosemary begins to wish that she had remained at the poetry group a few minutes longer so she would not have arrived home in time to receive Jamie's call. Why on earth did she allow herself to be persuaded?

'What time do you have to be back at work, dear?'

She checks her watch. 'In about twenty minutes. Look, mum, I'm sorry about the other night. I didn't mean to upset you, but I still have problems when I think about dad. When he left it was a big trauma for me. Sometimes I think I've never really come to terms with it.'

'Jamie seems to have coped all right.'

'Well I'm not Jamie. We keep avoiding talking about these things, mum, we sweep it all under the carpet, but it doesn't go away. Not for me anyway.'

'Well it has for me. I've been strong enough to get on with my life without your father. I think you're old enough now to do the same. Take a leaf out of Jamie's book. He embraces life, he doesn't allow these kind of things to drag him down.'

'Well, I'm sorry to be such a disappointment to you. Look, I'd better get back to work. Keep in touch.'

She scrapes her chair back and hurries towards the exit.

A shrill voice calls after her.

'Rosemary. Don't forget your jumper.'

In a corner of the living room, cluttered with dusty piles of magazines and newspapers, Rosemary browses through the photos and films on her computer. An image snaps onto the screen and she is transported through time: the beach at St Andrews in early autumn, deserted. The Play button starts the footage rolling. Sand is lifted by the wind, sculpted into liquid spiral shapes, like tiny tornadoes. A whirl of sand hits the lens but she keeps filming, observing later that the camera never worked properly again after that.

Next, a shot of the Forth Bridge from a window of the Hawes Inn in South Queensferry, the day before Adam's cousin is due to be married in a medieval monastery on Inchcolm Island in the middle of the firth. She hears Adam's voice behind her.

'This place has a lot of history. There's a notice on the wall here saying it's where Robert Louis Stevenson first had the idea for *Kidnapped*. He mentions the hotel in the novel.'

'You seem to collect historical snippets about pubs like other men collect toy cars.'

'I realise your experience of men is limited, Rosie, but most men don't collect toy cars. Anyway, I spend a lot of time in pubs. Maybe I just have the sort of mind that collects details others don't notice.'

'And I suppose you can tell me what Inchcolm means in Old Pictish or whatever obscure language your ancestors spoke.'

'Gaelic, actually. Which is not obscure, there are people who speak it today. There's even a Gaelic TV channel.' She gives a wide mock-yawn. 'And if you really want to know, Inchcolm means Isle of Columba. The abbey was dedicated to him.'

'How do you know all this trivia?'

Adam frowns. 'I'm a Scot.'

That night, she lies in bed listening to a gale-force wind driving torrential rain against the glass in their upstairs room, wondering if the trains rumbling across the bridge ever stop for the night. A pall seems to hang over the bed. She has told Adam she is not in the mood for making love, and now has to listen to him snoring like an asthmatic pig. Earlier she asked him: 'Suppose this weather keeps up tomorrow and the ferry can't sail? Does your cousin have a Plan B if we can't get to the island?'

'I doubt it. What Plan B could there be? Have the wedding on the jetty? All pile in here to the bar? Anyway, you don't know Scottish weather. It'll be fine tomorrow.'

Next morning, Rosemary sees through the gap between the curtains that the sky is blue. Trains have been running across the Forth Bridge since five o'clock, but as no more than a drowsy backdrop to her half-sleeping state, and even their rattling progress now seems vaguely comforting. Once outside, they find that the wind has died, the air is warm and the Scottish climate has indeed worked its magic. For now, at any rate. Judging by the volume of cleavage on display in these pictures, she must be at least five kilos heavier than now, having assimilated Adam's voracious appetite but not, sadly, his restless metabolism.

Sunlight glints on the water as they hang over the side of the ferry, watching seals bask on the rocks and buoys while fulmars and petrels patrol the sky above. They have the prospect of two hours on Inchcolm Island. It is bathed in light, but the ceremony takes place in the dark, barrel-vaulted refectory of the monastery, lit by more candles than she has ever seen in one place, where they sit on hard plastic chairs grouped too closely together. The happy, and now legally married, couple make their way back down the impromptu aisle to the sound of howling bagpipes, and the congregation processes out onto the lawn to drink champagne. While Adam consorts with kilted friends and family, Rosemary explores the ruins, the still-intact cloister, the now roofless chapel. Down on the beach, a seal bobs in the water, watching her without alarm. She waves, and the seal languidly slips below the surface.

On the ferry's return journey, it is decreed that the remaining champagne be consumed before they dock, so she and Adam make their contribution to the heroic task. The bride, she thinks, looks the happiest person she has ever seen. She turns to see Adam smiling at her, and in that split second they know that they are imagining the same possibility. The moment is as transient as the distant view of Edinburgh Castle before it is eclipsed by the headland.

Rosemary stares at the last image in the folder, the returning wedding party assembled in loose order in front of the main door of the hotel. At first she cannot make out herself and Adam, but at length spots a familiar figure, right at the back. Adam is tilting a glass of beer above her head, as if about to pour it over her. She enlarges the image until she can see her own face, and realises from her horrified expression that she believed at that moment that he was really going to do it.

She runs her fingers through her hair, sits back and stares at the screen. After a few minutes the screen-saver kicks in; images of exotic flowers, surfers, megalithic monuments and desert sand dunes dissolve into one another. She watches, unblinking.

4

At 6.30 on Friday evening, Rosemary has already decided to wind down for the weekend in the remaining half an hour before the library closes. A survey of Cambridge cinema and concert listings, a final check for any urgent e-mails, then she will go out and help the reading room staff to clear up. She has not seen Roger all day, but now he walks in.

'Have a look at this, Rosemary.'

She has no desire to look at anything Roger may have brought to show her. She casts an eye towards the clock, but a sense of propriety obliges her to feign interest. He passes her an old book, small enough, she observes, to slip into a pocket, contained within a worn and fragile brown leather binding. She opens it gingerly; the spine crackles, and it is clear straight away that damp and worm have done their insidious work over the centuries. The outer part of most leaves is heavily stained and, in places, almost illegible. The entire contents appear to be in the same spidery, cursive, late medieval hand, a hand either not trained for the work of a scribe, or perhaps working hurriedly. On the flyleaf, faded but still legible, is an autograph in a quite different hand, a florid Elizabethan one, that of its erstwhile owner, John Dee.

'Where did it come from?'

'To be perfectly honest, I'm not sure.'

'No, I don't mean where was it written, where did you find it?'

'That's what I'm saying. It just turned up.'

'Okay, is it one of ours?'

Roger pauses. 'I don't know. It appeared from nowhere on one of the reshelving trolleys.'

She scours the pastedowns and flyleaves for any sign of an old library mark, but none is evident. Even the Dee connection does not take them very far: a fair number of the library's manuscripts have passed through the hands of the Elizabethan astrologer/magician, an avid collector himself, particularly of the occult and the arcane.

'So, what are we going to do with it?'

'It'll need to go to Conservation to stop it falling apart, but can you do a contents list for me? Then we can check it against the old catalogues and see if it's a lost or stolen item. Which it presumably is. Strange how long it takes people to have pangs of conscience sometimes.'

The cursory examination she has made so far suggests that interpreting the contents will be as much a test of patience and eyesight as of palaeographic skills. The thought makes her rub her eyes.

'Okay. I'll look at it on Monday.'

At 7.40 on Saturday evening she dodges buses, bicycles and taxis on Bridge Street, knowing that Sharon will be unforgiving of her lack of punctuality. Living ten minutes from the restaurant, she has no appetite for fabricating stories of hair disasters and last-minute phone calls. The bullet will have to be bitten. Dr Sharon Turner, lately of a small town near Brisbane and now of King's College, Cambridge, will have her mind on higher things, she is bound to get over it. At least, she always has before.

Sharon is unmoved as she hurries to the table. 'I'm sorry, honey, I've eaten, I couldn't wait any longer. Don't mind me though, I'll wait while you catch up.'

'Don't be like that, Sharon. It's only ten minutes.'

'Which means that you left home at the very time you were supposed to be here.'

'Well, I know I'm sometimes late, but I'm worth waiting for, aren't I? Anyway, at least you had the foresight to pour me a glass of wine. Didn't Rousseau say that a day without wine is like a day without, something or other?'

'A hangover?'

'Don't think it was that. Anyway, prost, santé, bottoms up.'

Sharon sips from her glass without taking her eyes from

Rosemary. 'So, how are you going to make it up to me?'

'For what?'

'Keeping me waiting?'

'How about, I'll let you look at a manuscript next time you come into the library.'

Dr Turner stands, tosses her blonde hair behind her shoulders and walks towards the toilet. Rosemary begins to wonder if she has pushed her friend's tolerance too far this time. She looks around at the other diners, trying to filter out the incessant and excessive noise which emanates from the student-based groups. In darkened corners are tables occupied by couples, some clearly struggling for dialogue, seemingly either at the beginning or the end of their relationship. The most desirous of one another seem to be an attractive man and woman in their forties, barely noticing their food, talking with animation, never missing an opportunity to touch one another. Rosemary finds herself imagining them falling naked and passionate into bed as soon as they get home. They sense her staring and look round. She holds their eyes for a moment before turning away.

'You're a bit young to be having a hot flush.'

'It's just the wine going straight to my head. I haven't eaten today, let's order.'

The harassed waitress seems determined to ignore their increasingly frantic efforts to attract her attention. When finally she arrives at their table, beads of sweat are poised to drip from her forehead.

'Two large mushroom pizzas please.'

'Would you like green salad with that?'

Sharon mimes the act of spitting on the floor. The waitress's expression does not change.

'We'll have some olives though,' Rosemary says.

The waitress picks up the menus and hurries off without indicating whether she has registered the latter request or not.

'A smile costs nothing,' Sharon says.

'Go easy on her, she's rushed off her feet.'

'That's the restaurant's concern. Are they going to give us a discount for the poor service?'

'Perhaps someone called in sick at the last moment.'

Sharon scans the menu, even though they have already ordered, then tosses it onto the table.

'Have you seen Adam recently?'

Rosemary takes a large mouthful of wine. 'He appears from time to time.'

'Is it still a touchy subject?'

'No, it's okay.'

'But you wonder how long you've got left?'

Rosemary picks up her napkin and begins to twist it around her finger. The pizzas arrive sooner than expected and they smile at the waitress, who says in a weary monotone, 'Enjoy your meal,' and hurries to the next table.

'The bitch didn't even bring one of those priapic pepper mills,' Sharon says.

'Or the olives.'

'Right. Anyway, what were we talking about? Oh yes, Adam. Or … perhaps not.'

Rosemary allows the implied question to dissolve into the air. As soon as she begins to eat, she realises how in need of food she is, and has no further appetite for conversation until she has cleared her plate. Alcohol has stormed the fortress of her brain without pausing to unload its siege engines. She slumps back in the chair while waiting for Sharon, who has been eating at a more measured rate. At length they both sit back, hands clasped across distended stomachs.

'Sharon, do you ever wonder where your brain ends and your mind begins?'

'Well there's a light-hearted question for a fun-filled Saturday night. What's prompted this?'

'Our body cells die and get replaced, but we still look like us. Our brain cells die and get replaced, but we still have the same personality, with the same memories. Don't you think that's strange?'

'Only if I think about it too hard. Maybe our personality and our memories, which I imagine are intimately connected, are contained in the organic equivalent of a memory card, which just stays there until Alzheimer's or something else erases it. As for our bodies, presumably it's just a question of the programming that's in our DNA. The new cells are clones of the old ones. Unless they're cancerous or otherwise artificially mutated. But hey, what do I know?'

'If I ask you another question, will you promise to give me a straight answer?'

'What if I say no?'

'Then I'll punish you.'

'I might enjoy that.'

'No you won't. I'll make didgeridoo noises for the rest of the evening.'

'Okay, you win. Fire away.'

Rosemary tilts her head to one side. 'What do you think about when you lie in bed?'

'You wouldn't want to know.'

'No, I mean about the really big questions in life. Why are we here? Is everything just random, or is there a point to our existence? Why are there more questions than answers?'

Sharon dabs the corners of her mouth with her napkin. 'You already know my philosophy of life. Why ask me?'

'I want to know what are the ultimate questions that keep you awake at night.'

Sharon makes a show of checking the alcohol content of the wine they have been drinking, glancing from the bottle to her friend.

'Whether William Blake suffered from bi-polar disorder. Whether Shakeseare's plays were written by a chimpanzee who found a typewriter and got lucky. What would you expect?'

'All right. What do you believe about, let's say, what happens after we die?'

'Ah. The ultimate game-breaker. Come to my bed and I promise to explain all the secrets of the universe.'

'I'm serious.'

'So am I. Look, Rosie, I understand why you're asking this question, but I'm not the person to help here. I'm a boring old rationalist who doesn't waste time speculating on these things. Maybe I'm blinkered, but I'd rather just get on with my life.'

Rosemary fidgets with her napkin once more. Sharon reaches across and puts her hand on her friend's. 'You know what you need?'

'A personality transplant?'

'I was trying to pluck up the courage to suggest it. A change of scenery. Why don't we get away for a few days? I've still never been to Wales. How about a trip to Snowdonia?'

Outside, the night is still mild but it has started to drizzle. When she gets home, Rosemary decides that going to bed is the last thing she wants to do. Perhaps one of these days she will find herself taking up Sharon's proposal. Not yet, though. Sharon is too good a friend to risk losing.

She lies on the bed, turns on the radio and listens to the World Service. Even the voice of a BBC newsreader is better than no company at all. She can hear that the rain is getting harder, and within a few minutes it beats against her window. She gets up, holds a curtain back and looks out onto the street; people are sheltering in doorways and under trees, couples are running, laughing, holding coats over their heads. She closes her eyes and sees the Forth Bridge, huge and brooding in a storm.

5

Next morning, the rain has ceased but the air is still humid as Rosemary walks down Castle Hill in t-shirt and shorts to buy a Sunday paper. She finds herself continuing past the newsagent's shop and stopping to watch the river traffic below Magdalene Bridge. A party of Japanese tourists, many weighed down by the Nikons hanging from their necks, waits to be taken on chauffeured punt trips from Scudamore's Boatyard. She takes out her phone and goes to her address book.

'Hi Jamie. What are you doing at lunchtime?'

'Putting my feet up and watching the cricket.'

'Like hell you are. Meet me in the Champ at one.'

She arrives at the Champion of the Thames at 12.45 to find the only accessible section of the bar is sandwiched between two fat men on stools who, observing her attempts to attract the attention of the barman, make no effort to move to allow her through. Her frustration overflows.

'Bought a life indenture of this stretch of bar, have you?'

They respond to her tone of voice rather than the words, which they do not understand.

'You only had to ask, love.'

'A bit of politeness costs nothing.'

They mutter as she walks away with her drink, but her assertiveness has not been in vain: the little alcove next to the fireplace in the back bar remains unoccupied. She places her glass on the table and settles down to wait for Jamie. After a couple of minutes, she borrows a pen from behind the bar and begins to write on a beer-mat.

What's a day without you worth?
A day to feel time's cold grey hands,
the slings and arrows of sepulchral curse,
crimson cords to strangle the stars.

30

Wondering if she has been exposed to one too many of Polly's streams of consciousness, she turns the mat over.

Jamie walks in at ten past one, looks around until he sees her, waves, and a couple of minutes later brings over a pint of IPA and another glass of wine.

'We could have sat outside the Clarendon. Why do you want to be stuck inside on a day like this?'

'I'm comfortable here. Anyway, I thought you liked the beer.'

'I also like fresh air. Never mind, down the hatch.'

Jamie drinks deeply, and lowers his pint onto the beer-mat on which Rosemary has written. She lifts his glass and draws the mat closer to her. Jamie raises his eyebrows inquiringly, but says nothing. They sip their drinks and watch the people around them for a couple of minutes. Jamie begins to fidget.

'You sounded a bit agitated when you phoned,' he says.

'Not agitated exactly. More a feeling that I need to talk to someone I can trust.'

'If our last conversation is anything to go by—'

'I can hardly talk to mum, can I?'

'Don't you trust Sharon?'

'Yes, but not in that way. She's a bit … a bit too close, if you know what I mean.'

'She's still coming on to you?'

'Sharon's been coming on to me for as long as I've known her. I can deal with that, but I'm not sure I'd trust her with highly confidential information, any more than I'd share it with a man if I thought there was any chance I'd get involved with him.'

'So you think at some point you might get involved with Sharon.'

Rosemary ignores the question, turning the beer-mat over and over on its corners.

'Didn't you trust Adam?'

'I'd have trusted Adam with my life. I think. But that's neither here nor there now.'

Jamie drinks and takes his time responding. 'Do you

31

still see him?'

'He comes to me when he wants to.'

'Interesting how you turned my question around.'

'That's the way it feels to me.'

'So, is this what you wanted to talk to me about?'

Rosemary pauses. 'I suppose so, although to tell the truth I feel a bit foolish now. I've no idea what I expected you to say. Mum's always so dismissive. I just needed to talk to someone who might understand.'

'That's okay, you don't have to apologise. Sometimes it's good to offload even if you know your problem can't be solved.'

Jamie sees that his sister is staring, not at him, but over his shoulder. Her eyes appear glazed.

'What's up?'

After a few moments, she blinks hard. 'Sorry, I heard a Scots voice from over there. I was just checking.' She drains her glass. 'I'll get this one,' she says, negotiating her way around the table.

'I'm okay,' Jamie says to her back, 'I've still got—'

She returns with two more drinks. There is a clear hint of disapproval in Jamie's expression, and she recalls their phone conversation a few nights ago.

'Look, Rosie, I may as well come out and say this. I'm no expert on these things, but you do realise that the fact you're seeing Adam now, in the way you do, means that he must be, well, for want of a better word, dead.' She clasps the base of her glass with both hands, keeping her eyes focused on the table top. 'I'm sorry, Rosie. I know you want to keep believing, but there's no point pretending.'

She sits back and folds her arms, looks out of the window then back at Jamie. 'So, did you get a shag after you rushed away from mum's the other night?'

An elderly couple at the next table glance sideways. Jamie turns his back to them. Rosemary pays no attention, but lowers her voice.

'It's not true, Jamie, he's not dead. I refuse to accept it.'

'It's natural that you don't accept it. Who'd want to?

But sooner or later you have to face the facts. Until you do you'll never be able to move on.'

'Then why hasn't his body turned up? There's no evidence he had any sort of accident.'

'Except—'

'Except Byron's Pool, everyone says it must have been at Byron's Pool. But the sea gives up its dead, presumably rivers do as well, anyway they sent divers down to check. And Adam was a strong swimmer. He told me he once swam across the Firth of Tay. He couldn't have drowned.'

'Maybe unpredictable currents, who knows? But the Police have closed the case, Rosie. They must deal with lots of these situations, so they must know when it's not worth searching any more.'

'The Police know fuck all. You've said so yourself.'

A small audience is now eavesdropping. Rosemary takes a sip of her drink, oblivious to them.

'In a different context,' Jamie says, subdued. 'Look, maybe this is not the place to be having this conversation. I don't want to upset you, but there's not much else I can say.'

'You could say you believe I'm right.'

'Rosie, if Adam turned up alive today, I'd be as thrilled as you. But since you seem to want it spelled out, if he's not dead, then either he was abducted by aliens, or it means he cruelly disappeared out of your life, out of everyone's life, off the face of the earth in fact, without any thought for your feelings and how it would destroy you. Is that really what you'd prefer to believe?'

She allows her head to fall forward, shaking it slowly from side to side. When she raises it again, there are tears in the corner of her eyes.

'Oh Jamie, what am I going to do?'

Making no attempt to conceal her emotions, she stands and makes for the privacy of the toilet, followed by every eye in the Champion's back bar. When the murmur of conversation has resumed, Jamie picks up the beer-mat of

which his sister was so protective, turns it over and reads.
He replaces it, and downs his drink in one.

6

Navigating a course around the gridlocked cars on Queens Road on Monday morning, Rosemary tries to suppress a nagging, ill-defined sense of apprehension about the day which is about to unfold. She wheels her bicycle across at the lights at the end of Garrett Hostel Lane and continues along Burrell's Walk, then through the decorative wrought-iron gateway and into the wide, tree-lined approach to the University Library. She dismounts beneath the shade of a huge arching yew tree and stares up at the Italianate tower which dominates with supreme elegance the skyline of western Cambridge. Wispy clouds pass behind, creating the illusion that it is swaying. She has to lower her head and close her eyes until the giddy feeling passes.

Her office is at the opposite end of the building from the staff doorway, and on this occasion she takes a circuitous route, avoiding the most heavily-trafficked parts of the library, to avoid meeting anyone she will have to exchange pleasantries with. Once safely ensconced at her desk, she checks her e-mail and is relieved to find that no further excursion to the basement is required, for the moment anyway. From the corner of her eye, she glances at the locked drawer containing the manuscript Roger passed to her on Friday evening. She turns away, but not for long. Nothing else in her in-tray distracts her attention, and at last she succumbs and opens the drawer. The book sits exactly where she left it on Friday. Rosemary realises that she has been holding her breath.

A quick flip through the stained vellum leaves confirms that the manuscript will be as challenging to catalogue as her initial appraisal on Friday suggested. She decides to remove herself to the side room where she can study it under an ultra-violet lamp in the hope that this will render it decipherable. As she turns the fragile pages, it becomes ever more evident that the manuscript has been neglected. Has it been stored in some damp cellar? She struggles through the first item, a late medieval medical treatise devoted to the study of urine and the analysis of its colours and odours. Not the most salubrious of subjects, but she has encountered its like often enough. The second is more unusual, a collection of supposedly Babylonian astrological lore. Pseudo-Babylonian, no doubt. The third is on the signs of the zodiac and their supposed qualities and influences. Nothing so far to pique her interest.

She sits back and rubs her eyes. Her watch confirms that two hours have passed. The faded ink and the near-illegible script are already taking their toll. A knock at the door breaks her concentration.

'Rosemary, Dr Collins needs some help. Can you come out?'

She sighs and drapes a weighted string across the open page to hold it open, then drags herself up from the chair and out into the reading room, locking the door behind her. Half an hour later she returns, grinding her teeth and silently cursing the ever-demanding Dr Collins. After several deep breaths, she sits and leans over the manuscript.

Her eyes widen. Although the book-weight is still in place as she left it, the manuscript is open at a different page. She checks and re-checks in case her flagging vision is playing tricks, then slowly walks back out to the reading room's reception desk.

'Donald, who's been in there since I came out to see Dr Collins?'

'No-one, Rosie. You've got the key, and you locked the door after you.'

'Are you sure? Did you see me do it?'

'Yes. Why? Have you lost something?'

'My mind, possibly.'

She returns to the side room and closes the door. The manuscript is still open at the page which it seemingly presented to her of its own volition. It is the last item in the manuscript, and written in an even more frantic script than the rest. There is no sign of an original title, but one has

36

been supplied in the margin by the hand, it appears, of the book's erstwhile Elizabethan owner. She reaches for a magnifying glass, reads and re-reads John Dee's words to make sure she has interpreted them correctly.

De evitacione mortis et de revivificacione defunctorum.

On avoiding death and bringing the dead back to life.

The glass drops onto her lap. She reaches out to close the manuscript, to seal in whatever may be contained in this text, but is now afraid to touch it.

She stands up and paces from side to side. Think carefully. Dee's interest does not prove that he believed it was to be taken at face value, but it does prove that he considered it worth acquiring and reading. So what is to prevent Rosemary from reading it herself, perhaps the first person since the good doctor to do so?

But suppose there is a power in the words themselves, power of a kind she may not want to experience? It is possible, on the other hand, that she just needs to control her imagination. What can there be to fear? After long consideration, an answer forms: if we fear something without knowing why, if our rational mind is at war with our primal response and in danger of defeat, then a deep-rooted instinct is telling us to beware, and we ignore it at our peril. She sits down and stares at the fateful words.

There is another tap on the door. Too stunned to speak, she watches it open slowly.

'Rosemary, are you okay?'

Roger does not wait for a response before entering and closing the door behind him. He tries to smile.

'People have been getting worried about how long you've been in here.' He nods at the manuscript. 'That thing must be more interesting than I imagined.'

Seeing that the book is still open at the page which made her freeze, she removes the book-weight and closes it. Roger looks quizzically at the manuscript, then at her.

'I think you've been concentrating for too long. Take a break. You look as if some fresh air would do you good.'

'What time is it?' The question is foolish; she could as

easily look at her own watch.

'Half past five.'

'What? You're joking.'

'I'm afraid not. Don't worry, I remember how easy it is when you're young to get carried away when you find something out of the ordinary. What I wouldn't give to experience that again.'

She rubs her eyelids. Her watch belatedly confirms that she has indeed been in this small, dark room, off and on, for over seven hours.

'Come on, Rosemary, you've had enough. It'll still be here tomorrow.'

Will it? She sits bolt upright. Roger is still smiling, but he means what he says. He has come as close as he ever does, ever can do, probably, to issuing an order.

As she walks back out with him into the reading room, trying not to blink in the light, she knows that all eyes are on her. Back at her desk, the mouse shimmies over its pad and the screen bursts back into life. Roger is still watching her.

'Close it down and go home, Rosemary. Get some rest.'

Roger is pushing at an open door since she wants nothing more than to get out of this office, out of the building, into the normal world: Cambridge on a warm summer evening where people are too busy enjoying life to waste time on avoiding death. She locks the manuscript in her desk, places the key in its usual place behind the flower-pot and picks up her bag.

'I'll see you tomorrow, Roger,' she says without looking back.

Heading for the reading room door, she risks a glance at Donald. He watches her for a moment, then looks away.

At home, the memories continue to sidle onto her computer screen. Here is Adam standing in front of the doorway of the Cambridge University Press building on his first day there as an assistant editor. It is a bright winter's day and the horse-chestnut trees look like hydras,

38

their stark branches snaking like tendrils towards the chill blue sky, but Adam has refused to wear a coat on the basis that, by Scottish standards, the temperature is distinctly on the mild side for the time of year. She has insisted on walking there with him, joking that he might get lost on his first day at school. He pretended to be embarrassed, but did little to conceal his obvious pleasure at her pride in him. He is looking smarter, his hair shorter, than in the earlier folders; she demanded that he visit the hairdresser the day before, and he wears the grey-blue suit she chose for him because she thought that it set off his hair. She recalls the very moment of pressing the shutter, when she wondered if she hadn't made him look a little too handsome. Suppose the workforce of the University Press contained an unhealthy number of young females? Still, this is Adam, and what they have between them is like nothing which binds any other man and woman. As he bids her farewell, she raises her skirt to reveal that she has donned stockings and suspenders for the occasion, just as an astonished senior executive walks out of the building. When he is out of ear-shot, they laugh without restraint and fall back into one another's arms.

7

The manuscript remains in the drawer throughout the following day, its silent but increasingly strident appeals falling on closed ears. Rosemary busies herself with more urgent tasks, but knows that she cannot forever ignore its presence, torn as she is by the warring impulses of curiosity and fear. This inanimate object seems prepared to engage in a battle of wills, and her concerns grow as the hours pass that she will not emerge the victor. When her sore eyes tell her to pack up for the day, she locks her desk and goes to place the key behind the flower-pot as usual. This time, an alarm bell rings. She slips it into her bag.

She leaves the library through the staff door at five o'clock, ignores her bicycle and walks in the opposite direction from home. Grange Road beckons with its huge old houses, playing fields and student hostels. At the bottom she dodges the traffic racing towards the M11. Once across the main road, she heads for a turning which entices her away from the noise and fumes. Within a few minutes she is out of the realm of tarmac and concrete, leaving houses and cars behind. Ahead, a more rural vista opens up.

The footpath follows the course of the river, though in places out of sight of it. Between the path and the bank are meadows and grassy fields, grazed by the occasional huddle of cattle or horses. The sky is overcast, the air sultry, and although she is wearing only a light blouse and skirt sweat is already forming under her arms. She flaps them to create a draught and keep them away from her sides, but the cooling effect of this absurd activity is minimal. A young couple walking towards her stare long and hard; she smiles as they pass, but they look beyond her.

Checking that no-one is in view, she clambers over a stile with no concern for elegance or decorum and continues alongside a field of tall grass, then stops for a moment, staring towards the river. A young man is using the current to steer a punt languidly back in the direction of the city while his female companion, in a long, floral-print dress and sunhat, tips her head back and closes her eyes, allowing the gentlest of breezes to caress her face.

Just ahead is a mature ash tree between the path and the river, and she is sure it is the one she and Adam chose to conceal them last summer as they lay naked in that same field. She notes with the benefit of hindsight that the tree would have served no purpose at all as a screen. Their foreplay consisted of her pinching his waist and accusing him of developing love handles, in response to which he pointed out, not for the first time, that her breasts are asymmetrical. Closing her eyes, she feels once again the rough stalks rubbing against her back, her buttocks and her legs. As she holds her breath, Adam lowers himself towards her, kissing her passionately until she aches for him, and then they make love between the warmth of the earth below and the sky watching above. Every nerve in her body is alive.

'Are you all right, my dear?'

A trim elderly couple in hiking boots are standing alongside, frowning. How long have they been there? Rosemary realises that sweat is dripping from her face and hands, and for a moment she struggles to collect herself. The insides of her thighs are clammy.

'Yes. Yes, thank you. I thought I heard something. A bird. I think.'

'Well, as long as you're okay … '

'Yes, I'm fine. Thanks. Enjoy the rest of your walk.'

She strides away, knowing that they are still watching. Despite the heat she quickens her pace, and after another half a mile the rooftops of Grantchester loom ahead. The sky has grown darker, clouds of tiny flies have materialised from nowhere, and the air is heavy with the promise of thunder. For a moment the option of turning back without fulfilling her self-imposed mission seems tempting, perhaps not just for meteorological reasons. She presses on, however, diverts through an orchard and finds

41

herself in the welcoming garden of the Red Lion with its children's swings and slides, its gnarled cherry trees and its reassuringly traditional wooden benches and seats. She buys a pint of lager from the bar and finds a table in a shaded spot. She is generally bemused by the popularity of lager, but on this occasion cares only that it is chilled to the temperature of a melting Greenland glacier.

It would be all too easy to close her eyes once more and recall the times that she and Adam sat in this very garden, but she reins herself in. At a table a few yards away, oblivious to her presence, sit a student couple (you can always tell) whose easy intimacy makes her wonder if they also are no strangers to the sensual seclusion of Grantchester Meadows. She is torn between draining her pint and going straight in to buy another, or sipping this one to try to make it last. She drinks half and postpones a final decision.

There is a memory now, unbidden and not containing Adam. She sees herself walking past the parish church, complete with famous clock frozen in time, alongside Sharon, at that time a recent acquaintance who, somewhat out of character, has opted for summer dress, sandals and straw hat. Rosemary thinks she resembles one of the flighty females from a Bertie Wooster story. Sharon has been provoked by the location into expounding in strident terms her hypothesis that if Rupert Brooke had not died in the Great War, his piss-poor poetry (her words) would have been recognised for what it was. Sharon has grasped her hand, and she is looking for an opportunity to free it by pointing or gesticulating, but her new friend holds on tightly. Rosemary has no views on Brooke's poetry, having read very little of it, although she suspects that she would always prefer Wilfred Owen. So many poets, so little time. Ars longa, vita brevis. She allows Sharon to continue in full flow.

'The fêting of the War Poets is an expression of post-war society's guilt, not just at having allowed the horrors to go on, but at having survived the war themselves. They were desperate to believe that these young men hadn't died in vain, despite all the evidence to the contrary, so they told themselves that at least these guys had left a remarkable literary legacy.'

'As opposed to … '

'The reality is that they wrote poems about gruesome death, mud, mutilation and horrific injuries, not to mention nostalgia, because poetry was the only medium in which they could begin to convey the horror. They may have been brave and articulate, but no-one took any notice of them at the time. If they had, the war might not have dragged on for so long.'

Rosemary has never heard Sharon mention the War Poets before, let alone discuss their work in such vitriolic terms. She is out of her comfort zone, and eager to change the subject.

'So who's your favourite poet, then?'

She bites her lip at the inanity of the question. Its vacuousness reverberates around her skull, sends tremors through her spine and ribcage and on down her arms. To her surprise, Sharon seems to be deep in thought, and grips Rosemary's hand even tighter.

'I suppose it ought to be possible to answer that question. But in the end it's a bit like saying, who do you think should win the Man Booker, or the Oscar for best film? You can't make a judgement on aesthetic grounds because books and films come in so many different forms and have so many different purposes. How do you compare a comedy with a tragedy? A mind-bending piece of science fiction with a raw emotional drama? When it comes to poets, I could rattle off Gower, Dryden, Keats, Eliot, Plath, but then tomorrow in another mood I'd probably come up with a completely different list.'

They walk in silence for a while until Sharon asks, 'How about you? Who's your favourite poet?'

Rosemary grins. 'Pam Ayres.'

'Who?'

'Sorry. An English joke.'

It is Sharon who releases Rosemary's hand. 'Ah. There I was, labouring under the illusion that our intellects were in the process of forming subliminal connections. Remind me to make a note not to bother again.'

Back in the here and now, Rosemary recalls that it was in this precise spot in the garden of the Red Lion that she and Sharon first shared a drink, the atmosphere distinctly frosty despite the time of year after her unwise foray into faux-irony. A year after that exchange it occurs to her that, unlike anyone else she knows, Sharon sees intellectual endeavour not as an ultimately solitary activity, but as a channel for intimacy. She wishes Sharon were here now so she could tell her that she finally understands.

An empty glass sits before her, even though she has no recollection of finishing her lager. Checking the time, she reluctantly concludes that there is a need for urgency, so she regains the path which now follows the river bank more closely. The oppressive humidity has lifted, and a palette of blues stretches from zenith to horizon. Soon the river divides, one arm meandering into the tree-lined lagoon of Byron's Pool. She makes her way with difficulty over tree-roots and, removing her sandals, across lingering patches of sticky mud, until she reaches the seat which offers a view from which to contemplate the pool's enchanted waters. It would be reassuring to think that Byron really swam here, but who knows? The infamous Brooke certainly did. But there is no-one swimming here this evening, apart from a pair of mallards and a moorhen. Was this how it looked when Adam decided to take the plunge? Was he impelled by the prospect of joining the list of illustrious Cambridge men (and presumably quite a few women) who stripped off to rinse the sweat from their flesh here in the past? Did he imagine it might one day be known as McKenzie's Pool?

In her mind's eye, she pictures Adam swimming in these superficially calm waters, relishing the coldness on his skin, the weightlessness, the freedom of movement. But then what? Does he emerge unscathed? Does he find

44

himself sucked down as a sudden surge from the weir flows downriver and disrupts the serenity of the pool? The passageway of her imagination is sealed off at this point.

'Can you hear me, Adam?'

The words are spoken aloud. An image flashes into her mind, an arm rising from the waters holding aloft a sword. She smiles and shakes her head. Something breaks the surface of the pool, and she watches intently as a shoal of fish picks off the flies which have gathered just above on this still, damp evening. The light is starting to diminish.

What did she expect to see? What did she hope to find? Clues? An item of clothing inexplicably missed by the Police when they scoured the pool and its banks in search of his body? Or even a suicide note? At that moment there seems only one way of even beginning to understand. She takes off her clothes, folds them neatly and places them on the seat. Edging down the slippery bank, she loses her footing and lands in the water, struggling to maintain her balance, but the water is colder than she expected and the shock propels her forward. She struggles for breath as the chill bites into her, then slowly brings her breathing under control and moves her limbs to keep the blood flowing. Within moments she starts to relax and turns onto her back with only her face and breasts breaking the surface, floating beneath the same tree-ringed patch of sky Adam must have seen. She watches a flight of swans, hears their unearthly whirring, and turns her head to one side.

'Good evening, my Lord Byron,' she says, and laughs. 'Why, good evening mistress Torrance,' she replies to herself. 'It is my great good fortune to encounter such a comely and shapely wench on this fine summer's night. Perhaps you will agree to tarry and become my plaything.'

Before she can formulate her response to the poet's indecent suggestion, she feels a tugging at her hair, and instinctively moves to place her feet on the bottom of the pool, but she is out of her depth so tries to swim away from whatever new current is trying to draw her out into the main river. One foot has become entangled in the tall,

45

dense weed which lurks below the surface, and the harder she pulls the more firmly it secures its grip. She feels herself drawn down, but does not panic, looks around below the water, no longer struggling, not trying to extricate herself, but looking for Adam. She does not care that the depths of the pool have already been scoured for his body, this is the real reason why she came. Seeing nothing but mud and weeds, and unable to hold her breath any longer, she tugs at the fronds which have knotted themselves around her ankle, but they refuse to yield. Desperation growing by the moment, her writhing more and more frantic, she struggles until her lungs are ready to burst. The last thought which passes through her mind is that she and Adam really were always destined to spend eternity together.

The cold mud beneath her bare skin moulds itself to her shape as she lies on the bank, coughing and gasping for breath. There is no way of knowing how long she has been there. At length she draws herself up onto all fours and watches the drips from her hair forming tiny pools of their own. She starts to shiver uncontrollably, reaches up for the bench and hauls herself to her feet. Using her underwear to scrape off some of the mud, then throwing it into the undergrowth, she puts on her blouse, skirt and shoes with fumbling fingers. It will be dark in an hour; she stumbles back towards Grantchester, rubbing her arms and legs to try to restore them to life.

After attracting a number of concerned enquiries while making her way through the city centre, Rosemary arrives home at midnight, cold and exhausted, and runs a bath. Her body subsides into the hot, oily water, the scent of lavender helping to dilute the memory of her trauma, then closes her eyes and allows her head to sink back, but is soon once again below the malevolent waters of Byron's Pool. She sits upright and splashes her face.

'Careful, you might drown.'

'What the hell are you doing here, Adam? I just want to unwind in a hot bath, with some privacy if you don't mind.'

'There's no privacy between lovers, or so you once told me.'

'Well it just goes to show, you can't believe a word I say. Now please go, this really isn't a good time.'

'I just wanted to check that you were okay. Perhaps you'd like me to stop visiting altogether.'

'I didn't say that. It's just that this is – well, not normal, is it?'

'Adam's fourth Principle of Life: when you start hankering for normality, you know you're on the downhill run.'

'I thought the fourth Principle was, Never make eye contact in the changing room.'

Adam's nose wrinkles. 'Actually, you're right. I must be losing it.'

She closes her eyes, and when they open again Adam is gone. She slides back into the water until only her face is above the surface. Taken aback by his appearance, she has forgotten to ask him where he was a few hours earlier.

8

Rosemary remains awake through the hours of darkness, unwilling to risk closing her eyes. At two o'clock she gets up, pours herself a large gin and tonic and takes it back to bed, sipping it until the first distant birdsong drifts into the room. Soon the street lights extinguish themselves to reveal the dull light of early dawn. She sinks below the duvet and risks allowing her eyelids to drop.

Some hours later she looks at the clock, reaches across the bedside cabinet for the phone but knocks it off its stand. She turns over and goes back to sleep.

Waking once more, with a thumping headache, she draws back the curtains and sunlight floods in. Humanity moves in waves up and down Castle Hill, on foot, by bicycle, by bus and by car, firm in purpose, destination clear in mind. A young man happens to look up, sees her in the window and smiles. Even though she is wearing her dressing-gown, she folds her arms across her.

In the hall, a red light is blinking to tell her that someone has left a phone message. She tries to remember if it was there when she got home last night, but the result is inconclusive. She ignores it, rings the library to say that she is too sick to come to work, then goes back to the bedroom and collapses onto the bed.

It seems that she has only dozed for a few minutes, but when she opens her eyes the clock, if it is to be believed, is informing her that the time is now after eleven o'clock. It slowly dawns that she has woken because the phone is ringing. She pays no attention, but something in its relentless tone says that it will not be ignored. She gropes on the floor and picks up the receiver.

'Hullo.' The word reaches her ears as an incoherent mumbling.

'Rosemary, it's Roger. I'm sorry to disturb you when you're obviously unwell, but I think you should know that your brother has been ringing here, desperately trying to get hold of you. He said he'd rung you at home but without success. He sounded upset, so I said I'd see if I had any better luck. Sorry if it's a false alarm, but I'll leave you to judge whether you're up to contacting him. Hope you feel better soon. Bye.'

She listens to the click as Roger rings off without waiting for a response, rolls over and closes her eyes once more.

Fuck, fuck, fuck.

Brain refuses to send the message to fingers to tap Jamie's number into the phone. All she wants is sleep, happy oblivion. At last she gets up and runs the shower, stands beneath allowing it to massage her scalp, and eventually feels the warm cleansing bringing her skin back to life. Having towelled herself dry, she returns to the bedroom. When she gets there, the phone is ringing again. Her hand hovers before picking it up.

'Rosie, where the hell have you been? I've been trying to get hold of you all morning.'

'Sorry, Jamie, I'm sick.'

'Oh really. Well not half as sick as mum. She's in hospital.'

'What are you talking about? What's she—'

'They think she's had a stroke.'

'Wow. Is she going to—'

'They can't say yet. They've got lots of tests to do. All they'll say is that if it was a stroke, it was a big one.'

'So, where is she?'

'Addenbrooke's. A ward called Acute Admissions. I told them to expect you. I'm heading there now.'

The hospital's ascetic white corridors seem designed to foster the belief that sickness, pain and death have no place in these sterile surroundings, an illusion readily pricked by the large sign indicating the location of the mortuary. The hospital complex occupies an area equivalent to a small village, with population to match. At that moment, it seems that the rest of them are attempting to move in the opposite direction. Each time Rosemary stops to get her bearings, she is engulfed. The signs point to every conceivable department of a major hospital apart from Acute Admissions. She is tempted to scream.

A porter with an open face and smiling eyes appears, pushing an empty wheelchair.

'Acute Admissions? You're going the wrong way, love. That's right down the other end. I'll show you if you like. Better still, hop in and I'll take you there.'

Presumably this is standard hospital porter banter, but he nods down at the wheelchair and appears to be serious, so she takes him up on the offer.

'Just try to look a bit ill,' he says over her shoulder.

At first she feels foolish, but soon closes her eyes, growing into the role of dependent, invalid, victim. The journey seems to go on for miles. Thank goodness she did not have to walk it.

'Acute Admissions. Next floor for furniture and ladies' lingerie.'

She looks up reluctantly and finds it difficult to lever herself out of the wheelchair.

'Are you sure you're all right, love? If you don't mind me saying, you look worse than some of my real patients.'

The ward consists of a central corridor with rooms leading off on each side, punctuated by toilets, wash rooms and doors with 'Staff Only' signs. She glances into each cubicle as she goes past, but sees no sign of her mother. At the end is a desk behind which a young male doctor stands talking to three nurses. She waits beside it. One of the nurses looks up and sees her, then looks away again. From time to time, the four break into laughter. She looks around, and finally spots Jamie sitting reading a book. She walks over, and sees that it is Sartre's *Huis Clos*.

'"L'enfer, c'est les autres",' she quotes.

He looks up, but says nothing.

'"Hell is other people."'

'I know perfectly well what it means.'

'It just seems appropriate, you sitting here reading a

50

story about characters discovering they're condemned to spend the rest of eternity together.'

Jamie narrows his eyes, then turns to look at mum, who is lying on her back with her eyes closed, her face grey, the rest of her body concealed beneath blankets. An oxygen mask covers her nose and mouth, and a saline drip is connected to a canula in her arm.

'What do they reckon?' Rosemary asks.

'Still don't know. Apparently the next forty-eight hours could be critical, whatever that means.'

Apart from the gentle rising and falling of her chest, there is little to suggest that their mother is alive.

'Do you think she can hear us?' Rosemary says.

Jamie shifts position without looking at her, as if he finds the question unpalatable, even tasteless. 'Perhaps we should talk as if she can, just in case.'

Rosemary drags across a chair from beside the next bed, and they sit in silence staring at their mother. They watch for a long time, knowing that it is pointless, but what else is there to do? Perhaps, despite appearances, mum does in some way know that they are present. And if she does, will she want them to see her helpless, incontinent, hovering between life and death? Rosemary checks her watch and sees that it is coming up to half past one.

'Did you notice when visiting hours end?'

'As far as I can gather, there aren't any on this ward.' Jamie looks around furtively, drops his voice. 'Quite a few of them look like they're … ' He makes a thumbs-down gesture.

The men and women sitting at other bedsides are reading magazines, watching the over-bed TV or just yawning. Perhaps some of them, in their heart of hearts, are willing the reluctant relative to get on and die, just to end the inconvenience and the tedium. At least preparing for a funeral gives you something to do. Does she have the courage to examine her own conscience?

'Look, Jamie, I'm feeling really rough. I'm going to go home and put my head down for a few hours. I'll try to get back tonight if I'm up to it. You'll let me know if there's any change, won't you?'

It is clear from Jamie's expression, annoyed and pained at the same time, that he does not believe a word she has said.

'Yeah, sure. I'll stay. You go and get your head down.'

She cycles along the broad highway of Hills Road back towards town, head throbbing. The last twenty-four hours have been among the most traumatic of her life. Perhaps. How do they compare with losing Adam? Then, there was no pivotal moment, no drama, just a slow realisation that he was no longer around as he used to be. A bit like losing a favourite cat, and still half-expecting to see it curled up on its old chair.

Each revolution of the pedals requires a superhuman effort now. She wears stiff new jeans, the seams of which are chafing the inside of her thighs. Were she seen by anyone from the library, cycling along Hills Road is an activity she would find hard to explain on a day when she is supposedly not well enough to go to work.

The Lensfield Road traffic lights stay red for what seems an eternity, but soon she finds herself in the relative calm of the city centre, where only buses, taxis and other cyclists threaten her health and safety. Before realising that she has made a conscious decision, she crosses the traffic and heads along the edge of Parker's Piece, keeping the University Arms Hotel to her left. Past the bus station she enters Christ's Pieces and freewheels towards the narrow alleyway leading alongside the Champion of the Thames. Locking her bike against the railings, she walks around and through the front door.

Inside it is cool, the lighting subdued. Her favourite alcove seat is occupied by an elderly couple, so she contemplates walking out again, but notices that their glasses are empty. Will they refill them? She decides to take the risk, orders a glass of wine, then sits at an adjoining table. They put their jackets on and she grips her glass, ready to pounce, but then they fall back into conversation. She struggles to restrain the urge to tell them to piss off and finish talking somewhere else. At last they rise to their feet, and she observes that two young men standing at the bar have their eyes on the same prize. As soon as the couple move away, she rushes to take the alcove seat just as the young men try to do the same. She nearly knocks the table over in her eagerness to plant herself before her rivals, and several other customers look around to find the source of the commotion. In the face of this show of determination, one of the young men holds his hand up, open palm towards her in a gesture of submission. His partner mouths an obscenity. She mouths a worse one back.

If she happens to be seen in a city centre pub by a work colleague on a day when she has called in sick, she will face severe questioning or even suspension. What can be her defence? The trauma of seeing her mother's life-threatening condition?

So, Miss Torrance, if you were so concerned at your mother's state of health, why did you make your excuses and leave her on what might have been her deathbed in order to visit a public house?

'It wasn't like that. I'd had a rough time the night before.'

I'm not sure we wish to go into the details of that. And did an infusion of alcohol succeed in taking your mind off your mother's condition?

'I didn't set out to take my mind off it. I just wanted to be able to deal with it.'

I see. And do you cope with all your problems by using alcohol, Miss Torrance?

She leans back and closes her eyes. When she opens them again, the unforgiving young man is still staring, whispering to his drinking partner, as if plotting some form of revenge. She tells him to go and screw himself. No sound emerges.

9

Ignoring the obvious risk, Rosemary walks around the town centre for several hours, watching reflections in shop windows, drinking coffee in the Grand Arcade, listening to a Mozart trio played by young musicians in the Lion Yard. They are smiling at one another because they know how gifted they are.

Arriving home, she throws her jacket on the back of a chair, heads straight for the kitchen, turns on the oven and chisels a pizza from the ice-bound freezer. She removes a bottle of chardonnay from the fridge and unscrews the top, having long ago resolved never to spend more time and effort than necessary to access the contents of a wine bottle. Twenty minutes later, she slips into an armchair, plate and glass on tray, and turns on the TV, knowing that anything she elects to watch will need to be at an extreme end of the spectrum between mental challenge and mindless futility.

Mysteries of the Ancient Egyptians begins with a simulation (hopefully) of a dead pharaoh's brain being hooked out through his nose. *Nostradamus, Seer and Prophet* is based on the premise that the writings of the eponymous French soothsayer have predicted everything from the Great Fire of London to the 9/11 attacks. *Secrets in the Stars*? Perhaps the wonders of the cosmos will provide the required degree of distraction.

The programme, it transpires, presents not a survey of cosmological wonders but a secret history of alchemy and astrology amongst the intellectual community in Renaissance England. Something of a busman's holiday for someone in Rosemary's line of work, but when she tries to change the channel, the remote control refuses to function. As she prepares to put in a new set of batteries, a shot of the façade of Cambridge University Library stops her in her tracks. Indeed, not only does the programme feature her workplace, but it cuts to an interview with none other than Roger Thomas, Head of Manuscripts, holding the very book whose contents he recently asked her to itemise. Her astonishment transforms itself to anger at the realisation that the interview could only have taken place in the last few days, at least if what Roger told her about the circumstances of the book's discovery is true. It also means that he chose not to share something of considerable importance with her.

'The evidence within the manuscript,' Roger says to an unseen questioner, 'points unequivocally to a man named Richard Bonner. We know nothing about him, but his name appears in cipher at a number of points within the book. In one of these coded entries he names himself as the author or, as we would probably say, compiler of this collection.'

Rosemary bites her lip, wondering why she did not spot this salient fact.

'Bonner claims to have communicated directly with angels and with the ghosts of the dead. John Dee's interest in the work is therefore hardly surprising, although Bonner goes further than even his illustrious contemporary might have considered wise.'

So why is this man so obscure?

'Perhaps the most arresting of his extravagant claims is that the angel Uriel revealed to him that he would not suffer death, at least in the ordinary mortal sense. How he himself interpreted this revelation, we cannot tell.'

The screen starts to blur, the edges lose their detail. The effect of a largely sleepless night, combined with a fair amount of wine, is beginning to take its toll.

It is several hours later when she wakes, still in her chair. The channel she was watching is now offering discount jewellery for sale. The wine bottle is empty. The ticking clock mocks her from the mantelshelf. She gropes for the remote control and turns off the television, only several minutes later wondering why this seems surprising.

Nursing an ache above the eyes, she gives a pained smile to the library doorman. The back staircase seems steeper than the last time she climbed it, and the main corridor even gloomier. As she shuffles along, a more energetic figure moves up alongside, then slows down to keep pace. The voice is disturbingly alert.

'Hi Rosie, I would ask if you're feeling better, but you still look like crap if you don't mind me saying so.'

'Thanks Kerry, you look radiant as ever. Don't you have bad mornings?'

'I did once, I think. Guess I'm just a morning person.'

'Must be the prospect of spending the day within these gilded halls that fills you with joie-de-vivre.'

'Hardly. Not these days anyway.'

'How do you mean?'

'Well, since they installed this doomsday machine for reversing global warming.'

'The Big Freezer? It is a bit excessive. Perhaps you should wear more clothes.'

'You sound like my mother. But it's not just that. It's kind of – eerie.'

'Eerie?'

'Eerie. As in, unsettling, disturbing.'

'Is this to do with what you were saying in the basement the other day?'

'All the assistants are talking about it. You hear strange moaning noises that weren't there before. Doors blow open on their own. That kind of thing.'

'I suppose that's what happens when you try to update an old building. The dilithium crystals cannae take it, captain, as a friend of mine used to say. By the way, did you see the library on the telly last night?'

'No, I was out. Well, here's the punishment room. See you later.'

Rosemary enters her office and puts her jacket on the hook just inside the door. Roger is already at his desk, intent on whatever is on his screen.

'Morning, Roger.'

'Morning, Rosemary,' he says without turning round. She stares until he looks up.

'Are you feeling okay now?' he asks.

'Why didn't you tell me?'

He frowns. 'Tell you what?'

'That you already knew all about that manuscript you gave me. That you already knew who wrote it and what's in it, after all the hours I've spent on it. Why did you give me that cock-and-bull story about finding it on a trolley?'

Roger pushes his chair back from his desk and takes off his glasses. 'Could we start again from the moment you walk in the door, because I haven't got a clue what you're talking about.'

'Oh come on, Roger. I saw you on TV last night. *Secrets in the Stars.* Remember? Talking about the very manuscript that nearly made my eyes fall out.'

Roger tilts his head to one side without taking his eyes from her. She slumps into her chair and swivels it away from him.

'Rosemary, you've been working very long hours recently. To be honest, you've been looking a bit under the weather. I realise from yesterday that you're not well. Maybe you ought to take some time off.'

She clasps her hands and blinks hard. 'So that's what this is about? You want shot of me?'

Roger stands up, walks across and rests with his knuckles on the edge of Rosemary's desk. She refuses eye contact.

'Look, I've absolutely no idea where all this has come from. For the record, you're the best research assistant I've worked with. And I think you need to get your TV checked, because the programme you're referring to was about our astronomical manuscripts, all of which I'm sure you're perfectly familiar with. I have no idea what's in that manuscript in your desk, but I do know that if anyone can make sense of it, you can. Now, can we just take a deep breath and try to pretend this never happened?' He raises himself from the desk. 'And remember what I said, I know that life hasn't been easy for you in the last few months. If you need to take some time off, just say so. No-one will think the worse of you for it.'

He waits for a moment, then quietly leaves the room. Rosemary puts her elbows on her desk and buries her face in her hands, but after a couple of minutes sits up with a start, remembering that she took her desk key home the night before last. In her mind's eye it lies on the bedside table where she left it after taking it out of her bag when she finally arrived home from Grantchester. She leans back in her chair and closes her eyes, then hauls herself to her feet and delves forlornly in the jacket hung by the door. In the right hand pocket lurks a small silver-coloured key. She has no memory of placing it there before leaving the flat, and knows for certain that she did not go back into the bedroom after putting the jacket on, yet these convictions cannot alter the reality that the key is now lying in the palm of her right hand. She stares, half-expecting it to dematerialise or crumble into dust. It remains as it always was, solid, inert and inanimate. She returns to her desk, inserts the key into the lock and hesitates. What can there be to fear? That the manuscript will grow an arm and grab her by the throat? That it will have metamorphosed into something monstrous, a giant spider or scorpion, perhaps? Or will it be dripping blood? Holding her breath, she turns the key with trembling hand and inches open the drawer.

The manuscript lies exactly as before. It still feels the way she remembers, the coarse leather binding offering no clue to the portentous contents within. It opens itself readily at the last item: *De evitacione mortis et de revivificacione defunctorum*. The TV programme, or the dream she had of it, mentioned that Bonner was told by the angel Uriel that he would not die in the ordinary mortal sense, whatever that means. She holds the book up to the light which struggles through the grimy window behind her, trying to adjust her eyes to the tortuous script. One section has an apparently original heading: *Disputacio cum Uriele angelo*. A debate with the angel Uriel. She swallows hard.

Mihi dixit angelus, quod mortalis non sum, sicut alii.

Mihi explicavit quod deus vult me in terra remanere quod hic sibi utilior sum, sed fortasse non in modo humano.

The angel told me that I am not mortal like others. He explained to me that God wants me to remain on earth because I am more useful to him here, though possibly not in human form.

She re-reads the passage to make sure. This man may not have written Latin prose to challenge Cicero or Suetonius, but he clearly had no reservations about his importance in the grand scheme of things.

She replaces the manuscript in the drawer, slides it closed and locks it, then slips through the reading room to the toilet and throws up. Under merciless fluorescent light, the mirror does everything in its power to highlight the moist red eyes, pallid skin and cracked lips. Perhaps there is some truth in what Roger said about needing to get away for a while. She bathes her face in cold water, only to find that it has made her look even paler. The application of lip gloss succeeds in creating the impression that she has just consumed a bag of greasy chips.

Returning to the office, she finds Roger back at his desk. He looks up, his mouth hinting at a smile, but says nothing.

'Roger, does the name Richard Bonner mean anything to you?'

'I don't think so. Has he just started?'

'No, apparently he was a Renaissance scholar with a deep interest in the occult.'

'That hardly marks him out. Why do you ask anyway?'

'I – saw a reference to him, but I've never come across him before. He seems elusive.'

'Probably not a great loss.'

Staring at the still-dark computer screen in front of her, she feels a compulsion to discover more about this man, but all that she knows, if 'know' is the correct term, is his name from the TV programme which, according to Roger, she dreamed anyway.

At lunchtime, sitting on the grass with a cheese sandwich,

she phones Jamie.

'Hi, it's Rosie.'

'What do you want?'

She pauses. 'No need to mount a charm offensive on my behalf. I just phoned to see what the news is about mum.'

'Did you really?'

She holds the phone away from her ear, thumb hovering over the red button. She decides to have one more try.

'Look, Jamie, I'm not sure what's going on here. I don't get out of work till seven tonight, so I was hoping you could tell me how mum is.'

'Why don't you ring the hospital and find out for yourself?'

Jamie rings off. She drops the phone onto the grass, raises her knees and props her arms on them, allowing her head to sink. Instinct prompts her to raise it in time to see that two young men walking along the roadway are staring up her skirt. She elevates the middle finger of her right hand. They laugh.

The hospital switchboard puts her through to Acute Admissions, where she is told by a nurse that her mother is no longer there.

'Can you put me through to wherever she is now please?'

'I'm afraid I don't know where she is. I've only just come on duty. I'll have to put you back to the switchboard.'

'Wait. Before you—'

The nurse's voice has been replaced by the theme from the first movement of Mozart's fortieth symphony. A beep warns that her phone is critically, dangerously, life-threateningly low on battery. Under her breath, she urges the switchboard operator to answer or face eternal damnation. There is a longer, flat-lining drone before terminal silence. She lets out a muffled scream, and people around fall silent.

10

'Roger, is it okay if I leave a few minutes early tonight? I need to get to the hospital to see mum, and visiting finishes at eight.'

'Of course. Why don't you let me give you a lift?'

'It's okay thanks, I've got my bike.'

'How is she anyway?'

'I'm not sure. They've moved her to another ward, so I won't find out till I get there.'

Hills Road is long enough at the best of times, but seems to have been extended since the last occasion when she cycled the length of it. Even though she left work early, it is a quarter past seven by the time she arrives at the hospital, and she still has to find out where her mother is. The long narrow entrance hall is reminiscent of the nave of a cathedral, the retail outlets selling cards, flowers, chocolates and magazines taking the place of the side chapels where in earlier days prayers were said and offerings made for the sick and the dead. The shops are mostly closed now, and without their lights the foyer is a gloomy tunnel. Rosemary makes her way towards a radiant beacon, the information desk.

'I'm looking for my mother, Anne Torrance.'

'Torrance? As in the golfer?'

'I've no idea.' She spells the name patiently and the receptionist types the letters in. 'I gather she's been moved recently.'

'Torrance, Torrance, let's see. Yes, ward B3. Second floor, turn right when you come out of the lift.'

'Is B3 some kind of specialist ward?'

The receptionist is already on to her next task and does not look up. 'No. Why?'

The second floor is populated only by the trickle of visitors who are already leaving. The entrance to B3 is at the maximum possible distance from the lift. Rosemary wonders if she should have picked up some flowers on the way, although that would have made her even later, and aren't there rules about not taking flowers onto hospital wards these days?

A nurse is shuffling papers at the desk. Looking up and seeing Rosemary, she drops them into a drawer.

'Hullo, I'm looking for my mother, Anne Torrance.'

'Are you her daughter? You don't look much like her. She's over there, in the second side ward.'

Her mother is in a room with three beds on either side, occupying the middle bed on the right. The one next to her, in front of the window, has been cleared but not yet re-made. The other four patients appear to be in their seventies or eighties. All have their eyes closed, as does her mother, whose face looks bloodless, expressionless and ten years older than when she had her children round to dinner just days earlier. Rosemary pulls up a chair and takes hold of her mother's hand. Mindful that the others appear to be sleeping, she speaks in a whisper.

'Mum, it's Rosie. I've come to see how you are.'

There is no response. She tries squeezing her mother's hand, but it remains inert.

'You're wasting your time, I'm afraid, love. She can't hear you.'

In the bed immediately opposite, a gaunt woman with sparse white hair was, it seems, just resting. Rosemary nods to her, half-smiling. A few minutes later, a nurse wearing a disposable apron appears with a trolley on which are loaded discrete assemblages of drugs. She wakes the patients, apart from mum, and delivers pre-measured doses of liquids and pills. She does not look at Rosemary or her mother, and makes for the exit.

'Excuse me, I'm trying to find out what's happening with my mother.'

'I'm sorry, I can't talk while I'm on the medication round. One of the other nurses will be able to help you.'

The old woman opposite clicks her tongue and raises her eyebrows in an exaggerated way. 'They're always like that. You might as well try and talk to God.' She chuckles.

The nurses' station is unoccupied. Rosemary waits and waits, looks at the clock and sees that it is now ten to eight. At last a nurse hurries past, clearly too busy to stop.

'Excuse me, I'm trying to find out about my mother, Anne Torrance.'

The nurse's urgent pace has already taken her some steps beyond Rosemary when she spins round and replies.

'Yes, she was transferred here from Acute Admissions.'

'I know. I'd just like to find out what's happening.'

'You really need to speak to the consultant, Dr Bialkowski.'

'Is he here?'

'Goodness no. He starts his rounds at nine in the morning. Can you come back then?'

'No, I have to be at work by nine. I could try and get up here at lunchtime, I suppose.'

The nurse is taking slow backward steps. 'Try ringing him. About half ten's usually the best time.' She turns to walk away.

'Do you have a number for him?' Rosemary says to her retreating back.

'Switchboard,' she replies over her shoulder.

Rosemary returns to the bedside for the last few minutes of visiting time, watching her mother's face for any sign, even a tick or a twitch, to suggest that her brain is still operating her nerves and muscles, but a vital spark, the essence of consciousness and personality, has departed. At eight o'clock, she gets up to leave.

'You don't have to go, love. They never bother to chuck you out of here.'

She looks at the woman opposite, then back at her mother.

'Better not push my luck on the first night. I hope you recover soon, anyway.'

The old woman chuckles again. 'Don't you worry about that, love. There's no way I'll be getting better. They'll take me out of here in a coffin.'

As Rosemary unlocks her bike, it is starting to spit with

rain. Cursing under her breath, she takes advantage of the downhill gradient on the way back to town, but by the time she reaches the lights at the top of Station Road it is evident that at this rate she will be drenched long before she gets home. She wheels her bike back to the Flying Pig to await more clement conditions.

Peering into the semi-darkness within, knowing that this is a favoured haunt for some of her library colleagues, but recognising no-one, she buys a drink and sits in a corner. A copy of the Cambridge Evening News has been left on the table by an earlier customer so, ignoring the circular brown stain on the front page, she starts to peruse it. Her eyes skim idly over shop closures, threatened cuts to bus services and drink-driving convictions, until they are arrested by an item buried well after the main news.

Revealed After Five Hundred Years –
The Cambridge Magician

Cambridge University researchers have been uncovering the extraordinary tale of a sixteenth-century academic who lived a bizarre double life.

Richard Bonner was, on the surface, an unremarkable fellow of King's College, a lecturer in Greek and divinity, but newly-discovered letters reveal the hidden world he inhabited away from the lecture room. For Bonner, when not teaching his students about Christian theology and the Bible, had a passion for all things to do with the occult. In a letter to a friend who seems to have belonged to the same secret society, he reveals that

The rest of the article is missing, torn out. She turns over to find that a crossword occupying the same position on the next page has been removed for later consideration. She wanders around the bar in case another copy of the paper has been left lying around, but returns to her seat empty-handed. After two more glasses of wine, it becomes clear that new arrivals are no longer shaking umbrellas outside the door before entering. Her phone reveals that, although it has not made a sound, a new text message has arrived. According to the alert on the screen, it is from Adam. The phone drops to the floor. When, breathing hard, she bends down to retrieve it, the message has disappeared.

Outside, the air after the rain is cool and carries the earthy aroma of humus and wet leaves from the nearby Botanical Gardens. She fumbles with the bicycle lock, struggling to control her fingers, then begins the ride homewards. The lights are against her at the end of Station Road, but she checks and can see nothing waiting to turn across. She rides past the red light only to hear a car horn sound frantically a few feet away. With a howl of tortured rubber the car pulls to a halt with its bumper inches from her leg. Responding to the teenage driver's cascade of foul abuse with an apologetic outstretched hand, she dismounts and walks her bicycle along the pavement down to Lensfield Road, continues through the city centre and out the other side to Bridge Street, pauses outside the Pickerel, then crosses Northampton Street and toils up Castle Hill.

Slamming the front door behind her, Rosemary locks it with greater than usual care, throws her jacket on the bed, opens the fridge and pours a glass of wine which will without doubt be the last of the night. The television offers channel after uninspiring channel. Her computer suggests other possibilities; she googles the name 'Richard Bonner' and, despite the addition of the qualifiers 'Elizabethan' and 'occult', the request produces over five million replies. She tries 'Richard Bonner magician', and discovers that a certain resident of that name living in Kalamazoo, Michigan is available to perform magic tricks at children's parties. She tries adding 'Cambridge'. This brings forth the revelation that Richard Bonner-Jones runs a funeral parlour in New South Wales.

An hour later she takes her empty glass through to the kitchen, glancing at the draining board and wondering what happened to the money she started putting aside to buy a dishwasher. She pours a glass of water to take to bed, stops in her tracks, then checks the list of contacts on her phone. Adam's name and his old number are there even though, after much agonising, she deleted them after the inquest. She highlights the entry and suspends her finger over the Call button, then presses it. The phone rings for some time, but does not divert to a message service. After five minutes, she presses Cancel.

11

Typing 'Richard Bonner' in the search field of the university's intranet produces no result, as does a keyword search in the library's catalogue of holdings. She waits until her boss seems to be between tasks.

'Did you see the Evening News last night, Roger?'

'Yes, I have it delivered. Why?'

'There was an article on an inside page about a Richard Bonner who sounds very much like my bloke.'

Roger frowns, looks down and strokes his chin, then a flash of recognition lights up his eyes.

'Oh yes, your Elizabethan occultist. I'm surprised I didn't notice that. What did it say?'

'Unfortunately I only saw the beginning of the article, but it said that Cambridge University researchers, unspecified, had uncovered some correspondence from him. He lectured in Greek and divinity by day, but he was also involved in some kind of secret society.'

'It sounds like it was based on a press release. Why don't you try the University Press Office?'

'I did, first thing. They had no idea what I was talking about.'

'That's strange. Maybe some ambitious young postgraduate chose to go direct to the paper without running it past them. It happens. But if someone's really uncovered some original correspondence from the sixteenth century, I'm surprised we've heard nothing about it.'

'Have you still got last night's paper?'

'I should think so, if Alison hasn't emptied the cat litter into it. I'll try and remember to bring it in.'

At half past ten, in the open space in front of the staff lift, the only spot on this floor of the building where a mobile phone signal can be obtained, she rings the hospital. When she gives her name and asks for Dr Bialkowski, she is asked to wait while he is paged.

'Dr Bialkowski will ring you back. Can you let me have your number?'

'That may be tricky. I'm at work.'

'If you give me your number, Dr Bialkowski will ring you straight back.'

A minute later, a lightly-accented male voice addresses her. 'You're Mrs Torrance's daughter?'

'Yes. Rosemary. They said only you can tell me how she is.'

'Well, that's not strictly true.'

'What do you mean?'

'I'm not sure that anyone can tell you with any precision. Your mother has suffered a serious cerebral haemorrhage, leaving a blood clot on her brain. In the long term, there may be some very limited recovery, but at this stage we really can't judge. It's still early days.'

'So, in the worst case scenario she could be like she is now, in a coma, for years. The rest of her life, even.'

'We can't strictly say she's in a coma. But yes, it's possible that she won't regain her cognitive functions.'

The lift begins to rumble upwards from the floor below. She waits for it to grind to a halt in front of her, but it continues to rise until the doors scrape open on the floor above.

'You mean, she could spend the rest of her life in a nursing home?'

Dr Bialkowski weighs up his answer. 'Nursing homes are limited in the type of patient they can take. Even there, people have to be capable of a certain basic level of independence.'

'But her body's still functioning. Her heart's pumping, her lungs are still working. That must be a good sign.'

'They are working at the moment, and could continue to do so for months, or even years. But we'll need to monitor her liver and kidney functions. It's not so easy to predict what will happen with those. And if they start to break down—'

'But I've read about people waking up from a coma

68

after years. Surely even medical science doesn't always know exactly what's going to happen.'

'Indeed. But we also have to consider issues to do with quality of life. Whether, given a choice, your mother herself would want to go on living.'

'You mean, pull the plug?'

'That's a rather brutal way of putting it. It wouldn't be as abrupt as that. It's more a matter of allowing things to take the natural course they would take without active medical intervention. Withdrawing nutrition, for instance.'

'I couldn't possibly agree to let mum die. How could anyone just say, yes, go ahead and kill my mother?'

'No-one's suggesting that it's a decision you should have to take alone. You have a brother, don't you? And don't get me wrong, we haven't reached that stage yet. As I said, it's still early days. But I don't want to give you any false hopes.'

As she walks back towards her office, Rosemary considers what she has just been told: if the hospital decides that her mother has no chance of any meaningful level of recovery, she and her brother will be asked to sign a death warrant. She knows that this should have been a devastating revelation, and wonders why she is not shaking.

At eleven o'clock, she sees Sharon sitting alone at a table in the tea room, talking on her phone. As Sharon sees her approaching, she ends the call.

'I have to point out, Dr Turner, that the use of mobile phones is discouraged in the tea room. It upsets the old farts.'

'You can smack me if you like.'

'You're shameless.'

'I come from a land down under.'

Rosemary takes the seat opposite her friend, pouring coffee from her saucer back into the cup. Against the background of animated conversation in the high, echoing room, she is forced to speak more loudly than she would have wanted.

69

'Sharon, things are getting weird.'

'You should try my life.'

'I'm serious. Have you ever had the feeling that everything's just in the very slightest danger of spiralling out of control?'

'Constantly. I recommend the collected works of George Herbert. Never fails to put me back on an even keel.'

'I'll bear that in mind. But do you remember what I asked you about last Saturday night?'

'Of course not. I'd had a shedload of wine.'

'I asked if you believed in a transcendent realm, or something like that, probably not so coherent. You side-stepped the question.'

Sharon sits back and exhales through her nose. 'Yes, I side-stepped it. I thought you'd realise by now, I'm a born-again rationalist and humanist. Look, I don't want to upset you babe, but if you want to know what's going on inside your head, ask a psychotherapist or a neuro-surgeon. You've got some misfiring synapses. Look to science for the answer, not witchcraft.'

Rosemary sips her coffee while watching the queue at the till, male and female, young and old, scholars from all over the world united by their willingness to travel however far they have to in search of knowledge, and most of them looking pretty happy that they have done so. She meets Sharon's gaze and smiles, and for once it is Sharon who looks away.

'Never mind,' Rosemary says. 'Forget I spoke, I'll never mention it again. Let's change the subject. What are you working on at the moment?'

'William Blake. I'm doing research for a book on the sources of his belief system and their impact on the imagery in his poetry.'

Rosemary bursts out laughing. 'You're kidding. After what you just told me?'

'I don't see what's so amusing. It's a purely academic project. You don't have to see the universe the way Blake did to write about it. In fact today you'd probably be locked up if you did.'

'Maybe. But wouldn't life be more, I don't know, multi-faceted, exciting even, if there really were angels and spirits who appeared to us and talked to us?'

For some moments the two women stare one another out.

'Rosie, do you remember what I said last Saturday?'

'Nope. I plead the same excuse as you.'

'I suggested we go off somewhere, get away from Cambridge for a bit. Just to give you a break from everything that's happened.'

'I do remember that. The trouble is, even more's happened now.'

'Meaning?'

'Mum. She's had a cerebral haemorrhage.'

Sharon's eyes widen. 'Christ, why didn't you tell me? Honey, I'm so sorry, I wish I'd known.'

'It's okay. She's comfortable, as the hospital bulletins say.'

'So how is she? Can she talk?'

'It seems not. She hasn't regained consciousness since it happened.'

'Jesus. Rosie, how are you coping?'

Rosemary smirks. 'Coping? Sharon, how long is it since I've coped? My life's a car-crash. I'm seeing things that aren't there. Except mum unfortunately, she's definitely there because Jamie's seen her, unless of course Jamie's a figment of my imagination too.'

Sharon slides her hand across the table. Rosemary takes it. An elderly woman walking past with her tray looks down and frowns. Sharon's scowl puts an increased urgency into her step. She turns back to Rosemary and whispers.

'Rosie, I'm here for you. I'll tell you I believe in angels and spirits, whatever, if that's what you need. Just let me help. Promise me.'

'Okay. Thanks, Sharon. Look, I've got to get back. I'll

see you around.'

She gets up and heads for the door. 'Ring me,' Sharon calls after her. Rosemary raises her hand in acknowledgement.

It is a relief to find that Roger is not in the office. Even so, any residual power of concentration has fled. She walks out into the reading room and unlocks the door into the closed area behind the desk where the manuscripts collection is housed. She has no purpose in mind, but for the moment the cool air and the low light are a balm to her senses. A pile of folders encloses papers waiting for re-shelving. The first sheet in the topmost folder is from volume 13 of the Kellett papers, item 30, the very one she had to go and find. She holds it up to the dull yellow light.

To the London Society for Spiritual Studies.
30 November, 1822

My dear sirs. It is with the greatest pleasure that I am able to report the findings of my most recent researches. Once again, may I express my gratitude to the Board of the Society for agreeing to fund this work. The papers which we previously discussed I finally located in a restricted area of the Lambeth Palace Library, to which researchers are not normally given access, and it was only with the greatest difficulty that I was able to persuade the Custodian ...

She skims the next few lines, but her eyes widen at the beginning of the following paragraph.

The work is unmistakably in the hand of Richard Bonner, yet throws up a great enigma. My previous researches, as you know, have established beyond reasonable doubt that Bonner was born in or around the year 1530. Yet one passage in this work makes clear reference to the supposed apocalyptic significance of the execution of King Charles the First in 1649, by which time

Bonner would have attained in the region of 120 years. This astonishing discrepancy I am, at present, at a complete loss to explain. Needless to say, I trust that further investigation will shed light on this enigma, and will contact you again with a proposal to this effect.

Your humble servant, Andrew Kellett

So, Bonner isn't completely unknown. He was just forgotten.

Taking the letter with her, she returns to the reading room and searches the handlist of the contents of the Kellett collection, but the entry relating to volume 13, item 30, makes no reference to Bonner and describes the letter simply as 'routine correspondence between Andrew Kellett and the London Society for Spiritual Studies'.

'Donald, do you happen to remember who was looking at this letter?'

He casts a cursory eye over it. 'Sorry, no. We've been busy today. It could have been any of a dozen people.'

'How well do you know the Kellett papers?'

'All too well, sadly. A real hotch-potch. I don't know why anyone thought they were worth keeping here.'

'So why do you know them so well? Why does anyone look at them?'

'I'm not sure. A few people seem to have convinced themselves that they contain some sort of secret. I blame *The Da Vinci Code*.'

'What happened to Kellett himself?'

'Good question. Apparently he went off on a manuscript-hunting trip, around the mid-1820s if I remember correctly, and after that he just disappears from the record, thank God, otherwise we'd have even more of this rubbish to keep filing.'

Her finger traces the opening line of the letter. 'He seems to have been in correspondence with something called the London Society for Spiritual Studies. What do you know about that?'

'An obscure group of self-taught scholars with arcane interests. Thankfully, it seems to have disappeared about the same time as Kellett.'

'So, maybe these unexplained disappearances are the reason people go through the papers looking for some kind of secret.'

'Maybe. Anyway, I'm sorry Rosie, I've got to crack on.'

She lies outside on the grass enjoying the sun on her face. The warmth tempts her to succumb to drowsiness, but she forces herself to piece together what she has found out about Richard Bonner. A manuscript containing his writings suddenly appears from nowhere, at least according to Roger. It, or something like it, was last heard of in 1822 secreted away in the depths of Lambeth Palace Library. Kellett, the man who found it, disappears from the record soon afterwards, as do the people he told about it. The manuscript was written or compiled by someone called Richard Bonner who lived to be at least 120, who talked with ghosts and angels and considered himself immortal, in some form anyway. The other night Roger appeared on TV talking from the library about astronomical manuscripts, though in the soundtrack she heard he talked about Richard Bonner instead. Possibly. Oh, and since the climate control system was installed, people are experiencing strange noises and doors banging. Allegedly. Some, all or none of this may be a figment of her imagination.

There must be a simple explanation.

12

It is Saturday, so Rosemary cycles to the hospital just after lunch to take advantage of the afternoon visiting period. Before going up to ward B3, she sips tea in the cafe on the ground floor, wondering why she feels a strange reluctance to undertake the final stage of the journey to the second floor, even though there will almost certainly have been no change in her mother's condition. Perhaps therein lies the key. When the last dregs in her cup are cold, she heads for the lift.

Mum lies on her back with her eyes closed, her head propped up on two pillows, to all appearances not having moved a muscle since the last visit. Indeed, she looks like a corpse.

'Hi mum, it's me.' She takes her mother's hand and squeezes it, but it remains as limp as before. 'Can you hear me, mum?'

This time, the woman lying opposite does not stir. A new patient has been moved into the bed next to the window, but all that is visible is a head with gaping mouth, seemingly disembodied, poking out above the sheets. It could almost be the Roman woman in her coffin in the museum, but clothed in a paper-thin layer of skin. Rosemary walks out to the nurses' station and manages to gain the attention of the senior nurse on duty.

'I don't suppose Dr Bialkowski is about?'

'I'm afraid not. Your best bet is to ring him on Monday morning. About 10.30 is usually the best time.'

'Yes, I know. But you can probably tell me. Is there any news on Mrs Torrance's condition?'

'We're keeping her comfortable.'

'Yes, I'm sure you are. But do you know yet whether she has any chance of recovering?'

'Recovering?'

'Yes, as in, waking up, regaining consciousness.'

There is a long pause. 'I can't tell you that. You'll

really—'

'Have to ask Dr Bialkowski, yes, I know.'

She returns to her mother and takes a book out of her bag. She reads for a few minutes, but before long her mind is wandering. The absurdity of the situation begins to sink in: she is sitting at the bedside of someone who does not know she is there, pretending to be filled with concern and anxiety, promoting the illusion that her presence is making some kind of difference. She walks over and looks out of the window. Beyond the blank, flat grey roof outside, all that is visible is the car park far below. The barriers rise and fall like semaphore signals.

On the way home she stops at Sainsbury's to buy bread, milk and wine, places two orange carrier bags in the basket on the front of her bike and cycles back to the flat. The kitchen clock, through its patina of accumulated dust and grease, proclaims the time to be 3.30, and Rosemary has no idea what to do with the rest of the day. Until recently, she might even have considered going round for a dutiful chat with mum. She makes a cup of tea, sits on the sofa and turns on the TV. After a few minutes she turns it off again and picks up a magazine. Before long she throws that onto the floor, gets up and goes to the phone, listening while Sharon's phone rings eight times and then cuts to a recorded message.

– Hi, you've phoned at just the wrong time, but if you want to say something to Sharon, preferably polite, just speak after the beep.

Despite the temptation to hang up, she decides at the last moment to leave a message. 'Hi Sharon, it's me, Rosie. Don't know if you noticed, but the Arts Cinema is showing *Solaris* tonight, the original Tarkovsky version, not the re-make with George Clooney, and I know you're into Tarkovsky's films so I wondered if you fancied going. If you're not around, no probs, but if you fancy it give me a ring back. Otherwise … see you around. Bye.'

She reads until seven o'clock, looks at the phone, which has remained as lifeless as her mother, then gets to her feet and puts her jacket on. At this moment the phone decides to ring, and she rushes to answer it.

'Hello.'

– Have you had an accident in the last few years which wasn't your fault? Have you—

'Go fuck yourself.'

The evening sun casts the outside world in shades of red and gold, and she decides to leave her bike and stroll down Castle Hill into town, watching groups of young cyclists leave themselves a perilously short distance to brake before the traffic lights and then laugh about it. When did her circle of acquaintances shrink to its current perilous level? *Friends of Rosemary Torrance have been added to the Red List of Endangered Species, there being possibly insufficient remaining in their natural environment to ensure their survival.* It at least explains why she still feels drawn to Sharon despite her shameless advances. Was she this short of social contact during Adam's time? It did not appear so then, but looking back they spent an inordinate amount of time with his friends, who were as numerous as wildebeest on the African plains. That seems an awfully long time ago now.

Sidney Street leads to the narrow alleyway of Market Passage. In the foyer of the Arts Cinema there is, ominously, no queue at the box office. She takes a seat on the end of a row and looks around. The cinema is about a third full. She begins to wish she had bought some popcorn to give her something to do. When the house lights go down and the film starts, she sinks back and stretches her feet out beneath the seat in front.

It soon becomes apparent that the film bears little resemblance, stylistically at least, to the more recent Hollywood re-make, but she has nothing else to do and nowhere else to go, and before long this dark, brooding Soviet film is drawing her in. She has ceased to care that no-one has so far cracked a joke or been murdered or had sex. The alien planet somehow knows the longings and the most cherished, and painful, memories of the terrestrial astronauts orbiting it. She is torn between tears and anger, but everything around her has fallen away and the only world she knows at this moment is located in a distant part of the galaxy.

A head inclines towards her from the adjacent seat, and a voice whispers. 'I didn't think this was your kind of film.'

'Neither did I, Adam, but I want to watch it, so be quiet.'

'I can tell you the ending.'

'If you do I'll kill you.'

She hears Adam sniggering, but it is her the other cinema-goers are glaring at as they twist their heads. She slides further down into the seat.

'Serves you right,' Adam says. She ignores him but knows that, as far as the film is concerned, the spell is broken.

'We need to talk. Outside.'

She storms towards the exit, strides out into Market Passage and looks behind her. No-one has followed. She closes her eyes, leans forward and places her hands on her thighs, suppressing at the last moment the urge to scream.

It is 8.30 on Saturday night and she is in the middle of town, alone. She quickly decides that she cannot face mingling with the revellers in the Champion of the Thames, but is receiving a sharp reminder that she has not eaten since that morning. Her route takes her through the Market Square, past the Arts Theatre and into Bene't Street. Pausing to take in the squat outline of its eponymous church, glowing in the fading light, she enters the Eraina restaurant. It is not long before a young waiter strides up to her with a wide smile.

'I'd like a table please.'

Without any pretence of subterfuge, he looks over her shoulder.

'Okay. For how many?'

'Just me.'

'Right. We don't really … hold on one second.'

He holds an animated conversation with an older woman in the bar area, then walks past Rosemary into a recess at the far end of the restaurant. When he returns, his smile is less welcoming.

'There's some space on the big table at the far end. The customers there say they don't mind sharing.' He reads the disappointment on her face. 'It's the best I can do, I'm afraid. Saturday night, you know.'

The table he has indicated has six seats, four of which are already occupied by three thin young men who clearly believe in dressing down for a night out, and in the midst of them a self-assured young woman wearing a colourful scarf who does not seem to belong with them. Rosemary scans them one by one, quickly assesses them as undergraduates, first or second year. They are all watching her.

'Okay. If they're happy about it, so am I.'

She forces a smile as she walks briskly towards the table and says, 'Are you sure it's okay if I join you?'

The young men trip over one another in their eagerness to reassure her. 'Sure. Of course. Be our guest. You're more than welcome.'

'I'm Rosemary. Who are you?'

They look at one another nervously and then, as if responding to an unheard instruction, announce themselves from left to right.

'Andrew.'

'Tom.'

The woman hesitates. 'Rosalind.' Her accent reveals her to be North American.

'Jamie.'

'Jamie?' Rosemary says. 'That's my brother's name.'

'Really? Wow. That's weird.'

'Not really. It's quite a common name, isn't it?'

Jamie looks crestfallen. 'Yes, I suppose so. Still, a bit of a coincidence isn't it, don't you think?'

She smiles and looks towards Andrew, noticing for the first time his striking blue eyes and smooth pale skin.

Although the bottle on the table is half full, the glass in front of him is empty.

'I don't suppose there's any chance of nicking a drop of your wine until the waiter arrives, is there?'

Andrew knocks over a salt cellar in his rush to refill his glass and offer it to her. She sips it and licks her lips to reward him for his compliance. The wine is red and cheap, not one she would normally consider worth drinking, but at this moment it is infinitely better than nothing.

'So, what are you all studying? Andrew?'

'Engineering.'

'Mmm. Tom?'

'Engineering.'

'Rosalind?'

Rosalind's dark eyes are the only ones not welcoming her in. 'Computing.'

'Well, you won't be out of a job. And Jamie?'

'Theology.'

'Wow. You're the odd one out, aren't you?'

A waiter arrives, and she orders mushroom pizza and a bottle of valpolicella, speculating that the reluctance of her companions to drink is a consequence of the despicable quality of the wine they have in front of them. The bottle arrives within a minute, she samples it and agrees it can stay, offers it around and finds no takers, then pushes Andrew's glass back to him with a smile. He manages a smile in return, but there is disappointment in his eyes.

Rosemary turns her chair through ninety degrees to disengage from them, crosses her legs and allows her eyes to wander around the restaurant. The three young men engage in stilted conversation about their favourite bands and football teams, trying to pretend that her presence is not a distraction. Rosalind snaps.

'So, Rosemary, you've asked us stuff, but you haven't told us anything about yourself.'

'Me? Not much to tell really.'

'People always say that. You're obviously too old to be a student, so what do you do?'

Andrew, Tom and Jamie look uncomfortable at the implied hostility in her line of questioning, but say nothing. Rosemary sees that they are staring intently at her. Her mouth curls into a smile.

'I work in adult films.'

Three of the four lower jaws opposite drop in unison. Rosalind glances down at Rosemary's breasts and looks unimpressed.

'I rather doubt that. What do you really do?'

'Curses, foiled again. I really work in a library.'

'But have an active fantasy life.'

'Oh yes. Don't you?'

The waiter delivers a large mushroom pizza and offers Rosemary pepper from a mill the size of a gate-post. She declines. Before he leaves, Tom asks for their bill.

'So, Rosalind, whereabouts in the States are you from?'

There is a sharp intake of breath from Andrew, Tom and Jamie.

'A little town called Toronto, since you ask.'

Rosemary slaps herself on the back of the hand. 'Mea culpa, mea maxima culpa. You must get sick of people making that mistake.'

'Yep, pretty much. Anyway, we have to go so we'll leave you to your meal. Nice to meet you.'

'Likewise.'

Rosemary makes eye contact with the three young men as they leave the table. They all smile back. Rosalind is the last to stand up. As she is walking away, Rosemary says: 'Enjoy your night. However it ends up.'

Rosalind stops and turns around. 'Meaning?'

Rosemary checks that Andrew, Tom and Jamie are out of earshot, but lowers her voice anyway. 'Well, you're obviously not fucking any of these losers.'

Rosalind opens her mouth as if to reply, then turns on her heel and storms after her companions. Rosemary tucks into the pizza, glancing over her shoulder to see Rosalind talking animatedly to the waiter while pointing in her direction. No-one joins her at the table for the rest of the evening. By the time she has consumed the last of the valpolicella, she realises that she will struggle to rise to her feet, let alone walk home. She hails a young waitress.

'Could you get me the bill. And, look, I think I'm coming down with something, I don't feel too good. Any chance you can call me a taxi?'

The waitress looks uncertain. Rosemary's brain, even in its enfeebled state, reminds her that the appropriate answer to her question is, 'Certainly madam, you're a taxi,' and she suppresses a smile by distorting her face until she feels forced to put her hand over her mouth. The waitress panics.

'Of course. Just stay where you are. I'll get you some water.'

She is aware of being helped into the cab, and of relaxing against the comfortingly cool upholstery within. When she tries to say 'Castle Hill', the sound reaches her ears as a meaningless jumble of syllables, perhaps a folk memory of the Old Norse her ancestors probably spoke, but the driver seems to have made some sense of them. It belatedly occurs to her that she began the evening by watching a film about a distant planet which is more sentient than her mother. Just before falling asleep, she smiles at the recollection that the flustered young waitress never did bring her the bill.

13

The door bell rings intermittently but insistently, like a warning alarm. Rosemary unglues her eyes and squints; the gap between the curtains reveals that outside it is bright daylight. Turning her head towards the bedside clock sends agonising tremors up and down her neck muscles. Once the wave of pain and nausea has passed, it slowly emerges that the time is 1.30. The door bell refuses to be dismissed, so she peels back the duvet, hauls herself from bed and finds to her surprise that she is fully dressed. Unpeeling her tongue from the roof of her mouth, she makes with faltering steps for the front door, looks through the spy-hole and sees an overly rounded image of Sharon's face staring back at her. After a futile effort to brush a few creases out of her clothes, she opens the door.

'Christ, Rosie, what's happened to you? You look like—'

'Good to see you too. Come on in.'

Sharon steps inside and sniffs the air, screwing up her face. 'Have you thrown up somewhere?'

'Not sure. Possibly. Look, do you mind if I lie down?'

Rosemary meanders back to the bedroom, slumps onto the bed and closes her eyes. Five minutes later, Sharon appears with two mugs of tea and puts one down next to Rosemary.

'Here. You look like you could do with this.'

'Thanks. Sorry to be a wet blanket, but I don't feel too good.'

Ignoring her complaints, Sharon grabs her beneath the arms and hauls her to an upright position, then holds the mug to her lips. Rosemary wonders if this is what life is like on ward B3.

'Ugh, it's got sugar.'

'I know, it's disgusting, but you need it in your state. Trust Dr Turner, I know about these things.'

By the time the mug is empty, Rosemary is indeed

starting to feel less abominable. Sharon props a pillow behind her head, then kicks off her sandals and sits on the bed next to her. Rosemary has no energy to complain about this uninvited familiarity.

'I found your phone message this morning,' Sharon says. 'I tried to ring you but I couldn't get any answer, so I thought I'd better come round and make sure you were okay. Just as well, by the look of it.'

'I'm sorry.'

'Stop apologising. So, where did you go to get hammered?'

'It's a long story. Can I tell you another time?'

'No. Tell me now.'

'Well, let me see. I didn't fancy staying at home, so I went to see *Solaris* anyway. I was actually getting into it when Adam turned up.'

'In the cinema?'

'Yep. The seat next to me. He kept talking and ruined the film, so I told him to follow me outside. And when I got outside … '

'No Adam.'

'How did you guess. Anyway, I was starving so I went to get something to eat at the Eraina. It was pretty busy, so I ended up on a table with four fresh-faced undergraduates, three nerdy blokes and a feisty Canadian bitch.'

'They're the worst. What was she doing with the nerdy blokes?'

'That's what I wondered, but if I remember correctly, when I tried to quiz her about it I may have overstepped the mark. Canada has probably already severed diplomatic relations with the UK. Anyway, by the end of the evening I was too pissed to care.'

Sharon moves her hand across the bed with palm upturned, but Rosemary does not look down. Sharon withdraws it again.

'Maybe you should get your head under the shower. That always helps to perk me up.'

'Are you saying I stink?'

'I think it's probably the vomit down your top.'

Sharon insists on running the shower, and seems set to help Rosemary to undress, perhaps even to join her, until she pleads the need to use the toilet in private. Rosemary allows the jets of water from the shower-head to caress her scalp, and within moments the tautness in her skull begins to ease.

'Does that feel better?'

Under the noise of the shower, she cannot tell if Sharon's voice is coming from inside or outside the bathroom, or for that matter from inside or outside her head, so she ignores it. When she has finished, she puts her head around the shower screen just to be sure.

The TV is playing in the lounge, where Sharon is sitting on the sofa watching a 1930s Hollywood B-movie set in Scotland. It appears that genuine Scots actors were thin on the ground in Hollywood at that period. Rosemary sits beside her without bothering to dry her hair, which falls onto her shoulders in damp cords.

'Do you want me to dry it for you?'

'No, don't worry, I'm not going anywhere.'

They watch the film in silence. Each knows that the other has no interest in doing so.

'So, did you have a hot date last night?' Rosemary eventually asks.

'I went to the concert at Great St Mary's. With a man.'

'Wow, your standards are slipping.'

'He's just a friend. I'm not sure he fully appreciated that at the outset, but he certainly did by the end.'

'As in, a knee in the balls often offends.'

'Something like that. Let's just say, our friendship may be a bit more distant from now on. Anyway, how are you feeling?'

'I think I've left the knuckle-walking stage behind. I'm probably approaching Homo erectus in the evolutionary scale of hangover recovery.'

'Look, Rosie, I know I'm not one to talk, but don't you think you're hitting this stuff a bit hard at the moment?'

'You sound like my mother. Well, when she could still talk.'

'I'm serious. I know things haven't been easy—'

'Christ, I wish I had a hundred quid for every time someone's said that to me recently. And, as you say, you're hardly in a position to moralise on the subject.'

Sharon takes a deep breath and stands up. 'I'd better be going.'

Rosemary watches her walk out into the hall, listens for the opening of the front door, then rushes after her.

'Sharon, wait. Please.'

Sharon is already on the landing, her hand ready to slam the door from the outside.

'You don't have to go. Sorry. I'm being a miserable cow.'

'Look, I'd rather walk away than have us fall out. I've obviously called at a bad time. Let's just leave it at that.'

'There's something I want to talk to you about, Sharon. Please come back inside.'

Sharon looks down at the door-handle, then relinquishes her grip. They return to the lounge, sit back on the sofa, and Rosemary turns the TV off.

'Tell me honestly, Sharon. Do you think I'm cracking up?'

'As in … '

'Losing it. Having some kind of breakdown.'

'Hey, hold on. We all think the worst of ourselves when we've got the hangover from hell.'

'It's not just today. I tried to tell you in the tea room. I think I'm seeing things that aren't there.'

'Well, you're certainly seeing Adam when he's not there, but perhaps that's not so remarkable.'

'So you think he's dead too.'

'I'm not in a position to make a judgement. But it's what the Police and the coroner think. And don't hate me for this, but if he's appearing to you now … '

'That's what Jamie said. I hated him for it.'

Rosemary struggles to keep control, but soon her tears

86

are flowing freely. Sharon places an arm around her shoulder and waits for her to cry herself out. It takes some time.

'Look, Rosie, if you don't mind me saying so, maybe you need to get out and meet some normal everyday people. People are good for taking your mind off stuff.'

'I meet people all the time at the library.'

'I said normal people. Look, I'm meeting a few friends tonight in the Eagle. Why don't you come along? They're great fun. It'll do you the world of good.'

'You're inviting me to a pub? You just said I should go easy on the demon drink.'

'You're a big girl. Just because you're in a pub, it doesn't mean you have to get lashed.'

'So, how am I supposed to introduce myself to these friends of yours? "Hi, I'm Rosie. Sharon thinks I'm a sad cow with no friends."'

'Now you're just being self-pitying. You don't have to say anything, this is not some private members' club we're talking about, they're just a bunch of folks. Tell you what, I'll call by and walk down into town with you. About seven okay?'

Rosemary is smiling as she sees Sharon out the door, and is tempted to think that she does not deserve such a loyal friend. But she already knows that Sharon is not easily put off.

It is now just after four. She checks her e-mails; one offers a discount on weekend stays at a golfing hotel in Warwickshire, and another from Facebook advises that her virtual friends have been posting yet more photos of people at parties pulling faces. She opens a folder containing photos Adam took with her camera just before she went to meet his parents for the first time, saying he wanted to send the pictures on in advance to prepare them for the shock. They were taken on one of the bridges over the river just after she had been for a hair and beauty makeover. In these photos she looks, she thinks, as good as she has ever done in her life. Adam clearly thought so too, as he wanted to find somewhere secluded to make love. She insisted on waiting until they got home to avoid ruining her hair. By the time they reached her flat, the excitement had faded.

Maybe I'm not cracking up. Maybe I just need to get laid again.

She picks out her uniform for the evening: tight jeans (or at least they used to be), close-fitting black vest-top and cream linen jacket. She eyes herself in the mirror and decides that, whilst the look is not one she normally goes for, she is in the mood for it. But suppose the only person she ends up turning on is Sharon? And did Sharon actually say that any of the friends she'd arranged to meet tonight were men? If they are, what if they're married or ugly or smelly or just plain boring?

At five to seven the phone rings.

– Hi. It's Jamie.

'Oh, hi. The line's not very good.'

– I'm at the hospital.

'You're what?'

– I'm at the hospital. Hang on, I'm going to move outside.

After a few seconds there is a rush of noise as Jamie steps onto the pathway outside the hospital entrance.

– Can you hear me now?

'As long as you speak up.'

– It's mum. There's been a change in her condition, apparently.

'What do you mean, apparently? What does she look like?'

– Just the same to me. But the nurse seemed to be preparing me for the worst.

'Well, what did she say?'

– I can't remember exactly. Something about, in mum's current state they won't bother intervening if it looks like she's dying.

'Yes, I know about that. I've had the conversation with Dr Bialkowski. But all they'll do is stop feeding her and wait for events to take their course. Nothing's going to happen suddenly.'

– Well I'm just telling you what I've been told.

'Okay. Have they taken the drip out of her arm?'

– No.

'In that case, we haven't reached the final stage yet. We could still be weeks or months away.'

– Maybe that's what they've told you. But I don't trust them. You know how desperate they are for beds.

'Jamie, get real. If they think she's about to go, they'll contact us. In the meantime, we've still got our own lives to get on with. Hold on, there's the doorbell.'

She lets Sharon in. Sharon mouths, 'Who is it?' Rosemary shakes her head.

'Look, Jamie, apart from anything else, I've already agreed to go out with Sharon tonight.'

– And that's more important than seeing mum?

'No, but there's no point flying up there every time someone tells us what we already know.'

– Look, Rosie, it's on your own head. If mum dies tonight and you're too busy having a good time—

'All right, I don't need the sodding blackmail. I'll be there as soon as I can.'

Sharon frowns. 'I take it we're not going out tonight after all.'

Rosemary thumps the hall table. 'Jamie seems to have got it into his head that mum's going to die tonight, just because they've told him they're not going to go on artificially keeping her alive forever. I don't believe for a moment that she's going to die tonight, but what else can I do?'

'I'll come with you.'

'What?'

'We'll get a cab. Then, assuming it's a false alarm, we can go back into town afterwards.'

'Won't your friends be waiting for you?'

'I'll ring Steve, he can let the others know. They'll amuse themselves, don't worry.'

When they arrive at Addenbrooke's, Sharon insists on paying for the taxi.

'I'll go and find somewhere to have a coffee. Take as long as you need.'

'You don't have to,' Rosemary says. 'You may as well come on up. Have a chat with mum.' She giggles and puts her hand over her mouth. Sharon looks disapproving.

As they enter the room where mum lies on her side, Jamie does not look round.

'Hi Jamie,' Sharon says.

Jamie turns his head slowly. 'Hello, Sharon.' He eyes his sister up and down. 'I see you dressed for the occasion.'

'I told you I was going out. Anyway, I'm wearing something black just in case.'

Jamie scowls, and makes a show of taking his mother's hand. Rosemary looks around and notices that the bed opposite, formerly occupied by the laconic old woman, now has a different patient. Presumably her prediction came true. Rosemary finds herself hoping that she did not die alone.

'Mum seems just like the last time I saw her,' she says. 'She looked like death then.'

Jamie opens his mouth to speak, then seems to think better of it. The three of them sit in silence for several minutes watching the inanimate body on the bed, not knowing what else to do. Mum breathes, but her eyes do not flicker.

'Are they keeping her under any special kind of observation?' Sharon asks, looking at Jamie. Jamie shrugs. The nursing staff have not been in evidence since they arrived. The whole ward is silent.

'This is ridiculous,' Rosemary says after half an hour. 'We could stay at her bedside for days or weeks or months, and then she could die when we go out for a coffee. There's no point.'

She stands up. Sharon looks at Jamie and then slowly follows suit. He remains seated.

'Look, Jamie, they've got our phone numbers if anything happens.'

Jamie glares. Rosemary takes Sharon's arm and steers her towards the doorway. Sharon glances back to see him staring after them, looking forlorn rather than angry.

14

They decide that it will be quicker as well as cheaper to get the bus back to town rather than wait for a taxi. When it leaves, it is about a third full; they sit on the bench seat at the back. Outside, it is heading towards dusk.

'Tell me if I'm speaking out of turn,' Sharon says, 'but you seem a bit detached from what's happening to your mother.'

'There's nothing can be done. She's dying, even if very slowly. All we can do is watch.'

'I understand that. But it doesn't seem to be affecting you very much. Emotionally I mean.'

'She's not in any pain. And to tell the truth, I'm not sure I've ever been that close to mum.'

'Jamie obviously is.'

'I'm sure he'd like to think so. As far as mum's concerned, I'm the daughter who went off the rails. Jamie can be incredibly self-centred, yet he's always been her blue-eyed boy who can't do anything wrong.'

'Sounds a familiar story.'

The wide expanse of Hills Road is flanked by mature trees and some of the most expensive houses in the city, all long gravel drives, stone lions and security gates. The vista flashes past; on Sunday evening most of the stops have no takers, and the bus is making rapid progress towards the railway station. As they pass the Flying Pig, Rosemary remembers the news item on Richard Bonner which she saw there, and makes a mental note to ask Roger in the morning if he turned it up. The bus swings around and heads for the station at the end of Cambridge's longest cul-de-sac.

'How long is it since your dad left?' Sharon asks.

'Thirteen years, one month and an uncertain number of days. It was raining, I remember.'

'Jeez, you were, what, fifteen then?'

'Not a good age to lose your dad.'

'But you had some idea it was coming, right?'

'Nope. The first I knew was when I saw his case in the hallway. Mum had kept it from us.'

'Ouch. Do you ever hear from him?'

Rosemary pauses. 'Therein lies a tale.'

It takes several minutes for an exchange of passengers to take place at the railway station. They watch the new arrivals stepping on board, mostly students returning from a weekend away, some with rucksacks, looking tired and grubby. The bus is considerably more full for the last leg of the journey, the seats around them are all occupied, and they remain silent until it pulls into Emmanuel Street. They walk past the dark, empty shops in Petty Cury where occasional ragged figures slump in doorways, skirt the deserted market square, and soon the sign of the Eagle beckons. When they step through the door, it is uncomfortably warm. Sharon buys drinks, they wander around the bar but there is no sign of her friends. They manage to find two seats outside on the patio.

'Your friends apparently didn't think you were worth waiting for,' Rosemary says.

'It seems not.'

'You did ring this guy Steve to let him know, didn't you?'

Sharon wrinkles her nose. 'Now you come to mention it, in all the excitement I think I may have forgotten.'

'Why don't you try calling him now? They've probably just gone on to another pub.'

Sharon relaxes back in her seat. 'I could do, but to tell you the truth, now that we're sitting down with a glass of wine, I'm not sure I can be arsed to chase around town after them.' She pauses. 'I detect that response doesn't entirely meet with your approval. If you're getting bored with my company … '

'It's not that. After what you said about meeting new people, I was just feeling, well, you know.'

A broad smile spreads across Sharon's face. 'Ah, now I get the picture. Listen, honey, I'd better put you straight on a couple of things. Steve is married to a mega-bitch who looks like a supermodel, with personality to match. She treats him like something she scraped off her shoe and he adores her for it, so your chances there are zilch. His mate Tom is desperately sweet, and more camp than a boy scout jamboree. On the other hand, we passed plenty of men with lust in their eyes when we came through the bar. There are easy pickings in there if you're that desperate.'

Rosemary looks at her glass, then takes a sip, her eyes still downturned.

'Sorry, Rosie. Have I ruined the evening?'

'It's okay. I guess it was ruined as soon as Jamie rang.'

'Tell you what, I'll make it up to you. You can come as my guest to—'

'It's okay. A girl just has needs, that's all. Knowing my luck, Adam would have appeared half-way through anyway.'

'Wow, that's quite a thought. Still, if you're feeling ready to open up to someone else, if you'll excuse the expression, that's a good sign, isn't it?'

'I suppose so.' Rosemary picks up her glass. 'Anyway, down the hatch. Hoist the mainsail.'

'Shiver me timbers. Avast behind.'

'Speak for yourself. Let's tap open another barrel of grog.'

A group of loud young men intent on giving alcohol a bad name are blocking the way to the bar. Rosemary asks them to make way, but they pay no attention. She pushes her way past and manages to plant one elbow on the bar. The inebriate nearest to her inclines his head and delights her with the fragrant aroma of lager and nicotine.

'Darlin', if you don't give me a kiss, I'm gonna kill myself.'

'Good.'

'I mean it.'

'Piss off and get on with it then.'

He slides his hand onto her buttock. She takes hold of it, smiling into his eyes, raises it slowly towards her breasts and then slams his wrist against the edge of the bar. The young man screams in pain, and his friends convulse with laughter.

Arriving back outside with the drinks, she notices that Sharon is smiling. Her friend waits until she sits down, then says, 'Don't look now, but the dark-haired guy over there couldn't take his eyes off you as you walked over. Just thought you'd like to know.'

'It's okay. I've suddenly gone right off the idea of having a man anywhere near me.'

'Ah, so there's hope for me yet.'

'At least you wouldn't grab my arse.'

'Don't be so sure. Anyway, this conversation's getting smutty.'

'Quite right. Tell me about William Blake.'

'On a Sunday night?'

'Why not? The more I think about it, the more puzzled I am that a devout humanist wants to research someone like him.'

'I'm surprised you're surprised,' Sharon replies. 'If I was only interested in writers who were also humanists, that would exclude most of the important people in the history of western literature. I don't have to have sympathy with Blake's beliefs to be interested in where they came from, how they evolved and how they affected his poetry. And his art, for that matter, because you can't look at them in isolation.'

'I see that. But suppose you became convinced that he really did see all those strange things, angels and spirits and God knows what? If you concluded that, to him at least, they were as real as his wife, or the desk he wrote on?'

'Ah. Is this leading somewhere, by any chance?'

'You'd either have to argue that he suffered from some kind of delusional disorder, or you'd have to accept that he somehow tapped into a secret dimension most people are excluded from.'

'I know where you're going with this,' Sharon says.

'For the record, I've not drawn either of those conclusions about you, even though you apparently see something others would call a spirit.'

'We don't know Adam's dead.'

'You don't.'

Rosemary grips the stem of her glass more tightly, and her eyes darken.

'Look, Rosie, to return to your original question, if I decided that only two options were possible, that Blake was mad or there really was a secret world of spooks and people with wings, I could then go back and conclude that there must have been a flaw in my original premise that Blake really did literally believe in the things he wrote about.'

'You mean, you could decide he was a fraud.'

'Not necessarily a fraud. I could question whether we've misunderstood his use of language. Maybe as a poet he just wanted to stretch people's imaginations away from their mundane daily lives, away from the tired certainties of the teaching of the established Church. I don't know, I'm making this up as I go along. But as Einstein used to say, zere are always uzzer possibilities.'

'So the bottom line is that, despite being a dyed-in-the-wool sceptic, you might have to suspend judgement if you couldn't draw a firm conclusion from the evidence available.'

Sharon frowns. 'Isn't that what we do in life all the time?'

An hour later, Rosemary is nursing a full glass of wine, wondering why for once it is she who is struggling to keep up.

'So,' Sharon says, her voice raised a few decibels above its normal level, 'what kind of a tale hangs by the question of whether you still have any contact with your dad?'

'Mum and Jamie don't know this, and mum never will now, but on my eighteenth birthday dad phoned me. He said he'd never have lost touch if it hadn't been for the fact that mum was so determined to prevent him from contacting us.'

'And you believed him?'

'You don't know mum. Anyway, I didn't care, I was just so pleased to hear from him. I went to see him in London shortly afterwards, had to pretend I was going shopping, and since then I've always had Christmas and birthday cards from him.'

'No effort spared, then.'

'Sorry?'

'Is he with someone else now?'

'Yes, but I've never met her. She's got kids from a previous marriage. I suppose he didn't want to complicate things.'

'Hmm. So you reckon your mum would have disowned you if she'd known?'

'Certainly would. But that's a problem I'll never have to face now.'

'And, let me guess, in the back of your mind you blame your mum for the fact that your dad left in the first place.'

Sharon's voice is strident, and people at neighbouring tables are making no secret of listening in. Rosemary leans forward and lowers hers.

'No. In the front of my mind.'

'So now,' Sharon says, not taking the hint, 'you're not sure if you really care if she dies or not.' There is a cold stare in Rosemary's eyes. Her friend inclines her head and bites her lower lip. 'Sorry, shouldn't have said that. In vino veritas. Sorry.'

For once it is Sharon who appears sad and remorseful. Her blonde hair has fallen in front of her eyes, and she makes no attempt to brush it away.

'Do you ever get homesick, Sharon?'

Sharon's voice drops a notch. 'No. If I wanted to go back I could, but I don't.'

'You don't miss your family?'

'Not really. You have to understand what it's like growing up in a small town in Queensland. My parents see the world just like everyone else there. I suppose it's not really their fault.'

'So they didn't approve of your, how shall we say, predilections?'

'Not after they caught me in bed with one of my classmates. Carole, her name was. Carole Pickering. Mum and dad came home earlier than they were supposed to. And what galls me is that if it had been my brother in bed with her, dad would have laughed it off. Bastard. After that, I just knew the only thing I could do with my life was to get out of there with extreme prejudice and never go back. Which has turned out to be no problem whatsoever. If the whole town got flushed down the toilet, it would be no more than it deserves.'

'Didn't you say it nearly did get flushed away the other year, in the floods?'

'Yep. And once I'd made sure mum and dad were safe, I didn't give a flying fuck what happened to the rest of it.'

Rosemary notices that Sharon's head is starting to look strangely unstable on her shoulders.

'I'm sorry, Sharon, I didn't mean to—'

'Stop apologising, for Christ's sake. It's not your fault where I was born.'

'But talking about your family seems to have upset you.'

Sharon appears to be on the verge of tears. Rosemary has never seen her in tears before, has always thought of her as too hard-faced to cry. She starts to move her hand towards Sharon's, but something makes her hold back. It occurs to her that the normally tactile Sharon has been unusually reserved this evening.

'I hope we're close enough friends that you can tell me if something's wrong.'

Sharon lets her head roll back and releases a hollow laugh into the warm night air. Several people at neighbouring tables look round.

'Oh yes, there's something seriously wrong. Can you keep a very, very big secret?'

Sharon is now very drunk. Rosemary has a bad feeling

about what is to come.

'If you're about to tell me that you've murdered someone, then I can't promise to keep it a secret. Otherwise, probably yes.'

Sharon looks down at her wine. 'Oh, for Christ's sake, I may as well just say it. I don't expect you to do or say anything, but I miss you when you're not around, I'm on edge if I don't know when I'm going to see you next, there's something gone from my life when we part. There, I've said it. I promised myself I never would, and I already wish I hadn't, but there it is. I'm sorry, I've ruined everything.'

Rosemary was half-expecting something like this, but still feels hopelessly tongue-tied.

'Good,' Sharon says, 'you're doing and saying nothing. So we never have to mention it again. We can just get on with our lives.'

Rosemary is not sure that they can. Although she is not the one who has made the confession, she feels strangely disempowered, as though now condemned to walk on eggshells every time she meets the friend who has been her closest confidante. She wishes as intensely as she has ever wished for anything that Sharon had remained sober enough to keep her feelings to herself. All she can think to say is: 'Do you want to share a taxi?'

Back at the flat, Rosemary realises that she feels more weary than for a very long time. She drinks a coffee, brushes her teeth, goes to the bedroom and undresses. Adam is lying in her bed, half-turned away from her. She slips under the duvet and lies behind him with her arm around his chest and her breasts pressing into his back. He stirs and twists his head towards her.

'Hi, Rosie.'

'Hi. This is a surprise.'

'You know me. Full of surprises.' His voice sounds faint, strained.

'Before you disappear again, tell me one thing.'

'All right. It's not true, East Fife do occasionally win.'

'I was rather expecting to choose the question myself.'

'All right. Fire away.'

'Did you save me from drowning in Byron's Pool?'

He turns away again. 'I don't know what you're talking about.'

'Adam, please, I have to know.'

There is no reply. After a few minutes, she turns onto her back and stares at the ceiling.

15

In the office on Monday morning there is no sign of Roger, but he has clearly been in because on Rosemary's desk is a crumpled copy of the Cambridge Evening News, thankfully uncontaminated by cat litter. She fumbles through the pages, finds the crossword, takes a deep breath and turns back to the previous page. The item occupying the space where she read the Bonner article is entitled 'Landmark For Hospice Fundraisers'.

In the bottom drawer lurks a superficially unremarkable late-medieval manuscript, sitting where she left it. She takes it out into the reading room, where no-one pays her any attention, takes the key to the side room, locks herself in and turns on the ultra-violet light. Checking once again that the door is locked, she flexes her fingers, then opens the manuscript at the last item and skips straight to the words she is looking for. They stare up at her, as she remembers them: *Mihi dixit angelus, quod mortalis non sum, sicut alii. Mihi explicavit quod deus vult me in terra remanere quod hic sibi utilior sum, sed fortasse non in modo humano.*

No wonder Dee was so interested. And no wonder the Church of England was determined to keep this material under wraps. Although, despite its apparently blasphemous and heretical contents, keep it they did.

Was Bonner no more than a charlatan, trading on the gullibility of his patrons at a time of national crisis and religious turmoil? Or did he really believe that an angel had spoken to him? William Blake was apparently convinced the same happened to him. And if so, what on earth did Bonner make of Uriel's pronouncement? How could he have interpreted the idea of being spared death, of living way past his normal life-span, *sed fortasse non in modo humano*? And what did he imagine to be the special purpose God had in store for him?

The text becomes discontinuous at one point from the

end of one leaf to the beginning of the next. When she pulls the binding open a little wider, a neat cut made by a sharp instrument presents the tell-tale evidence that a leaf has been removed. But why, and by whom? Did the missing leaf contain material Dr Dee for some reason did not want to be passed down to posterity? Or perhaps the reference to the execution of Charles the First of which Kellett made mention? Was it he who removed it, perhaps to show to his colleagues in the Society while he kept the rest of the manuscript somewhere secure?

She returns to her office and looks at the clock to find that, on this occasion, only an hour has passed. On her desk is a pale green envelope with her name on it, in purple ink, in a delicate calligraphic hand she knows only too well. She takes a deep breath before opening it. Inside is one of the library's own greeting cards, the image on the front taken from an illuminated Persian copy of the Qur'an.

Hi Rosie

So, so, sorry about last night, I lost the plot. I hope you won't hold it against me, I'd hate anything to come between us. I won't bother you until you decide you can bear to see me again.

Yours, as always,
Sharon

She opens the door, still holding the card, and looks out into the reading room. The young female assistant on desk duty looks up, smiles and raises her eyebrows. Rosemary hurries back to her desk, re-reads Sharon's card then slips it into her bag, walks over to the murky window and looks out. People are scurrying along Burrell's Walk, bracing their umbrellas against a sudden summer squall. Youthful cyclists in t-shirts laugh as water drips from their hair and sodden clothes cling to their bodies.

'Morning, Rosemary.'

She spins around.

'Did I startle you?'

'Oh, you know what it's like when you start gazing out of the window.'

'Did you find what you were looking for?'

'Sorry?'

He indicates the newspaper still lying on her desk. 'In the Evening News.'

'Oh. No. The article didn't seem to be there. I must have got mixed up about which night I saw it. Still, not to worry. Thanks anyway.'

'Try their web site. It may still be up there. Oh, by the way, is there any chance of you finishing your contents list of the manuscript this week?'

'The manuscript?' Rosemary has no idea why she has pleaded ignorance. He nods towards the drawer in which it lurks.

'The one you've been working on. I'd like to get it to Conservation before they're overwhelmed when the Helsing Collection arrives.'

'Yes. Yes, of course. I'll let you have it by the end of the week.'

At lunchtime, on her own in the office, she phones Jamie. His voice sounds tired and bored.

'Jamie? It's Rosie. Look, we need to talk.'

'Do we? What about?'

'About mum. The hospital may decide any time that there's no point in keeping her alive, and they'll ask us to agree to withdraw intervention. We need to know what we're going to do before that time comes.'

'You didn't seem bothered about it last night when you had Sharon to distract you.'

'And what's that supposed to mean?'

There is a long pause. She closes her eyes and drums her fingers on the desk. 'Jamie? Are you there?'

'I just don't see what there is to talk about. If they want to kill mum, we tell them no. End of story.'

'No, it's not end of story. We'll need to examine the evidence about mum's condition, and we may end up agreeing that there really is no point in keeping her alive. That it would be a kindness to let her go.'

'Ah, I see where this is leading.'

Rosemary does not. 'What the hell are you talking about?'

'I spoke to dad the other day.'

'You what?'

'Thought that would surprise you. I decided the old bastard had a right to know about mum, so I managed to get a phone number from the solicitors who dealt with the divorce. I thought he wouldn't know anything about what you've been doing since he left, but I was wrong. He already knew a surprising amount. What do you make of that?'

Rosemary holds the phone away, squeezing it until her fingers turn white, then slowly returns it to her ear, buying time to think.

'So, what's your point?'

'Don't piss me about, Rosie. You've been in contact with him for years, behind my back.'

'Behind your back? What did it have to do with you? Look, if you must know, dad contacted me, not the other way round.'

'Oh, that's all right then. As long as it's dad's fault you've been deceiving mum all this time.'

'I never lied to her. She never asked me about dad, so I never told her.'

'You know how betrayed she'd have felt if she'd known.'

'Don't be ridiculous. I'm an adult, Jamie, I'm grown up. Even she can't tell me I can't speak to my own father.'

'You know what he did to her.'

'No I don't. Nor do you. All we've got to go on is what mum told us after he left. We don't even know if it's true.'

'Oh really. And why would she lie about it?'

'Well, let's think about that. Has it ever occurred to you

104

that she hated him so much for walking out on her and shacking up with another woman that she decided to poison our minds against him? Or, more charitably, that she felt alone and vulnerable after he left, and wanted to make sure she didn't lose us as well?'

Jamie takes a few moments to think about this. 'That's just stupid.'

'God, are you so blind, Jamie? Loyalty to mum is all very well, but she's no saint for Christ's sake. Dad wouldn't have been capable of half the things mum claims he did. He just wasn't like that, you know as well as I do.'

'All I know is that dad's managed to twist you round his little finger.' Jamie pauses. 'I always thought you and he were suspiciously close.'

Rosemary tries to suppress a gasp, without success. It is several seconds before she can reply. When she does, her voice is low and staccato.

'And just what is that supposed to mean, for fuck's sake?'

Jamie's laugh becomes increasingly distant, then the line goes dead.

That evening, before leaving work, she checks the catalogue and heads upstairs to a long, narrow, gloomy room containing thousands of volumes of English literature. Skimming along rows of long-untouched books, she alights on the catalogue number she seeks and picks out one which has evidently received more attention, entitled *William Blake: Songs of Innocence and Experience*. Outside, the long hot summer has been abruptly interrupted: the sky is overcast, the clouds low and threatening and the temperature has plummeted. She brushes drops of water from the saddle of her bicycle and heads for Burrell's Walk feeling as low as at any time since Adam disappeared. Beyond the gateway several people are standing, gazing upwards and smiling. At the top of a tall tree, a thrush is performing a song of joy, its rapid, melodic arpeggios fit to shame any coloratura soprano. A cyclist who has paused there is recording it on his mobile phone. It is the most beautiful music Rosemary has ever heard. After a few minutes, the bird flies away to repeat its performance for another audience. She rides on, smiling.

At home, she opens the Wikipedia entry on William Blake. Humble beginnings, father a hosier, apprenticed to an engraver at the age of ten. Parents were Dissenters, possibly members of the Moravian Church (a mental note to find out what that was). Influenced by the teachings of Swedenborg (another mental note), including, some believe, in following the philosopher's belief in free love. Hmm, more interesting. As a young child, Blake saw God appear at his window, a vision of angels in a tree with wings like stars, and angels walking among some haymakers he was watching. She skims through much of the long article, but stops when she comes to the accounts of his death, on the day of which he was working, ironically enough, on illustrations to Dante's *Inferno*. When approaching the moment of death, he was said to have started singing hymns and describing the heavenly delights he saw awaiting him.

There is more. He promises his wife Catherine that he will still be with her, and after his death, although she continues to administer the promotion of his work, she declines to take any major decision until she has consulted with her late husband. On her own deathbed, she talks to William as if he is in the next room, telling him that she is looking forward to being reunited with him.

Rosemary decides that she has a lot more research to do.

She opens a folder and looks at photos from the holiday she and Adam took in Crete. There they are still, surveying the ruins of the Minoan palace at Knossos, the artificial ochre-painted columns seemingly made from plaster-of-paris from a misshapen mould. She and Adam are pointing, smiling in awe, the picture taken before they became disillusioned to discover that the reconstructed palace is the fantasy of a British archaeologist. There is Adam pushing against a boulder on a hillside, recreating the torment of Sisyphus, his teeth gritted less in physical exertion than in his effort not to laugh. Here she is, mimicking the bikini-clad models at the Motor Show, draped seductively across the bonnet of the less-than-sexy hatchback which they hired because it was the cheapest vehicle available, little suspecting that it had insufficient grunt (Adam's word) to cope with the island's severe inclines. In this one, she is leaning back against the trunk of one of the specimens in what is apparently the only stand in Europe of a certain species of palm tree with a long Latin name. The image is more Playboy shoot than Motor Show; her body is arched forward to avoid the palm's sharp spines, and she is pouting, bare-breasted, her right leg held at an angle, head tilted seductively to the left as her eyes make love to the camera. She stares at the final picture, the two of them surrounded by their cases in the Arrivals lounge at Stansted Airport. She can't remember who they asked to take it. She has put on a suitably gloomy expression; Adam is already looking for the exit.

It feels at that moment as if Adam was the pivotal point on which another dimension of reality revolved, a collection of memories which, in his absence, now feel strangely dislocated. They may as well belong to someone else.

16

The sinister presence in the drawer of Rosemary's desk continues to exert its influence. Is it the presence of evil? She decides that, as Roger is agitating for the much-delayed contents list, she will have done with the accursed manuscript. She is not sure how she will describe the last item, but she has plenty to occupy her before she has to make that decision. She grasps the brittle leather of the cover, takes it out to the side room with a pad and pencil, and begins to itemise the contents.

Working through the book page by page, she finds little else to detain her. A number of the works are poorly copied and error-strewn, and constitute little more than compendia of popular superstition, as John Dee's acerbic notes in the margin indicate he observed more than four centuries ago. Within a few hours, she has catalogued in as much detail as she can bear all the items but one. Her hand hovers before she takes a deep breath and turns the page. It occurs to her, strangely for the first time, that once she has completed this list and the manuscript disappears into the bottomless void of the Conservation Department, it may not be available again for many months, perhaps even years. Surely this can only be a good thing; the sooner this pernicious piece of work is out of her life, the better. But a deeper instinct is ringing alarm bells, warning that she is already bound to it, has made the mistake of delving into a mystery which must be unravelled before she can feel at peace again. She leans back in the chair and rubs her hands over her weary eyes.

There is a background voice which at first seems to be drifting through from the reading room. It is no more than the faintest of whispers, on the threshold of audibility. A few words become audible, and they are not in English. Over time they grow more distinct.

Sum legatus dei, audite me. Audite me sive ad inferna parate.

Her eyes snap open. She takes up her pencil and begins to transcribe the whole work onto her writing pad, working as fast as Bonner's gnarled handwriting will allow, fearing that, if she is interrupted, some kind of spell will be broken. She cannot help but pause, however, as she reaches the words she already knows by heart: *Mihi dixit angelus, quod mortalis non sum, sicut alii.* Somehow, the words do not seem as shocking as when she first read them. She hurries on; approaching the end, she already knows the coda which will greet her as she completes the last line.

Sum legatus dei, audite mea verba. Audite mea verba sive ad inferna parate.

I am the ambassador of God, listen to my words. Listen to my words or prepare for hell.

She closes the manuscript for the last time and puts it to one side, then returns to her contents list, tapping the blunt end of her pencil on the paper. How to describe what she has just read? After several minutes she rises to her feet, gathers up the manuscript and her writing pad and prepares to leave.

This is for just you and I to know, Richard. This is our secret.

Roger looks up as she re-enters the office. 'Are you okay, Rosemary?'

'Fine, thanks. Why?'

'It's just that, you're smiling.'

'Am I? Well, I've just finished the contents list for that manuscript you gave me. I'll type it up and let you have it.'

'That must explain it. Nothing like finishing a job you've not been looking forward to to put a smile on your face, eh?'

At five o'clock, Rosemary gets ready to leave work. She makes to lock the transcript of *De evitacione mortis et de revivificacione defunctorum* in her desk, then at the last moment folds it and places it in her bag, just behind *Songs of Innocence and Experience*. Outside the staff exit, she gets on her bike and cycles towards Addenbrooke's

Hospital, resolving that she will no longer put herself through the torment of sitting aimlessly at mum's bedside: if she has to be there, she may as well fill the time by reading. The denizens of ward 3B seem to share as little consciousness as before. The bed opposite is now occupied by a man who appears to be a little older than her mother. His body, what she can see of it, looks gaunt and pale, clearly ravaged by some debilitating illness. His hair, though still thick, is pure grey. As she walks in, to her surprise he looks up and smiles, and his eyes are bright, clear and blue. She smiles back, then pulls up a chair at mum's bedside.

She begins to take out the transcript, then decides against it, instead removing the volume of Blake poems. On the title page is a picture of a youthful, smiling, winged figure emanating light; he dances away from darkness, towards the viewer and out of the frame. She finds herself smiling at the infectious joy of the image. The *Songs of Innocence* are aptly named, poems about rural idylls in which children play and lambs gambol. One or two, however, contain surprising messages: 'The Little Black Boy' seems nothing less than a plea for racial tolerance, presumably a controversial theme at a time when British colonialism was gathering pace and slavery was still tolerated throughout the Empire. A similar theme is to be found in 'The Divine Image', which ends:

And all must love the human form
In heathen, turk or jew.
Where Mercy Love & Pity dwell
There God is dwelling too.

The man opposite is watching, seemingly trying to make out what she is reading. She holds up the book, and he nods and smiles.

The book's introduction indicates that the *Songs of Experience* were written several years later, and that they represent the state of humanity after its expulsion from the

110

Garden of Eden, as opposed to the pre-lapsarian world depicted in the first book. The opening lines of the initial poem grab her attention.

Hear the voice of the Bard!
Who Present, Past and Future sees

She shifts in her chair, half-wishing that she had Sharon there to explain what she is reading. She lowers the open book onto her lap.

'Blake, eh?' the man opposite says. '"Tyger, Tyger, burning bright in the forests of the night." First poem I ever learned off by heart. Sorry, the name's Derek, by the way.'

Rosemary notes from his clipped consonants and long, liquid vowels that his roots lie to the east of Cambridge, somewhere in the hinterland of the fens.

'Rosemary. Pleased to meet you.'

'Likewise. Is that your mother?'

'Yes. Her condition doesn't seem to change much.'

'That's why she's here. Sorry, I should be more careful what I say.'

'It's okay, I know what the deal is. What's your prognosis?'

Derek raises his eyes to the ceiling. 'They try to tell me they're still doing tests and assessing this, that and the other, but they must think I'm stupid. They just haven't got the balls to tell me. Excuse my French.'

'No need to apologise. At least Dr Bialkowski's been pretty straight with me about mum.'

'Not good news?'

'Reading between the lines, he doesn't seem to think there's much chance of her improving.'

'That's sad. You're the only one who's been to visit her since I've been here.'

She is tempted to ask if he has seen any sign of Jamie, but knows that her question has already been answered.

'Do you get many visitors, Derek? Friends, family?'

Derek smiles, but not in a way to suggest he is thinking fond thoughts.

'They've sent cards saying they hope I get well soon. That's a joke. They say it's difficult to get into Cambridge, but I know deep down they can't cope with seeing me like this, knowing I'm – well, you know how it is.'

'Lots of people do find it difficult, I suppose. Probably don't know what to say.'

'That's true enough, but it also makes them think about things they'd rather not, so they just bury their heads instead.'

Derek brings his hands out from beneath the blankets; the knuckles and finger-joints are swollen and distorted, ravaged by arthritis.

'That must be really painful,' she says, nodding at his hands.

Derek shrugs. 'It's all relative.'

Rosemary realises that on first hearing his accent she did not expect him to be articulate. She feels disappointed with herself.

'Is there anything I can do for you before I go?' she asks.

Derek laughs, then coughs from the depth of his lungs. 'If this were me ten years ago, you could have done a lot for me. Tell you what, though, you could just read me a poem before you go. If you've got time, that is.'

Rosemary picks up the Blake volume, glancing to see that her transcription from the manuscript is still in her bag. She pulls up a chair next to his bed, opens the book at random and reads from the *Songs of Experience*.

'This is called, "London".

I wander thro' each charter'd street
Near where the charter'd Thames does flow,
And mark in every face I meet
Marks of weakness, marks of woe.

In every cry of every Man,
In every Infant's cry of fear,
In every voice, in every ban,
The mind-forg'd manacles I hear.

How the Chimney-sweeper's cry
Every black'ning Church appalls,
And the hapless Soldier's sigh
Runs in blood down Palace walls.

But most thro' midnight streets I hear
How the youthful Harlot's curse
Blasts the new born Infant's tear,
And blights with plagues the Marriage hearse.

'Sorry, that wasn't terribly cheerful, was it?'

'I'd enjoy listening to you read the phone directory, Rosemary. Mind you, I've never been to London.'

'Never? Wow.'

'Nope, and I don't think I'll bother after hearing that.' He smiles. 'I've never been a great one for travel. Oh, I know they say it broadens the mind and all that, but I reckon what broadens your mind is people and books. In that order.'

Rosemary ponders for a moment. 'I don't think I'd disagree with you. Mind you, people can bring you pain as well as pleasure.'

'That's why they broaden the mind.'

She rises to her feet and takes one of Derek's distorted hands in hers.

'Well, I'll see you next time I come in if you're still here. That is – sorry, that didn't come out quite right, I meant … '

'I know what you meant. And don't you worry, they won't be carrying me out in a wooden box just yet. Especially if I've got something to look forward to.'

As she makes her way out of the hospital, Rosemary wonders if befriending someone seemingly in the latter stages of a terminal illness, and who already seems to have taken a shine to her, is an unmitigatedly good idea. Dodging buses on her bicycle to rejoin the main road she concludes that, even if Derek does fancy her, he is hardly in a position to do anything about it. Before long, she feels guilty for doubting the value of bringing a short period of pleasure to the life of a dying man. Anyway, Derek seems interesting. Talking to him has to be an improvement on staring at her mother's inert and expressionless face.

When she reaches the town centre, she detours to the Champion of the Thames. Wine-glass in hand, she is making for her alcove seat when a voice calls her name. Behind her are two library colleagues, Jayne and Mary, sitting at the end of a large table.

'Pull up a stool and join us,' Jayne says.

'Sure I'm not intruding?'

'We like to be inclusive,' Mary says. 'I'm bored talking to Jayne anyway.'

They clink glasses. Jayne sips a tonic water, Mary grips a pint.

'I haven't seen you two in here before,' Rosemary says to get the conversational ball rolling.

'We were going to a concert in Jesus Chapel,' Mary says. 'But it got cancelled at the last minute. Soloist went down with syphilis or something.'

'Laryngitis,' Jayne corrects. 'Anyway, it would probably have been crap, Mary's ideas usually are. So, what brings you out, Rosie?'

'I'm on the way back from Addenbrooke's. I've been visiting my mother.'

'Nothing serious I hope,' Mary says.

'They're, as you might say, still doing tests.'

'That's what they always say.'

Jayne frowns. 'Mary, I don't think that's what Rosie wants to hear.'

'It's okay,' Rosemary says, 'in this case I suspect Mary's right. Mum's suffered a cerebral haemorrhage. I don't think there's much they can do for her.'

Mary puts her hand on Rosemary's shoulder and grips it powerfully. 'Wow, that's awful. You must feel terrible about it. Especially so soon after Adam.'

Jayne scowls at Mary. Mary mouths, What?

'Strangely,' Rosemary says, 'I don't feel very much at all. Perhaps it just hasn't sunk in yet. Anyway, I guess it's in the lap of the gods.'

She watches Mary consume half of her pint in one go, then pass wind without the slightest attempt at concealment. Jayne grimaces.

'How lady-like.'

'Better out than in. Did I ever tell you about—'

'Yes you did, and it's disgusting. Don't go there.'

'Not as disgusting as when you had to take penicillin and couldn't stop—'

'Never mind about that, I'm sure it's the last thing Rosie wants to hear.'

Through her amusement, Rosemary knows that she is picking up distinctive undercurrents in their conversation. She drains her glass of wine.

'Same again?'

'You bet.'

She places the replenished glasses back on the table, sits astride her stool, takes a deep breath, leans forward and speaks in hushed tones.

'Look, I may be about to commit the most horrendous faux pas here, but are you two, you know, an item?'

They stare at her for some time in apparent bemusement. At last Mary cracks. 'You mean you didn't know?'

'Don't be stupid,' Jayne says, 'of course Rosie didn't know or she wouldn't have asked.' She turns to Rosemary. 'Sorry, we thought everyone knew. It's just not something you put an announcement on the intranet about. Does it appal you?'

'Of course not, it just never occurred to me until now. To be honest, I thought I'd seen you both out before with men. I know I'm naive, but I took you to be pretty much regulation hetero.'

Jayne and Mary look at one another. Rosemary wonders if they are unsure how to reply, or if indeed their replies are different.

'Sometimes,' Jayne says finally, 'you have to try both before you decide which feels right.' Her hand brushes Mary's and then retracts. 'I felt with men that I might just as well have been trying to see eye to eye with a different species. Sometimes it was as if we didn't speak the same language. Being with Mary is much more, I don't know, easy, natural. Even if she is uncouth.'

'And what about your friend Sharon Turner?' Mary says.

They are both staring at her expectantly. 'What about Sharon?'

'She doesn't exactly hide her light under a bushel, does she?'

'What, you mean, you think she and I … '

'You're among friends,' Jayne says. 'Sharon's a lively, attractive woman. Anyone would be tempted.'

'Yes, but I'm not like that. At least, I don't think I am.' They continue to stare. 'Hang on, what am I saying? Adam and I were totally happy and fulfilled. We had great times together, we weren't like different species talking different languages. Often we didn't have to talk at all to communicate. Sharon's a good friend, but that's all.'

Rosemary wipes her right eye with the back of her hand.

'Sorry,' Mary says. 'Didn't realise I was going to touch a raw nerve.'

17

On Saturday morning, a young man and woman are performing in the open space in front of the west end of Great St Mary's church, while a portable stereo system behind them fills it with the sound of electronic trance music. The man is slim, dressed in a silver outfit the top of which is open to the waist, like a gaudy version of the costumes traditionally worn by flamenco dancers. He poses, arms extended, as the woman, presumably his partner, performs with a diablo. She is blonde, pretty and very skilful, effortlessly bouncing the disc to outrageous heights, then pirouetting several times before nonchalantly catching it without needing to watch it descend. She is clad only in a tight sequined leotard, and has attracted the focused attention of a ring of male bystanders. She sends the disc high again, and while it is in the air pushes the bucket in front of her towards them with her foot, appearing for a moment to have forgotten to catch the disc but turning and retrieving it just before it reaches the ground. The dull thud of coins striking thick plastic provides a rewarding accompaniment to the music. Her performance over, she takes a low bow, holding the position to prolong the time during which her breasts are partly revealed.

The man now takes centre stage, while it is the woman's turn to strut behind and to either side of him. A number of the audience are clearly having difficulty in focusing their attention on the new main attraction until he produces from somewhere behind him a scabbard, from which he draws, with agonising slowness, a long and fearsome-looking sword. A muted gasp rises from the audience. He holds it up to reflect the light of the sun from its blade, then walks around the semi-circle of watchers, whirling it from side to side. The woman holds up a sheet of white paper and he slowly draws the blade through it. The cut is clean, the edge evidently sharp. Now she stands

117

to one side and extends her arms towards him as he raises the sword, takes hold of it part-way down the blade, tips his head right back and lowers it slowly towards his open mouth. He holds the tip poised between his lips for what seems like an eternity, then it slowly begins to disappear. A young child screams, another begins to cry. Little by little, the blade descends into his body. At length, only the pommel and handle remain visible. The man is motionless, so too his partner, the audience not daring to breathe. Then, with increasing rapidity, he withdraws the blade from his mouth until it is clear. He jerks his head forward, throws the sword into the air, catches it by the handle, sweeps it horizontally before him and takes an extravagant bow. The audience erupts into wild cheering and surges forward to add to the coinage already in the bucket.

Rosemary, standing on the edge of the crowd, smiles and applauds, then realises that someone is very close. She glances sideways.

'Morning, Dr Turner.'

'Morning, Dr Torrance. I thought about pretending I hadn't seen you, but then decided that would be stupid and childish.' She nods towards the performers. 'They were good, weren't they?'

'It's not just the ability to do the tricks that impresses me, it's how they make a show out of it. Not to mention having the nerve to wear a skimpy leotard in public.'

'I might have done when I was her age, I suppose.'

They watch the performers tip the contents of the bucket into a thick blue bag, then pack it with their equipment into a suitcase. The man puts on a track suit over his costume, the woman unfolds a summer dress.

'Have you had lunch yet?' Rosemary asks.

'No, but you don't have to do this. I wouldn't blame you for—'

'Sharon Turner, stop behaving like a platypus. Thanks for your card by the way.'

'I didn't know what else to do. I was a bit upset when I brought it in. I'm afraid your colleagues probably gave you some strange looks afterwards.'

'Just as well I don't care what they think. From what I can gather, some of them assume we're an item anyway.'

'Really? Sorry, Rosie. I've never said anything to suggest that to anyone.'

'What are you apologising for? A bit of racy gossip makes the world go round. So, where do you fancy for lunch? Better give the Eraina a miss if that's okay.'

'Is there a place locally where you haven't disgraced yourself, young lady?'

'Hang on, I'm sure I can think of one. Fascinating creature, by the way, the platypus.'

They ensconce themselves at a corner table and peruse the multilingual menu.

'I'm tempted by the thick pork sausage,' Sharon says.

'That'll be a first for you. I had you down for the tarte vaginale.'

'I think that's viennoise. And if you don't mind my saying so, you're acquiring the tongue of a guttersnipe, Ms Torrance.'

'Keep your thoughts to yourself, you rapscallion.'

'Rosie, you don't even know what that means.'

'Of course I do. It's a cross between a rascal and a postilion.'

A faint shadow falls across the table.

'May ah tek your order?'

They look up to see a young waiter who is good-looking, bright-eyed and, from his accent, outrageously French. He holds Rosemary's eyes for just longer than necessary. She gives no sign of discomfort.

'Just a few more minutes,' Sharon says. She is not smiling.

'Of course. Just wev to me when you are ready. Ah will cuhm at wuhnce.'

As he walks away, Rosemary is grinning.

'How crass is that?' Sharon hisses. 'He's exaggerating that accent just because he thinks we're turned on by it.

"Ah will cuhm at wuhnce." For God's sake.'

Rosemary shrugs. 'It can't be very exciting waiting on tables. You can't blame him for flirting a bit.'

Sharon sits back in her chair, ignores the menu and folds her arms. Rosemary tries to catch her eye, but she looks away. This goes on for several minutes.

'Have you made any progress with William Blake?' Rosemary says at last.

'Depends what you mean by progress.'

'Well, maybe as in finding out something you didn't know before.'

'In that case, no.'

'Can I ask you something?'

'If you must.'

Sharon keeps her eyes fixed on the window, even though it is impossible to see much through the frosted glass. Rosemary gives an exasperated sigh. 'Sharon, this is like pulling teeth. Maybe I should just get up and leave now.'

Sharon takes so long to reply that Rosemary thinks she is about to agree, but she looks back and says, 'No, don't do that. I'm sorry, I get jealous, and yes I know it's childish. Ask me what you want to know and I'll do my best to answer.'

'Not sure I want to now.'

They stare at one another, then simultaneously erupt into laughter, not caring that they have attracted the attention of most of the other diners.

'Go on, ask me, you cow, get it over with.'

'It's really boring.'

'Don't bother then.'

'Okay. In your research, have you come across an early nineteenth-century group called the London Society for Spiritual Studies?'

Sharon ponders for a moment. 'I don't think so. At that time there were a lot of obscure bodies dedicated to matters philosophical, scientific, religious and plain crackpot, but some of them are barely more than a footnote

120

in the records. Do you know for certain that this society existed?'

'Oh yes, there are odd items of correspondence in the Kellett Papers.'

Sharon looks askance. 'So what's your interest in it?'

Rosemary wants to unburden herself, to ask for her friend's help in resolving the mystery into which she has been drawn. Instead, she says, 'Nothing that exciting really. One of Kellett's letters mentions a character who may be the same person who crops up in a manuscript I've been working on.'

'Hang on, I thought you said this was in the early nineteenth century. You work on medieval and Renaissance manuscripts.'

Rosemary hesitates. 'Well, it's … quite a tenuous connection. Never mind, forget I asked.' She looks down at the menu. 'Shall we order? I'm starving.'

Sharon pushes her chair back and rises to her feet.

'What's the matter?'

'Ah em guhing to wev to ze wetter.'

An hour later, Sharon pours the last few drops from their wine bottle into Rosemary's glass.

'You're not drinking much,' Rosemary says.

'I've learned my lesson. Now, are you going to tell me what this is all about?'

'What what's all—'

'Come on, Rosie, you've piqued my curiosity. How can a character mentioned in a medieval manuscript have anything to do with this nineteenth-century society?'

'I'm not sure you deserve to know. You were a naughty girl earlier.'

'Do you want to find out how naughty I can get?'

'Probably not.' Rosemary studies her glass. 'He was called Richard Bonner. Possibly still is. Look, I'm going to order another glass, do you want one?'

'No thanks. So who was, or is, and I'm confused already by the way, this Richard Bonner?'

'An obscure Elizabethan with an unhealthy interest in the occult.'

'But not too obscure to be mentioned in a letter hundreds of years later.'

Rosemary's mind begins to race. She wishes that she had stayed more sober, but senses that it is now too late to go back. 'It seems that Richard Bonner never died.'

Sharon waits, her face betraying no emotion. 'Go on.'

'Andrew Kellett had a particular interest in Bonner. He'd discovered that he was born sometime around 1530. In 1822, Kellett wrote to the London Society for Spiritual Studies about a manuscript he'd discovered in the depths of Lambeth Palace Library, and in which he'd identified Bonner's handwriting. This work, according to Kellett, mentions the execution of Charles the First.'

Sharon still looks unexcited. 'This is only interesting if Kellett was right in identifying Bonner's hand in the manuscript, and in establishing the year of his birth. Which clearly he wasn't in one or the other case, or both, because otherwise Bonner would have been 120 years old when Charles was executed. Which, unless he'd spent his life in a remote village in the Carpathians, is impossible.'

'Hang on, though, there's more. I've come across a manuscript in the library which sounds suspiciously like the one Kellett was referring to.'

'Your point being?'

'No-one knows where it came from.'

'Lambeth Palace Library, from what you just said.'

'No, I mean no-one knows how it turned up in Cambridge. It's not in the catalogues. It just materialised on a trolley the other day. We've absolutely no record of it.'

'All right, someone stole it from Lambeth Palace Library, got cold feet and decided to abandon it.'

Rosemary holds her glass up to the waiter to indicate that she would like it refilled. He smiles and gives the faintest of bows. This time she does not smile back.

'I know more than this, Sharon, but I don't know that

you'll thank me for telling you.'

'Doesn't it just piss you off when people say things like that?'

The waiter arrives with a fresh glass of wine. Being met by silence, he moves quickly away. Rosemary speaks so quietly that Sharon is forced to lean forward.

'In this manuscript, Bonner says he met the angel Uriel, who told him that God wanted him to remain on earth in some form or other, instead of dying in the usual way.'

Sharon nods. 'Now I see where this is going.'

'Bonner's still here,' Rosemary whispers. 'Now. I think he's trying to contact me.'

Something just out of her field of vision attracts her attention, a figure seemingly watching from the adjoining table. She turns and sees it occupied by a group of complete strangers totally involved in one another's company.

'Rosie, are you okay?'

'Fine, thanks. I seem to be having difficulty working out what's real and what isn't these days.'

'Talk to a quantum physicist, that'll cheer you up. Look, Rosie, can I say something to you, as a friend? It may be you're suffering some kind of delayed reaction to everything that's happened to you. You've had one trauma after another. It would be enough to make anyone, how shall I say, temporarily mentally fragile.'

Rosemary's voice suddenly sounds drained. 'I'm not cracking up. I'm strong enough to get over it.'

'I know you are. But there's nothing weak about allowing yourself to take it easy for a while. We all need to do that sometimes.'

'I didn't ask for any of this.' Rosemary is close to tears. Sharon reaches her hand across the table.

'Of course you didn't. Life's just thrown you a triple whammy out of leftfield, or whatever illiterate bollocks people talk these days. Look, perhaps it's time to go and see someone. Just to talk all these issues through. I'll come with you if you like.'

Rosemary watches her friend through moistened eyes.

'Come on, Rosie, I'll sort the bill on the way out.'

As Sharon steers her by the arm out onto the street, the strength of the sunlight is punishing.

Rosemary and Adam are running naked into the Mediterranean Sea in broad daylight, whooping with delight. The secluded cove they were told about, judging by the number of young, slim and unclothed sun-worshippers on its beach, must have its own section in the Lonely Planet guide. The two lovers are unconcerned about the lack of privacy, at this moment do not care in the slightest who may be watching them. They swim out through vigorous waves, squint up at dark, winged shapes in the cloudless sky, then make their way back towards the shallow river which flows into the sea at one end of the beach. On one bank are huge rushes, out of which swallows and kingfishers dart and dive. Adam speculates that the rushes are papyrus.

'Have you actually seen papyrus, Adam?'

'It doesn't grow very well in Scotland.'

'Then how do you know what it looks like?'

'From Sunday School. Moses in the bullrushes. We had a book with all the stories in it, complete with drawings. This is just like the picture of the river bank where Moses was found.'

'Well, no need to consult a botanist then.'

The shallow river has been warmed by the endless sun and, floating on their backs with their eyes closed, they soon become drowsy. Rosemary feels her head being pulled under the water, tries to jerk it upwards but her neck muscles refuse to respond. She flails her arms and legs, opens her eyes wide, sees the sunlight fading.

Strong arms enclose her, she grasps them and begins to cough violently. A hand strokes her head. The voice is a soothing whisper.

'It's okay, Rosie. It's okay.'

Slowly returning to consciousness, she begins to sob,

but the voice she has heard is a familiar and reassuring one. Sharon has one hand on her head, the other around her waist.

'Everything's okay. You're safe. Just let it go.'

She allows herself to sink into Sharon's body.

'I'll look after you,' Sharon whispers. 'I can help you.'

Rosemary opens her eyes and sees that she is in Sharon's house, on the pastel green sofa in the lounge. All is silent, no radio plays, no TV, no music. It occurs to her that Sharon has been just sitting there, waiting for her to wake. A rotund ginger cat lies along the back of the sofa, watching her through half-closed eyes.

'Why don't you stop here for the weekend? Just to give you some breathing space. I don't like the thought of you being on your own at the moment.'

'Are you putting me on suicide watch?'

'Of course not. But sometimes it's not good to be alone. Don't worry, there's no hidden strings attached, I just think you'd be better off with some company.'

Rosemary's head sinks forward onto Sharon's chest.

'I do a mean baked trout.'

'Okay. Thanks, Sharon. I'll need to go home and fetch a few things, though.'

18

Walking into her flat, Rosemary feels the hairs rise on her arms. She checks every room but finds nothing out of place. Returning to the hall, she sees that a message has been left on her answering machine. She does not particularly care who it is from, but decides to check it anyway. The voice is Jamie's, the message succinct to the point of abruptness.

'Ring me.'

No further explanation is forthcoming, and a click indicates that the message is at an end. She curses under her breath, then packs some clothes and toiletries into an overnight bag. She hesitates at the front door, and takes a reality check. It is true that she has no wish to be alone, and, considering the number of occasions on which she has misbehaved in Sharon's company, an objective observer might well judge that she has no right to expect such loyal friendship.

'Cheer up, love, it might never happen.'

The relentlessly jovial Mr Barnes lives on the ground floor. He is the full-time carer of his invalid wife, and is himself riddled with arthritis, yet appears to live each day as if he has just won the lottery. At this moment, however, Rosemary loathes his irrepressible optimism and his refusal to be dragged down by his circumstances. She manages to mumble 'Hi', accompanying the half-hearted greeting with a wan smile.

'Worse things happen at sea, you know,' Mr Barnes calls after her. He is also very fond of platitudes.

As she walks along Chesterton Road, Rosemary wonders whether Sharon will have organised some gesture of welcome. Will she have baked a cake? Will she have donned a seductive negligee? On reflection, it seems unlikely that Sharon owns such an item of apparel. The effects of lunchtime drinking are beginning to take their toll in the form of a headache just at the edge of her awareness. If in fact Sharon seems unconcerned and is merely pottering about, will she even feel the slightest bit disappointed?

Sharon's front door is unlocked so she lets herself in. In the hallway, a vase containing fresh lilies has appeared; she pauses to take in their intoxicating scent. The lounge has been tidied, in the kitchen the dishwasher is working. Out in the courtyard garden, Sharon is reading a magazine through dark glasses, stretched out on a recliner. An unoccupied one waits alongside. Seeing Rosemary, she tips her glasses up onto her forehead.

'Hi. I was beginning to wonder if you'd had second thoughts about coming back.'

'No, I'm too fond of trout.'

'Everything okay back at the flat?'

'Yes. A message from Jamie, that's all.'

'What was it about?'

'He just said, "Ring me".'

'That's it?'

'That's it.'

'He's obviously been on an assertiveness training course. Anyway, sit yourself down. No time like the present to start unwinding.'

Rosemary lies on the spare recliner. Sharon returns to reading her magazine, so she closes her eyes. Try as she may, she is soon forced to acknowledge that she is not relaxing: her fingers are fidgeting restlessly.

'Rosie. Are you okay?'

She opens her eyes. 'I'm fine. I was just thinking.'

'I know what you need, young lady.'

Sharon reaches down and picks up a small tin and a lighter from the ground. She opens the tin, takes out a roughly constructed roll-up, lights it, inhales and then passes it across. Rosemary draws deeply. She speaks in mock-conspiratorial manner from behind her hand.

'This isn't pure tobacco, right?'

'Let's say it's a tobacco-related product,' Sharon replies in a stage whisper, holding out her hand for another turn at the joint.

Rosemary soon feels the tension in her muscles begin to dissipate, and her anxieties to lift.

'Hey, Rosie, it's working. You're smiling.'

Rosemary has seen plenty of her friends doped-up and grinning inanely. Is that how she appears at this moment? Thankfully, her companion will soon be in no position to pass judgement.

'Have you seen Adam recently?'

Even Rosemary can tell that Sharon's voice is becoming slurred. Presumably this is not her first joint of the day.

'Are you determined to break the mood of calm reflection?'

'No, I'm just curious, but if you don't want to talk about it, that's fine. That's totally fine by me. Yes indeedy.'

'Actually, now I think about it, I don't mind talking about it. Him. Adam. It might even do me good.'

'So, what's the answer to my question?'

'What was your question?'

'Jeez. Are you still seeing Adam?'

'Oh. Yes, I still see him.'

'Does he talk to you?'

'Sometimes.'

'And does he, you know, look the same?'

'He still looks the way I remember him, curly red hair and, when he's not in bed, wearing the same scruffy jeans and lumberjack shirt he had on the last time I saw him. In fact, he's watching us from the back door now.'

Sharon sits bolt upright. Rosemary sniggers. 'Sorry, that was cruel. A bad joke.'

Sharon slumps back onto her recliner. 'Well, since only you can see him, Rosie, you could say any old bollocks and I wouldn't know if you were telling the truth. You can be a bitch sometimes.'

Sharon takes another joint from her tin, lights it, inhales and passes it to Rosemary.

'So, do you think Adam visits you for a purpose?'

Sharon asks.

'You've been watching *Truly, Madly, Deeply* again. Anyway, I'm still not prepared to accept that he's dead. If he'd drowned, his body would have turned up by now since there are no crocodiles or piranhas in the Cam, and even the Police have said there's no evidence of foul play. Ergo … '

'Ergo, if he's not dead, where is he?'

Rosemary draws hard on the joint before handing it back. 'There has to be a reason, an explanation, even if it turns out he's robbed a bank and escaped to South America. The mystery will be solved one day. I just know that he'll walk back through the door.'

'Life isn't a film script, honey.'

'We'll see. Anyway, you asked if there's some purpose behind him appearing to me. As a matter of fact, wherever he is, he seems to be looking out for me.'

Sharon half-turns her head. 'In what way?'

'A couple of weeks ago, I think he saved me from drowning.'

'What? Rosie, for God's sake, why didn't you tell me about this? How did it happen?'

'I walked out to Byron's Pool one evening to revisit the spot where Adam was last seen. It was warm so I decided to go for a dip. Suddenly there was a strong current, it came out of nowhere and I was being dragged under. Next thing I knew, I was back on the bank coughing my lungs up.'

Sharon is staring at her open-mouthed, like a fish on a slab. She laughs.

'Shit, Rosie, I'm glad you think it's funny. Did you actually see Adam while you were in the water?'

'No. But somehow I just knew.'

Sharon is struggling to fit the last couple of centimetres of the joint between her lips without burning herself. She gives up and throws the butt into a flower tub.

'I feel like a crazy woman for even suggesting this, but have you tried asking Adam whether he had anything to do with it?'

'Of course I have.'

'And?'

'He said he didn't know what I was talking about.'

'Well, doesn't that rather suggest … '

'But he would say that, wouldn't he?'

Sharon sighs. 'I give up. Look, I know I promised trout, but I really don't think I'm quite up to doing it.'

'Good, I'm still full from lunch.'

The sun has dipped behind the rooftops at the back, but the air is still warm. Rosemary allows her eyelids to droop, listening to the drone of a plane somewhere high overhead, a bee exploring honeysuckle flowers, the distant murmur of traffic.

The light has faded and the air is cool. There is no sign of Sharon. She swings her legs around and tries to stand up but has to steady herself, then walks carefully towards the back door. In the kitchen, Sharon is setting out a tray of hors d'oeuvres, olives, cashew nuts and crisps. Her eyes are bright.

'Hi, don't know about you but I feel great.'

'I'm a bit of a lightweight, I'm afraid. You're obviously a more hardened user than me.'

'I plead the fifth amendment. Anyway, I sorted out some DVDs. I thought we could have a quiet evening, just a few nibbles and something not too challenging to watch. Does that sound okay?'

For a brief moment, Rosemary contemplates the option of saying that she feels less than great, would really rather go home. Sharon is smiling, waiting for her response.

'Sounds perfect. I'm not sure I can cope with a complex plot, though.'

'Don't worry, you'd be surprised at some of the crap I buy. Romantic weepie, chick-flick, we aim to please.'

'That seems a strange collection for a Tarkovsky-lover.'

'I'm a woman of many facets.'

'Okay, I'm happy for you to choose. As long as it's not

The Drowning Pool.'

'Consider it cast into the outer darkness. Plenty more to choose from, anyway.'

Rosemary hits the sofa in the living room more heavily than she expects. Sharon frowns for a moment, then breaks into a broad smile.

'Sorry, I should have warned you. The stuff we were smoking earlier was quite strong.'

'Now you tell me. You seem to have coped with it.'

'I think of it as inhaling the spirit of Coleridge.'

'Coleridge used opium.'

'Yes, but this is twenty-first century Cambridge.'

'Did Blake use drugs?'

'Not that we know of. I don't think he needed drugs to see strange things.' Sharon tilts her head. 'Why do you ask?'

'Just curious. Anyway, what have we got to watch?'

'Well, there's the Hollywood re-make of *Solaris*, but as you've recently seen the original that's probably not a good idea. There's *Blade Runner*, the director's cut of course, all of the *Star Wars* sextet, though the only one I ever watch these days is *The Empire Strikes Back*. Ah, and *Event Horizon*, that's one of my favourites—'

'I never knew you were such a science fiction fan.'

'There's a lot you don't know about me, my girl. But if you're serious about watching something unchallenging, there's that lot over there.'

Rosemary slumps to the floor, slides across on her knees and picks one from the centre of the pile.

'*Gladiator*? Good choice. I've always had a soft spot for the sword-and-sandals genre.'

Rosemary continues to wonder at Sharon's ebullient good humour, and decides that habitual use must have rendered her immune to the after-effects of cannabis. Sharon puts the DVD on, heads for the kitchen and returns with an open bottle of wine and two glasses.

'May as well finish the job off.'

By the time that Maximus Decimus Meridius has had

131

his vengeance, been reunited in the next world with his murdered wife and murdered son, and the final credits have finished rolling, the bottle is empty and Rosemary is struggling to keep her eyes open.

'Sorry, Sharon, I think I'm ready to crash. Do you want me to make a bed up or something?'

'Already done. I'm afraid my spare room doubles as a junk room, just like everyone else's, but the bed's comfortable enough.'

Is it Rosemary's imagination, or do Sharon's blue eyes convey just a hint of longing, of desire unspoken? She risks hugging her friend. 'Thanks for looking after me.'

Sharon clamps her arms firmly around her, and seems to have no intention of letting go. When Rosemary feels Sharon's heart begin to pound more rapidly, she pulls herself forcibly away.

'See you in the morning. Not too early, probably.'

'Okay. Sleep well.'

The moistness of Sharon's eyes gives them an extra glint as Rosemary turns to head up the stairs.

It is still dark, and Rosemary has no idea how long she has been asleep. She tenses as she hears footsteps on the landing, then Sharon opening the door of the bathroom opposite. A couple of minutes later the cistern flushes, the tap runs and she steps out onto the landing, pauses as if listening, then returns to her bedroom.

Next morning, the balmy weather of recent days has given way to a cool drizzle, so they sit in the living room with Debussy's *Preludes* playing softly in the background. Sharon reads the *Observer*, while Rosemary has helped herself to a book from the shelves, a biography of William Blake thick and heavy enough to be used in flood defence. The bibliography alone fills twenty pages, and the index another twenty-five. She heads there first and checks for entries under 'London Society for Spiritual Studies' and 'Richard Bonner', but finds neither. Why did she imagine she would? Thumbing through the list of contents, she decides to start on a chapter entitled 'Spiritual Messengers'. Mr Keats is curled up on her lap, his purring vibrating through her thighs. After a few minutes Sharon says, 'You must have found something pretty interesting.'

She looks up. 'Why do you say that?'

'You're chewing your bottom lip. You only ever do that when you're concentrating hard.' Is this true? Rosemary herself has never observed it. 'Don't be fooled by the size of that thing. I've come to the conclusion there's quite a lot of fanciful speculation in it.'

'I'll have to trust your judgement. But according to this, Blake wrote some extraordinary things in his letters. In 1802 he said, "I am under the direction of messengers from Heaven daily and nightly." In a letter in 1800 he said, "Thirteen years ago I lost a brother and with his spirit I converse daily and hourly in the Spirit and see him in my remembrance in the regions of my imagination. I hear his advice and even now write from his dictate."'

'Blake was always saying things like that. But how do we know what he meant by "in the regions of my imagination"? Look, Rosie, I know why you're interested in this, but trying to make sense of Blake's visionary world can be a minefield, particularly for someone who's – oh jeez, I don't know how to put it. In a suggestible state? You know what I'm trying to say.'

'Or, to put it another way, Blake knew what he saw and didn't worry how other people might try to explain it. Which could also be said about me.'

Sharon watches for some moments, then returns to her newspaper. Rosemary ejects Mr Keats and walks to the window. The drizzle has stopped.

'Let's go punting this afternoon,' she says.

'Can you punt?'

'No. But I'll treat us to one of the chauffeured jobbies.'

'Okay. But the chauffeurs are all good-looking blokes. You'll have to promise not to flaunt yourself like a tart.'

'Don't worry. I'm not in the mood.'

133

Sharon's eyes narrow. 'Moods can change.'

That evening they sit at the dining table, replete with baked trout and two bottles of wine. John Coltrane plays in the background, the last of the evening sun is filtering through the window, casting their skin in a golden glow.

'I'll take this stuff out and get it washed up,' Rosemary says half-heartedly.

'Just leave it. The maid can sort it out tomorrow.'

Rosemary picks up the last of her wine and gazes at Sharon, who frowns back at her.

'I want to do some research, Sharon. Something at the library that's caught my interest. It would be great if you could give me a bit of help.'

Sharon picks up her glass and takes a sip. 'Would this be anything to do with what you started to tell me about in the restaurant yesterday?'

'No, not at all. Not directly. Well, perhaps just a bit. You never know, my research could help yours, and we could achieve more working together.'

'Rosie, I know I said I wanted to help you in whatever way, but I'm just not sure this is healthy. You're getting too hung up on this spiritualist stuff. In the end, I just don't think it's going to help you to deal with what you're trying to deal with.'

Rosemary puts her glass down, screws up her napkin and throws it on the table, then slumps back in her chair and folds her arms.

'Whoa, hold on there, missy. Tantrums at bedtime?' Rosemary refuses to meet her eyes. 'Tell me more about what it is you want to find out, and why. Then I'll tell you if I can, and will, help.'

Rosemary takes her time in replying. 'There's more than I told you in the restaurant yesterday. Some very strange things have been happening. Like I said, this manuscript appears in the library from nowhere, most of it's complete crap, but while I was looking at it in the side room I was called away, and when I got back it had opened

134

itself at the last item. The one written by Bonner.'

'The manuscript … had opened itself.'

'I'd left a book weight holding it open about half-way through, and I checked that no-one went into the room while I was away. When I finally got to read through this last item, I knew what the closing coda was going to be even before I got there. It was as if a voice inside my head had been chanting it to me. There's other stuff too, but I'm not sure even I believe it.'

'And how do you know this piece is even written by Bonner, apart from Kellett's identification?'

'I don't. Well, there was something on TV, but never mind. In a way it doesn't matter what his name was, it's the content that's important. John Dee acquired the manuscript, clearly just for this one work as the rest's rubbish, and was interested enough to give it a title. Anyway, I transcribed the whole piece, I've got it at home. How good's your Latin?'

'Young lady, I may have grown up in Australia, but I did receive a basic education.'

'Well, I'll let you read it. You can tell me what you think.'

Sharon drains the last drop of wine from her glass. 'So, what might any of this have to do with William Blake?'

'Possibly nothing. I suppose I'm following a hunch. But once you start learning about Blake, it's difficult not to be drawn in anyway.'

'I'll grant you that. Okay, let me get this right. The long and short of it is that you want to see if there's any reliable information about this Richard Bonner and that society with a long name you keep talking about—'

'The London Society for Spiritual Studies.'

'Whatever. And the creme de la creme would be to find that Blake had some connection with the London Society blah blah because he too was visited by angels and talked to dead people. Is that just about the gist of it?'

'You make it sound very prosaic, but that's about the gist of it.'

Sharon fingers her unused dessert spoon. 'Look, Rosie, you'll understand if I find this rather a lot to take in. I need to think about it. Let me sleep on it, and I'll give you an answer tomorrow. I can't say fairer than that, can I?'

Rosemary ponders, looks up and smiles. 'No. That's fair.'

'Now, I need to crack on tomorrow morning. I'm going to turn in, if that's all right with you.'

Rosemary sits on the bed in her nightdress, listening to Sharon visit the bathroom, open and close drawers and get into bed. She walks along the landing to Sharon's bedroom and opens the door.

'Are you still awake, Sharon?'

'I've only just got into bed. You okay?'

She checks that the light from the landing is directly behind her, then slips her nightdress from her shoulders. Sharon's eyes widen.

'Rosie, what's going on? You don't have to do this. I ... '

Rosemary puts her index finger to her lips, walks forward, lifts the duvet and slides beneath it. In the half-light she can see the mixture of confusion and excitement in Sharon's eyes.

'Look, Rosie, are you sure?'

She moves across and lowers her lips onto her friend's.

19

The curtains are open and sunlight streams onto the Matisse print on the far wall. Rosemary turns over in bed and sees that Sharon is already up. There is no sound from any other part of the house. Squinting at her watch, she manages to make out that it is already 8.30. She does not have her bicycle to get her to work.

Fifteen minutes later, showered and dressed, she finds Sharon working in her study.

'I've got to go. Sorry to dash off, I didn't realise how late it was. Thanks again for everything.'

Sharon looks up, her lips slightly apart. 'That's okay, any time. Look, why don't you leave your bag here? You can pick it up later. It'll save having to carry it all the way to the library with you.'

'It's okay, I can manage. Anyway, must fly. See you.'

She hurries to the front door, knowing that Sharon is following every step.

She crosses the river behind St John's College while contemplating the additional pleasure to be gained from taking in her surroundings at walking pace, rather than having to focus on arriving without serious physical injury. Past the college gardens and through onto Queens Road; walking beneath the avenue of trees she is aware that she will be late for work, but also knows that she has never heard Roger reprimand anyone in the years she has been working with him. In any case, she can make up the time later in the day.

Half an hour after her appointed time of arrival, Roger looks at her bag, her unadorned face and ruffled hair and says, 'Good weekend?'

'Yes, thanks. The train I planned to get back this morning was cancelled, I had to wait half an hour for the next one.'

Roger's eyebrows rise just high enough to plant the possibility in her mind that he does not believe her, but without further comment he turns his attention back to the report sitting on his desk. She is tempted to go straight to the tea room for a therapeutic intake of caffeine, but senses that this would be strategically unwise. Instead, she checks her e-mail, noting in passing that her attendance would be very welcome at a conference on watermarks at a mid-western university she has never heard of. She has also been offered the chance of a lifetime to attend a day school on the music of Guillaume de Machaut in Manchester. Her attention is drawn, however, to a message from the British Library attaching the agenda for a meeting the following week of an inter-library working group on 'The Fast Track to Digitisation'.

'Roger, do you know anything about this meeting at the BL?'

'Sorry, I should have mentioned it on Friday. I took the liberty of volunteering you. I thought you might appreciate a day out in the big city. Is it a problem for you?'

'No, not really. Don't know how much use I'll be, though. It sounds a bit technical.'

'Tracey's attended previous meetings from the IT side, but the working group wants to start prioritising between different fields of study. Who knows, you may even find it interesting.'

'Maybe.'

While Roger is out of the room, she goes onto the Cambridge Evening News website to try to locate the article on Richard Bonner which seems to have appeared in one edition but not others. Despite going back through the last four weeks, just to be on the safe side, she finds nothing. The Dictionary of National Biography is the next logical port of call; if Bonner is known to have been a Cambridge academic, the DNB should have some reference to him. It does not. Out in the reading room, the major histories of Cambridge University ignore his existence; Bonner seems to have left no footprint.

If he didn't die in the conventional way, whatever that means, perhaps Bonner staged a disappearance at some point in order to avoid any inconvenient questions. The absence of any record of his death would help to explain the difficulty of tracking him down. Has he been active in some way during the intervening centuries? If so, in what way and to what end? With a shudder, she recalls the curse he added at the end of the piece which she transcribed: *Audite mea verba sive ad inferna parate.* Listen to my words, or prepare for hell. Is Bonner pure spirit, or can he take corporeal form? Could he help himself to any woman he wanted, knowing he could never be traced? Has he been systematically covering his own tracks over the centuries? In all likelihood, he would only have to adopt a series of pseudonyms to achieve this. Recent events would also suggest that he has the ability to make evidence appear and disappear at will. But if so, why is he choosing to reveal himself here and now? Is he trying to convey some kind of message? And, most important of all, is Rosemary losing her mind?

'Is everything all right?'

'What? Oh, yes, fine thanks Roger.'

Roger closes the door behind him. 'Look, Rosemary, I've noticed you seem to spend a lot of time just staring at that screen these days. Tell me to mind my own business, but is there a problem I can help you with?'

She takes her time, thinks hard before replying. 'This Richard Bonner I've mentioned to you before: according to the Evening News article, which I now can't turn up, he was a fellow of King's, so it seems strange there isn't at least something known about him. Any idea where I could go to track him down?'

He nods in the direction of the reading room. 'I presume you've tried all the standard reference works?'

'Yes. There's nothing.'

'In that case, King's itself would seem to be the obvious place. Mind you, I've had dealings with their archivist before; I wouldn't say he's the most co-operative.'

If the King's archivist is unwilling, she will need the

help of someone within the college, and fortunately she happens to have such a contact.

That evening, she sits on the sofa with a glass of wine and turns on the TV. Moments later, the doorbell rings. She finds Jamie on the doorstep, and his eyes are fiery.

'Why haven't you rung me?'

'Perhaps because you've become an obnoxious twat.'

'Where have you been all weekend?'

'It's none of your sodding business. Now, do you want to come in and start this conversation again in a more civilised way, or are you going to just bugger off?'

Within a moment, Jamie's face becomes that of the kid brother she knew years ago. His expression is full of apology, although there are no words to back it up. Once inside, he accepts the offer of a beer and turns towards the TV. Rosemary switches it off.

'So, what was so urgent at the weekend that you just had to speak to me?'

Jamie wrings the neck of his bottle. 'It doesn't really matter now.'

'So, you came all this way to abuse me on my own doorstep because whatever you were harassing me about doesn't matter. Well in that case, if you'll excuse me—'

'I needed someone to talk to. I couldn't think of anyone else.'

'Fine. Just let me know any time I can be your listener of last resort.'

'I didn't mean it like that. I couldn't think of anyone else I could talk to about this.'

'"This" being what, precisely?'

'Agnieszka's pregnant.'

Rosemary waits. 'I see. Well, I've no idea who she is, but if you give me her address I'll send her a congratulations card.'

'You do know who she is. I've talked to you about her.'

'Jamie, you must have talked to me about a dozen women this year already. How am I supposed to keep up with them all?'

He shrugs his shoulders and looks down at his beer.

'So which one is Agnieszka?'

'The one who's about to start postgraduate research in London.'

'Ah. Perfect timing. And how do you both feel about this impending event?'

'I'm horrified. She's not.'

'What, even though it's potentially going to set back her academic career?'

'She thinks it doesn't necessarily have to. As long as she gets enough support.'

'Right. And when she says "support", I take it she's not referring to the ante-natal clinic.'

Jamie shakes his head and drains his beer. Rosemary silently takes the empty bottle from his hand, goes to the fridge and replaces it with a full one. His head seems to be sinking lower and lower.

'Are we just talking money?'

'No, she's not bothered about money, she lives on fresh air. She wants me to go down to London with her.'

'But she knows about mum, right?'

Jamie hesitates. 'No. I've never mentioned mum to her. I didn't want to complicate things.'

'That's handy. So, what was your answer?'

'Initially I said no, of course. But the more I think about it, the more I feel I'm being a coward, trying to run away from responsibility. If I'm the father of her child—'

'If? You mean she's not even sure?'

'It was a rhetorical "if". Given that I'm the father of her child, I can't really turn round and say, sorry, that wasn't meant to happen, you'll have to deal with it.'

'Indeed you can't. But isn't there some way short of uprooting yourself and going to live with her?'

'Not as far as she's concerned. And to tell the truth, I don't want to lose her.'

'Ah. So a woman has finally broken through the firewall around your heart.'

141

'Rosie, this isn't funny.'

'Damn right it's not. I just hope you're not asking me to tell you what to do.'

Jamie runs a finger down the side of his bottle. 'No, of course not. I'm saying that I've pretty much made up my mind. I know the timing's awful in terms of what's happening to mum, but what else can I do? I'm in a lose-lose situation.'

'Oh I don't know. It means you're not losing the thing that's apparently most precious to you. For now anyway.'

He looks up abruptly. 'And what the hell do you mean by that?'

'Just that, if she's prepared to use emotional blackmail against you over this, she probably won't stop there. She'll always use the fact that you got her pregnant against you. Every time something goes wrong in her life, it'll be your fault for putting a bun in her oven.'

'How can you say that? You've never even met her.'

She gives an audible sigh of frustration. 'Look, Jamie, why did you come here? What do you expect me to say? If you've already made your mind up, then it's not for me to tell you if you're right or wrong. Thank you for informing me of your decision. Now, is there anything else?'

She watches him descend the stairs. Before disappearing from view, he turns and scowls.

Back inside the flat, she writes a letter to Adam telling him all the things that she never seems to remember to say when she sees him. That not knowing if he is dead or alive is preventing her from moving on, has left her trapped in her past. That his erratic appearances are becoming progressively more difficult to deal with, and the possibility that they are generated within her own mind is becoming ominously real. A mind she fears is becoming unstable.

Will the mental act of composing the letter somehow broadcast it to Adam? What will she do with it now? Post it to the North Pole? She refills her wine glass and decides to leave the letter out on the coffee table. A little, she

142

reflects, like leaving out a glass of brandy and a mince pie on Christmas Eve for Santa Claus. Oh, and a carrot for his reindeer.

20

The next morning, Rosemary remembers belatedly that she has the day off work. Her initial reaction is to wish that this were not the case, that her day will be ordered for her, that she will be surrounded by other human beings however indifferent she may be to the prospect of interacting with them. She puts on her dressing gown and looks out of the window. High summer has bleached any vibrant colour from the scene; the small area of grass across the road resembles the fringes of the Sahara and, apart from a few crimson pelargoniums in a window box, there are no flowers in sight. Even the sky has taken on the hue of dried mud.

A warm bath tries its best to ease the tension in her muscles, but thoughts will not allow her to unwind. She begins to understand the agony of Jamie's dilemma, and realises that she has been too wrapped up inside herself to care very much what is happening to others, even those closest to her. The thought leads inexorably to Sharon. Would it be a good idea to phone her? The chances are she will already be in the library. Perhaps she will come looking for Rosemary in the reading room. A picture of mum is forming itself, mum trapped: in the bed in which she can't even turn over without being manhandled; in her head, perhaps, willing her eyes and tongue and lips and muscles to move, wanting to scream, to tell the world she is still in there; and trapped by those who hold her fate in their hands, who can decide at any time to begin the process of ending her life.

She watches the water drain away before hauling herself to her feet, then dresses and decides that thinking about her mother has made her want to visit the hospital again. The weather still looks uncertain, so she packs a cagoule in a small rucksack. On the way down, she sees Mr Barnes at the bottom, sweeping out the entrance hall. She stops in her tracks, is tempted to go back upstairs and wait for him to finish, but hesitates too long: he looks up and waves. She smiles and continues her downward progress.

'Lovely morning, Mr Barnes,' she says, before remembering that it is not. Mr Barnes does not seem to have noticed.

'Every day's a gift from God,' he replies, curling his gnarled fingers around the broom handle. 'And let's face it, we're a long time dead.'

Rosemary feels the forced smile drain from her face. 'Well, better crack on, I suppose.'

'Quite right,' he says. 'Procrastination's the thief of time.'

Walking towards the road, she shudders as the outer door of the flats bangs behind her. Perhaps Mr Barnes and his relentless can-do attitude can mend door-springs too.

On ward B3, the curtains have been drawn around mum's bed. She waits outside, listening for any clue as to what is taking place behind them. All that emerges is a muffled rustling sound.

'No need to worry,' says Derek from the bed opposite. 'Just the nurses doing their rounds. They'll be finished in a minute, I expect. Sit over here while you're waiting, if you like.'

'Thanks. How's it going with you?'

'Oh, not much change, really. They seem to have stopped even pretending they're going to do more tests. I'm quite relieved, to tell you the truth.'

'Oh. Why's that?'

'Well, it's ridiculous giving people false hope. I don't know what they think I'm going to do when they tell me. I know my own body better than anyone.'

A gull strutting along the window-sill catches her eye. It stares at her for a moment, then with leisurely strokes of its wings soars into the air.

'But if there's nothing they can … don't you feel you'd rather be at home, in your own surroundings?'

Derek thinks for a moment, and his eyes become

distant. 'I remember what happened to my neighbour Alec. They sent him home to die, told him the nurses would call in three times a day to do the necessary. Oh, a nurse called three times a day, all right, for a few minutes at a time. That's all she was allowed, God knows how many patients she had to get round in a day. I met her coming out of Alec's place once, just about to rush off to the next one, and she was almost in tears. She was exhausted, and she knew poor Alec wasn't getting the help he needed. I wouldn't wish that on anyone.' He lowers his voice. 'The nurses here don't know they're born.'

'What happened in the end? Did Alec die peacefully?'

'Who knows? They just found him dead one morning. The doctor told us he'd died in his sleep, but how could he have known that?'

The curtains opposite are drawn back, and she sees her mother lying supine with hands folded, for all the world like a corpse laid to rest. She asks one of the nurses how she is.

'No change,' the nurse replies over her shoulder as she walks away, tossing a yellow plastic sack into a waste bin as she passes.

Rosemary walks across, looks into her mother's face. Mum's breathing remains shallow but regular. She takes one of her hands, and it is warm and limp. She resumes her seat next to Derek.

'I get the feeling they're not telling the whole truth about mum either.'

'Don't take this the wrong way, but sometimes the kindest thing that can happen is pneumonia. Apparently that does take you quietly in your sleep. I hope that's what happens to me. The nurses call it "the old people's friend".'

She looks across, and thinks that perhaps he is right.

'Derek, do you think there's anything after death? Any part of us that lives on, in any shape or form?'

'Nope. They put you in the ground and the worms eat you. End of story.'

146

'That just seems so … I don't know … bleak.'

'Not to me. I find it comforting.' He chuckles. 'After all, who'd want my soul reborn in them?'

Rosemary forces a smile. Outside, the sun is beginning to break through. She turns back to Derek, but he is looking past her, over her shoulder. She turns to see a tall, dark-haired, good-looking man in his fifties. She leaps to her feet and throws her arms around him.

'Dad!'

'Hi, baby girl.'

'Why didn't you let me know you were coming?'

'I didn't know you'd be here. Anyway, we've met up now, that's all that matters.'

He ignores Derek and looks across at his former wife. 'How is she?'

'What you see is what you get, I'm afraid.'

Dad walks over to take a closer look. He stoops to peer into mum's face but makes no physical contact with her. He speaks her name and, receiving no reply, shrugs.

'I see what you mean. What do the doctors say?'

'As little as possible.' She drops her voice to a whisper. 'Reading between the lines, I don't think they hold out much hope, if any.'

'Hmm. Shame.'

He walks over to the window and stares out, clearly ill at ease, folding and unfolding his arms, pushing his hands into his pockets then removing them and leaning on the window-sill. Rosemary notes that Derek is watching her rather than her father. At length, dad turns and walks briskly back.

'Well, there doesn't seem much point in hanging around here, does there? Have you had lunch? Let me take you out. How about Grantchester?'

'I'd rather stay away from Grantchester at the moment if you don't mind.'

'Okay. What about the Spade and Becket then, on the river? I haven't been there in years, they always did a good lunch.'

147

'I don't think it's called that any more. And it's a long way from here.'

'I've got the car.'

'And I've got my bike. Look, dad—'

'No problem, it's a big four-by-four, your bike'll go in the back.'

As they leave, Rosemary holds up her hand, waves her fingers towards Derek and mouths, 'Bye. He manages to raise one skeletal hand in response.

The day is warming up, so they sit at a table outside overlooking the river. On the bank, two small children feed over-sized chunks of unwanted sandwich to a pack of squabbling ducks. The distant hum of traffic on Chesterton Road is filtered by the trees at the top of the far bank. Dad places an empty glass over a wasp which has landed on the table. They watch its increasing irritation as it hurls itself against the side.

'So, how have you been keeping?' he asks.

Rosemary knows that the question is no more than a conversation-opener, and is tempted to respond accordingly, but does not know when she will have the chance to speak to her father again.

'Up and down, I suppose. As you'd expect in the circumstances.'

He nods, as if happy that this has provided a full answer to the question. 'Anyone new on the horizon? Hope that's not an indelicate question, but it's been a while since Adam, after all.'

'Yes. I suppose it has been a while. Doubtless someone'll turn up once I'm good and ready.'

'Sometimes you have to do a bit more than wait for life to turn up. You have to go out and—'

'I get the point, dad. Now can we change the subject? Look, I'm going to get another drink. Do you want one?'

'No thanks. One's my limit when I'm driving.'

She returns with a wine glass filled nearly to the rim. Dad raises his eyes, but says nothing. He takes a sip of his beer, and watches a young woman with long black hair and mobile hips in a short summer dress sway along the towpath. Rosemary wonders how to reconnect with the father she knew all those years ago. This one seems quite changed.

'What made you feel you wanted to come and see mum?'

His eyes follow the girl on the towpath as he speaks. 'Would you believe me if I said it was nothing more than a sense of duty?'

'Of course. Why should you feel anything more?'

'Call me callous, but when I looked at her in Addenbrooke's I found myself thinking that, if she were dead, then maybe I could start to rebuild some kind of relationship with you and Jamie. Does that seem strange?'

'Why would it? And why are we exchanging questions like a couple of rabbis?'

Dad laughs, and for the first time she sees the sparkling grey eyes she remembers so well.

'To be honest, dad, I've sometimes looked at her and thought, if this is all she's ever going to be, like a breathing corpse, then what's the point of keeping her alive? I know that sounds terrible, but there's no point pretending we don't have these thoughts. I imagine her doctor has them all the time.'

Dad nods, and rubs the tip of his finger up and down the condensation on the outside of his glass.

'Anyway,' she says, 'let's talk about something more cheerful. How's life in the smoke?'

'Not too bad, now you mention it. The last of Karen's kids goes off to university in September, so we're looking at downsizing to a better area.'

'They'll still keep coming back, you know.'

'Not if we haven't got room for them. Anyway, it's time they stretched their wings. Karen and I have earned a bit of us-time at our stage of life.'

'What's all this "at our stage of life"? You've got decades to go.'

'Yes, I expect your mother thought the same.'

Rosemary takes a sizeable sip of wine. 'Are you going to call in on Jamie?'

'I'm not sure. He may not be around, and I expect it would be a bit of a shock.'

'Dad, it would mean the world to him if you went to see him. You can't come all this way and not even try. I can give him a ring and let him know you're coming. Or he could come and join us here if he's free.'

'No. I'd really rather not.'

Rosemary's eyes narrow. 'Why?'

Dad looks over her shoulder. 'I think seeing one of you is enough to be going on with, that's all.'

She brings her palms together in front of her mouth. 'Why did you keep in touch with me all this time, and never with Jamie? He was bound to find out one day. Don't you realise how much that hurt him?'

'Look, I don't want to talk about it. I'm beginning to think it was a mistake coming up here after all. Maybe I should just have stayed well out of it.'

'Excuse me? You were saying a minute ago that when mum's dead you'd like to build a new relationship with me and Jamie. That didn't last long, did it?'

'Rosemary, stop twisting my words. You know I've always cared about you.'

'No I don't, dad. I don't know that at all, because you've not been here to tell me.'

'I had no choice about that. You don't know what I had to go through with your mother. Maybe one day you'll understand.'

'God, I hate it when people say things like that.'

'Stop it, Rosemary. You're being ridiculous.'

'"Stop it, Rosemary"? Not your baby girl any more when I challenge you, am I?'

'I'm not going to listen to any more of this. I'll keep in touch with the hospital from time to time to see how your mother's doing. I don't know when we'll speak again.'

He drains the second half of his pint, gives his daughter

a final stare, then gets up and strides towards the car park.

'Oh, dad. Thanks for the lunch.'

A huge Range Rover pulls out of the car park, accelerates hard and then brakes even harder. Her father opens the driver's door, slams it violently behind him, opens the tailgate, lifts out her bicycle and dumps it against some railings, then climbs back in and races away, tyres screaming for mercy. Onlookers stare after him. Rosemary has another sip of wine, then props her jaw on one fist. The trapped wasp is now crouching, subdued. She raises the upturned glass and grants it its freedom.

Not for the first time recently, she decides that it may be safer to walk her bicycle home, but decides to detour via the city centre. She locks the bike outside Heffers bookshop and heads for the English Literature section, taking care to grip the handrail tightly as she negotiates the stairs. She is surprised to find an extensive section on William Blake; forests have been felled, it seems, to advance or counteract theories about nearly every aspect of his life and work. She finds herself clinging on to three volumes, an edition of the complete collected poems, a biography which is hopefully more reliable than Sharon's, assuming the imprint of the Cambridge University Press can be considered a guarantee of scholarship, and a large, lavish colour volume of Blake's drawings, prints and engravings. She tries to tot up the cost of acquiring these works, but soon gives up the unequal struggle, knowing in any case that it is more than she can afford at this stage of the month. The moments pass in a dream until she is standing at the cash desk, credit card in hand.

Relaxing at home, she sits on the sofa with a mug of strong tea and reads the introduction to the biography and the collected poems, then starts browsing through the art volume. She knows that the style of no artist or writer, however singular, arrives fully formed without antecedents, but at the same time she has seen nothing quite like some of the pictures in this book. Blake's characters have muscles of raw, stretched sinew like early anatomical

151

drawings, and faces which portray joy or wisdom or suffering in their most visceral state. She knows some of the images well from book or album covers, or from her residual memory of an exhibition she saw as a teenager. She turns the pages with a growing sense of wonder.

When she awakes it is several hours later. She is still on the sofa, and wondering why she feels unseasonably cold. Little by little, it dawns on her that the phone is ringing. She decides to ignore it, but for some reason the answering machine does not cut in. The ringing is insistent. When she answers, the voice at the other end sounds relieved.

– Rosie? I was beginning to think you were out.

'Hi Sharon. I'm sorry, I fell asleep on the sofa. Hang on, I need to sit down.'

– Been celebrating something?

'Not as it turned out. I bumped into dad at the hospital. He insisted on taking me out to lunch.'

– That's great. After all this time, you must have been really happy.

'I don't know. Something didn't feel right. We didn't connect somehow.'

– Well, it's been a long time. You can't make up for all those years in a few hours.

'I guess you're right. I still can't help feeling I fucked up, though.'

– It usually takes two to create a fuck-up. Speaking of which—

'How are you anyway?'

– Oh, I guess I'm okay. I called into the reading room today in case you were around, I didn't realise you had the day off.

'Nor did I until I woke up.'

There is a pause.

– Anyway, I just wondered if we were going to hook up again at some point.

'We've been hooking up for the last couple of years, so I guess the answer's yes.'

– I didn't mean quite like that. Look, I may as well just

152

come out with it. Did Sunday night mean anything to you, or should we just try to forget it and carry on as before?

Rosemary has not been looking forward to this moment. 'I'd never slept with a woman before. I was, in common parlance, bi-curious. For that night.'

– I understand that. But you haven't answered my question. How do you feel now?

A pause. 'I feel fine about it. No problem.'

– Christ, Rosie, you're really pulling me through the wringer. Would you feel that it's something you'd want to do again?

'Maybe. To be honest, most of the time, I don't think a lot about sex with men or women.'

– Except over-the-top French waiters.

'Oh, come on, I was just in a jovial mood. Okay, the mood didn't last. But I still have to deal with Adam, apart from anything else. Things are just, well, difficult at the moment.'

There is a lengthy silence at the other end of the phone. When she speaks again, Sharon sounds weary.

– Okay. Are we at least still friends? I'd hate anything to ruin that.

'Of course we're still friends. Like Mary and Martha. Or Thelma and Louise.'

– That's reassuring. We're heading for the edge of a cliff.

'I'm not suggesting a suicide pact. Look, I know this is not the most appropriate moment, but can I ask you a favour?'

– You can try.

'This man Richard Bonner I was talking about apparently taught at King's some time in the second half of the sixteenth century. Just wondered if you could have a word with your archivist for me and see what you can find out. I'm sure he'd be more helpful to you than to me.'

There is a pause. Perhaps Sharon is scribbling a note for herself.

– I'll see what I can do. You know, Rosie, sometimes I

think you don't deserve a friend like me.

As she replaces the receiver, Rosemary knows that her friend is right.

21

In the tea room, Donald sits at a table on his own, absorbed in his newspaper. Rosemary buys a coffee, walks past him towards an empty table, hesitates and turns back.

Hi, Donald. Mind if I join you?'

'Why, am I coming apart? Sorry, I can't believe I said that out loud.'

'Your words, not mine. What's that you're drinking?'

'Ginseng tea. Good for the digestion, apparently. Or is that camomile? Anyway, it's good for something.'

'Does it straighten out your head when you've got a hangover?'

'If you're drinking ginseng tea, I think it's assumed you're too spiritual to have things like hangovers.'

'Perhaps I'd better stick to strong coffee then. Look, Donald—'

'How are you doing these days, Rosie? If you don't mind me asking.'

'How am I doing? In what way?'

'Well, generally. You've not been yourself recently. People notice these things. People are concerned about you.'

She winces. 'Well, feel free to tell people I'm doing fine, thank you.'

Donald looks hurt. 'I see I've spoken out of turn.'

'Forget it. Look, there's something I want to ask you. I'm sorry to talk shop, but I need to know more about the Kellett papers.'

'I suddenly feel the beneficial effects of my tea wearing off.'

'I know, I suppose it has become a bit of an obsession. But I want to find out more about Kellett's relationship with this London Society for Spiritual Studies. Any ideas?'

'As far as I know, what exists is in the Kellett papers, but scattered at random, and as you already know the cataloguing leaves a lot to be desired. I can't say I'm surprised, though, you'd need the patience of a saint to wade through all that dross to find the odd gem of interest.'

'So, until someone gets round to cataloguing the collection properly, there's nothing I can do.'

'You could always volunteer for the job. In your spare time, of course. To be frank, I can't see that task ever becoming a priority when staffing's as tight as it is these days. Maybe this London Society did keep records, but you have to remember that they seem to have started up in the 1790s, when the English ruling class were gripped by paranoia about the French Revolution and you could be executed for breathing in a treasonous manner. Even poor benign old William Blake was tried for sedition. It wasn't always wise to write things down.' He shrugs. 'Conversely, they may have kept very detailed records which got burned to ashes or are rotting in someone's attic. The survival of these kind of things is often a lottery.'

'Do the Kellett papers mention any of the Society's other members by name?'

'As far as I recall, they only referred to each other by code names or initials. Like I said, these were dangerous times.'

'Do any of these code names or initials suggest that the individual might be someone actually known to history?'

'I'm not sure. I don't even know if anyone's been interested enough to check. Why, what sort of person do you have in mind?'

'Oh, I don't know, someone known to have been involved in fringe religious activities around that time. Someone like William Blake, for instance.'

Donald strokes his chin. 'As far as I recall, Blake and his wife initially joined the New Jerusalem Church set up by followers of Swedenborg.'

'I've come across that name.'

'Swedenborg believed that the Last Judgement had actually taken place in 1757, and that angels were now passing messages through him. Sound familiar?'

'All too familiar. But I can see why people got interested in his ideas at that time. From what I've read, lots of people saw the French Revolution as some kind of apocalyptic event.'

'What with that and the American War of Independence, it must have felt as if the whole established world order was being turned upside down. Still, I suppose we shouldn't be too judgemental. I heard a sermon once in which the preacher insisted that the formation of the European Union was the fulfilment of a prophecy in the Book of Revelation. Anyway, as far as I recall, the Blakes quickly became disillusioned with the New Jerusalem Church when it started getting as regulated and autocratic as the Established Church they'd turned their backs on. After that, William seems to have ploughed his own highly individual furrow.'

'So, unless I spend the best years of my life immersed in the least rewarding collection of documents in the library, I'm screwed.'

'Your words, not mine. Otherwise, I can only suggest you try the British Library. It's just possible that some of this Society's papers are lodged there, assuming they still exist. But I wouldn't get your hopes up. If there's anything there, it'll probably be in some forgotten archive, and no-one will want to search it out for you.'

After lunch, Donald comes to find Rosemary in her office.

'Hi Rosie. I thought you might be interested in this.'

'The Kellett catalogue. Thanks very much. Just what I always wanted.'

'Not just any old Kellett catalogue. One that Wainwright has been scrawling over with his pencil. I've told him so many times, but short of barring him from the reading room … '

'I take your point. It doesn't really bear thinking about. So, are you asking me to go through and rub it all out?'

'No, of course not. But he's obviously got very interested in particular items. Unfortunately, his scrawl might as well be in ancient Sumerian for all I can decipher of it, so God knows what he's marked them for. It's not much, but at least there'd be nothing to lose by finding out if they've got anything significant in common. Just a thought. I know it's a long shot.'

'You're right Donald, there's nothing to lose. Is his stuff still out the back?'

'Sadly, no, it's been re-shelved.'

'Never mind. Thanks anyway.'

Donald is right, Professor Wainwright's idiosyncratic script makes as much sense as snail trails on a damp morning. Still, there are about half a dozen items he's clearly very interested in. It shouldn't take long.

Down in basement room 3, in the subdued light, she presses herself against the external wall and, through the relentless buzz of the strip lights overhead, seems to hear sounds filtering through from outside, below the ground: moles and earthworms burrow through the soil, leaving echoing chambers in their wake; tree-roots hiss as they spread their tendrils in every direction; the constant ebb and flow of life in the subterranean world beyond.

The boxes containing the Kellett papers are in their usual place. Wainwright's first item is missing; so also the second and third. I suppose I should have checked for myself, she thinks, rather than taking Donald's word for it.

Striding through the reading room, she opens and closes doors with more force than strictly warranted. She checks the back room and finds no Kellett papers waiting to be returned.

'Donald, who's supposed to have done the last lot of shelving?'

'Supposed to have?'

A thin young man with curly hair in jeans and baggy jumper looks up from the end of the counter. Donald nods towards him.

'Julian did. Why?'

She stares pointedly towards Julian and lowers her voice. 'Well he didn't do a very good job. These Kellett items must have been misfiled. They're not where they should be. What's going to happen next time Wainwright wants them?'

'Rosie, I only mentioned this to you because I was trying to help. If this is your response, perhaps it would be better if you forget the whole business.'

Back in the basement, she sits on the icy flagstone floor and stares at the offending boxes until dizzy, then leaps to her feet. She begins to go through the first box searching for any item which is out of order, but finds none. By the end of the second box, her hands are trembling with anger. Half-way through the third and final box, she screams and hurls it to the floor, scattering the contents in all directions and under neighbouring stacks, then sinks to her knees and holds her head in her hands.

When the wave of despair has begun to pass, she looks up to see Julian standing a few feet away.

'Donald was worried that you'd been gone a long time. He sent me down to check on you.'

She sniffs and wipes the back of her hand across her nose. 'Did he indeed? Well, you've checked on me. What are you waiting around for?'

'We'd better not leave things like this. I'll give you a hand to pick them up.'

Julian begins to collect the papers from the floor; Rosemary makes no move to help. Within a few minutes he has picked up all but those which she is sitting on, so he holds out a hand, inviting her to rise. She looks up slowly and takes it. As she stands, she has to grab his shoulder to steady herself. She stares into his eyes, and he does not seem uncomfortable.

'Believe it or not,' he says, 'I know what you're going through.'

'Do you really. How's that?'

'I had a breakdown when I was at university. I had to take a year out to recover.'

She feels her body relaxing against his. 'A breakdown? Is that what you think's happening to me?'

159

'I'm not sure there's a clinical definition of it. But I'd say it's what happens to anyone when things just get too much for them.'

She turns her head and leans it against Julian's chest. He strokes her hair.

'I'm sorry I had a go at you earlier,' she says in a near-whisper. 'The papers I was looking for have just disappeared. It's not your fault.'

His body tenses just enough to put her on guard. 'How do you mean, disappeared?'

'It's difficult to explain. It's been happening quite a bit recently. Someone's messing with my head.'

Julian grasps her by the shoulders and takes half a step back. 'Rosie, there are people who can help you. When I … when I had similar problems, I was lucky enough to have friends who cared enough to push me in the right direction. I know a therapist, he's really good. Not a bullshitting Freudian, someone who really understands what it's like to be under pressure. I can have a word with him if you like.'

Rosemary tries to quieten the anger in her voice. 'I don't need a therapist. I just need to know who Richard Bonner is and why he's leading me towards William Blake. And why he's fucking with my head.'

Julian steers her to one side until she is leaning against a rack of shelves, then bends down to pick up the remaining papers.

'I'll take this lot back upstairs and sort them out. No point trying to do it down here.'

'Please don't tell anyone. About this.'

He looks pained. 'What do you take me for?'

Julian does not head straight for the exit. Instead, he places the box on the floor, takes a stub of pencil and a scrap of card from his pocket and scribbles.

'Have a think about what I said. If you want to talk, give me a call. Any time.'

'Julian, why are you doing this?'

His shoulders sag. 'I just want to help. All I'm doing is

trying to help.'

Rosemary looks through more pictures on her computer. They suck her in, images of a life which seems more real than the one she is living now. Adam is rarely without a genial smile, at ease in front of the camera in a way she senses she has never been. He had nothing to conceal, he lived life in full view of his friends and colleagues and couldn't understand why people felt the need to keep secrets. Well, that's where taking life by the throat gets you. Dead. Probably.

She works through a folder headed 'Private'. It soon becomes clear why she gave it that name. She is about to close it again when her eyes focus on the tiny icon of the last image. She double-clicks and opens it. On the screen is a photo clearly taken by Adam. With one hand she is holding out a small plastic cylinder towards the camera, in the other she has a cardboard box on which it is possible to make out the words 'Pregnancy Testing Kit'. On the cylinder is a strip coloured blue. She is grinning, looking as happy as she has ever been in her life.

22

Next morning, Rosemary chances to arrive at the staff entrance at the same time as Donald. He does not smile, in fact seems anxious to avoid conversation as they walk to the reading room. The atmosphere becomes tense.

'Look, I'm sorry, Donald. I was a bit stressed yesterday. I know I was out of order.'

He is in no hurry to reply. She begins to worry that her apology has been too little, too late.

'Rosie,' he says finally, 'it's your life, but I think you need to take a step back. Everyone's made allowances for you, but their patience is starting to wear thin.'

'When you say "their patience", you really mean "our patience".'

'After yesterday, yes. Taking out your frustrations on a junior member of staff who's not in a position to answer back is not acceptable.' His voice softens a notch. 'Maybe it would be better if you forget this whole business about the Kellett papers. It seems to be having a bad effect on you.'

She swallows hard. 'You're right. I've spent far too much time on it. I'll give myself another week. If I haven't made any progress by then, I'll give it up.'

Donald's silence makes clear that this is not what he wanted to hear.

'Look, if you're determined to go on with this, there's one person who can probably tell you if you're on a wild goose chase or not. Someone who seems to know the Kellett stuff better than anyone.'

'You mean Wainwright?'

'Of course. Why not just talk to him?'

'Because he's highly irascible and as mad as a skunk.' She bites her lip, waiting for Donald to point out that this is a fair description of her own recent behaviour, but he resists.

'Some might call it self-focused. But if you can get past

his daunting exterior, you may find he's quite human.'

'So, what, you think I should ask him out for a drink after work? See if he wants to take in a film?'

'I shouldn't think Professor Wainwright's been out on a date for fifty years. But you might get a few minutes from him in the tea room. Just a thought. But promise me one thing. If even he doesn't know what you're talking about, give it up. Immediately, not in a week's time.'

She opens the office door to find Roger waiting for her in a state of agitation. She hangs up her jacket and sits at her desk. He shuffles some already tidy papers on his desk.

'Is something wrong, Roger?'

'No. Well, yes, there is. There's no point in beating about the bush, I may as well come right out with it.'

She waits for him to do so. He takes a deep breath.

'Donald spoke to me last night. He said he'd had some difficulties. With you.'

She purses her lips. No wonder Donald was reluctant to talk this morning.

'I think the Kellett papers have been taking up too much of your time. They're not even your responsibility. It would be better if you refocus on more immediate tasks.'

She forces a smile. 'Okay, you're probably right.'

Roger does not smile back. It dawns on her that, in his inimitable way, he believes that he has given her an instruction, not friendly advice. He continues to stare.

'Okay, Roger, point taken. So be it.'

A little later, she is checking a reference book in the reading room when a stooping, grey-haired figure in a threadbare check suit, frayed off-white shirt and stringy tie walks in. She glances at Donald, who quickly looks away. Last night he asked Roger to bar her from any further contact with the Kellett papers, this morning he suggested that she speak to Wainwright about them. She is in the last chance saloon.

Professor Wainwright is a creature of habit. At eleven o'clock precisely according to the reading room clock, he closes the lid of his ancient laptop, tucks it under his arm and leaves for the tea room. Five minutes later, she sees him sitting alone at a table, apparently in discussion with his coffee cup.

'Professor Wainwright?'

He does not look up, and his lips continue to move soundlessly. She decides to take the risk of touching him on the arm. He jumps and stares at her, wide-eyed.

'Sorry to startle you, Professor Wainwright. Do you mind if I sit with you, just briefly?'

It seems that he is staring intently at her breasts, until she realises that he is trying to read the identity badge hanging on a chain from her neck. She holds it towards him.

'Rosemary Torrance. I work in the reading room. I've seen you there many times.'

Professor Wainwright remains silent. She waits for a moment, then slides into the seat across from him. From the corner of her eye, she notices that several people at nearby tables are looking on with curiosity.

'I thought it would be easier to talk here than upstairs. It's just that, I know you're an expert on the Kellett papers.'

His eyebrows rise, lifting the furrowed forehead above them.

'I have a passing interest in them myself,' she continues. 'I wondered if I could talk to you about them, just for a moment.'

Wainwright takes a sip of his coffee with trembling hand, leaving a brown pool as he places the cup back on its saucer. When he finally speaks, Rosemary realises that she has never heard his voice before. It is surprisingly fluid, musical, legato.

'I can't imagine why you'd want to know about them. They're very dull.'

'But they obviously keep you interested, given how long you've been going through them. What do you make of Kellett himself?'

'Kellett? A dilettante. He knew nothing very much

about anything, as far as I can see.'

'So ... what is it that interests you about the Kellett papers?'

'His correspondence with others of greater significance. I'm not remotely interested in the man himself.'

She leans forward and lowers her voice. 'How much do you know about the London Society for Spiritual Studies?'

He screws up his face as the name rattles around his cerebral cortex. 'Nothing. Never heard of it.'

Rosemary takes a sip of her own coffee while she collects her thoughts. 'I remember you recently ordered up a letter from the collection which Kellett wrote to this London Society for Spiritual Studies in 1823. It specifically referred to an Elizabethan occultist called Richard Bonner. Doesn't that ring any bells?'

His eyes glaze over for a few seconds, then snap back into focus. 'No. Never heard of him either. Must be a letter I haven't got to yet. You've no idea how painful it is dredging through all the dross in that collection. If I saw something like that I'd remember it.'

'In that case, I'm sorry. It must have been another reader who was looking at it.'

'I doubt it. No-one else has looked at this stuff for ages. But if I happen to come across something like that, I'll let you know, Miss ... ' He stares towards her breasts once more.

'Torrance.'

'Rosemary Torrance. Hmm. You can call me Montague.'

On the way back to her office, Rosemary wonders who on earth could have been looking at the infamous letter from Kellett if not Wainwright. There is a pile of slips hundreds deep under the counter which, had she the time and inclination to search through them, might indicate the identity of the reader who called it up. Given the recent history of vanishing evidence relating to Richard Bonner, such a search would surely be unlikely to be fruitful. Why did she not photocopy the letter when she had it in her grasp?

On leaving the library that evening, she makes a last-minute decision to cycle to the hospital even though the sky looks threatening. She is a quarter of a mile away when a downpour soaks her in seconds. On arrival, she heads straight for the toilets and attempts to remove as much water as possible from her hair by directing the hot air dryer towards it. After several minutes, the reflection in the mirror causes her to flinch in fright. She runs her fingers through her hair to flatten it, tries to mitigate the damage with a comb and, resisting the inclination to head straight home, takes the lift to 3B, thankful that at this time the hospital is quiet.

Derek lies on his back, snoring. Across the way, her mother lies apparently asleep as always, but there has been a change. Mum's expression, rather than that of one experiencing unending rest, has twisted in such a way as to project anguish, perhaps pain. Her skin feels dry, paper-thin, ready to crack at any moment. She finds the senior nurse at the desk.

'Can you tell me what's happened to my mother, Mrs Torrance? She looks worse.'

'Dr Bialkowski is continuing to monitor her condition. If there's any change, I'm sure he'll let you know.'

'But I can see it on her face. She looks like she's in distress.'

'If you're concerned, I can only suggest that you ring and speak to him directly. The best time is—'

'After ten thirty, yes, I know.'

At home later, a strange restlessness, immune to any attempt at distraction, takes hold of her. She flicks through channels on the TV, then turns it off and picks up several of the books which she is reading concurrently, but is unable to dispel the urge to hit the wall and scream. Her watch confirms that the time is nearly ten. She puts on her coat and walks down Castle Hill, crosses Northampton Street and enters the Pickerel. She wanders from room to room in search of anyone she knows, but finding no-one sits on a bench with her back to the wall between two groups of young men. She takes a sip of wine, leans back and closes her eyes. How would she feel if Sharon were to walk in at this moment? Relieved, probably; after all, she came here in urgent search of human company. Her eyes flick open as she hears a middle-aged man call 'Rosie'. A portly figure in corduroy embraces a woman at a table some distance away. After a few more minutes, the relaxant effect of the wine begins to kick in. Draining her glass, she goes to the bar and orders another. From the corner of her eye she catches sight of Jayne and Mary. How did she miss them?

'Hi, you guys. Didn't see you when I came in.'

Jayne and Mary look at one another. 'Are you here with Sharon?' Mary asks.

'No. Why?'

'She was looking for you earlier. I just wondered if she'd managed to contact you.'

'No. No, I haven't heard from her.'

There is a pause. Rosemary observes that on this occasion Jayne and Mary have not invited her to sit down and join them.

'Ah well, I'll leave you two in peace.'

'See you tomorrow, Rosie.'

The two groups of young men have spread themselves to fill the space where she was sitting. She finds a vacant stretch of bar, checks that it is out of sight of Jayne and Mary, and leans against it, running her finger up and down the glass, checking her phone, restlessly sipping her wine. A few minutes later she empties the glass and turns to leave, keeping her eyes fixed on the door.

Back at home, sleep seems the only remaining place of safety, but she is taken aback to find Adam already waiting, this time sitting fully clothed on the side of the bed. She tries to smile. He leans on his hand as he watches her undress and then slip under the duvet.

'You seem to be around quite a bit at the moment,' she says.

'And how do you feel about that, Ms Torrance?'

'Okay, I suppose.'

'Charmed, I'm sure.'

'I did think of you the other night. I found the picture.'

'You'll have to be a little more explicit.'

'The pregnancy test picture.'

'Ah. Is it still painful to think about?'

'Sometimes I think that having a baby would have felt the most natural thing in the world. But then, as things turned out, I'd have ended up as a lone parent, wouldn't I?'

Adam averts his eyes.

'Wouldn't I?'

'It depends how you view the nexus of cause and effect.'

'What's that supposed to mean?'

'Just that, if one factor had turned out differently, like you'd not miscarried the baby, for instance, then you can't assume that things which followed wouldn't also have been different.'

'So it's my fault you went to Byron's Pool that night? If I hadn't carelessly, thoughtlessly, negligently passed the remnants of our baby down the toilet whilst doubled up in agony, we'd still be a normal happy couple.'

'Rosie, please, you know that's not what I'm saying. Look, I didn't come here to argue.'

Her head slumps back on the pillow. 'Well you're making a stunning success of that.'

'If you must know, I came here to warn you.'

'About what?'

'About Richard Bonner.'

Now she is wide awake. She waits for him to continue.

'Bonner isn't all that he seems to be.'

'Since he seems to be positively unearthly, I'm quite relieved to hear it.'

'I'm saying you need to be very careful, Rosie. Think hard before you carry on down the road you're travelling. You could be putting yourself in danger.'

'Of what?'

'Of things which you won't understand, and which I can't explain to you.'

She stares at an ancient cobweb on the ceiling. 'And what am I supposed to make of that? Just because you're ... why should I believe that you know any more than I do? I hate people who say things like, "Ah well, if you knew as much as I do, you'd understand." You're just getting on my tits, Adam.'

There is no reply. Rosemary keeps her eyes fixed upwards. When she turns to look back at Adam, the other side of the bed is empty.

23

At 10.35, Rosemary makes her way to the landing in front of the lift shafts to obtain a mobile phone signal and rings the hospital, only to be told that Dr Bialkowski is not on duty that day. She rings Jamie's number, but gets no answer.

Returning to her office, she finds Roger fielding a call at her extension. He asks the caller to wait, then hands the receiver to her. She asks who it is, he shrugs.

'Rosemary Torrance, how can I help?'

'You can just talk to me, babe. It's been a long time.'

'Hi, Sharon. I guess life has been a bit busy.'

'Just wanted to make sure you weren't avoiding me.'

Rosemary glances at Roger, but is unable to decide whether he is listening. 'No, of course not. Why would I?'

'That's okay then. I guess. You doing anything tonight?'

'Not that I know of.'

'How about the Pickerel at eight o'clock then?'

'Can we make it somewhere else?'

'Sure. The Eagle?'

'Perfect. I'll see you there.'

'See you there. I'll be looking forward to it, Rosie.'

She puts the receiver down. Roger clears his throat loudly.

In the tea room, Donald sits at one table, Jayne and Mary at another. None of them looks up as she walks past. Bringing her coffee back from the counter, she sees Julian sitting with another young man, trying to do a crossword. She sits opposite Julian, and they both look up. Julian tries to conceal his surprise.

'Hi Rosie. Are you any good at crosswords?'

'No, I'm crap. Not much good at lateral thinking, I guess.'

There is a long silence, at the end of which Julian's

friend excuses himself and leaves. Rosemary leans her elbows on the table.

'What are people saying about me, Julian? I'm sorry, I have to ask you as no-one else seems to want to talk to me.'

Julian looks around, scratching his head. 'Look, Rosie, I don't know why you're asking me this.'

'I just told you, everyone else is avoiding me.'

'But why do you assume I know what other people are thinking?'

'Because I see you and the other assistants all talking together. You're a close-knit group.'

'But why would we talk about you?'

'Julian, don't treat me like an idiot. I know people think I'm losing it. Do you think I'm losing it?'

'Hang on, I do when you talk like this.' He looks around once more and lowers his voice. 'Look, more to the point, do you think you are?'

'Oh, undoubtedly. I communicate with dead people, you know.'

'Okay. Well, I suppose that doesn't prove much in itself. But since you put me on the spot, you are behaving strangely. Like I said the other day, I know a guy who might be able to help.'

'And like I said, I'll bear that in mind. Anyway, you've told me all I wanted to know.' She sits back. 'I'm grateful to you, Julian. At least you're not afraid to give me a straight answer. Reasonably straight, anyway. And I like your eyes.'

At five o'clock she puts on her jacket, says goodbye to Roger and heads out of the office door. Rather than making her way to the exit as usual, she takes out her keys and diverts through a door and down a flight of stairs. Checking that no-one else is around, she enters basement room 3 and heads for case 38. The climate control system sends a constant low whistling through the vents. She pulls up a stool next to the boxes containing the Kellett papers and prepares for a more thorough trawl.

Some time later, the familiar sense of despair arrives which seems to accompany any attempt to make sense of the few tantalising fragments she has already picked up. The collection has so far revealed nothing further out of the ordinary. Kellett certainly had an interest in the occult, but it was all familiar territory: séances, mesmerism, secret writing. There are a few other references to the London Society for Spiritual Studies, but all elliptical, as if Kellett were reluctant to commit too much to writing. Most important of all, there is no further mention of Richard Bonner.

A slight breeze signifies that someone has opened a door at the far end of the room. She looks up and waits for the sound of footsteps, or the tortured wheels of an ancient shelving trolley. The room remains silent. She waits. Her hands are clammy despite the cold.

'Who's there?'

She looks along the passageway at the end of the racks, but sees no-one. Perhaps someone realised they had come to the wrong room and did not enter. She returns to the task in hand with greater urgency. Here's box 13, from which emerged the now infamous letter, item number 30. The adjacent items 29 and 31 bear no relation to its content. She is about to give up and go home when, right at the bottom of the box, appears a sheet which has one corner turned over. It is unnumbered, as if a later addition which has been secreted there. It could be just a scrap of waste paper, but she unfolds it with trembling hands.

My dear sirs,

I have recently met with Richard Bonner, at his instigation. The information which he conveyed to me, I cannot write to you about openly, and will follow up this communication with a further letter in cypher, as per our normal practice in these matters. Suffice it to say at this stage that the content will cause shock and disbelief.

I remain as always ....

Andrew Kellett
2 November 1822

All Souls' Day. How appropriate. So, Kellett may have been mad or gullible; or, just possibly, he really did meet with a man who was by that time nearly three hundred years old. No wonder Bonner had some surprising things to tell him.

A frantic search through the remaining boxes produces no sign of the promised encoded letter. Assuming, of course, that it was ever written. If Kellett indeed disappeared shortly afterwards, then perhaps he never had time to write down what he believed Bonner had told him.

She replaces the boxes carefully, trying to avoid leaving any evidence that they have been rifled through, just in case. In case of what? 6.40: if she does not leave soon, she will be in danger of being locked in. Not for the first time, the search for Richard Bonner has taken far longer than expected. She heads for the door.

A current of warmer air from the vents overhead stops her in her tracks. It is fragrant, carrying heady scents of incense, and as she inhales it she closes her eyes. She is back in her student room, surrounded by candles and joss sticks, discussing with friends the meaning of life and love and how to spend the summer vacation. She is in a Greek Orthodox monastery in Crete, taking refuge from the punishing heat, a censer leaving a smoky trail as it swings above her head, staring up at the image of Christ Pantocrator in celestial majesty behind the altar, dark and overpowering, so different from the benign realisations of his earthly life in the western iconography she is used to. Now she is in a church in the centre of York, seeking spiritual refreshment while Adam breathlessly peruses the material wonders of the National Railway Museum's historic collection. The building is silent and calm, illuminated by flickering candle flame, and she wonders why, minute by minute, she is becoming increasingly agitated. The comments in the visitors' book reflect this tension; half describe the church as peaceful and uplifting, the other half as sinister, threatening. It is only later that she discovers this was the site, during the middle ages, of a massacre of Jewish families who had sought safety inside during one of the periodic pogroms in that city.

But now she is in a place she has never visited in life. A dark room, the atmosphere polluted not by sweet incense but by acrid chemicals, ammonia and arsenic. Choking smoke swirls and dances, parting briefly to reveal phials and tubes on a heavily stained wooden table, bubbling liquids in clouded glass chambers over charcoal fires. At the far end of the table a figure, half obscured, staring at the pages of a book. He is dressed in black, but his hair is long and grey, and swirls like a horse's mane as he turns his head to stare at her. His eyes are red.

The door from basement room 3 is weightless as she steps outside. Her footsteps echo along the library's empty corridor, and from the now-sealed rooms on either side escape whispers from men and women long dead. She knows what they are telling her without needing to stop and listen. A door at the far end admits her to a stairwell down which music filters, voices singing in a complex polyphony which makes her think of Byrd and Tallis, but based on a harmonic structure which defies analysis, as if several different choral pieces are being performed simultaneously. It draws her up the staircase but, although she rises past several floors, becomes no louder. By the time she reaches ground level, it has ceased.

The library's main thoroughfares are as she has never seen them, deserted and unlit. She is ruler of all she surveys, emperor of academia, czar of studious endeavour, caliph of the corridors of learning. She removes books from the shelves at random, takes them to the window to survey their contents, replaces them with care, dizzy with power. She explores places she has never had occasion to explore before: the map room, oriental studies, periodicals, biology, anthropology, thinking that perhaps her lifelong quest for knowledge and understanding has been insufficiently ambitious. The principal reading room, normally entombed in a breathless hush, with its panelled walls, its long tables punctuated by desk lamps, is her playground. She turns every alternate lamp on, stands back to survey the effect, then decides that one at the end of each table produces the best atmospheric effect, the light fading to leave a small area of darkness in the centre. She goes to switch them off again, but realises that leaving them on is in fulfilment of a higher purpose, the optimal balance between light and dark.

Another staircase beckons. She takes flight after slow flight, the air in her lungs becoming more rarefied with each level. Reckoning that she is about half way up, she stops to get her bearings, staring out of one of the narrow, grime-coated windows through which daylight struggles to infiltrate. Now each further flight is an ordeal, and she has to pause on every landing to catch her breath. At long last the summit of the staircase is in sight. When she reaches it, a heavy door presents itself which she knows should be locked, but knows will not be. Outside, she steps onto a small platform, surrounded by a parapet wall to waist height, at the very summit of the library tower. To the east, Cambridge spreads across the land like an exotic carpet, with alternate patches of green and red punctuated by squares and lines of grey. After a while, if she focuses hard enough, she can zoom in on individual landmarks: the frosted windows of the Champion of the Thames, the incongruous frontage of her mother's house, the stark façade of Addenbrooke's Hospital. By concentrating a little harder, she can pierce the walls and see the interior of ward B3, its occupants lying motionless, eyes loosely shut. By turning her head slightly, she can hear the rattling in Derek's lungs.

She raises her eyes to look beyond the bounds of the city. A supreme effort of will starts the globe below rolling towards her, so that she can look beyond her former horizon. Far to the north lie the Cheviot Hills, which Adam always saluted as they crossed the boundary into Scotland. Before long, the turrets of Edinburgh Castle pierce the sky, and to the east a long iron bridge the colour of rust spanning the Firth of Forth. A plume of smoke marks the passage across it of a southbound train; the girders creak as they take its weight, then settle back. Above is a sky of unbroken blue. A man and woman lie together in an upstairs room of the hotel on the southern bank of the firth. A tear runs down the woman's cheek.

24

A voice intrudes, and it does not sound happy.

'What in fuck's name is going on, Rosie?'

She knows the voice, but has not heard it as angry as this before. In fact it is disconcerting in the intensity of its displeasure. When she opens her eyes, she is in the familiar surroundings of her bedroom.

'Sharon. How did you get in?'

'Via the front door, which you'd thoughtfully left open for me, not to mention any passing rapist or psychopath. Jeez, just what is going on in that head of yours?'

Rosemary hauls herself to an upright position to find that she is wearing only her knickers. There seems little point now in any false display of modesty. Her brain is taking time to clear itself. The bedside clock reveals that it is just after nine, but is it a.m. or p.m.? Perhaps Sharon will let slip some clue.

'It was good of you to call by.'

This remark feels inappropriate even as it emerges, but her mind struggles to pin down the reason. Worryingly, her friend looks more cross than ever.

'Have you been drinking already?'

This word 'already' rings alarm bells, even though Rosemary does not recall that she has been drinking. Sharon is on her feet.

'I came round to tell you that this is the last time I'm going to be pissed about by you, Rosie, and now I'm even more convinced that you deserve it. True friends don't stand one another up just because of some drunken fucking sexual escapade. If we meet in the library, don't even bother to say hello.'

'Sharon. Wait. Please.'

Sharon is already heading towards the staircase. Rosemary rushes after her and calls to her from the top step. From the landing below, her friend, or former friend, looks up.

'Rosie, for Christ's sake, get back inside. Look at you.'

The door of an adjoining flat edges open, but Rosemary does not notice.

'I need to talk, Sharon. Please. Come back.'

Sharon looks from Rosemary to the thinning male head which has emerged from the other flat, strides back up the stairs, grasps her by the arm and drags her back inside. Rosemary is as compliant as a rag doll. Sharon takes her dressing gown from the back of the bedroom door, forces her arms into it, pushes her into the lounge and sits her on the sofa. Sharon positions herself at the other end.

'You don't even remember what we arranged, do you? That's obviously how important it was to you.'

'I do remember.'

'Oh? What were we going to do, then?' Sharon stares as Rosemary's head sinks, but resists stating the obvious.

'Oh, Sharon, I'm so sorry. I seem to have lost the last few hours. I don't know what's happened to me.'

'Yeah, well I lost a whole weekend once, but I didn't expect anyone to feel sorry for me. I told you, I came round to say that I've had it up to here and I'm going to do what I should have done some time ago. I feel like I've been kicked in the guts once too often, and it's not going to happen again.'

'I'm sorry.'

'Stop saying you're fucking sorry. And you could at least have the decency to tell me who he was and why he's so special he takes precedence over me.'

'I don't know what you're talking about.'

'What, you lie on your bed undressed all evening just in case?'

'I haven't been with anyone. The last thing I remember I was getting ready to leave the library tonight.'

Sharon is frowning, but says nothing. Rosemary starts to weigh up how much it is safe to tell her, and concludes she now has little to lose.

'I seem to have been to a strange place. I can't decide if it was real or inside my head. I still feel disoriented. And scared.'

She risks looking at Sharon, whose face seems to have softened just a little.

'What's the last thing you remember?'

'I was in a basement room in the library, just about to leave for the night. There was a sudden draught of warm air, and a smell of incense. You know how it is with smells, it immediately triggered a string of memories.' She decides to pause there. 'The next thing I knew was that you were yelling at me.'

'Any headaches recently? Dizzy spells?'

'I know what you're thinking. I'm sure it's not that.'

'How? Why don't you get checked out just to be on the safe side?'

'If I start falling over and having blackouts, I promise I will.'

'By your own admission, you've just lost several hours of your life. How much worse do things have to get?'

Rosemary knows that she cannot risk telling her friend the whole truth, not least for her own sake.

'Why don't we stick to our original plan?'

'Which was?'

'Going out.'

'Where?'

'Wherever you want. Just say the word. Give me five minutes to throw some clothes on.'

'You really don't remember what we agreed, do you?'

'I think my memory's been erased.'

Sharon waits a few moments, then gets up and walks towards the hallway. 'Look, Rosie, I've no idea what's going on here, but I don't think I can cope with being a part of it. I'd hoped that things would turn out differently, and I still have strong feelings for you, but either you're playing me for a fool, or you really do need help but are refusing to accept it. Either way, this doesn't feel like a good place to be.'

'Wait. Please wait. I do need help, but not the sort you mean. Will you help me?'

Sharon shakes her head. 'The sort of help you need isn't going to come from someone who knows about literature. Look at you, Rosie, you're falling apart. You need to get a grip, or find someone to do it for you.'

'It's literature I want your help with. That's what will help me get back on track.'

Sharon seems to debate with herself, then perches on the arm of a chair. 'How?'

'I need to find out more about William Blake.'

'A perfectly worthy object of study, but I fail to see how knowing more about a man considered by many of his contemporaries to be deranged is going to help your mental state. Unless you want someone even more deranged to compare yourself with.'

'I just feel he's a kindred spirit.'

'Oh. Do angels visit you too?'

'No. Not exactly.'

'If not exactly, then how?'

'I don't know. Adam's acting as a kind of spirit guide for me, isn't he?'

'Ah. Well if that's where you're coming from, I'm not sure there's much point in going over old ground again.'

'It doesn't matter. I'm not asking you to see things the way I do. But you're a renowned expert on Blake.'

'Hang on, that's going a bit far.'

'On the way to being one, anyway. All I'm asking for is your help on some academic research. I don't want to hold a séance or anything.'

Sharon glances down at the seat of the chair as if tempted to make herself comfortable for a longer stay after all, but remains on the arm.

'Look, Rosie, you know how I feel, but maybe this is not the time to talk about this. I'm still feeling hurt. And you, to put it bluntly, don't seem to be in full control of your faculties. Perhaps we should cool things a bit. Let's talk again in a couple of weeks or so.'

'Why don't you stay? For the night?'

Sharon stands. 'Because, tempting though the offer is,

in your current state I could never be sure why you were doing it and, I suspect, neither would you. Like I said, let's talk again in a couple of weeks and see where we go from there. Do you want some smokeable substances to help you relax?'

'No thanks, I'm good. Well, you know.'

'Okay, hasta luego. Oh, by the way, there's no trace in the King's archives of your friend Bonner.'

When Sharon has left, Rosemary sits on the sofa for some minutes watching the light fading outside, then throws on jeans and a top and walks down Castle Hill. Crossing Northampton Street, she pauses for a moment outside the Pickerel, then moves on towards the city centre, turns left into Jesus Lane, passing its eponymous college, then right towards King Street. Entering the Champion of the Thames, she sees that her alcove seat is occupied by one member of a group of noisy teenagers drinking garish alcopops. Looking around for an alternative refuge, she finds none and walks out. Cutting across Jesus Green, she makes her way out onto Chesterton Road, stops at the late-night convenience store and buys a box of chardonnay. Back in the flat she puts it into the freezer to chill as rapidly as possible, pouring first a lukewarm glass to keep her going. On TV she finds that her favourite film channel is showing *Terminator 2*. Although it is part-way through and she has seen it at least three times, she settles down willingly to watch, and speaks softly.

'Adam, if you can hear me, despite what I said I could really do with your company now.'

She continues to watch the film, from time to time checking out of the corner of her eye.

'You said it was more my choice than yours when you turn up. Why can't you come to me now?'

She chews her fingers as the final credits roll, then retrieves the box of wine from the freezer and pours another large glass. The film channel has moved on to a recent Disney animation. She sits and stares at the phone, gets up and checks her empty bedroom and finds herself longing for company, for the touch and sound of another human being, wishing that she had tried harder to persuade Sharon to stay. She drains her glass and pours another, picks up the phone, dials Jamie's number, then presses the red button. Every TV channel now seems to be showing something she does not want to watch.

'That's it, Adam, I've had it with grieving for you, making do with your unpredictable appearances instead of moving on and having a real relationship with a real living man. It seems I'm going to have to come to terms with the idea that you really are dead. I'll feel a lot better when your body finally turns up and I can feel some sense of closure, but until then I can't go on living in limbo like this. Let's say goodbye now and get it over with. I can't take any more. I'd never have wanted things to end this way, but it seems like we're fated not to have a clean break so I'm making the decision. I'll always love you, I'll always cherish the time we had together. Thanks for everything, I hope you can rest in peace now.'

Rosemary takes her replenished glass to the bedroom, seeking only the oblivion of sleep. Before drawing the curtains, she looks out on the human traffic making its way up and down Castle Hill. A couple walking hand in hand stop every few yards to embrace and kiss. Through the darkness she can make out a small group sitting on top of the grassy mound which is the only surviving relic of the city's Norman castle. She perches on the window sill and stares out; circumstances have conspired against her, but no matter. It is time for her to become more self-sufficient, to stop living her life through others; it is time she learned to be content with her own company.

25

The reading room is already open for business when she walks in the next morning, and Donald and Julian are at the desk whispering in what seems a conspiratorial manner. She stops and watches them; as soon as they see that she has noticed, they return to shuffling papers. She stares for a couple of seconds longer, then walks to her office. Several readers follow her progress.

In the tea room a couple of hours later, Julian sits at a table on his own, reading a newspaper. His eyes register alarm as she takes the seat opposite. She watches him without speaking.

'What's up?' he says eventually, the merest quiver in his voice.

'I was rather hoping you could tell me.'

'About what?'

'About what's up.'

'We seem to be going round in circles.'

'Isn't life just like that.'

'Rosie, this is tortuous. Have I done something to upset you?'

'I was rather hoping you could tell me.'

'This is ridiculous.' Julian snatches up his paper and prepares to leave. 'I'm beginning to think you're beyond help.'

She returns from lunch to find her computer on standby, even though she knows she logged out when she left. The moving mouse restores the screen to life, revealing that it is open at her e-mail inbox. As far as she can tell, nothing has been moved or deleted. She is still staring at the screen when Roger enters the room.

'Do you know who's been at my computer?'

'Just the IT people, as far as I know.'

'As far as you know.'

'Yes. Security checks or something. Why?'

'Why would the IT people want to check my e-mail, and make sure I know they've done it?'

'Rosemary, I've no idea. If you're bothered about it, why not ask them?'

She slumps back in her chair. Roger is sorting through papers on his desk.

'Oh, by the way,' he says without looking up, 'there's no need for you to go to this meeting at the BL tomorrow. Donald's agreed to go instead. I'm sure you've got better things to do.'

She grips the arms of her chair. 'It's no problem. Actually I'd quite like to go. The more I think about it, the more I think I might have some ideas to offer.'

'Well, not to worry. I'm sure if you pass them on to Donald—'

'I really want to go, Roger. Please.'

Roger looks up from his desk and turns toward her. 'When I first mentioned it we agreed it would be anything but exciting. I can't see what you're getting so worked up about.'

'It just feels like I'm being elbowed aside. Like I'm dispensable.'

'No, on the contrary. As I've already explained, I've decided that at this moment Donald's time is less valuable than yours.'

'Or that you want to keep a close eye on me.'

Roger's shoulders tense. He is suddenly reluctant to maintain eye contact, staring at the door as if hoping for an interruption. None materialises.

'What is it that you're not telling me, Roger?'

'We need to talk about you and Julian. You seem to be forgetting that he's several levels junior to you.'

This is unexpected. 'We're not having a relationship, if that's what you mean.'

'That's not our concern.'

'Our?'

'From what's been reported back, on more than one occasion you've been guilty of making inappropriate

184

remarks to him. Speaking in a way which could even be considered as harassment.'

'That's crazy. What am I supposed to have said to him?' Roger seems to be pondering whether to answer this question. 'Look, he's cooked this up with Donald. I've seen the two of them whispering whenever I walk in.'

'I suspect there's more to it than that.'

'But you don't know.'

Roger takes several seconds to examine his hands before continuing. 'What I do know is, for the last few weeks you've been like a stranger, and a pretty odd one at that. We all appreciate you've had a lot to put up with—'

'God, I wish people would stop saying that.'

Does Roger roll his eyes? 'The long and short of it is, Rosemary, that your behaviour is starting to have an effect on other people in the department. HR feel that you might benefit from some bereavement counselling. I don't know how you feel about that, but it seems to me that it can't do any harm. Sometimes psychological problems can manifest themselves a long time after the event.'

Rosemary feels her alarm and confusion slowly morphing into anger. She stares at the ceiling for a few moments, then leans forward in her chair and exhales loudly. Roger remains motionless.

'And if I agree to have some counselling, will people start treating me as a normal human being again? Can I get on with my job without people staring at me all the time?'

Roger shifts in his chair. 'We think – that is, HR think – that counselling would be more effective if you weren't subjected to the pressures of your day-to-day job at the same time.'

It takes a while for these words to sink in. 'You mean you want to get rid of me?'

'No, of course not. We're just talking about a period of leave – sickness, compassionate, whatever we agree to call it – until you're back to your old self again.'

'Oh, I see. And which old self would that be?'

'I'm sorry?'

'Well, are we talking about the old self that started here four years ago, thinking I'd just landed the best job in the world? Or the old self from when Adam and I were together, when I'd take time out at work just to daydream about how blissful life was? Or the old self from just about a month ago, before I found out that my mother had turned into a living corpse? Because if I'm going to conform, I need to know which one I'm supposed to be.'

She buries her head in her hands, determined that her boss will not see her tears. She hears him pick up the phone and dial a four-figure extension, mutter a few inaudible words, perhaps from behind his hand, and then replace the receiver.

'We can do this quietly, Rosemary. No-one else need know why you're not here. Your job will still be waiting for you, that I promise. What do you say?'

She wipes her eyes as she lifts her head. 'All right. But if I'm going to do what you say, I think I'm entitled to ask just one thing before I go, if only to convince people that this conversation hasn't happened.'

Roger declines to offer the obvious prompt.

'If I just walk out now and I'm not seen again for – well, however long you've got in mind, then everyone will just put two and two together.'

'Your point being?'

'So let me go to this meeting at the BL tomorrow. It will at least throw people off the scent. After that I'll need a few days to clear up, and it'll look strange if I leave in the middle of the week. Give me until the end of next week and I'll go quietly. In the meantime, I'll keep out of everyone's way. It's not a lot to ask, is it?'

She senses the speed at which Roger's brain is working out the pros and cons of her proposal.

'All right. I've no idea why this extremely routine meeting is so important to you, but since it is, I don't see any reason why you shouldn't go. Use the time until the end of next week to tie up any loose ends here. HR will let you know the arrangements for your counselling.'

186

'You mean they've already organised it?'

'I didn't say that.'

'Fine. I just need to know one more thing. Was this Julian's suggestion?'

Roger looks appalled. 'Rosemary, are you seriously suggesting that I'd discuss a matter like this with a library assistant?'

After a walk around the building to clear her head, she gathers up the papers she will need for the following day, and starts to consider which of her personal belongings, photos, pen holder, cat ornament, she should remove when she goes. In the end she resolves to leave her desk as people always see it, remembering the pictures of the dining room on the *Mary Celeste* with its china, cutlery and serving dishes still in situ. For a moment she considers the dilemma inherent in leaving her workplace on seemingly indefinite leave; there are people she would like to say goodbye to in case things do not go according to plan, but she cannot do so without alerting them to her situation. She has also pledged to minimise contact with other library staff. Still, Cambridge is sufficiently small that there is a good chance of bumping into them anyway.

Cycling home, she struggles to swallow the cocktail of relief and foreboding. Her life, until recently on a stable if unrewarding course, now looks to be heading for more turbulent waters, perhaps for Scylla and Charybdis. On the other hand, if there really are psychological issues to deal with, at least she can do so sooner rather than later, and at someone else's expense. What is more, she will have no access to the Kellett papers. The whole matter of Bonner and Kellett and the London Society for Spiritual Studies will be behind her, at least as soon as she has explored one final avenue.

26

The day is already warming as Rosemary leaves her flat and encounters Mr Barnes up bright and early, sweeping the already pristine foyer. Without breaking step, she hails him breezily.

'Morning, Mr Barnes. Lovely day for it.'

'Looks like it could be a scorcher. You off anywhere nice?'

'Up to the smoke. The fleshpots of the big city.' Mr Barnes frowns. 'London.'

'Ah. Of course. Could never abide the place myself. Too busy and noisy. Still, I'm sure you youngsters see it differently.'

'I suppose so. Well, better crack on. Mustn't miss my train.'

She sings to herself as she cycles along Bridge Street and Trinity Lane, enjoying the morning sun on her face as she turns into St Andrews Street, eyebrows rising indulgently as a taxi pulls up in front of her, forcing her to swerve. Having parked her bicycle among thousands of others outside the railway station, she finds herself waiting in a throng on platform 1 for the next King's Cross train. When it arrives, she is not in a mood to jostle to the front, so settles for asking a fellow passenger if his briefcase has bought a ticket since it is occupying its own seat. He moves it with minimal grace and no apology. The train is already nearly full as it pulls out, leaving precious little space for anyone getting on at Royston, Letchworth or Hitchin. Indeed, at Letchworth she gives up her seat to an elderly man whom everyone else is making great efforts to avoid noticing. By the time the train crawls through the succession of tunnels on its final approach to King's Cross, her early morning bonhomie is in danger of evaporating.

The danger is not mitigated as she sets out along Euston Road to the din of weaving and darting traffic, but within a few minutes she turns gratefully away from the noise and fumes to enjoy the relative calm of the paved courtyard, complete with statuary and reminiscent of a twenty-first century Italian piazza, which leads to the main entrance to the British Library. A short while later, she is admitted to an austere window-less meeting room where, it seems, she and other librarians are to be imprisoned for the day. About a dozen are already there, but only one or two look up as she enters. Most of the others are checking their laptops. No-one speaks, and the silence soon becomes oppressive.

By lunchtime, she is losing the will to live. Rather than join the other delegates for small talk over the sandwich buffet provided, she leaves the building and makes for the nearest pub, checking that she has remembered to include in her bag a packet of extra strong mints. With a glass of wine and a bag of cashew nuts, she sits in a corner where it seems unlikely that she will be troubled, and is soon enjoying the soothing effect of alcohol hitting her bloodstream for the first time that day. Her mind begins to wander, but it does not have time to travel far.

'Penny for them, love.'

An elderly couple have seated themselves a few feet away. The man, short, bald, rotund and red-faced, is staring at her with his mouth slightly open, actually expecting a response. His wife's expression is inscrutable. Rosemary forces herself to smile.

'I wasn't thinking about anything. Sorry.'

'You can't think about nothing. Pretty girl like you, you must have been thinking about your boyfriend.'

This time she does not smile. 'I can assure you I wasn't.'

'Leave her alone now, Tom,' his wife says in a stage whisper.

'I wasn't bothering you, was I, love?'

'Um, no, not really.'

'There, she says I wasn't bothering her.'

The old couple argue for several minutes. She tips a handful of nuts into her mouth, leans back and closes her eyes

When the meeting finally draws to its conclusion at four o'clock, she heads for a terminal where she can consult the main catalogue. She keys in the name Richard Bonner, only to find that there is no precise match, so instructs it to search for the exact words 'London Society for Spiritual Studies'. Despite the precision of her command, a daunting number of entries relating to other London societies appear, but on the fourth page one vaults from the screen. She makes a note of the catalogue number, takes it to the reading room, fills in an ordering slip and joins the queue to hand it to the counter staff. It is added to a very thick collection of similar slips. Rosemary takes a seat at an adjoining table, and waits. Energetic assistants return every few minutes with bundles of documents, which are then claimed by eager readers and researchers. At length she looks at her watch and walks up to the counter to point out that she has been waiting for three-quarters of an hour, to be told coldly that she has arrived at one of the busiest times.

A bound volume with a burgundy cover arrives at the desk, and the assistant after some discussion looks in her direction.

'Thank you. Better late than never. What time does this reading room close?'

The assistant, uninjured by the barb, looks over his shoulder at a large wall clock. 'In about half an hour.'

She skims through the minutes of successive annual general meetings of the London Society for Spiritual Studies. They appear to be no more illuminating than the bulk of the Kellett papers. Just as she begins to feel that the whole expedition has been in vain, she turns a page and her eyes widen.

'Excuse me. Excuse me. Is there any chance of getting a photocopy of this?'

'No, it's far too late now. We're closing soon.'

Writing faster than she knew she was able, Rosemary transcribes as much as she can of the relevant pages, ignoring the injunction broadcast to all readers that they must immediately return whatever items they have borrowed to the desk. When most readers have already left the room, a middle-aged man rather like a younger version of Professor Wainwright stands in front of her with his hand out. When she can no longer ignore him, she hands back the volume and leaves the reading room, clutching her notebook to her chest.

In a shop on King's Cross station, the full-sized bottles of wine in the fridge shamelessly flaunt their sensual delights, but she forces herself to move down to the small, plastic 175 millilitre versions. She picks up one, estimates the number of mouthfuls within, and adds a second. On the train she tries to sip slowly, but the first bottle has disappeared by Potters Bar, the second by Hitchin.

After Letchworth, the train's occupants are unusually sparse. She begins to take out her notebook then, prompted by a subliminal warning, replaces it. She looks up and notices for the first time, she is not sure how she has missed him, the young man sitting opposite. He is slim, good-looking, athletic. His blond hair falls in what seem to be natural ringlets. When she narrows her eyes, he reminds her of Julian when they met in the basement of the library and her imagination begins to take over. The young man senses her attention, looks up and smiles. She smiles back, hoping that the effect of the wine did not distort her expression too badly. He returns to his reading.

No other passengers are sitting within clear view, and the toilet is only a few feet away. She looks at the young man again, and her foot slides forward until it brushes his. He looks up once more. She glances towards the toilet, then stares into his eyes. He looks back quizzically, turns to see where her gaze is leading, and raises his eyebrows. She mirrors the gesture. He still seems confused. She leans forward and strokes his thigh.

In the cubicle, bending over, grasping the hand-basin with her trousers and knickers around her ankles, she makes a show of enjoying the experience without excessive vocalisation. In the grimy mirror she half-expects to find the young man's face transformed into Adam's. Instead she sees her own eyes, dark and sunken, and thinks that she resembles a valkyrie, or better a vampire drawing out the life-force from the stranger who, in his innocence, thrusts into her with ever-increasing energy. When, groaning and swearing, he ejaculates inside her, she knows that she has sucked out his soul.

27

To Rosemary's surprise, Donald brings his morning coffee to her table in the tea room. He is even smiling. He clearly knows.

'Did you enjoy the BL trip, then?'

She thinks hard before replying. This seems to be becoming a habit. 'The day had its moments. Though I always find a trip to the BL makes me glad I work here.' For now, anyway.

'And did you manage to find out any more about the Society?'

'The what?' She has almost forgotten that it was Donald who suggested searching at the British Library in the first place. 'Oh, the LSSS. Well, yes and no. I found a volume of AGM minutes, but most of the content was as tedious as you'd expect.'

'And the rest?'

'Sorry?'

'The parts that weren't tedious.'

'Well, there are plenty of references to Kellett, as you'd imagine, but sadly nothing which sheds light on his mysterious disappearance, or the demise of the Society itself.'

It is not clear from his expression whether Donald believes her or not. 'That's a pity. Even so, it would be useful to include a reference to the volume you found with our papers. I don't suppose you kept a note of the catalogue number?'

Rosemary hesitates. She knows she did, but will it prove wise to set Donald off on this track? On the other hand, the catalogue entry gave little away about the content. At least, the content which interests her.

'I think I've got it upstairs. I'll let you have it when we go back up.'

Heading across the reading room, she detours alongside

the counter to avoid being noticed by the always-demanding Dr Collins. Donald holds up his hand as she passes.

'Are you sure that was the right number, Rosie? According to the BL's catalogue, that refers to some obscure eighteenth-century commentary on *Paradise Lost*.'

It is on the tip of her tongue to tell Donald that he must have searched carelessly, but Donald does not do things carelessly. Perhaps she was just in too much of a rush. A shiver passes through her as another explanation enters her mind.

'I probably jotted it down in a bit of a hurry. They were about to close. Sorry.'

In her office she double-checks the number she gave Donald and confirms it as the one she noted down at the time. She is about to consult the BL catalogue herself in case the usually-infallible Donald has actually got something wrong, but wearily accepts that there is no point.

Richard Bonner certainly enjoys playing games.

In her bag, the transcription she scribbled down before leaving the BL has disappeared. Her panic quickly turns to anger. She looks around for the most likely place to search. Or should it be the least likely? Deep down, she knows that it will re-appear when and where her nemesis chooses.

Preparing to leave the library that evening, she picks up her bag and senses even before checking that the transcription is back where she left it. She walks across the car park to retrieve her bicycle, mobile phone in hand.

'Hi Jamie. I'm sorry we didn't part on the friendliest of terms last time. I wondered if you fancy meeting for a drink tonight.' There is a long pause. 'Jamie?'

– Sorry. Just not sure I'd be very good company. What with one thing and another.

'All the more reason to get you outside those four walls. Meet me at eight. Usual place.'

– Not the Champ if you don't mind.

'Okay, how about the Pickerel?'

– That'll do. But remember what I just warned you.

'I told you, you'll feel better just for getting out of the house. Trust me, I know about these things.'

There is a hollow laugh before the phone goes dead.

Back in her flat, she finds to her surprise that neither the transcription nor her memory has been tampered with.

Mr Kellett gave a detailed account of his recent discussions with BW. BW had also been visited by Erliu, and had found him both affable and informative. BW had stressed the seriousness of Erliu's warnings about Mr Norben who, it seems, has significantly over-reached himself, to the extent that anyone who has dealings with him is unlikely to come out of it well. The chairman accordingly stressed to all members present the importance of avoiding contact with him if at all possible, and to report any approach from Mr Norben to Mr Kellett without delay.

What the Society was clearly most in need of was an expert in cyphers. Who did they expect to confuse with code-names like these? BW? William Blake's initials in reverse. Erliu? An obvious anagram of Uriel. As for Mr Norben … Ignoring for a moment the clumsy attempts at cryptology, Rosemary knows she should be more concerned by the warnings about Bonner, but somehow the sheer amateurishness of everything about the LSSS makes it difficult to take the whole thing seriously. In any case, what did Kellett mean by 'has significantly over-reached himself'? Perhaps Kellett simply got cold feet when he realised that Bonner really was who he claimed to be.

Rosemary is at the bar ordering her second glass of wine when Jamie finally appears at 8.25. Her determination to be in good humour is already being tested. He kisses her on the cheek.

'Sorry Rosie. Didn't mean to keep you waiting.'

But still did. 'Something come up?'

'Shall we sit down?'

Although it is Friday night, the table she has been reserving for them has not been taken in the thirty seconds since she vacated it. Jamie seems determined to ignore her question at the bar, until she asks it again. He shifts in his seat.

'To be honest, I had a bit of a panic attack. At least I think that's what it was. It's never happened to me before. Don't laugh.'

'Why the hell should I laugh? It's not something to joke about. Anyway, considering some of the experiences I've had recently, I'm hardly in a position to mock.'

'I wanted to ask you about that, Rosie. Don't take this the wrong way, but at your darkest times, when you didn't know if Adam was coming back and everything was shit, did you ever think about, you know, doing something dramatic?'

'What, like sky-diving?'

'I'm being serious. Just, I don't know, upping and disappearing without telling anyone and never being heard of again. Turning up somewhere you're not known and starting afresh.'

Rosemary's first thought is that she knows someone who seems to have been doing precisely this for centuries. She is not sure, however, if she can remember the answer to his question.

'There were dark times, but I don't think so. Problems don't disappear just because you try to run away from them. In any case, however depressed I got, I think I always believed that life would eventually take a turn for the better.'

Jamie nods, then looks down at his drink.

Why, where's this going?

'I suppose your situation was different,' Jamie says. 'When someone close to you dies, you grieve for them, but you always know that the pain will fade in time. It's not

196

like a life sentence stretching out in front of you.'

'Jamie, is this all about Agnieszka?'

His silence confirms the answer. He seems about to break down.

'Look, what's the hold this woman's got over you? You've never been like this with anyone before. What happened to love 'em and leave 'em?'

Jamie grips his glass. He has hardly touched the contents. 'Ironic, isn't it? She's on such a high, she's got everything planned down to the last detail and it's as if I've just been swept along in her wake. If there ever was a time when I could have told her that this is not what I want, that I'm not ready to make this sacrifice, it's long gone now. I'm caught up in the tide of events.'

It crosses her mind to tell her brother about her euphoric reaction to her own short-lived pregnancy. She decides that it might not be helpful to either of them.

'I may be speaking out of turn, Jamie, but it seems to me that even if you don't tell her outright she's soon going to work out for herself that something's wrong.'

Jamie nods to indicate that he already knows this.

'Do you feel like you're starting to get over Adam now?'

'At the beginning, the worst part was not knowing if he was dead or alive. If I was supposed to be grieving for him or not. I suppose now I've managed to accept that, whatever actually happened to Adam, he's never coming back into my life. I told him out loud that I'm moving on. Somehow, that seemed to help.'

'You told him. Out loud.'

She shrugs. 'Whether someone dies on you or just leaves, you still grieve. Everyone deals with it in their own way.'

'Like when dad left, you mean?'

This turn in the conversation throws her. She decides not to pick up the theme.

'Grieving's like being a recovering alcoholic, you just focus on surviving one day at a time. That's all you can do.

197

And make sure you've got someone close to talk to whenever you really need it. Anyway, I hate to raise this painful subject again, but we've got the little issue of mum. Whatever Agnieszka wants, you've still got responsibilities here.'

'Yes, I know.'

Jamie falls silent, staring through the window at the darkening sky. He finishes his drink, makes his excuses and leaves. It is still only 9.15, and Rosemary does not feel like going home. A few minutes later, Jayne and Mary walk in. They acknowledge her without smiling, and talk animatedly at the bar as they order their drinks. She decides that, if they snub her again, she will leave. Having bought their drinks, they walk straight across and ask permission to sit at her table. They even force a smile.

'On your own again then, Billy No-mates?' Mary says.

'I came here to meet Jamie, but he didn't feel like hanging around and I didn't feel like going home. You know how it is.'

'Jamie? Is this—'

'My brother.'

'Ah. Don't think I've ever heard you talk about your brother. Have you, Jayne?' Jayne gently shakes her head.

'Jamie's going through a hard time.'

'Seems to be a family trait,' Mary says. 'Sorry, that was a bit harsh.' Jayne scowls.

'It's okay, you're right, Mary. Between me, Jamie and mum, it's a bit like a union between the House of Atreus and the House of Usher. The post-nuclear family, you might say.'

Jayne introduces a diversionary tactic. 'What's the news about your mum, Rosie?'

'None, really. None they're telling us anyway. I'm pretty much resigned to the idea that every day without progress is a day closer to the inevitable.'

'You don't think there's any chance she'll recover?'

'Well, there are precedents for people rising from the dead, I suppose. Don't think it's happened too often

198

though.'

There is an uneasy silence for a few moments. Mary dives in to fill it.

'Do you see much of Sharon these days?'

Rosemary flinches, and realises that Jayne and Mary have noticed this. 'I haven't seen her for a few days. Any reason you ask?'

Mary checks with Jayne. 'We heard she was applying for jobs,' Jayne says. 'In America.'

At closing time, she trudges back up Castle Hill to her flat, sits on the sofa, allows her head to fall back, then after a few minutes picks up the *Songs of Experience*. Her eye alights on the final stanza of *The Clod and the Pebble*:

Love seeketh only Self to please
To bind another to Its delight:
Joys in another's loss of ease
And builds a Hell in Heaven's despite.

A few pages on, the prologue to *A Little Girl Lost*:

Children of the future Age,
Reading this indignant page,
Know that in a former time
Love! sweet Love! was thought a crime.

Sharon suggested a trip to Wales. Soon, Rosemary will have a fair amount of leisure time on her hands. Her eyes flick towards the phone, but it is late now. In any case, can she unwind even in the Welsh mountains until she has in some way resolved the mystery which is at the root of her unease?

28

The steps in front of the main entrance to the Fitzwilliam Museum lead to an atrium which is not large in relation to the scale of the building, but which manages to pack in a mouth-watering melange of styles. Italianate staircases curve away at either side of the reception desk to give access to the floor above. In niches and recesses lurk neo-classical statues, all sensuous curves and flowing drapery. The figures' noble features and raised arms guide the eye upwards to the richly coloured Victorian stained glass windows, worthy of the splendour of St Pancras in its long-gone heyday. Topping off this riotous confection is a Baroque ceiling, complete with cupola, which would not look out of place as the crowning glory of one of Wren's more decorative churches. The numinous effect of this pageant of human creative evolution serves, as always, to keep the overawed visitor in her humble place.

One of the first floor exhibition rooms allegedly holds four works by William Blake, but they elude Rosemary's searching eye. Finally resorting to the catalogue which is presented there for precisely such moments, she discovers that they in fact reside in a gallery which, now that she looks up, runs around the upper reaches of this room. Access is gained with some difficulty through an inconspicuous door and then a narrow spiral staircase, and it is with some relief that she steps out at the top onto a lofty passageway. The Blake pictures turn out to be on the far side. They are not among his best-known, although one, *Ugolino and his sons in prison*, she recognises from what is possibly another version of the same scene in one of her books. The painting, tempera on canvas according to the catalogue, which she finds most arresting is entitled *The Christ Child asleep on a cross*; it depicts a clearly anxious Mary and Joseph looking down at their young son, who has chosen to sleep spread-eagled on a cruciform wooden bed. No wonder his parents' faces show their concern.

The central lending library offers, by and large, less refined delights, and is considerably busier. In one corner, behind some bookcases, a group of young children is learning the words and actions to 'What shall we do with the drunken sailor?' Rosemary sits down to peruse a couple of tourist guides to Wales, but within a few minutes the soundtrack of unsuppressed chatter and mobile phone ring tones leads her to check the books out and repair to the Champion of the Thames for lunch. Her favourite seat is already occupied, but after a morning spent at least partly in the worship of high culture she feels that it would be churlish to make too much of a fuss about this, so sits at a neighbouring table, close enough to make a lurch for the alcove should it be vacated. Returning after fifteen minutes with her second glass of wine, she studies the guide books and begins to make a mental itinerary: a few days walking in the hills around Dolgellau, the Ffestiniog Railway which she has not visited since she was a child, Harlech Castle, Caernarfon, a jaunt across to Anglesey, which she promises to think of from now on as Ynys Mon … She begins to wish that Adam had been Welsh. The occupants of the alcove seat show every sign of having settled in for a long stay, but for once she feels too relaxed to consider this a matter of pressing concern. Her wine is chilled to perfection and the dry roasted peanuts are her favourite brand. She is at one with the world. Surely nothing could disrupt this idyllic state of affairs.

As if waiting for the moment to pounce, her memory reminds her that it is now some days since she went to visit mum. She pushes the thought away, but it is primed and ready to fight back. There is always tomorrow, she tells it. Sunday is a good day for hospital visiting, there is little else to do. This, apparently, is not a convincing response. Soon a needling sense of guilt is eating away at her earlier bonhomie. She shows a willingness to negotiate: one more glass of wine and one more packet of peanuts, then she will go to the hospital. The third glass takes three-quarters of an hour to consume, the guide books proving a sufficient distraction in the meantime.

Assessing her blood alcohol level as she steps outside into the fresh air, she decides against returning home for her bicycle and walks across Christ's Pieces to Emmanuel Street, where a bus is already waiting. Twenty minutes later, she walks into Addenbrooke's Hospital. Up in the ward, Derek is not in his bed, although his dressing gown is still on the chair and his book on the bedside cabinet. Seeing her momentary confusion, the red-faced woman in the next bed says, 'They've taken him for tests.'

'On a Saturday?'

The woman responds with a shrug of the shoulders. Rosemary sits next to her mother, who remains as impassive as ever. She takes her hand, with the same result as on every previous occasion. Mum's breathing is flat and regular, as always. She considers trying to find a nurse, but recalls from previous visits that weekends are not the best time to discuss clinical matters. The hospital's warm, stuffy atmosphere is making her feel that the third glass of wine may not have been such a good idea after all.

Looking out of the bus window on the journey back, she sees groups of fresh-faced and clear-headed young people heading out for an evening's entertainment, and possibly more. How many of them will find their aspirations dashed and end up spending the night on their own, and how many will feel as miserable about it as she will? How can a life so promising until so recently have veered so far off course?

She is walking along Bridge Street heading for Castle Hill when a young man hurtles out of the front door of the Mitre and knocks her into the road. A cyclist narrowly avoids her and directs a volley of abuse at the young man. Rosemary is too stunned to be sure whether she has suffered any injury, but before she can assess the damage numerous hands are helping her to her feet. A sea of anxious faces tries to talk simultaneously. One voice seems more insistent than the others.

'I'm so, so sorry. That was utterly idiotic of me. Are

202

you okay? Please tell me you're okay. Can I do anything to help? Here, let me dust you down. Oops, sorry, didn't mean to do that. Look, can I do anything to help? Oh God, I think I've already said that.'

She concludes from the location of the pain that her head hit the road, but otherwise no great harm has been done. The young man with the line in frenetic monologue is presumably the one who ran into her, and he now stares intently with furrowed brow. His eyes are shocked and fearful, but his sandy-coloured hair looks naturally wavy, and his jaw-line firm.

'It's all right, I'm sure there's no damage done.'

'Look, please come in and let me buy you a drink to help you over the shock. It's the least I can offer to do. Come and sit down for a few minutes. Just to make sure you're okay.'

'I'm fine, I really don't need a drink.'

A voice cuts in from behind him. 'Come on George, we'll be late.'

George turns angrily. 'Well piss off then and I'll catch you up.' Tosser, she hears him add under his breath. An involuntary smile plays on her lips. The crowd of voyeurs begins to melt away as she checks her clothing to make sure that it has not been too obviously dirtied or damaged.

'Well, perhaps one drink. Purely to settle the nerves, you understand.'

She watches George at the bar, and assesses from his self-confident stance that he is ex-public school, from his accent that it is probably an expensive one. The forearms protruding below his shirt sleeves indicate a muscular physique, although perhaps not from rugby, given the lack of any obvious facial blemishes. Rowing, more likely.

'Thanks George. Cheers.'

'Cheers. I really am so, so sorry about earlier. Hey, you have the advantage now in that you know my name.'

She thinks for a moment. 'You can call me Ingrid.'

'Ingrid. Wow. Don't think I've ever met an Ingrid. What a fabulous name.'

'Why? It's just a name.'

'You know, Ingrid Bergman and all that. It suggests someone sultry and mysterious.'

She touches the growing lump on the back of her head. 'Does it? In that case, you'd be very disappointed if you got to know me.'

'I rather doubt that somehow.' George is already leaning forward in a way which suggests he is testing her openness to intimacy. 'In fact, I very much doubt that.'

Rosemary's head is beginning to throb. 'What does your father do then, George?'

'My father? He has a pretty uninteresting job. Why do you ask?'

'I don't believe you. Tell me what he does. I bet he's really a Shakespearian actor or a Cabinet minister.'

'Well, Ingrid, if you really must know, he's the Bishop of Salisbury.'

She bursts out laughing. 'You're kidding. The Bishop of Salisbury?'

George's mood alters abruptly. 'I told you it wasn't very interesting. And I suppose some people would find it amusing.'

She smiles to soothe his irritation. 'It's not boring at all. Or amusing really. It's just strangely appropriate given that we're in the Mitre.'

George looks quizzical, then smiles. 'Do you know, I drink in here several nights a week, and the significance of the name never struck me until you mentioned it. You see, you're broadening my horizons already.'

Rosemary is still weighing up whether she wants to broaden George's horizons any further. The wine is topping up her residual blood alcohol level from lunchtime with some enthusiasm. She senses that the next few minutes will be critical.

'How are you feeling now?' George asks.

'I'm okay. Why?'

'You keep touching the back of your head and wincing. Perhaps I should have a look at it.'

'No, it's fine. It's not bleeding. I'll take a paracetamol when I get home.' George's expression betrays a level of disappointment at this reference to parting. 'Where were you and your friends about to head off to, anyway?'

He waves his hand. 'Oh, just some tedious wine and cheese do put on by the Master.'

'With free wine it can't be all bad. Which college?'

'Magdalene. To be honest, I wasn't that keen on going in the first place. Anyway, what does yours do?'

'Excuse me?'

'You asked me about my father. Tit for tat and all that.'

'Oh, I see. To be honest, I've no idea what my father does. I've no idea what he looks like or what his name is. He could be dead for all I know.'

'Oh. I'm sorry.'

'Really? Why?'

'Well, it must be difficult never having known your own father.'

'No it's not. What you've never had you don't miss. The family story goes that my mother and father got together for one night on the hippie trail in Samarkand. Or was it Tashkent? Anyway, they were following the Silk Route to China, except that you couldn't get into China in those days. Mum's never confirmed or denied the story, so perhaps it's better to leave everyone to believe what they want to believe.'

'Christ, I wish my parents had been that adventurous.'

'Not the sort of thing future bishops get up to, I suppose. The Church of England probably frowns on the fathering of illegitimate children.'

George has visibly relaxed since they first started talking. His broad shoulders are no longer hunched, and he has slipped his right ankle across his left knee. His thoughts are becoming progressively more easy to read.

'So, Ingrid, it's Saturday night, I hope I'm not keeping you from your boyfriend.'

She laughs. 'I can't remember the last time a young man made such a cack-handed attempt to find out if I'm beddable.'

George stares open-mouthed, clearly debating whether to show his indignation, or to demonstrate that he can take a joke at his own expense. Rosemary finds herself revelling in his dilemma.

'To be honest, George, that crack on the head has given me a splitting headache. I'm going to go home and lie down. Alone.'

'Well, can I see you home, just to make sure you get there okay?'

'That won't be necessary. But thanks for the drink. I've enjoyed your company.'

Giving him no time to respond, she pushes her chair back and makes for the door. Outside, a picture forms in her mind of a young woman with a remarkable resemblance to her lying in bed wondering, What if I had? After fifty yards, she stops. Perhaps George has come out onto the street and is staring after her. If he has, should she take a lead from her temporary namesake and rush back into his arms? On the other hand, he must be at least six, maybe seven years younger. And what if he loses interest when he discovers her name is not really Ingrid?

She walks on slowly, listening hard in case a voice calls after her, and hears nothing but traffic.

29

After work on Monday, Rosemary makes the all-too-familiar journey by bicycle to Addenbrooke's Hospital. As she walks into the ward where her mother lies, her eyes move first towards Derek. It is obvious from his laboured breathing and sunken eyes that he has taken a turn for the worse.

'Not so good today, Derek?'

It is clearly an effort for him to turn his head. 'Could be something to do with the new medication they've got me on.'

His expression tells her that he knows this is not the explanation. He cannot even manage a smile. She takes his hand. It is cold and limp.

'Well, I'd better leave you to get some rest. Mustn't go tiring you out, must I?'

She pulls up a chair next to her mother's bed. After a few minutes she looks across and sees that Derek's eyes are closed, his bony hands balled into fists. A little later, a nurse approaches her.

'Dr Bialkowski would like to have a word with you when it's convenient. Can you come in one morning after 10.30?'

'I can from next week, if it's not screamingly urgent.' Her eyes drift back towards her mother. 'I don't suppose … '

'We're doing everything we can to keep your mother comfortable.'

A few minutes later, Rosemary decides that being present to receive the message from Dr Bialkowski fulfils her responsibility to mum for that day. Derek is now snoring in a laboured and irregular manner, his mouth open and his head tipped back on the pillows. She watches him for a few moments, wondering if it is for the last time.

Cycling back towards town, she finds herself thinking of

Derek rather than her mother. By his own admission he has no visitors, and he believes that when he dies, which cannot be long delayed, nothing of him will remain. When she first met him, he would have had the strength to get out of bed and hurl himself from a window had he chosen to do so, though even that option is surely beyond him now. Still he clings onto life. A wave of sadness swamps her as she considers how short a time of strength and good health we have to achieve our goals, to make our mark, to grasp life by the scruff of the neck until it pleads for mercy. Her thirtieth birthday looms a couple of years over the horizon. It suddenly feels that she has been treading water.

At the traffic lights at the top of Cherry Hinton Road, the sadness begins to transform itself into something more rounded, a sense that a turning point in her life has arrived. Perhaps she has been spending too much time with dying people, but she is no longer prepared to drift. She has some serious thinking to do.

Nursing a glass of sauvignon blanc in her favourite alcove, Rosemary wants to tell anyone within hearing distance that she has done with dabbling in mysteries beyond her understanding, she has done with Richard Bonner and John Dee and the London Society for Spiritual Sodding Studies. From now on she will not succumb to the dictates of ghosts or hobgoblins; she will live the life which she chooses for herself, and she will live it hard.

Her diary reminds her that one dictate which has not gone away is the monthly meeting of her poetry group, always held on the final Thursday of the month. The meeting starts at 8; it is now 7.30. Is attending the poetry group in accord with her new approach to life? After a few moments' consideration, she concludes that turning up without having spent the previous few weeks labouring to give birth to her latest magnum opus and then to polish it to perfection is very much in accord. She finds a piece of paper in her bag, chews the end of her pen and begins to scribble. The experience is reminiscent of the stream-of-consciousness writing exercises they used to engage in when the group first formed: write for five minutes without stopping, put down whatever words form themselves in your mind even if they constitute meaningless gibberish, and if you have indeed come up with gibberish, do not make any attempt to correct it. Within ten minutes, three four-line stanzas with regular abab end-rhyme have appeared in front of her. Are they in iambic tetrameter? At one time she would have known. She throws the pen down on the table in front of her, takes a sip of wine and peruses the words she has written. Each time she tries to find a more apt or colourful synonym for a word in the poem, it transpires that none exists, at least within the bounds of her vocabulary. Was it Verlaine who on principle never edited his poems, trusting always to his first instincts? Perhaps it was Rimbaud. Anyway, if it was good enough for a dead Frenchman …

She takes a large glass of wine up to the meeting with her, and this time is content to leave it resting on the table, taking only the occasional sip. Politely applauding the efforts of her former antagonists proves to be no effort. This time she is the last of the group to present her work. She allows herself a wry smile at the raised eyebrows when she pulls a scruffy scrap of paper from her bag. Her eyes scan the hurried, spidery script to make sure she can still read it. She did not notice it at the time, but her rushed handwriting looks strangely like John Dee's. She completed the poem not much more than an hour ago, but the words already feel like someone else's.

Passion: A Prophecy

If suffering makes the soul grow strong
and patience makes a fool a saint,
inflicting pain can cause no wrong
and misery should have no restraint.

When love and hate share common goal
and oft their faces interchange,
let senses rule the human soul
and self-control no profit gain.

Let angels for our fate contend
with spirits of malign intent.
Then every human soul must bend,
heaven-born, but hell-ward bent.

When the poem has ended, an uneasy silence settles. Rosemary looks up and sees the others glancing at one another with puzzled expression.

'I guess that didn't go down too well. Sorry. I ignored the first law of poetry composition and didn't give it time to gestate.'

'It's not that there was anything wrong with the poem, Rosie,' Sally says. 'It's just that we all thought you were a modernist. You're normally the first to condemn anything you see as a pastiche of an antique style.'

'Well, I suppose so, but—'

'Unless you've been engaging in shadow-writing, Rosie, you seem to have somehow imbibed the spirit of William Blake. That poem could almost have come from the pages of the *Songs of Experience*. Quite uncanny.'

On the way home, Rosemary realises that today was her mother's birthday.

30

On her last day, she enters the library humming to herself, offers a breezy 'Good morning' as she passes the porters' office, climbs the stairs and walks along the main east corridor smiling at each person she passes. The central courtyard is still in shadow, but up above the sky is an untarnished blue. Entering the manuscripts reading room, she finds that most of the staff have not yet arrived. The clock high on the wall above the counter reassures her that this is probably the earliest she has ever turned up for work. She feels wide awake, and totally alive.

Roger has not yet arrived either. She takes out of her bag the transcriptions she made of the fateful last item in the newly-discovered manuscript and of the LSSS minutes from the British Library. Should she take them outside and burn them? Deciding that this would be an unnecessarily dramatic gesture, she folds them over and over and stuffs them into the bottom of the paper recycling sack which sits in the corner of the office. She turns on her computer and peruses the paper correspondence in her 'in' and 'pending' trays while waiting for it to boot up. There proves to be very little which she can realistically finish; most of the outstanding tasks represent continuing projects on which, for one reason or another, she cannot at present make progress. Will Roger feel confident enough in the healing ability of therapy to leave them for her return, or will he hedge his bets and reassign them? She does not allow the question to fester in her mind and turns to her e-mail inbox, which is reassuringly empty.

There is a staffing shortage in the reading room, so she volunteers to help out for an hour behind the counter. Donald glances across from time to time, looking anxious. Have her standards of customer care dropped that low recently? Even some of the library users seem to prefer to queue to speak to another member of staff.

'Anything wrong, Donald?' she asks during a quiet

moment.

He looks around and keeps his voice low. 'I, um, just thought you'd have a lot of other things to do. What with one thing and another.'

'One thing and another? Oh, you mean the fact that I'm being forced to take a period of sick leave due to stress. To be honest, most of my work isn't the sort you can finish off at short notice. In any case, I'm not going to be gone long, am I?'

In the tea room, Sharon sits at a table on her own, staring at the screen of her laptop. Rosemary is tempted to pretend she has not noticed her, but quickly realises that this would be inconsistent with her new outlook on life. She sits opposite her friend, who does not look up. Is Sharon ignoring her, or just utterly absorbed?

'Hi, Sharon. Found something interesting?'

There is no response. After a few seconds, Sharon closes the lid of her laptop and looks up. She is not smiling.

'Just tell me if my presence is unwelcome. I'll go and sit somewhere else.'

'No, Rosie, your presence isn't unwelcome. It never has been.'

'Then why the ice treatment?'

Sharon sighs and sits back in her chair. There are dark lines around her eyes. 'I'm sorry, I'm just tired. Haven't been sleeping too well. How's your mum?'

'Apparently Dr Bialkowski wants to see me. I suspect he wants to switch mum off.'

'You seem remarkably sanguine about that prospect.'

Sharon seems to have aged since they last met, but Rosemary has no wish to open up the likely source of her malaise for discussion.

'I suppose I've just come to terms with the fact that it's one more facet of my life I've got no control over.'

Sharon stares hard. 'I know what you mean,' she says. There is bitterness in her tone. Rosemary begins to wish she had sat at another table.

'How's William Blake coming along?' she asks.

'Kind of on the back burner. I'm trying to focus on day-to-day things. You know.'

'No, not really.'

Sharon casts her eyes down. No answer to the implied question is forthcoming. After frantically weighing up the pros and cons, Rosemary slides her hand across the table, palm upwards. Sharon stares at it, frowning, then pushes the laptop to one side and allows her own hand to rest limply on top. Rosemary squeezes it, but the gesture is not reciprocated.

'Anything I can help with?' she asks.

Sharon smiles without mirth, slowly shaking her head. 'What a question.' She leans forward. 'Look, let's just pretend this conversation never happened. In fact, let's pretend everything never happened. I'm sure you'd prefer it that way.' She tries to draw her hand away. Rosemary does not release it. Sharon struggles, scrapes her chair back, gets to her feet and people on other tables start to watch. At length she pulls her hand free, picks up her laptop and hurries towards the exit. Rosemary sits open-mouthed. Jayne and Mary stare at her from three tables away. Her forehead drops onto her fingertips and she closes her eyes, praying that when she looks up again everyone will have gone back to their own business. Her prayer is not granted.

She works through most of her lunch-break, pausing only to go outside for fresh air. When she returns, the transcriptions she carefully placed at the bottom of the recycling sack are sitting on her desk, showing no sign of the rough treatment she gave them before disposing of them. She looks towards heaven, knowing that Roger is watching her.

'Do you know how these got here, Roger?'

'I didn't see who put them there. I assumed they were yours. It's your handwriting, isn't it?'

Three hours later, she puts on her jacket and sits back at

her desk to await the departure of most of the reading room staff before making her exit. If there were a secret door through which she could depart unseen by anyone, she would use it. From the corner of her eye she can see Roger anxiously shuffling papers, apparently as discomfited by the situation as she. When the reading room has emptied out, she stands and opens the door.

'Bye Roger.'

'Bye Rosemary. Good luck.'

Good luck. Is that all? As she pedals towards Queens Road, the air is warm and humid and the sky heavily overcast, a little like on the night she walked to Byron's Pool. While crossing the river she stops for a moment to watch the punts passing and to gaze at the timeless classical proportions of Wren's Trinity Library. Below lies the willow-shaded spot where she rested on the way to her mother's house for dinner, when mum was still capable of cooking, after a fashion, and of provoking an argument. Freewheeling down the other side of the hump-backed bridge, she turns to ride along the narrow street which flanks the high, austere walls of Trinity College.

Someone is following her. It is not immediately clear which sense has alerted her to this fact, but she stops and looks over her shoulder. The road behind is empty. Two young male students sweep round the corner on bicycles, and she waits for them to pass. They leer at her as they do so. Her eyes check for alley-ways down which a pursuer could have disappeared from view, but there are none. Nevertheless, the sense of a malevolent presence is almost tangible. Her trembling hands grip the handle-bars and she rides as fast as she can for the safety of Trinity Street with its throngs of tourist shoppers and café-goers spilling from the pavements onto the roadway.

She throws her bike against a wall and leans back, breathing fast. A number of passers-by stare, but none thinks to check if she is all right. What could she say in any case? When her pulse is no longer racing, she walks her bicycle back towards Bridge Street and the route which will take her home, looking carefully up each side street along the way. Her surroundings appear unchanged and the presence, whoever or whatever it was, has gone. As she starts the long toil up Castle Hill it begins to rain, a few large spots initially, then rapidly blossoming into a full-blown downpour. She casts around for somewhere to take shelter, ducks under a tree for a while, but when its branches become saturated she grits her teeth and heads for home.

Entering the flat, carelessly dripping rainwater across the carpet, it occurs to her that it would make her happy if there were a phone message from Sharon. The red light whose responsibility it is to indicate 'message waiting' remains idle and sullen. She stares at the phone for a while, but this does not cause it to ring. Her cold, wet clothing is making her shiver. Last night, when she adopted her new life-affirming philosophy, suddenly seems a very long time ago.

31

The next morning, the first of her enforced vacation, Rosemary allows herself to sleep in. Feeling no pressure to get up and clean the flat or toil down to the supermarket, she turns over and buries her face in the pillow, trying to formulate positive thoughts about the opportunity being afforded to her to defibrillate her life and place it on a more regular path. There is still the not-inconsiderable obstacle of resolving her mother's future, but surely even this can be kicked into the long grass for the moment. The radio plays somewhere in the background, just below the level at which it might impact on her conscious mind. It is high summer, she can see the sun through the curtains and hear muffled, happy voices in the street outside.

She becomes increasingly restless and agitated. The sheets are rough against her skin, as though they have transformed themselves into sackcloth. The radio has developed an underlying hiss. A symphony of car horns begins on Castle Hill. The phone rings and she hesitates too long, picking up the receiver just as it rings off. The caller does not leave a message.

Just before mid-day she rises, showers and decides to put on a bright summer dress in the hope of raising her mood. She walks into town, striding with conviction past the Pickerel, enjoying the breeze on her legs and more than a few admiring glances, which she studiously ignores. There is even a chance she will bump into Sharon; would that be a happy encounter? While window-shopping in the Lion Yard she decides on a whim to enter the central library, in whose reference section sits a self-professed Encyclopedia of the Esoteric and the Occult. She takes it from the shelf, sits down at a table and finds the entry relating to Uriel. After a good deal of familiar material, it describes the archangel's role in a magical ceremony known as the banishing ritual of the lesser pentagram, used to ward off evil. In this the magician, after first creating a magical circle, uses a sword to inscribe pentagrams in the air whilst invoking the archangels Raphael, Gabriel, Michael and Uriel at the four quarters. Uriel, it appears, is summoned in the northern quarter and is associated with the element earth. So, Uriel keeps pretty exalted company. And any magician with such powerful spirits at his disposal would be pretty powerful himself. If you believe that such rituals work, of course. No wonder Dr Dee became so obsessed with contacting the spirit world. Speaking of which ...

The Dictionary of National Biography, not surprisingly, has a long entry on Dee. She skims the section about his early life, but discovers one arresting fact. In 1563, Dee visited Venice. There, he made the acquaintance of one Thomas Philologus Ravenna, author of a book entitled *De vita hominis ultra CXX annos protrahenda*. She reads and re-reads the title: On extending the life of man beyond 120 years. One hundred and twenty years: the age which, according to Kellett, Richard Bonner must have attained when he wrote about the execution of Charles the First. A coincidence, perhaps, though an extremely spooky one. But read on: from the early 1580s onwards, Dee devoted himself to making contact with the realm of angels and spirits, working with a man who may have gone under various aliases, including Edward Talbot and Edward Kelly. It seems that this man, by means of prayer and intent staring into a crystal globe, was able to receive messages from the spirit world, or so he convinced Dee. Early in their endeavours, Uriel, no less, appeared to them and gave instructions for invoking other angels.

She props her elbows on the table and rubs her eyes; the feeling that different strands of this story are beginning to interweave is hard to resist, but the key to unlocking the sense of it all as elusive as ever. The tone of the DNB article is sceptical bordering on hostile. Rosemary decides that she needs a second opinion. After consulting the catalogue she tracks down a detailed and apparently studious biography of John Dee, books it out and heads for home.

Deciding that a summer's day is too good to waste, she allows herself to be waylaid by the garden of the Pickerel where, over a glass of wine and a sandwich, she peruses her temporary acquisition. It quickly becomes clear that, whether charlatan or not, Talbot/Kelly was a most persuasive man. Dee remained under his spell for some years, even accepting at face value his assurance that the angels wanted them to have their wives in common, a belief which Dee not surprisingly had difficulty selling to his own wife. More interesting still is the role of Uriel, who plays an important part in some of the apocryphal works inspired by the early books of the Old Testament. In 1553, a French scholar named Guillaume Postel published a book recounting a meeting with an Ethiopian priest who described to him the Book of Enoch, long-since lost to western Christianity but still known in Ethiopia. According to this work Uriel, as well as being able to forewarn Noah of the great flood, revealed to the patriarch Enoch the secrets of the stars and planets. The Book of Enoch even contained a record of the primal divine language taught by God to Adam, and subsequently lost to humanity after the Fall. Dee owned a copy of Postel's book.

Uriel is clearly a useful archangel to have on your side. No wonder Bonner was ready to invoke the name to lend authority to his claims of immortality. Perhaps he was convinced that he actually had communicated with Uriel. But how many people in sixteenth-century England really believed that they had the knowledge and the ability to make contact with the spirit world? Dee met a man who wrote a book claiming that he could extend human life beyond 120 years. Could there be some connection between Bonner and Talbot/Kelly? Given the apparent fluidity of the latter's identity, and the former's invisibility in the historical record, could they even be the same person? Rosemary has to concede that she can only guess at the answer to any of these questions. All she does know beyond doubt is that, for the first time in living memory, she has allowed her chilled white wine to grow warm.

Walking home up Castle Hill, she finds that the memory of her haunting experience while cycling past Trinity College the previous night is still fresh in her mind. If anything, it seems even more vivid now than at the time. What she cannot be sure is whether the visitation, for so she considers it, constituted a threat or a warning. Either way, someone clearly wanted her to be afraid. It seems equally clear that someone, perhaps the same someone, also does not intend to allow her to duck out of trying to solve the Bonner mystery, despite the promise which she made to herself so recently. Not for the first time, she wishes that she could still confide in Sharon, albeit preferably a less sceptical Sharon. The simple truth is that she is starting to miss Sharon's company badly.

At home, there is a message waiting on the phone. When she plays it back, she hears Sharon's voice say, 'Hi Rosie,' after which there is a long pause, punctuated only by a sniff, followed by 'I'll try you later'. She checks her mobile to see that she has missed a call from Sharon even though she did not hear it ring. The time of the call suggests that it was made while she was engrossed in her reading in the garden of the Pickerel. Perhaps the noise of a passing bus drowned it out. There is no reason to suspect anything more sinister. She tries ringing Sharon, but gets no reply.

It crosses her mind to cycle round to Sharon's house to check that she is all right, but if Sharon is not answering her phone then she is most likely out. She did say she would try again later. But suppose she is now convinced that Rosemary is trying to avoid her?

She makes a cup of tea, sits down at the table and takes from a box a greeting card with an aerial photo of Tintern Abbey on the front. She opens it and her pen hovers over the pristine white interior. After considerable internal disputation she writes: *Hi Sharon. Sorry I missed your call earlier. It would be good if we could meet up. Any plans for the rest of the weekend? Rosie xx.* With hindsight she wishes she could erase the kisses at the end but decides that, to paraphrase Pontius Pilate, what she has written, she has written. She cycles to Sharon's house and puts the card through the letter-box without checking if her friend is actually at home. Mr Keats gazes out of the front window. He confirms to her that the house is empty.

32

Sunday dawns cloudy and grey. Rosemary considers this to be consonant with her own mood as, mug of coffee in hand, she stares through the window. Sleep has been elusive. Her enforced sabbatical from the library already feels as if, far from an opportunity for renewal, it will be a simple test of endurance. So far she has received no response from Sharon.

Shopping for clothes may offer at least a temporary respite from this melancholy. Cruising the glossy, brightly-illuminated emporia of the Grand Arcade, she has no clear idea what she is searching for. The items which catch her eye are ones which, in a different frame of mind, she would reject as being dowdy, and taking home clothes she knows she will never wear will do nothing to lighten her burden. At length she settles for a pair of white jeans which struggle past her hips after some heroic conflict but which, if she carries on losing weight at the current rate, will soon be a perfect fit. She complements the jeans with a white top designed to disclose a modicum of cleavage, assuming that, by the time she can wear the jeans comfortably, she has any left to reveal.

She finds herself wandering through the door of a large electrical retailer for no reason other than to review the ever-broadening range of electronic equipment for which she has no use. Her attention focuses momentarily on a compact camera with a small subsidiary screen on the front next to the lens; the purpose of this arrangement is apparently to facilitate the taking of selfies. This does not, however, seem a sufficiently sound motive for parting with the outlay involved. Rosemary recalls that she has never taken a selfie in her life, although Sharon once tried to persuade her to photograph them jointly on her mobile phone as part of some drunken escapade, the purpose of which had been lost by the next morning. A new laptop, on the other hand, might be a worthwhile investment, since her existing specimen will soon need to be booted up first thing in the morning to give her access to it by the evening. Unlike other electronic equipment, however, laptops do not seem to have become noticeably cheaper over the years. More to the point, the shelves are now full of slim, ultra-portable tablets which might be a better investment. Still, there must be a drawback with them or else there would be no point in continuing to sell laptops. These are issues probably better postponed to a later date.

Just after midday, she heads out of the mall with a view to lunching in the Eagle, but as she arrives decides on a whim to look inside St Bene't's church just across the road. She descends the steps to the main door and enters cautiously, checking from side to side. A service has not long finished, and the last few worshippers are preparing to leave. She exchanges a smile with them, places her carrier bag on the table inside the door and picks up a small leaflet offering visitors a brief guide to the building's salient features. The interior is bright and pleasantly cool. She runs her fingers down the smooth stones of the Saxon tower; after a thousand years they appear capable of remaining intact for another thousand, perhaps beyond. She smiles on reading that high in the tower are round holes believed to have been made to attract owls to keep down the level of vermin. She checks the floor carefully, just in case.

In one of the aisles, an auburn-haired woman in late middle age is ferrying trays of used cups and saucers into the kitchen, her rounded face seemingly locked into a permanent smile. Now and again she sings softly to herself, presumably recalling one of the hymns used in the recent service. When all the crockery has been removed, she begins what will be the lengthy task of stacking rows of folding chairs against the wall.

'Can I help you with that?' Rosemary asks.

The woman looks up and smiles even more broadly. 'Why, thank you my dear. You know what they say.'

'Many hands make light work.'

'Worth remembering if we have a power cut.' The woman chuckles.

Rosemary finds that engaging in a purposeful task of this kind, however unchallenging, is surprisingly fulfilling. She takes pride in stacking the chairs in neat groups of three, each group equidistant from its neighbours. The job takes about ten minutes, but clearly would have been an arduous undertaking without her assistance. Her cheerful companion makes no attempt to initiate conversation, but continues to sing to herself. When the task is complete, Rosemary surveys the outcome. The woman watches her.

'Thank you for your help. Bit late for introductions, but I'm Eleanor, by the way.'

'Rosemary. Glad to have been of service.'

'I don't think I've seen you before, Rosemary. Are you visiting Cambridge? We get lots of visitors at this time of year.'

'No, I'm that rarest of beasts, a resident of Cambridge who was actually born here.'

Eleanor laughs again. 'It does seem that way sometimes, doesn't it? Still, the place wouldn't be half as interesting if it weren't so cosmopolitan.'

Eleanor places a hand on her shoulder and gently steers her towards the back row of permanent seats in the nave. They sit and look forward towards the chancel.

'The Victorians pretty much rebuilt the chancel. Strange to think they considered they could make a better job of it than skilled medieval masons. I suppose they meant well, but just knowing that part of the church is modern makes it feel a little, how shall I say, inauthentic.'

I know what you mean,' Rosemary says. 'It must be a bit like seeing an ancient circle of standing stones tipping over at odd angles, then going back later and finding they've all been set neatly upright. In a way it hasn't really added or removed anything, but it's taken away the mystery. Like putting Seahenge in a museum.'

Eleanor says nothing for a while, although Rosemary senses that she is paying her close attention.

223

'Is there something you'd like to talk about, my dear?'

Rosemary frowns. 'How do you mean?'

Eleanor smiles yet again, a gesture which evidently comes to her easily. Rosemary does not feel uncomfortable, simply puzzled that an offer of help to stack chairs has led to this interrogation. She looks into Eleanor's eyes; they are brown and warm, welcoming.

'Do you get a lot of people wandering in to talk about their problems?'

'No. No, we don't. People tend to wander in hoping that they'll find a way of resolving their problems for themselves. It can take a while to persuade them that it's okay to ask for someone else's help. Many times it's a health issue, physical or mental.'

'My mother's dying, but I can cope with it. Not that I don't care, of course, but, you know, I'm dealing with it.'

Rosemary wonders at what point she began to lose the ability to construct a coherent sentence. Eleanor nods in encouragement. 'And what about you, Rosemary?'

'I'm fine. Really. Thanks all the same.'

'Well, that's good to hear. I suppose I'd better get back to the kitchen then. Those coffee cups won't wash themselves. It's been nice talking to you, Rosemary. And thanks again for your help.'

Eleanor gets to her feet and turns to head for the kitchen. Rosemary feels an unexpected frisson of panic.

'Do you believe in ghosts, Eleanor?'

Eleanor calmly returns and resumes her seat. She appears not to be disconcerted by the question. 'If I believed that the whole of our being is extinguished at the death of our physical body, I wouldn't be here now, would I?' She tilts her head. 'Why, has someone been in contact with you?'

'Two people. One's my fiancé. He died, apparently drowned.'

'Apparently?'

'His body was never found.'

Eleanor nods. 'Many people feel an ongoing

224

connection after death with someone they've loved deeply in life. William Blake's wife claimed that even after his death she never took an important decision without consulting him.'

'Yes, I've read that.'

'It must be comforting to know that you've not truly lost someone. What was your fiancé's name?'

'Adam.'

'Adam. Scottish?'

'As Scottish as they come. Red hair, deep husky voice. Put him in a kilt and give him a claymore and he could be a throwback to the days of the warring highland clans.'

'You still think of him in the present tense.'

'Yes, I suppose I do.' Rosemary smiles. 'Being Adam, he's had a habit of turning up at the most inconvenient times.'

'And the second?' Eleanor asks.

'Second?'

'You said there were two people in contact with you.'

Rosemary picks up the Book of Common Prayer from the shelf in front of her and runs her fingers over the embossed lettering. 'It's a very strange story. I sometimes wonder whether I believe it myself.'

'I'll bet you I've heard stranger. Why don't you try me?'

'It's also quite a long story.'

'I'm in no hurry.'

Who will she ever be able to trust if not this woman she has known for about twenty minutes? Eleanor seems infinitely patient, and in no hurry to pass judgement. Rosemary finds herself relating the history of her encounters with Richard Bonner. Her companion never feels the need to raise her eyebrows, let alone gasp in surprise. By the time she has completed the tale, she feels exhausted and emotionally drained. Eleanor seems happy to give her as long as she needs to recover, offering her a tissue. Rosemary sits up straight and takes a deep breath, waiting for the verdict.

'This man Bonner, when you encounter him, how does he seem to you?'

'In what way?'

'Well, do you sense him as benevolent, like Adam?'

'To tell you the truth, I'm afraid of him. And yet it seems that he's on some kind of mission from God. Speaking to archangels and all that.'

'Things are not always what they seem, Rosemary, especially in the realm of spirit.'

'But I heard the voice, I even read the words.'

'Ah, the power of the written word. Some things are not meant to be written down, you know. I'm interested in one thing, though. From what you say, Bonner isn't strictly a ghost if it's true that he never died. Which of course may be a lie. It may just be what he wants you to believe for some reason.'

'But if it's not true, then … I'm sorry, I'm struggling to get my head around this.'

'Look at it this way. We all know that there are people in this world who claim to have a hotline to the Almighty because, if they can persuade enough people to believe it, it will advance their own ultimately self-serving ends.'

'Like charlatan evangelists, you mean?'

'And, in some countries, unscrupulous politicians. But as I said, in the spirit world too things are not always what they seem. Do you know anything about John Dee?'

First Blake, and now Dee. Is Eleanor reading her mind?

'I've been finding out about him recently.'

'Then you'll probably know that he suffered constant anxiety wondering whether the messages supposedly passed on to him by friendly spirits were actually coming from malign ones, demons in disguise. He took nothing at face value.'

'But Dee did believe what he heard from the archangel Uriel. And that's who Bonner claimed had spoken to him.'

Eleanor sighs. 'To be honest, Rosemary, I have no idea whether there really are such beings as angels and archangels, and if so whether they have Hebrew names, and if so whether one is called Uriel. It doesn't affect what I believe one way or another. All I can say to you, from what God has taught me in all my years on earth, is that when trying to distinguish good from evil your best guide is your own heart. Your gut instinct, to put it another way. If you feel that Bonner's influence is malign, then it probably is. And you should be careful.'

'But I never asked him to make contact with me. How am I supposed to know what he wants? How do I make him leave me alone?'

While they have been talking, the interior of St Bene't's has grown darker. Thunder sounds in the distance. Rosemary turns to Eleanor who, she knows, can read the fear in her eyes. Her new friend smiles and takes her hand, at the same time retrieving a simple silver cross from below her collar and holding it loosely in front of her. The thunder grows steadily louder.

'You're safe here, Rosemary. Nothing can overcome the power of the cross. A power greater than any other.'

A huge thunderclap overhead rattles every object in the church which is not fixed or inordinately heavy. Rosemary flinches. Eleanor remains calm, unfazed.

'Remember what I said. No evil can harm you here.'

'But Bonner said his message came from God.'

'That's what evil spirits always say.'

A few minutes later, the sun shines dimly through the windows, and the recent chaos in the heavens seems a bad memory.

'You see, my dear? Even summer storms can be ferocious, but they soon pass.'

Rosemary decides that she needs a drink after all, thanks Eleanor for her help and gives her hand a last squeeze. As she is opening the door, she hears a gentle voice.

'Oh, Rosemary. Don't forget your shopping.'

33

By Monday morning, Sharon has still not made contact. Perhaps she decided to go away for the weekend. Perhaps it is time to stop behaving like a schoolgirl. But Rosemary's sense of restless irritation has not disappeared; rather, it has been yoked to a growing anxiety fuelled by her encounter the previous day in St Bene't's. Eleanor's warning seemed heartfelt enough, but she did not explain how Rosemary was to protect herself against Bonner, a man who has the power to appear to her at any time in any place, who has the ability to move objects remotely, and whose interest in her is itself entirely unexplained. Perhaps Adam might have some idea what she should do. But she has already said her farewells to Adam.

She decides to return to St Bene't's on the off-chance that she will bump into Eleanor again. An elderly couple are wandering around the church whispering to one another in German. They are too absorbed to notice her presence. Of Eleanor there is no sign. The Book of Common Prayer does not appear to contain a prayer for protection from evil spirits, such entreaties being presumably not common or dangerous, or if it does Rosemary does not know where to look for it. She checks her watch and sees that it is still only ten o'clock. The rest of the day stretches out formless before her.

As she wheels her bicycle towards King's Parade, it dawns on her that if she sets off immediately she will arrive at Addenbrooke's towards ten thirty, the window of opportunity in Dr Bialkowski's hectic schedule. On reaching the ward she is informed that the doctor is extremely busy and may not have time to see her.

'Excuse me, Dr Bialkowski asked to see me.'

'Did you phone to make an appointment?'

'No, every time I've tried I've just been told that the best time to see him is ten thirty.'

'Well, yes, but he is very busy, you know.'

She wanders towards her mother's bedside, but before she arrives a voice hails her from behind. She turns to see the elusive Dr Bialkowski, and has to work hard to contain her surprise: tall, dark-haired, a little podgy but younger than she expected. His accent seems less pronounced than it did over the phone.

'Miss Torrance, I assume. Thank you for coming. Let's see if we can find somewhere to talk in private.'

The only private space available turns out to be an untidy store cupboard where they sit on upturned cardboard boxes. Dr Bialkowski appears to be accustomed to this.

'Thank you again for coming to see me. I wanted to talk to you about your mother.'

'I rather suspected that.'

'I think it's better to be upfront with you. Am I right in thinking you're her next of kin?'

'I suppose so. There's nobody closer.'

'Look. We've done every test we can on your mother. None of them has shown up any sign of meaningful cerebral activity.'

She waits, but Dr Bialkowski is clearly waiting for her.

'You're not saying there's nothing you can do, surely?'

'We have already done everything we can do for your mother.' He pauses. 'I realise how difficult this must be for you.'

'But you hear of people regaining consciousness unexpectedly after years. How can you know that won't happen to mum?'

Rosemary is surprised to hear that her voice is conveying anger rather than grief. Dr Bialkowski seems familiar with this reaction.

'I'll try to explain it to you as best I can. You're right in saying that people do sometimes return to consciousness after a long period, but only if they have retained a certain level of cerebral functioning all along. To put it simply, these people wake from a long period of unconsciousness. But your mother is not unconscious in that sense. Key

229

areas of her brain are no longer functioning. They have lost the ability to function.'

She looks around at the dusty packages, boxes of cotton wool, dressings, syringes and sanitary pads. Part of her feels that she should explode in rage at this confirmation that medical science has washed its hands of her mother. It seems inappropriate to remain calm in the light of such news. Yet she has neither the energy nor the will to fight what the doctor is telling her.

'So what happens now?'

'Of course we'll continue to make sure your mother is comfortable. But any medical intervention is no longer appropriate.'

'You mean you're going to allow her to die.'

'We're going to allow nature to take its course. I think there's an important difference.'

'Do I have any say in this?'

'Miss Torrance, believe me, it would be no kindness to your mother to prolong her life in her present condition. We really have tried everything, but now there's nothing further which can be done.'

Back at mum's bedside, Rosemary watches her face for some time to try to detect even the tiniest flicker of activity, but has to concede that there is none. If some element of our individuality, a soul or spirit or whatever we choose to call it, carries on after our physical death, where is mum's now? Has it already abandoned the sinking ship? Is it floating away on a lifeboat at this moment? Or is it trapped inside her for as long as she continues to breathe and her blood continues to flow? Is it trying to claw its way out at this very moment, like the prematurely buried in the Usher crypt?

She takes her mother's hand. The arm seems thinner, the hand more bony than she remembers from her last visit. It occurs to her that the tube which previously kept her fed is now supplying nothing but a clear liquid. So, for all the good doctor's assurances and his sympathetic manner, he only wanted to inform her of what was already a fait accompli. Her first instinct is to find him again and berate him for taking her complicity for granted. And yet. Suppose the line were still in place keeping her mother alive, and Dr Bialkowski had informed her that the final decision on whether to remove it, now that she understands the full implications, would be hers. Her breathing begins to slow. She lifts one of her mother's eyelids; if the eyes really are the window to the soul, this one is barred and shuttered.

Cycling back down Hills Road, she wonders if she should share the news. Even if Jamie is hopelessly consumed by his own problems, surely it is only fair to give him one last chance to see her before she passes away. And what about dad? He has shown no sign of giving a toss since the day he left, but he might now, even if only out of guilt. Then again, when he turned up out of the blue a few weeks ago, he seemed determined to make sure no good came out of it. Come to think of it, why did he come anyway? Surely not just to invite her out to lunch. Little by little she draws towards the conclusion that those who have left her to deal with the whole nasty business up to this point have forfeited their right to be involved. Hopefully this is a decision she will not live to regret.

Back at the flat, the doormat supports a letter from the local health trust informing her that a place has been found for her in a new therapy group due to start in exactly two weeks. This probably constitutes urgent treatment in the Cinderella world of mental health, but still leaves her kicking her heels in the interim. What, indeed, is the point of her being off work during the intervening period? Moping around the flat can only do more harm than good. More to the point, her meeting with Eleanor has left her even more convinced that the source of the problem does not reside within her own head. One thing seems certain: whatever Bonner is up to, his timing will not be subject to the constraints of health trust resources.

That night she dreams of a family holiday when she was small. She, Jamie and their mother and father are on

231

the sandy beach in a very traditional English seaside resort, complete with candy floss, donkey rides and Punch-and-Judy show. She and Jamie are competing to build the largest and most plausible reconstruction of Windsor Castle. She looks up to see her mother sitting on the sand, legs outstretched, a towel over the lower half of her body as she wriggles into a one-piece bathing suit. At the last stage of the process she removes her bra, allowing her breasts to fall free, before pulling up the bathing suit to cover them. Her father is watching this unfold. Although he has taken a close interest in displays of female flesh in other areas of the beach, his face at this moment carries an expression bordering on disgust. He is clearly about to remonstrate with her mother when he sees Rosemary watching him. Biting his lip, he runs down the beach and into the sea. Her mother, unaware of any of this, is still intent on straightening the straps of the bathing suit.

When she wakes, she remembers the dream vividly, but has no recollection of any such family holiday.

34

Rosemary, curled up on the settee with her William Blake books, is drifting into a mood of reverie when the doorbell rings. Sharon is standing outside.

'Hi, Rosie. I came to say thanks for your card.'

'Oh. Right. You didn't need to call in person. Come in anyway, now you're here.'

As she crosses the threshold, Sharon says, 'Not interrupting anything, am I?'

'Well, I've got Johnny Depp in the bedroom, but he won't mind waiting.'

Sharon sits on the settee and peruses the Blake books as Rosemary makes coffee. She re-enters the lounge with two mugs on a tray and transfers them to the coffee table.

'Did you get up to anything interesting at the weekend?' Rosemary asks.

'Might have done if I'd known you were around. To be honest I didn't fancy being on my own, so I went to stay with a friend in Norwich.'

'Good old Naaaruch.'

'Quite so.'

'Male or female?'

'Male, as it happens, not that it's any of your business, young lady.'

'You were obviously happy to tell me.'

'I may be lying.'

'You're descended from convicts, we expect it. Anyway, who is this male friend? If you don't mind me asking.'

'A guy I once had a fling with. Just testing, I suppose.'

'And what was the result of the experiment?'

'What you see in front of you. I meet up with Mark occasionally just to reassure myself I made the right decision.'

They clink mugs and watch one another sip coffee. Sharon licks foam from her upper lip, rather more slowly and deliberately than necessary. 'I did, by the way,' she says.

'Did what?'

'Make the right decision.'

They hold one another's gaze. Neither feels uncomfortable enough to break the silence, until a question occurs to Rosemary.

'How did you know I'd be here rather than at work?'

'Well, you weren't in the manuscripts room, so I used my feeble antipodean brain to deduce you'd probably be here.'

'Liar. I could've been in a dozen other places in the library.'

Sharon now seems less keen to maintain eye contact. 'Promise you won't get mad?'

'I promise I'll try.'

'Donald told me what happened.'

'He did what? He had no right. What the hell—'

'You said you wouldn't get mad.'

'I said I'd try, and I failed. Now I'm mad.'

'It's not Donald's fault, Rosie, it's mine. I told him I was worried about you and I just wanted to make sure you were okay. I used emotional blackmail to make him tell me. If you want to vent your spleen on someone, vent it on me.'

Rosemary turns away and sips her coffee while wondering what to do and say next. She is soon forced to acknowledge that she is not really as angry as she made out. And no doubt Donald did feel that he was helping.

'Okay. At least you've been honest. Before you told me that, I was just about to say that I was pleased you'd called round. I've been feeling a bit, I don't know, lost. Pathetic, isn't it? I may as well say my life has no meaning. Don't you hate people who say things like that?'

Sharon reaches across and touches her on the shoulder. 'Yes, I do. But that's not your problem, is it?'

Rosemary drains her coffee mug and stares out of the window. The sky is a nondescript blue-grey, like a faded water-colour.

'How's your mum?'

'They've unplugged her. She'll probably be dead soon.'

'Ouch. Sorry for raising it. You seem quite calm though.'

She thinks for a moment. 'Yes, I am. The calm before the storm, I suppose.'

'How's Jamie taking the news?'

'I haven't told him yet.'

'Don't you think you should? He kind of has a right to know, doesn't he?'

'Maybe. I'm still thinking about it.'

'Well don't think for too long. Look, Rosie, I know everyone always says this, but if there really is anything I can do to help—'

'I know. I know you'll be there for me if I need you.'

They fall into an uneasy silence. Rosemary glances down at the books she has been reading. 'How's Mr Blake coming on?'

Sharon wrinkles her nose. 'He's elusive, to be honest. I keep feeling there's a lot hidden in a room which I don't have the key to. Maybe I'm not the right person to be doing this research. There were so many sects around at the time, and I'm struggling to get my head around any of them.'

'Why don't you start with his pictures? A picture paints a thousand words. Sorry, I sound like a lexicon of clichés.'

'I've spent countless hours on his pictures. It's impossible to make sense of many of them without the commentaries, and yet when I read the commentaries and look at the pictures again I can't help thinking, "that's not what that picture says to me". Does that make sense?'

Rosemary ponders for a moment, then opens one of her books to a section containing pencil sketches by Blake. 'What do you see in that?'

Sharon raises her eyebrows. 'I see that Blake liked to dabble in a bit of porn on the side.'

'Be more specific.'

'Okay. I see a fuzzy image of what appears to be a large

man whose dick is proportionately large, which is not surprising as two full-breasted naked women have thrown themselves at his feet, and two more are hovering in the air alongside him.'

'Turn the page and look at the next one.'

'I see a similarly large male who looks to be descending from heaven, with his hand stretched out towards a naked woman's lower abdomen, to put it delicately, while she looks away and strokes her thigh. Things are obviously hotting up.'

'Try the next page.'

'Ah, now they're getting down to it. The woman, her shaven genitalia brazenly on display, has a large man floating on either side of her. They appear to have flashes of light coming out of their dicks. She's staring at the dick to her right with a look somewhere between horror and fascination, while grasping the dick to her left. Or maybe my imagination's working overtime. Is it me, or is it warm in here?'

'No, that's pretty much how I see them. Blake drew them to illustrate a passage in a translation of the Book of Enoch.'

'I didn't pay much attention at Sunday School, but I don't remember that one.'

'That's not surprising, it never made it into the Bible. The story goes that the sons of God, angels or Watchers as they're called, looked down from heaven and noticed that the daughters of men were a bit tasty, so came down and had their wicked way with them, presumably without asking politely. The daughters of men gave birth to monstrous giants with unquenchable appetites. This pissed God off right royally, so he buried the Watchers and their hideous offspring beneath the earth.'

'Serves them right. Bloody men. Only ever after one thing. Did you show me these for a reason, by the way?'

Rosemary pauses. 'The commentaries always say that these drawings illustrate Blake's view that sin doesn't all stem from the Garden of Eden, it partly originates in male oppression of women. But I think you can read them as showing the daughters of men more than a tad impressed by the sight of these guys hung like carthorses. And who's to say my view isn't just as valid?'

Sharon watches her askance, as if deliberating. 'Do I sense some kind of sub-text here? A still, small voice is telling me that you didn't open the book at that page by accident.'

Rosemary brings her knee up onto the sofa and leans back into the upholstery. 'I bumped into a woman the other day who warned me Richard Bonner may be dangerous. She told me not to get involved with him.'

'Sensible advice. I've been trying to tell you the same.'

'True. But I still can't get my head around why it's me he wants.'

'How do you mean?'

'Of all the multitude of women he could have chosen, he's picked on me.'

Sharon rubs her finger-tips back and forth across her forehead. 'You're not trying to tell me he's like one of these Watchers? That he's looked down from heaven and decided he fancies trying to get your knickers off?'

'I don't know, I've got nothing to go on. It could be as likely an explanation as any.'

'Then, frankly, what's to stop him just turning up in your bed one night? From what you've said he's hardly likely to stop and ask for your consent.'

'So you still think I'm crazy.'

Sharon takes a deep breath. 'To be honest, I was hoping that we wouldn't be having this sort of conversation any more. I've already told you that there's only so much of your obsession that I can take. At this rate we're soon both going to need help.'

Rosemary looks away for a moment then turns back, smiling. 'Sorry, Sharon. You're right. I start therapy in a couple of weeks, by the way. The sooner I can get my head straight and put all this behind me, the better.'

'You're just saying what you think I want you to say.'

'Nope. No more mind-forg'd manacles for me. Watch this.' She stands and gathers up the books from the coffee table. 'One pile of books on William Blake into the bin.' She places them carefully into a nearby waste-paper basket. The unbalanced weight tips it over. The release of emotion makes them both laugh.

'Bonner at his tricks again?' Sharon says.

'Just the law of gravity this time. Come on, I'll treat us to lunch.'

'I've got work to do this afternoon, so it'd better be the non-alcoholic kind.'

'Is there any other?'

That night Rosemary sits up in bed, naked with a book in her lap. The bedroom is warm and the duvet has been replaced by a thin sheet. As she reads she discovers that, according to his diary, on Thursday 8 March 1582, at about nine in the evening, John Dee looked up at the sky above his house in Mortlake and saw the clouds turning to the colour of blood, as if a heavenly fire were spreading through them. He recorded that it was like nothing he had ever seen. Earlier that day, he had first made the acquaintance of Edward Kelly, aka Talbot.

She gets out of bed and, even though the night is sultry, retrieves an old pair of pyjamas from the bottom of a drawer and puts them on. She double-checks that she has locked the front door, closes the bedroom window and without turning out the light returns to bed, unwilling to close her eyes.

35

After drifting in and out of restless sleep, Rosemary is awoken by the phone ringing. A nurse on her mum's ward wants her to know that she seems to be slipping away more quickly than anticipated. There is not likely to be much change in the next few hours, but Rosemary should know that the end may not be long delayed.

She rings Jamie, but disconnects the call before he has a chance to answer. The feeling is stronger than ever that this is not going to be a family occasion; that if she is the only one to have stayed the course during her mother's final illness then, however much they fought like cat and dog over the years, she and her mother will see this out together. Her father likewise will have to face the guilt; he deserves to suffer. Mum will never know who was there during her last hours; this is about punishing the living.

Rosemary has never watched someone die, but from what she has read it seems likely that the process will not be quick and decisive, more a slow, steady descent into a drawn-out twilight state. The ideal scenario would be to arrive an hour or two before her mother's final extinction. The worst-case scenario would be to delay just too long. She determines to set off for the hospital at mid-day. Should she take plenty of reading material, or would that seem callous? Should she take a toothbrush and toothpaste? She decides to pack a shoulder-bag in case of a lengthy vigil.

Having absorbed the twelve o'clock news on the radio, she picks up her keys and stares at the front door. Should she ring the hospital for an update before setting off? Deep down, she already knows that what terrifies her is the thought that this will be the last time she will ever see her mother. She will feel duty-bound to remain at her bedside until the end. This reaction causes some surprise; ever since she entered hospital, her mother has barely looked alive anyway, and in her heart of hearts Rosemary has

239

always suspected that things would end this way. But now the moment has arrived, and nothing seems black or white.

She takes a deep breath, walks out onto the landing, closes the door behind her and, as she turns the key in the lock, reflects that this is almost as much of an ending for her as for her mother, at least if relative states of consciousness are taken into account. She takes her time cycling through the city centre, stopping now and again to take in a favourite view as if seeing it for the first time, or indeed the last: the widening ripples left in the wake of punt poles, the cloistered splendour of Trinity Great Court, the first glimpse of the turrets of King's College Chapel. Once she has cleared the centre, the rest of the journey passes in a mist, and it comes as a surprise to see the hospital's most prominent feature, its sky-scraping incinerator chimney, looming above the houses to her right. As she locks her bicycle to a rack outside the entrance, it begins to rain from a seemingly cloudless sky.

For the only time she can remember, the nurses' station is all smiles. She pauses with a view to asking mum's condition, but instead simply smiles back and makes her way to the bedside. At first glance it is hard to tell that there has been any change, but after a while it becomes clear that her mother's breathing is more laboured and, at times, erratic. She takes the skeletal hand from beneath the blankets and holds it tightly. If there is even a faint trace of awareness left, she will try to let her mother know that she is there for her. Even the slightest twinge might suggest that mum knows she is present, but the hand remains lifeless.

She sits there, inert, until mid-afternoon, when the warm, dry atmosphere leaves her craving a trip to the hospital café. Dare she leave her mother's side? How long does it take to drink a cup of tea? In the end, she insists on leaving her mobile phone number at the nurses' station even though it is clear that the nurses see no point in this. She takes the lift down to the ground floor and sits at a corner table in the café. What emotions should she be experiencing at this time? If only she knew how this is supposed to go, but all she can honestly feel is fatigue. To her surprise, she is not anxious to gulp the tea down and return to her mother's bedside. She even contemplates the idea of food, gets as far as surveying the rows of cellophane-wrapped cheese and ham rolls on the counter, then returns to her seat empty-handed. All around are people who, despite the setting, are chatting in a happy and animated fashion. Rosemary cannot remember when she has ever felt more alone. She takes out her phone, types a message to Jamie, selects his number, but cannot bring herself to press Send.

Back on the ward, all remains quiet, and Rosemary resumes her vigil. No-one in the adjoining beds is awake, perhaps even capable of being so. She wanders over to Derek; his eyes are shut, and his tautening face is grey. She takes his hand and whispers what she hopes will be comforting words, but Derek is now every bit as unresponsive as her mother. She returns to mum's bedside, takes out a book and starts to read. At first she looks up every few minutes to check for any change, but after a time the futility of this gesture becomes obvious. She walks around every hour or so to stretch her legs, breaks the monotony with an occasional visit to the toilet, but otherwise finds nothing to mark the passing of the hours. Dylan Thomas' refrain from *Under Milk Wood* resonates across the years: Listen. Time passes.

During the evening, she makes a final visit to the café before it closes. On returning to the ward, it is clear even from the limited view over the flat grey rooftops that it is now dusk. A nurse comes to check Derek's pulse, then her mother's. So, Derek has also reached the end of the line, but with no-one to maintain a death watch on his behalf. Perhaps he would have preferred it that way.

'Any idea?' she asks the nurse.

'Excuse me?'

'How much longer? Sorry, I didn't mean it to come out like that. Has there been any further deterioration in mum's condition?'

The nurse smiles. 'Her pulse is slightly weaker. I'm afraid I can't talk to you about time-scales though.'

Rosemary looks across. 'How about Derek?'

The nurse gently shakes her head. 'If you want to stay, I can make you more comfortable.' She drags over a padded chair from beside a neighbouring bed, then wanders back with a pillow and a blanket. 'Not much, I'm afraid, but do try to get some sleep. We'll keep an eye out for any change in your mother's condition.'

Like death, presumably. Rosemary wants to bury her head and sob, but feels too exhausted. She decides to text Sharon to let her know the situation. Sharon immediately texts back offering to come straight to the hospital. Rosemary replies that she feels the need to deal with the situation alone, and hopes that her friend will understand. Sharon responds with a row of x's. She rests her head back against the pillow, pulls the blanket around her shoulders and finds it surprisingly easy to slide into sleep.

Her eyes flick open at the sound of a pulsing alarm. A nurse hurries past to a bed next to the window, presses a button on the wall which silences the alarm, then pulls the curtains around the bed. Rosemary leans across and checks that her mother is still breathing, then puts her head back and closes her eyes, but this time sleep is slippery and evasive. Her mother lies alongside in the half-light; it is hard to identify this insensible body with the mother who, for better or worse, has been an indelible part of her life since the day she was born. Her head is beginning to throb.

There is more activity on the ward as a new shift of nursing staff comes on duty. The sun has been up for a couple of hours; her mother has somehow survived through another night and, who knows, will perhaps survive for another day. If only there were some way of knowing. At seven thirty the morning rounds begin, and an unfamiliar nurse comes over to check mum's pulse, though Rosemary suspects that this is more for her benefit than for her mother's.

'Do you think she's got long? Honestly?'

'I'm sorry,' the nurse says. 'It's impossible to know how long these things will take.'

'I feel knackered, but I don't know whether to risk going home and having some sleep. I'd hate to, you know, not be here when she goes.'

The nurse smiles and gives a slight shake of the head. 'It doesn't always work like that. You'd be surprised how often patients hang on for as long as their loved ones are at the bedside, even when they don't appear to be conscious. When they're finally left alone, they decide that it's time to go. It's almost as if they're determined that you're not going to see the end. As if they've decided to go at a time of their own choosing.'

Rosemary, exhausted and despairing, begins to cry. The nurse leans over and speaks softly. 'You can't do any more. Whether you're here when she dies is not under your control. It may be that she wants to go, is ready to go, but doesn't want you to see it.'

Rosemary takes her shoulder bag to the nearest bathroom, washes her face and brushes her teeth. She returns to her mother's bedside and takes her hand.

'I'm going home to get some rest, mum. I'll be back later. I want to be here with you. I'm not leaving you on your own. We'll see this through together.' Has she said these words for her mother's sake or her own? She takes a final look back before leaving the ward and notices, somehow for the first time, that during the night the curtains have been drawn around Derek's bed. She wants to ask at the nurses' station if he has died, but does not want to know the answer.

The traffic on Hills Road passes in a blur. All that keeps her moving is the prospect of collapsing on her own bed and closing her eyes. When she reaches the traffic lights at the Northampton Street junction, her strength fails and she wheels her bicycle across and up Castle Hill, almost weeping with fatigue. She abandons it in the shed outside the flats without bothering to lock it.

Inside, she drops her shoulder bag onto the floor, kicks off her shoes and lies on the bed fully clothed. Sleep overtakes her almost immediately, but not for long. The image of her helpless mother refuses to depart. For several hours she wanders between anxious sleep and fretful wakefulness. When finally a more profound rest takes hold, it is interrupted after what seems only moments. Having finally identified the sound which has woken her, she answers the phone with trembling hand. A female voice responds.

'Could I speak to Rosemary Torrance please.'

'Speaking.'

'Miss Torrance, I'm calling from Addenbrooke's Hospital. I'm afraid I have some bad news.'

Rosemary showers and puts on fresh clothes then, succumbing to the inevitable, calls a taxi to take her back to the hospital. The curtains have been closed around her mother's bed. A nurse nods to her to go through, and she takes a deep breath. Her mother lies on her back, fingers entwined over her chest, a single red flower placed between them. She looks at peace, but then when did she ever really look distressed? Rosemary sits on the bed and puts her hand over her mother's. Although it has been over an hour since the phone call, mum's hands are still warm.

'I'm sorry I was too late, mum. I tried to make sure I was here with you, but … well, I guess that's the story of my life. Anyway, what I wanted to say is, thanks everything you did for me. I'm sorry I didn't always appreciate it. I know I've been an ungrateful bitch. But I love you and I'll always remember you. Goodbye, mum.'

Slowly but perceptibly, her mother's hand turns cold.

36

On the way home, Rosemary texts Sharon to tell her the news. Sharon replies that she is really sorry, and asks if Rosemary wants someone to talk to. She waits for a few minutes, then texts back to ask if Sharon is free that evening. The reply is strident: Will be there at 7. Don't think of going out.

When she gets home she knows that, however dreadful the prospect, she must phone her father and Jamie. It takes moments to decide to contact Jamie first, but nevertheless it is a relief when his mobile goes straight to its answering service.

'Hi Jamie, it's me. Hate to have to tell you like this but there's no easy way to say it. Mum died this morning.' She pauses. 'Guess that's about it. See you soon, I suppose.'

It occurs to her that her father will be out at work, and phoning him may not be advisable until the evening. Having reassured herself on this point, she makes some tea, sits down and waits. Before long her eyelids are insupportably heavy. When she comes round, her tea is no longer steaming. Jamie is leaving a message on the answering machine. She struggles to her feet and plays it back.

– Just got your message. I'll talk to you later.

Jamie's tone is nondescript, cold even. Did he actually listen to what she said? She hauls herself back to the sofa, lies down and closes her eyes. She does not want to feel this tired when Sharon comes round. In fact she is not sure now if she wants Sharon to come round. On the other hand, one thing she does know is that she feels helpless and alone.

The afternoon passes in a blur of altering states. An increase in the level of traffic noise outside on Castle Hill signifies that the evening rush hour has started. Rosemary checks her watch and sees that it is 5.15. Her head is thumping. She makes some fresh tea and forces down two paracetamol tablets. At six o'clock the phone rings. Jamie is on the other end.

– How are you doing?

'No better than can be expected, thanks for asking. How about you?'

– Okay, I guess. Your call was a bit of a surprise.

'Why? You knew mum was dying.'

– Yes, but I didn't know she was that close – you know what I mean.

'Well, let's not have that discussion now. Look, there's going to be a lot to do in the next few days. You are going to be around, aren't you?'

– How do you mean, around?

'What do you think I mean? I can't do this on my own. I'm going to need your help.'

– To be honest, I've arranged to go flat-hunting in London with Agnieszka.

'Well, in the circumstances I think you'll need to unarrange it, don't you?'

– I kind of assumed you wouldn't be going into the library for a bit anyway. You'll have a lot more time than me.

'Jamie, I don't necessarily need loads of your time, I just need some emotional support, for God's sake. How do you think I feel right now? Don't ask, I feel like shit. I know all this seems to have washed straight over you—'

– And what's that supposed to mean?

'You know good and fucking well what that's supposed to mean. Oh, just don't bother. If you want to know when the funeral is, ring me.'

She ends the call, then waits by the phone for Jamie to ring back, but he does not. She ambles back to the lounge and begins to watch the six o'clock news. When it ends half an hour later she has no recollection of any event which has occurred anywhere in the world that day. The local news has just started when the phone rings again.

– Jamie just rang. Why didn't you tell me?

Thank you Jamie. She holds the receiver away from her

246

ear and tries to compose herself.

– Rosemary? Are you there?

'Yes, dad. I just thought it would be better to wait till you got home, that's all. It's not the sort of news anyone wants to get at work.'

– How could you? I had a right to know.

She feels something tighten inside. 'Well, now you do know.'

– No thanks to you, Rosemary. Look, I'll try to get to the funeral if I can. Can I rely on you to at least keep me informed about that?

She feels close to tears again, but will not allow her father to hear her weeping. 'Don't you want to know if she suffered? Don't you even care that much?'

– How dare you talk to me like that, Rosemary. You don't know the half of what I went through—

'And now it doesn't matter any more because she's dead. Your ex-wife, my mother, is dead. That's all that matters, not how much you went through years ago, not how she drove you into the arms of another woman. No-one gives a fuck. And if you think—'

– There's obviously no point in continuing this conversation if you're going to talk like a foul-mouthed slut. Must be the company you keep these days.

The line goes abruptly dead. Rosemary stands with the receiver in her hand, staring in confusion. The door-bell rings.

'Christ, Rosie, you look terrible. What am I saying, of course you do, anyone would. Look, sorry, I'm a bit early.'

'Sharon, I'll forgive you everything as long as you stop apologising. Just come inside.'

'Hold on, I haven't come empty-handed.' From outside the door, Sharon retrieves a large shopping bag. 'All the provisions essential for human existence: an extra-large deep pan spinach and ricotta pizza, two slices of lemon cheesecake and a large quantity of alcohol.' Sharon kicks the door closed behind her.

'I'm not really hungry, thanks all the same.'

'You think you're not. When was the last time you ate? Yesterday? The day before?'

'I can't really remember. The last couple of days have been a bit of a blur.'

'Right, I'm putting the oven on. In the event of any objections, I shall put my foot down with a firm hand, my girl.'

While the pizza is cooking, Sharon retrieves a bottle of malt whisky from the bag and places it on the kitchen table with a smile.

'I thought you knew,' Rosemary says wearily, 'I don't really drink whisky.'

'You do now,' her friend replies, and takes two tumblers from the kitchen cupboard. 'Think I'd better give these a wash. Your standards are dropping, young lady.' She dries them with a tea-towel, places them on the table and pours a large shot into each, then sits down and indicates to Rosemary the chair opposite. At that moment, Rosemary is content for her home to be taken over. They clink glasses and she sips cagily, knowing she has not drunk scotch since Adam was around. It rasps her throat on its way down.

'Foreign squaw bring fire-water,' she says.

'Fire-water from mountains of north country. Good. Drive away evil spirits.'

Rosemary drinks freely, and the whisky begins to slide down more smoothly. 'I trade you kitchen knife for fire-water.'

'Foreign squaw already have set of Kitchen Devils. Fire-water gift for friend. Later we smoke hash-pipe of peace.'

After a few half-hearted mouthfuls, Rosemary acquires a taste for the pizza, belatedly recalling that the last serious meal she had was two days ago. Those white jeans should be a perfect fit, though possibly not until tomorrow morning. The cheesecake disappears with equal rapidity. They dump their plates in the kitchen sink and take the scotch through to the lounge.

'How did Jamie take the news?' Sharon asks.

'With the same self-focus he's been showing for some time. Even now he doesn't want to get involved, he just assumes I'll deal with it all.'

'I'm not saying a word. Have you spoken to your dad?'

'I'm so glad you asked that. Jamie's sole contribution has been to wind dad up before I could even talk to him. We had a row and dad put the phone down on me just as you arrived, hence the reason I was gawping like a fish.'

'Ouch. They say trouble comes in threes.'

'I must be over that number already. You coming round is about the only good thing that's happened recently.'

'Look, just tell me how I can help, Rosie.'

She strokes Sharon's arm. 'Just stop me from going insane.'

'I thought your employers had decided you already were.'

'Touché. It's ironic, isn't it? If they hadn't told me to take time off, I'd have had to do it now anyway.'

'God's a master of irony.'

'I've never had to deal with anyone dying before. I'm sure there are loads of things you have to do, but at this moment I haven't got a clue what any of them are.'

Sharon runs an index finger up and down her nose, then takes a notebook and pencil from her pocket. 'Right, let's do a list before we're too wasted. First, where's your mum now?'

'In heaven, I hope.'

'Let me rephrase that. Where are her mortal remains?'

'In the hospital mortuary, presumably.'

'Okay. We need to get the death certificate from the hospital and contact a funeral director. Did your mum leave any instructions about that?'

'I don't think she was expecting to die quite so soon.'

'Leave it to me. I'll contact the Co-op. Tomorrow morning, you go to the hospital and collect the death cert, then take it to the Registry Office to register your mum's death.'

'I think I can just about manage that.'

'Now, what kind of funeral do you think she'd have preferred?'

'A long-delayed one.'

'Rosie, you're not making this easy.'

'Sorry. She wasn't religious. I think a church service would be a bit hypocritical.'

'The crem, then?'

'I guess so.'

'Leave that to me too. I'll phone them tomorrow morning and see what times they've got free. Now, funeral invitees. Who do we need to contact? Friends, relatives?'

Rosemary ponders for a moment. 'To be honest, I'm not sure she had many friends. I'll let her neighbours know, obviously. She used to talk about people she worked with, but I never met any of them and certainly wouldn't know how to contact them.'

'Okay, in that case we put an advert in the Evening News and hope that word of mouth does the rest. Family?'

'Just me and Jamie.'

'And your dad?'

'He's not family any more. But he'll have to be invited.'

'Right. How about the reception after the funeral?'

'Is there any point? There'll be so few of us there.'

'Looks like you're a cheapskate if you don't. Anyway, it's an excuse for us to get wasted at your mum's expense. It's what she would have wanted.'

'Right, the back bar of the Champ it is, then.'

'No it isn't. I'll have a look at some more suitable venues.' Sharon tears off a sheet of paper and hands it to Rosemary. 'Those are your jobs. Think you can deal with that?'

'Depends how much more of this scotch we drink. Look, Sharon, I really am grateful—'

'Don't want to hear it. Look, I'm sorry, I didn't mean to take over. How are you feeling now? I mean, apart from the obvious?'

'Better now I've got something to focus on. They say that people often cope with bereavement up to the funeral because there's so much to do, then they fall apart.'

'I won't let you do that. Anyway, you always gave the impression you didn't feel that close to your mum.'

'I didn't. How can I explain it? I thought there would be years and years to put things right, that my angry feelings towards her would eventually fade and one day magically things between us would be okay. Now I suppose I feel guilty because the last couple of times we had together before she went into hospital, things didn't go too well.'

Sharon takes a large mouthful of scotch. 'You blame her rather than your dad because he went off with another woman?'

'I don't know. I suppose I blame them both really. Which leaves me a bit isolated.'

'Perhaps this would be a good time to patch things up with Jamie. Let bygones be bygones. It sounds like he's all you've got left now.'

'I've still got you, haven't I?'

Sharon tucks her legs under her. 'For as long as you want, though I won't go so far as to say unconditionally. Oh, I nearly forgot, what about flowers?'

'I quite like them, but I don't have anywhere to grow them.'

'That's interesting but irrelevant. Did your mum like them, or do you think she'd rather people donated the money they'd have spent to an appropriate charity?'

'Like the National Association for the Brain-Dead? Or the Royal Society for the Terminally Uncommunicative?'

'Okay, well perhaps we've gone far enough for tonight. Sufficient unto the day, as my dad used to say ad nauseam, the old bastard.'

Sharon places the pencil and notebook on the coffee table and brings her knees into contact with Rosemary's thigh. Rosemary looks hard at her. 'I'm not sure I want to be on my own tonight,' she says.

To her surprise, Sharon's face is not wreathed in smiles. 'Why, what are you afraid of?'

'I don't know. Myself, maybe.'

'Look, Rosie, I said I'd be here for you and I will, but I'm not going to take advantage because you're in a vulnerable state. It's natural you're feeling pretty shot, but even so … you can call me any time day or night if you need me.'

'I'm not inviting you to take advantage. I'm too knackered to do anything but sleep. You can tell me I'm being ridiculous if you want to, but I feel vulnerable to more than just grief.'

'Ah. Are we heading in the direction I think we might be heading in?'

'I think Bonner preys on negative emotions. And I can't get those Blake drawings out of my head. Sharon, I've just got a really bad feeling.'

Sharon looks away, clearly thinking hard. She takes her time replying. 'All right. I'll stay on one condition. One way or another, once the funeral's out of the way, we have to find some means of putting this Bonner business to bed once and for all. It's eating you up.'

'Agreed. A bonfire of the vanities. As soon as the funeral's over.'

Rosemary has decided to wear her anti-Bonner pyjamas in bed, but sees that Sharon, who is already there waiting, is naked, so changes her mind. She lies on her back, desperate for sleep, but not the in-and-out kind to which she has become accustomed. Sharon, lying alongside, takes hold of her hand. Rosemary turns over and rests her head on Sharon's shoulder, feeling her fingers gently stroking her hair. Sharon seems happy to let their intimacy end at this point.

'Does Adam still come to your bed?' she asks.

'I haven't seen him at all for a few weeks.'

'Do you think that means he's, you know, at rest?'

'I don't know what to think. I've said my goodbyes to

252

him, but whether that's the end of it, who knows. I'd like to think that he's at peace too.'

They exchange a glancing kiss, then Rosemary closes her eyes. Sharon continues to stroke her hair until she is sleeping.

37

After she has collected the certificate from the hospital and registered her mother's death, Rosemary returns home and turns on her computer, having formed a vague notion that it would be therapeutic to look at old photos of mum, even though she cannot recall the last occasion when she might have taken any. A birthday party? Jamie's graduation? She trawls back to the earliest folder, but is unable to locate a single image of her mother. Perhaps she has not checked thoroughly. Or perhaps this very absence sums up the nature of their relationship, at least during the years since Rosemary bought her first digital camera.

One folder is simply named '!!!!!' It turns out to contain half a dozen photos taken on Grantchester Meadows on the summer day she made love (or had sex, as he would insist on putting it) in the long grass with Adam. They must have been taken with her camera since Adam refused to own one, and indeed scorned the very idea of recording anything for posterity. Or professed to. He never expressed any aversion to looking at other people's photos, especially if he featured in them. But these pictures are all of her, and her lack of inhibition suggests that she was significantly aroused by the context in which they were taken. Are they from before or after? She quickly decides from studying her hair that the photographic act must have been a form of foreplay. Her body was certainly more curvaceous in those days. She pouts provocatively at the lens, pursing her lips, legs heading off in all directions. It feels as if she has never seen these pictures before, but surely she and Adam must have looked at them together, or what was the point? From the Properties menu she sees that the folder was last opened a few days ago. But not by her, unless she is suffering from severe amnesia brought on by sleep deprivation. Only Sharon has been in the flat in that time, and she would never breach anyone's privacy in such a way.

Rosemary closes her eyes. Is Adam really 'at rest'? Somehow it does not feel that way. Despite having bid him farewell, she has not lost the sense that he may be somewhere in the background. And yet, how real have his appearances since his death, as she must now think of it, actually been? Have all his visitations been simple hallucinations, self-generated fantasies? Has some psychotic corner of her sub-conscious allowed her to play out scenes, to hold conversations, she wishes had taken place while he was alive? Did Adam become like the invisible friend with whom a lonely child shares its secret thoughts?

Adam's appearances have felt quite real, too real to be confined solely to the recesses of her own imagination. Hallucinations do not leave a trace on the pillow the next morning. But perhaps our other senses can be deceived as easily as our eyes. We use the term 'hearing things' specifically to mean hearing non-existent sounds. Then again, if they exist in our imagination, can they truly be termed 'non-existent'?

She shivers. Perhaps her sensitivity to Adam's spirit, or however she should think of that part of him which remains, somehow created a pathway enabling Bonner to reach her. Was Adam hinting at this on those occasions when he seemed to be warning her to be careful? Did Bonner recognise Adam as someone who lived on in her affections even if no longer physically a part of her life? Did he therefore see Adam as a rival to be removed from his path before he could fulfil his ambitions with Rosemary? Are the two of them even now battling it out somewhere on an astral plane?

Maybe her speculations are getting out of hand. Perhaps she has been kidding herself all along that she has been specially selected, when in fact Bonner would have latched onto the first person who happened to look at the fateful long-lost manuscript. By chance, it turned out to be her.

Or, perhaps, Sharon has been right all along.

38

Rosemary sits on the front bench of the crematorium chapel, with Jamie on the left and Sharon to her right. Sharon is wearing a formal jacket and dark skirt which Rosemary would not have suspected she owned; she deduces her friend has bought them for the occasion. Sharon rhythmically strokes the inside of Rosemary's upper arm in what she takes to be a gesture of solidarity. Jamie wears a creased white open-necked shirt, black jeans and trainers, and has his arms folded. The rest of the bench is empty, as is the one behind. Two rows back sit half a dozen of mum's neighbours and a couple of her old work colleagues who must have seen the newspaper announcement. The coffin is already positioned at the front of the chapel on the conveyor belt which, hopefully unseen and unheard by the mourners, will take it to its rendezvous with fiery annihilation. Bach's *Jesu, joy of man's desiring* plays softly through speakers positioned high on the walls.

They have asked for a secular commemoration so, rather than a priest, a serene man in his sixties wearing a sober suit and black tie sits behind the lectern waiting to begin the proceedings. He looks up at the clock; although it is two minutes after they should have begun, he seems to realise that someone important is missing. He catches Rosemary's eye and mouths the words, Shall I start? She checks her watch, then nods.

The president, or master of ceremonies as Rosemary has come to think of him, begins by emphasising that this is a celebration of mum's life, designed to enable everyone present to participate regardless of their personal beliefs. He has just begun to outline the key events of that life when a door crashes open at the back of the chapel. He pauses and looks up. The mourners twist their necks to watch the former husband of the deceased striding up the side aisle sweating and clenching his fists. He hurls himself onto the front bench beside Jamie and says with barely-suppressed fury to no-one in particular, 'How the hell are you supposed to get parked in this place?' The master of ceremonies, despite the brutal interruption to his oration, smiles benignly, waits a moment for the hubbub to subside and then continues as if nothing has happened. He focuses on mum's role as a working mother, tactfully skimming over the circumstances which led to her performing this role latterly without support. He closes the address with a reading of Christina Rossetti's *Remember*.

Despite the secular nature of the proceedings, the key participants have decided to include one hymn in order to hedge their bets, and because they have no recollection that mum ever expressed affection for any piece of music apart from *Mandy* by Barry Manilow. Jamie had proposed *Abide with me*, one of his few contributions to the planning of the event. This was vetoed in favour of *Teach me my God and King*, a concession to Sharon's affection for George Herbert. The pre-recorded keyboard accompaniment drowns out the voices of the dozen mourners. The period of silent reflection which follows is allowed to run on for longer than planned simply to fill the half hour allotted for the funeral. Jamie stares down at his hands. Their father is gazing around, his lips pursed as if whistling to himself in silence.

Rosemary does not at this moment wish to contemplate what her mother's life meant, so she focuses on trying to clear her mind, but whatever space she manages to vacate another force seems determined to fill, as if taking advantage of her weakened defences. She breathes deeply to still her pounding heart, but without success. Her forehead, her armpits and the palms of her hands are wet with sweat, and she starts to shiver. Sharon takes her hand and grips it hard. Rosemary now cannot stop shaking and begins to panic, weighing up whether to make for the exit while she still can. Sharon's arm is tightly around her shoulders and her voice whispers, 'It's okay, you're going to be okay.' The president has clearly noticed this turn of events as he jumps to his feet and brings the silence to an end by thanking everyone for turning up and wishing them a safe journey home. With a final death-rattle, the curtains close mechanically across the front of the coffin. Rosemary finally stops shaking and starts to sob.

Even though all the mourners have been persuaded to take advantage of the offered hospitality, they still rattle around the private function room of a small hotel near the crematorium. They have catered for twenty-five guests, twice the number present, so as Rosemary dutifully circulates from table to table thanking people for their attendance she urges them to take food with them when they go. From the corner of her eye she spots Jamie and Sharon sitting together, talking with some animation. From their expressions, the conversation is not amicable. Her father is at the bar ordering his third drink even though he clearly intends to drive home afterwards. She decides that she has neither the energy nor the inclination to remonstrate with him; he can calculate the risk for himself.

An hour or so later, the central core of four are left alone. Few guests have taken up the offer of helping to clear the food tables, and the uneaten sandwiches are already starting to curl at the edge. Rosemary waits for her father to make his own excuses, but he still has a drink in front of him, and on this of all occasions seems in no hurry to escape.

'You haven't properly introduced me to your friend,' he says to Rosemary, but without taking his eyes from Sharon.

'Dad, this is Sharon. Sharon, this is dad.'

'Pleased to meet you, Sharon. I'm surprised Rosie hasn't mentioned you before.'

'Oh. Why?' Sharon asks, poker-faced.

'Well, you're clearly very close.'

Sharon looks at Rosemary, whose face is set in something approaching a grimace. 'Yes Mr Torrance, we are. I suppose Rosie just didn't have the chance to talk to you very often.'

He smiles, seemingly not having spotted the hidden

barb. 'Please call me John. All my friends do.'

Sharon waits just long enough, then says, 'I'll bear that in mind.'

There is a cold silence. Jamie rises to his feet. 'Anyone want another drink?'

'Just get a bottle,' Rosemary says. 'There's plenty left on the tab.'

While Jamie is at the bar, dad leans across to Sharon as if to share a secret or an intimacy. She remains bolt upright in her chair.

'If you wouldn't mind, Sharon, there is some family business the three of us need to discuss. Could you give us a few minutes?'

'What family business?' Rosemary asks.

Dad inclines his head towards her, still watching Sharon. 'Family business,' he enunciates, as if to someone hard of hearing.

'This is hardly the time, dad. We've just said goodbye to mum. There can't be anything that urgent that we have to deal with it here and now.'

Jamie returns and places an opened bottle of pinot grigio on the table. Rosemary picks it up, scans the label and screws up her face, pours some into Sharon's glass and some into her own, then pushes the bottle into the centre of the table. Sharon takes her glass and stands up.

'Look, I'm going outside for some air. Let me know when you're done.'

She disappears through the open patio doors which give access to the garden. Rosemary watches her sniffing roses. Jamie looks anxiously between her and their father, realising that he has missed out on some moment of conflict, but having no evidence to work from.

'Now,' their father says, as if pronouncing the first word of a sermon, 'does either of you know if your mum left a will?'

Jamie's eyes widen. He looks towards his sister for guidance.

'So that's your "family business",' Rosemary says.

'You really think this is the most important thing to talk about when mum's body's just been burnt to ashes?'

Dad directs his reply to Jamie. 'If there's no will, things can get messy. It makes sense to talk about this while the three of us are together.'

'Well, maybe … ' Jamie begins, glances at Rosemary, then tails off into silence.

'What's it got to do with you anyway?' Rosemary says. 'You've no call on mum's estate. She wouldn't want anything to go to you. You left her on her own.'

'For your information, Rosemary, there are items which I assume are still in the house on which I do have a claim. Items which I could have insisted on as part of the divorce settlement, but allowed her to keep because I didn't want to cause her any further distress.'

'Very magnanimous of you. Well you're not touching anything in that house.'

'Rosemary, may I remind you that you're talking to your father.'

'More's the pity.'

Her father makes to rise out of his chair, and for a moment it seems that he is about to slap her. 'Dad,' Jamie says, shaking his head. Rosemary stands up, pushing her chair over onto its back, and hurries out to the garden, where she finds Sharon sitting at a table beneath a pear tree, fending off wasps. She sits opposite and beats the side of her fist against the table until a sharp pain shoots through her wrist. She releases a grunt of anger and frustration, and lowers her forehead onto the table. The surface is coarse and rough.

When her fury has subsided, she looks up and sees Sharon watching her, smiling.

'The nuclear family, eh?' Sharon says. 'It's the bedrock of western civilisation, that's what I say.' She stops as her attention is drawn to a movement back inside the function room. Rosemary follows her gaze and sees her father, car keys in hand, ushering Jamie out the door.

'Looks like now I really am alone.'

'Either they'll make it up to you,' Sharon says, 'or else they don't deserve you anyway. Bollocks to the lot of them, that's what you ought to say.'

'You antipodeans are blessed with such silver tongues.'

A young, dark-haired barman is walking towards them carrying the pinot grigio bottle and Rosemary's glass. 'I am sorry to interrupt you, ladies,' he says in a pronounced Slavic accent. 'I thought you might be in need of these.'

He places them on the table, and Rosemary finds that she is grinning at him. He smiles back and takes his leave.

'Hey, ask him if he's got a room while you're about it, why don't you?'

Rosemary laughs and tops up their glasses, then raises her own. 'And then there were two.'

Sharon lifts her glass in response. 'In the words of a famous Australian philosopher, fuck 'em all.' She drinks, then looks at her watch. 'Hey, it's still only half past three. What shall we do with the rest of the day?'

'The number of activities we can safely undertake in our present state is limited, I'm afraid.'

'In that case, why don't we finish this bottle, round up anything that's still edible from in there, get another bottle and head back to mine? We can watch crap or something.'

Rosemary looks back inside, to where she watched her father and Jamie disappear, probably from her life. The door through which they made their exit is still open.

'It's okay,' Sharon continues. 'Perhaps it wasn't such a great idea after all.' She reaches across and takes Rosemary's hand. 'One way and another, you've had to say goodbye to a lot of people in a short space of time. I don't know how you've coped as well as you have. But if you'd rather be on your own, that's fine. I understand.'

Rosemary grips Sharon's hand, hard. 'No, I wouldn't rather be on my own. You've got a plan, that's more than I have. It sounds just fine by me.'

The wasps have returned in force, attracted by the now dried sugar around the neck of the bottle. They compete in blowing them towards one another, laughing.

'I know we said we'd watch crap, but I'm sure my telly has a filter to prevent anything as awful as this getting through.'

'You're nearer the remote control than I am,' Sharon says.

'I don't know how to work it.'

'You see the button that says Channel next to it? Have a guess what that does.'

'You're just being a lazy cow.'

'Hey, remember you're a guest in this house. Didn't your mother teach you any manners?' There is a long pause. 'Oops, sorry, don't know how that slipped out.'

'It's okay. I can't spend the rest of my life bursting into tears every time someone mentions mothers, can I?'

The two women are recumbent like spoons on Sharon's long sofa. Sharon lies behind, her arm draped lazily around Rosemary's waist. They have consumed the bottle of wine they brought back from the hotel, and most of the food is in Sharon's composting bin. They are trying to ignore a TV game show in which two teams of contestants compete to offer the most banal and predictable answer to any given question.

'Shall I put a DVD on?' Sharon says.

'As long as I don't have to move. What have you got in mind?'

'How about *Prometheus*?'

'A story about doomed people, set on a hostile world. Yep, at this precise moment that would fit the bill.'

Sharon rolls across Rosemary, giving her a peck on the lips just before sliding to the floor in a heap. 'Oops. Must be that dodgy quiche.' She crawls across the floor on all fours and tips over a pile of DVDs to retrieve *Prometheus* from the bottom. After several prods at the machine she manages to open it and insert the disc, then clambers to her feet and makes her way back to the sofa, raising her arms to her sides and mimicking the actions of a tightrope-walker to conceal her unsteadiness. Rosemary shuffles to the back of the sofa to make room for her. She ponders for a moment, then drapes her arm around Sharon's midriff. Sharon rests her arm on Rosemary's.

They watch the film in silence. At one point Rosemary suspects that her friend has fallen asleep, leans forward and sees that her eyes are wide open. Sharon looks up at her and smiles. The film ends at midnight.

'It's been a long day,' Rosemary says. 'I'm not sure I can stay awake much longer.'

'Do you want me to call you a taxi?'

'Okay.'

'You're a taxi.' Sharon giggles.

'As I suspected, Dr Turner, you're twatted. You're no more capable of using a phone than I am.'

'That settles that then.'

With considerable difficulty, Sharon wriggles around until she and Rosemary are face to face. She brings her head forward until their noses touch.

'I'm sorry, Rosie.'

'For what?'

'For your loss. I don't think I said it earlier. I should have done.'

'I know you are. You didn't need to say it. You're sorrier than my own family are.'

Sharon gently places a finger on Rosemary's lips. 'Shhh. Let that go. Try not to think about it now.'

'I haven't thought about it for the last few hours. You're good at distracting me.'

'I'd like to say I'll try and distract you a bit more, but I think I'm just toooo pissed.'

'Really? God, you concealed that well. Anyway, thanks for being there for me today. I really needed you.'

'I'll be there for you whenever you want me. And when you don't.'

39

She has woken with a sense of alarm, the cause of which she cannot identify. It is still dark; the eerily luminous hands of the bedside clock, glowing as if coated in ectoplasm, indicate that it is shortly after three. Her head is thumping and she could drink Niagara Falls dry. She throws back the sheet, rises unsteadily to her feet and begins the tortuous descent of the stairs.

In the kitchen window, with the light behind her, the reflection of her naked body looks nearly as cadaverous as that of the Roman woman in the museum. Any insomniac neighbour will have a perfect view of her from the waist up, but all she cares about is imbibing as much water as she can stomach. Her digestive system is threatening to retaliate for the systematic abuse it has suffered during the previous day. The urge to vomit is not far over the horizon.

Her grip weakens and she drops the pint glass she has been drinking from into the sink. There is a face at the window, disembodied, as if some form of animated mask. Its features are indistinct, but she knows who it belongs to. She would like to scream but her vocal cords are paralysed, so she shuffles back and crouches down with her forearms over her head. When she dares to look up, the face has gone.

Once the kitchen light is extinguished, the back garden is faintly illuminated by the street lights beyond. The tall oleander in the sheltered courtyard casts the vaguest of anthropomorphic shadows, but she knows that has nothing to do with what she saw. It is clear who was at the window and why, and she is afraid. Groping her way back upstairs, she shivers even though it is a warm August night. She makes use of the toilet as quickly as physically possible, then climbs back into bed and grasps Sharon tightly. Sharon stirs but does not wake. Rosemary listens for every sound while waiting for sunrise.

Once it is light she begins to drift in and out of heavily dream-laden sleep. Her dreams take hold of her anxieties and contort them, then mingle them with real life until it becomes difficult to distinguish wakefulness from sleep. Her mother opens her eyes in her hospital bed and demands to know why she is dead. She wakes to find her father lying between her and Sharon, licking his lips. The only dish on the restaurant's menu is scorched lasagne.

It is mid-morning before they are in a fit state to face the day.

'Holy shit,' Sharon says. 'I must have gargled with the contents of a cess pit during the night.'

'I wondered where you disappeared to.'

'How are you feeling?'

Rosemary thinks hard before replying. 'I've had better nights. Still, I suppose we're the architects of our own downfall. I blame the cold garlic bread. How about you?'

'I'll blame it too given that it's not around to argue its own case.'

'Do you think there's a cure?'

'Everyone knows the only cure is a strong cup of tea made by someone whose name begins with R.'

'Quelle surprise. This time I'll borrow your dressing gown if that's okay.'

'This time?'

She hesitates. 'I just don't think I'd make a very attractive sight at the moment. Anyway, two industrial-strength teas coming up.'

'Any chance of a fried egg sandwich with that?'

'Do you have any eggs?'

Sharon considers. 'Just tea will do fine.'

Rosemary buys sandwiches for lunch from the local convenience store. While walking back, she wonders why she does not feel that her mother's funeral has brought any sense of closure. The loss of Jamie and her dad may not be irreparable, but at this moment that does not present itself as a pressing issue. Dad has barely impinged on her life for some years, and his performance when he came up to see mum and took her out to lunch a few weeks ago should have forewarned her how things were likely to play out. Her father, she is forced to accept, wanders in and out of other people's lives as and when it suits him. As for Jamie, he now seems little more than a blank canvas, stripped of personality and will, perhaps by the prospect of impending tragedy, but more likely by his incapacity to take responsibility for the unpleasant consequences of things going wrong. Can he really have led such a charmed life up to now? Rosemary is forced to acknowledge that she does not feel a clear and present need to re-establish contact with Jamie or her father. If it happens in the fullness of time, so be it. The truth which dare not speak its name, however, is that her life really would be empty now if anything happened to Sharon.

On opening the front door she is enticed by the smell of freshly-brewed coffee, and more existential thoughts are relegated. She sits with Sharon at a small green wrought-iron table out in the courtyard, having first cleaned it and its accompanying chairs of bird droppings, and the sandwiches do not take long to consume. The coffee is strong, but nevertheless the hum of bees probing the lavender behind them has an inevitably soporific effect. They are both content to lean back and allow the heady atmosphere to wash over them.

'I could go to sleep,' Sharon says at length, 'but to be honest I'm getting behind on my research. I really ought to go into the library and do a few hours' work. You okay with that?'

'Fine. I'll play with my imaginary friend.'

'That's probably a bit more information than I needed.'

'Actually, I think it would do me good to get some exercise and fresh air. Maybe I'll do the riverside walk out to Waterbeach. Must go home afterwards, though, and clean up and put some fresh clothes on. I feel a bit rank.'

There is a tremor of anxiety in Sharon's expression as she gets to her feet.

'I didn't mean to drive you away,' Sharon says. 'You're welcome to stay here.'

'It's okay, it'll do me good. I'll leave you to it. Have a productive time in the library.'

She raises her hand in a farewell gesture, then makes her exit before Sharon has the chance to say more. By the time the end of the road approaches, she has decided that it is too hot to walk to Waterbeach, and in any case she is not dressed for it, being still clad in the black trouser-suit she wore to mum's funeral. Instead she goes home, runs a bath and soaks in it for half an hour. As she considers her surroundings, the cracked wall tiles, the shrinking grouting, the plastic shower curtain which she has been meaning to replace for the last six months, she realises that the space she has called home for the last few years suddenly does not feel so comforting. The flat remains exactly as it was, so the change must be in her. Perhaps this should not come as a surprise, given the sequence of unwanted events since Adam's disappearance. But somehow that does not seem to explain it. It is as if the flat really belongs to someone else.

She dresses in a light summer skirt and sleeveless top and meanders aimlessly towards town. At least she starts out with no purpose in mind, but soon realises that her feet are directing her back towards St Bene't's church. She descends the steps from the street to the main door and basks in the coolness within. The only other person present is arranging flowers in front of the altar. She turns around as she hears Rosemary's footsteps approaching, and is all smiles.

'Well hello, my dear. Rosemary, isn't it?'

'Yes. Fancy bumping into you again. The flowers look lovely.'

'Why, thank you.' Eleanor stands back to survey her handiwork. 'A simple addition to the place, but flowers make such a difference, I always think. Not that I'm any kind of expert at flower-arranging, I just sort of jiggle them around until they look right.'

Rosemary laughs. 'Well, you're obviously an expert at jiggling.'

Eleanor smiles, indulgently as it seems. 'How's your mother? You said she was poorly when we met before.'

'Yes, I did. Her funeral was yesterday.'

'Oh, my dear.' She takes Rosemary's arm. 'I am so sorry. I hope her last days were peaceful.'

'I think so. To be honest, I doubt she knew much about it.'

Eleanor looks sideways at the front pew. 'Would you like to sit down and talk for a minute?'

Rosemary is not sure that she would, but before she can respond she is being led by the arm. Perhaps it will do her good to talk to someone detached. And Eleanor, she recalls, is nothing if not insightful. She also does not hesitate to come to the point.

'You were very interested, I recall, in whether there are such things as spirits and ghosts. Do you feel any clearer about that in your mind?'

'Because of mum's death, you mean?'

'Her life and her death. Do you still sense that she's with you in some way?'

'I'd have to say no. Perhaps we weren't close enough in life. Or perhaps it's because she'd lost her personality some time before she died. According to the doctors, she'd been brain-dead for some weeks before they turned everything off.'

'How awful for you. What about the other person you said was trying to make contact with you?'

Rosemary's mind flips back to the previous night. 'He's still around.'

'And still malevolent?'

'Increasingly so.'

'Oh. In what way?'

Rosemary stares down at a memorial stone which has been incorporated into the floor of the church, its inscription worn and faded with the friction of centuries of feet. 'It's difficult to say. He seems to turn up when I'm at my most vulnerable.'

Eleanor places her hand on Rosemary's forearm. 'Perhaps, my dear, you're just most receptive when you're feeling vulnerable.'

'Yes. I expect you're right.'

'But you don't really think I'm right.'

Rosemary shrugs. Eleanor is watching her intently, but smiling.

'It's just me being stupid.'

'Sometimes we say things like that because we're not confident about opening up to someone else. It's all right, just forget I spoke, I was being presumptuous anyway.'

'No, you weren't. You're right. It just seems very far-fetched. I don't want to make an idiot of myself.'

Eleanor continues to smile benignly, inviting her to do just that, if she wishes.

'Recently, people have been disappearing from my life at a rapid rate. My fiancé and my mother have died, and my father and my brother, the only close family members I have left, seem to have disowned me. And I feel like he's ruthlessly manipulated events to bring this about.'

Eleanor nods. 'That's serious, if it's really true. But sometimes life does just deal us a dud hand, so that we wonder if a trail of misfortunes is ever going to come to an end.'

'Yes, I know. I can't explain why I feel this. Call it intuition, call it paranoia. I just know deep down that his ultimate goal is to get rid of everyone around me, to leave me on my own.'

'I see.' Eleanor strokes her chin as she ponders. 'Do you have any clue yet what he wants?'

'I think he wants me.'

'Oh. For what purpose?'

Rosemary pauses. 'Do you know the story of the Watchers?'

'Let me think. Think. No, to be honest I'm not sure I do.'

'They were angels who came down to earth to have sex

with human women. Their offspring were a race of giants. God buried them under the earth. Allegedly.'

'Ah. You mean in the time of the Nephilim.'

'Sorry?'

Eleanor leans forward, takes a Bible from the ledge in front of her and opens it near the beginning.

'Genesis, chapter 6. "When mankind began to increase and to spread all over the earth and daughters were born to them, the sons of the gods saw that the daughters of men were beautiful; so they took for themselves such women as they chose. But the Lord said, *My life-giving spirit shall not remain in man for ever; he for his part is mortal flesh: he shall live for a hundred and twenty years.*'

'A hundred and twenty years?'

'Yes. It goes on: "In those days, when the sons of the gods had intercourse with the daughters of men and got children by them, the Nephilim were on earth. They were the heroes of old, men of renown.'

'So, who were the sons of the gods?'

'God knows. The early chapters of Genesis can be a minefield, they often seem to be obscure and self-contradictory. We get hints that the ancient Hebrews believed that other gods existed beside their own. And, just to confuse things further, we've already been told in effect that God withdrew his life-giving spirit, in other words immortality, in the Garden of Eden when Adam and Eve ate the forbidden fruit. Who knows what we're to make of all this in the twenty-first century?'

'Then just indulge me for a moment, Eleanor. If you felt threatened, even in your fervid imagination, by some kind of being who seemed to be taking these sons of the gods or Watchers or whatever we're to call them as his role model, what would you do?'

To her surprise, Eleanor laughs. 'I can't see a son of a god wanting to have his wicked way with me. But if I were as young and attractive as you, I'd go back to wherever I felt to be a place of safety. Somewhere I felt protected. Preferably with someone who loved me. But I'd warn them to be very careful.'

As soon as she is outside the church, Rosemary rings
Sharon's home phone, but she does not pick it up and it
switches to the answering machine. She tries Sharon's
mobile with the same result, then runs to the taxi rank on
St Andrew's Street, barges her way to the front of the
queue with profuse apologies and demands to be taken
with all alacrity back to Sharon's house. They crawl
through traffic queues and wait interminably at red lights.
She tries phoning Sharon again, but still without response.
When the taxi finally pulls up outside the house, she does
not wait to find out the fare but thrusts a twenty-pound
note into the driver's hand, rushes up to the front door and
finds it ajar. Inside, she hears only silence.

40

Fearful now, and wary of announcing herself by calling out, Rosemary gently closes the front door behind her and searches the house up and down on tiptoe, but there is no sign of Sharon. Realising that it has not so far occurred to her to check the garden, she looks out of the kitchen window and sees her friend sitting in the courtyard, apparently staring into space. A sheet of paper lies on the patio table next to her. When Rosemary opens the back door, Sharon does not look up.

'You had me worried. The front door was open.'

Sharon looks round, her eyes seemingly struggling to focus. 'Was it? How careless of me.'

Rosemary eases herself into the other chair. 'Are you okay, Sharon?'

Sharon seems to be trying to stare through the fence into the next garden. Rosemary glances at the paper lying on the table, but it is upside-down.

'Is it something to do with this?'

Sharon takes a deep breath as she nods, looks at Rosemary and then at the paper, to indicate that she has permission to read it. Rosemary turns it over and sees the printed letter-heading: University of Toronto, Department of English. She does not bother to read on.

'I'd have thought you'd be pleased,' she says.

'You're not surprised?'

'Jayne and Mary mentioned they'd heard you were applying for jobs in America.'

'Close. I had a problem with taking the yankee dollar, I suppose. Canada seemed more, I don't know, ethical.'

'But you're from Australia. You'll never stand the winters in Canada.'

'I'll stay indoors and watch TV for six months.' Sharon looks down at her hands.

'You're going to take the job then?'

Sharon's voice is flat, weary. 'I don't really have much

273

choice, do I?'

'What do you mean? You've still got a job here for next year, haven't you?'

'You know that's not what I'm talking about.'

'No, I'm sorry. I've got no idea what you're talking about.'

Sharon tilts her head back and stares at the sky. 'I guess I need to move on. Make a fresh start. Isn't that what people always say in these circumstances?'

Rosemary folds her arms and rests them on the table. 'Look, I must be really thick or something, but what circumstances?'

Her friend continues to study the clouds. 'Yesterday I dared to dream. But I saw the look in your eyes when you left earlier.'

The silence hangs in the air. Rosemary shivers. She knows that the next sentence she speaks could be one of the most important in her life. Various options run through her mind, only to be rejected as inadequate. The longer the silence continues, the more irrelevant it will be what she comes out with.

'I don't want you to go.'

'That's not what your eyes said earlier.'

'Never mind what my eyes said. You're the only person alive who means anything to me. You're all I've got, Sharon.'

Sharon finally looks straight at her. 'Until the next man comes along.'

'That's not fair. I've never claimed to be like you. But I always felt there was something special between us. Even when Adam was still here, I had something with you that I could never have got from him, or from any man.'

Sharon releases a melancholy sigh. 'Yes, I thought that too. Maybe I'm just getting older. Believe it or not, I've become such a sad cow that I have fantasies about settling down with someone. But I know that's never going to happen with you. And it'll never happen with anyone else while I'm around you, because you'll always be more special to me than anyone else.' She wipes her eye. 'You can be a cruel bitch, you know that?'

Rosemary cups her hands around her nose and mouth, then lets them rest in her lap. 'So you're going to take the job?'

'I rang them when I got the letter in case there was anyone in the office. I couldn't even work out what time it was in Toronto. I got an answering machine, and I didn't want to tell them by just leaving a message.'

Rosemary thinks back to her earlier conversation with Eleanor in St Bene't's. *I'd go back to wherever I felt to be a place of safety. Somewhere I felt protected. Preferably with someone who loved me. But I'd warn them to be very careful.*

'Please, Sharon, will you promise me one thing?'

'I can't promise until I know what I'm promising.'

'Don't do anything today. At least sleep on it. Think what you're giving up. You love Cambridge, you've always said that. You could have a successful career here and be world-famous and do TV documentaries and stuff. Isn't that what you always wanted?'

Sharon shakes her head. 'It's what I wanted once. It doesn't seem so important any more.'

'But will you promise me?'

'What's the point? What can you do during the rest of today that's going to change anything? Just being with you screws up my emotions so much that I make most teenagers seem level-headed. I can't cope with this roller-coaster any more, Rosie. I'm sorry.'

'You'll see what I can do if you just give me a chance.'

Sharon looks drawn, lines etched on her face where there were surely none yesterday. Rosemary has never seen her with so little fight, the spirit vanished from her eyes.

'All right,' Sharon says at last. 'If I spoke to them in this state they'd probably withdraw the offer anyway. But I'm only putting it off until tomorrow.'

Rosemary feels a sense of relief that she has at least

bought some time, but has no idea what to do with it. Take Sharon out for an intimate meal? Give her a night to remember? If she fails, Bonner has his final triumph and she will be defenceless against him. If Sharon stays, they may both be at risk. Unless, of course, she has been deluded all along. In the end, Sharon will decide her future. Her own at that moment looks irretrievably bleak.

They sit in silence in the garden of the Fort St George. Rosemary has dressed in a skirt and tailored jacket to show her friend how much this evening means to her, but her efforts are bearing little reward. In the suddenly cool evening air, banks of dark cloud edged with red roll in from the north-west like a celestial tsunami. The dramatic meteorological spectacle has the attention of their fellow drinkers, who from time to time make suitably awe-inspired noises. An unseasonably cold wind has sprung up, and Rosemary and Sharon decide to retreat indoors before the rush. They find a couple of spare stools and perch against a low table.

'You could come out and see me,' Sharon says, as if continuing a conversation which has been taking place in her mind.

'What?'

'In Toronto. We don't have to assume we'd never see each other again.'

Rosemary does not feel comforted by this thought, indeed is irritated to be dragged back to the subject she is finding it unbearable to consider. She sips her drink and looks away. Outside, even at eight o'clock it is growing darker by the moment. The first drops of rain are thudding against the windows.

'Hey, look who's just arrived.'

Across the bar, Jayne and Mary are shaking out their telescopic umbrellas and laughing. Jayne looks over and waves to Sharon, then spots her companion and nudges Mary, who is already ordering their drinks. After a brief whispered exchange they walk straight across.

'Hi, you two. Mind if we join you?'

'Be our guests,' Sharon replies with enthusiasm suggesting more than a hint of relief.

They cast around for more stools, but by now every one is taken. At that moment, four people at a table behind get to their feet to leave. Jayne and Mary rush to position themselves between the table and another group who have noticed the same opportunity, and hold them at bay until it is free.

'Nice manoeuvre,' Sharon says. 'Bit ruthless.'

'It's a dog-eat-dog world,' Jayne replies. 'Nice girls come second.'

'Better than not coming at all,' Mary adds, clearly having to enunciate her words carefully, and with autonomous volume control disabled.

'I detect that this is not the first drink of the night for you two.'

'Or the last,' Mary says. 'It's my birthday. Hey, did you see the sky? Something apoc–, poc–, something bad's gonna happen tonight, you mark my words.'

Jayne looks askance. 'There'll be an apocalypse in your head when you wake up tomorrow.'

Mary conspiratorially taps the side of her nose at the second attempt. 'Don't care. Day off tomorrow.'

A rainstorm of diluvial proportions is falling outside, hammering on tables and chairs and overflowing from gutters, and the noise has become a distraction. Rosemary, sitting near the window, is struggling to hear what her three friends are saying, and cannot bring herself to care. She toys with the idea of leaving them to it. Would Sharon follow her? At that moment, it does not seem certain that she would.

'How's the job-hunting going, Sharon?' Jayne asks.

Sharon looks at Rosemary for the first time in some minutes. 'I've been offered a job in Toronto.'

'Hey, that's great,' Mary says. 'Er, isn't it?'

'I guess so.'

Rosemary turns to look out of the window. Even Mary

spots the dysfunctional body language.

'But what are you two going to do without each other? You're insep – oh fuck it, you know what I mean.'

Jayne looks at her drunken partner and shudders before turning back to Sharon. 'There must be lots of things you'll miss about Cambridge.'

'Yes, there will. But you can't stand still, can you? It just seems like the right time to move on.' Sharon's expression conveys that even she is unconvinced by this sequence of platitudes. Mary's mind has clearly been working, albeit at reduced efficiency.

'Hey, Rosie, you could go with Sharon.'

Jayne winces. 'Mary, you're not funny any more.'

'I'm being bloody serious. Look, Rosie, you've got nothing to keep you in Cambridge now your mum's dead. Really sorry about that, by the way. And when you've worked at CUL you can get a job anywhere in the world, that's what I've heard anyway. It's the obvious solution.'

Jayne loses patience. 'Mary, have you considered in your charmingly pissed state that maybe Sharon and Rosie have discussed all this, and this is the way they want it?'

Sharon and Rosemary glance at one another as Jayne's question is left hanging in the air. Lightning momentarily illuminates the garden outside in pure white light. Sharon's eyes seem to indicate that she would be interested in hearing a response to Mary's proposal.

'It's okay Jayne,' Rosemary says at last. 'To be honest, I've never thought of working anywhere else but Cambridge. It was always my dream to work at CUL, and it's been a dream fulfilled. Most of the time anyway.'

Now Sharon is frowning. Mary downs her drink. 'Come on then, girl. Green Dragon's next on the list.'

'As long as you don't expect me to keep up.'

'You always were a lightweight. Bye, you guys. Let us know how it works out.'

When they are alone once more, Sharon smiles at Rosemary, raising her eyebrows playfully at the same time. 'Out of the mouths of babes and inebriates.'

278

'In the general breakdown of social inhibitions, why didn't you just tell them you were moving to Toronto to get away from me?'

'Because it's not necessarily true.'

'Was I tripping when we had a certain conversation this afternoon, then?'

'It's not necessarily true I'm going.'

'Sharon, if you think it's funny to piss about over something like this—'

'I wouldn't dream of it. Look, I said I wouldn't do anything about it today, and I was true to my word.'

'Except that, as you helpfully pointed out, nothing will have changed tomorrow.'

'Who knows? I may have changed.'

'Into someone who doesn't want to go to Toronto?'

'I could equally turn the question round and say, what was the point of you asking me to put off a decision until tomorrow? What did you think would have changed?'

Rosemary sighs with an air of defeat. 'I was hoping I'd think of a way to make you change your mind. I even toyed with the idea of suggesting we try living under the same roof for a while, see how it works out.'

'Toyed with it, but rejected it.'

'On the grounds that we've got our respective homes the way we want them, and we'd be bound to resent someone else coming in and changing things around.'

Sharon rubs her fingertips back and forth across her lips. At length she says, 'I'm going to get some more drinks in. Whatever you do, don't go away.'

While Sharon is at the bar, a young couple walk over, eyeing up the seats vacated by Jayne and Mary. The girl says, 'Excuse me, is anyone using these seats?'

'Yes. Yes, they are. I'm sorry.'

The couple, having clearly been watching the empty seats for a while, walk away muttering dark imprecations. Sharon seems to be taking an age to return. Rosemary looks around and sees that there is a lengthy queue at the bar. Her friend has somehow negotiated or elbowed her way to the front, and is now waving her hand dismissively at a man behind her. She returns just in time to prevent another assault on the empty chairs.

'That was a close one. I thought the guy at the bar was going to hit me. Fellow Aussie too. What's the world coming to? Bet he's from Melbourne.'

'If you colonials will bring your convict heritage back to the old country, what do you expect?'

'I suppose you're right. Now, where were we?'

'Disagreeing.'

'Ah yes. In the time it's taken me to get to the bar, get into a fight and walk back again, I've formulated a proposition.'

Sharon waits. Rosemary tilts her head, but says nothing.

'I'll take that as an invitation to go on. Maybe you're right about the two of us having our own precious personal space that we'd find hard to share. So let's try it another way. We talked a while ago about getting away and spending some time in Wales. I did, anyway. So let's find a cottage and try sharing someone else's space. There's nothing to stop either of us from going, as far as I can see. What do you think?'

'I think it's a great idea. Unfortunately, there are in fact two things stopping us from going. No, make that three.'

'Oh? Like what?'

'One, Wales is full up at this time of year. You can't rent a cottage worth staying in for love or money.'

'A friend of mine in the department has a little place in Snowdonia. I can ring him tomorrow and see if it's free.'

'Okay. Two, you've got a job offer outstanding which won't sit around for ever.'

'Already thought of that. I can pretend the letter arrived after I'd gone away. They haven't phoned or e-mailed to follow it up. If I get back and find they've got fed up with waiting and offered the job to someone else, that'll settle it once and for all.'

'And you're prepared to take that risk?'

Sharon's tone becomes less jaunty. 'Maybe I'm taking a

bigger risk if I don't.'

'You're doing well so far. But the third is, I'm supposed to start therapy soon, paid for by the library. If I don't go, I may not get my job back.'

'That's tricky, I grant you. When's your first session?'

'Next week.'

They sip their drinks in silence. This conundrum presents itself as more of a Gordian knot than its predecessors. Sharon looks up and shrugs.

'There's got to be a way round it. Let's take things a stage at a time. We need to find out if the cottage is available first. But does this sound like a plan?'

'I'm only sorry I didn't think of it.'

Sharon holds out her hand across the table, palm upwards. Rosemary takes it. A group of women at a neighbouring table notice and begin to whisper.

'Look, Rosie, do you really want to give us a chance? If you're humouring me, just come out and say what you really feel. There's no point pretending.'

Rosemary looks down at their entwined fingers. 'I've had a vision, perhaps a foretaste, of what life would be like without you. In the past I was guilty of taking it for granted that you'd always be there. But I want to give this a go. If the worst comes to the worst, I'll skip the therapy and take a chance on convincing the library I got better without it.'

'No more sorcerers and ghosts and archangels, then?'

Images of the Watchers and their earthly women spring unbidden into Rosemary's mind. She closes her eyes to erase these unwanted reminders. When she opens them, Sharon is still waiting for a reply.

'No more sorcerers and ghosts and archangels. Only in books.'

With their free hands, they clink their glasses together. Outside, the storm has abated but, beyond the garden of the Fort St George, all is in darkness.

41

The night is still and star-filled over Midsummer Common. In the tree-tops, incorporeal white shapes flow and weave like wisps of cloud between the upper branches. Rosemary observes with some concern that Sharon does not seem to have noticed them. She blinks hard, but to her they remain visible. The more she tries to focus on them, the more quickly they twist and transform. As the women walk along these formless shapes keep pace, just far enough ahead to remain always in view. Rosemary risks a sideways glance at Sharon; sensing the attention, she turns and smiles broadly. Rosemary takes her hand and grips it, tightly, then hears distant thunder and, turning to look over her shoulder, sees that another storm is approaching. Sharon is oblivious to it.

They cross the river by the quaint old iron footbridge and head through streets of terraced houses until they reach the main road where they continue hand in hand, indulgently ignoring the taunts of a group of pot-bellied men smoking outside a pub. Rosemary continues to glance upwards from time to time. She feels the silence between them has gone on for too long, but Sharon still looks serene.

'Look, Sharon, if we're going to be together for a bit longer, well, hopefully a lot longer, there's something I really need to tell you.'

'A dark secret? That sounds alluring. But if it's the fact that you talk in your sleep, I'm already well aware of that.'

'I'm being serious. I think I may have inadvertently put you in danger.'

Sharon laughs. 'Of what? Cirrhosis of the liver?'

'No. Of Bonner.'

Sharon is suddenly unamused. 'Rosie, what conversation were we having no more than an hour ago? This is over, we've agreed. End of discussion.'

When they reach the house, Sharon fumbles for some

time in her bag for her keys. Noctilucent clouds cascade in an aerial cataract. Once safely in the hallway, Sharon turns on the light and rubs her hands.

'Small nightcap? Or are you ready to go straight up?'

'Good job I'm not a man or I'd have taken it that you were getting straight to the point.'

'And you'd be nursing sore testicles.'

'In that case may I suggest, in the great British spirit of compromise, that we pour ourselves a nightcap and take it up with us?'

'That's my girl.'

They make their way upstairs, each carrying a large glass containing significantly more than a single measure of cognac, then toss a coin for first use of the bathroom. After brushing her teeth and combing her hair, Rosemary studies an image in the mirror of someone who may once have been her: lifeless hair, shadowed eyes and thin pale lips. It is clear that the last few weeks have taken their toll. She has said goodbye to her mother, and hardly thought of it since. She has come close to losing her best friend, and is still unsure how much she has been forced to sacrifice to avoid this fate, or indeed how far her actions have been motivated by the simple fear of being left alone. The face in the mirror crumples.

A few minutes later, Sharon returns to the bedroom to find Rosemary sitting up in bed sipping her cognac. Sharon undresses facing the wardrobe mirror, then turns and climbs cat-like onto the bed and kisses Rosemary before sliding her legs under the cover. She takes a sip of her own drink, then rests her head on Rosemary's shoulder. With her free hand, Rosemary runs her fingers through her friend's hair. 'I wonder what kind of state Mary's in now,' she says.

'I don't think Jayne could carry her home.'

'Still, I'm glad we ran into them tonight.'

Although she cannot see Sharon's expression, Rosemary feels the ripple at the front of her scalp as her eyebrows rise. 'You didn't give that impression at the time.'

'No, perhaps not. But it feels like they helped to break a logjam.'

'Perhaps they did,' Sharon says, then, after a pause, 'but would you really have considered doing it?'

'Doing what?'

'Coming with me to Toronto.'

'I could have renewed my acquaintance with Rosalind, I suppose. But you do realise the temperature there went down to minus 35 last winter.'

'You really took the trouble to check that?'

'I read it somewhere so it must be true.'

Sharon slides onto her pillow and wraps her arm around Rosemary's waist. Rosemary takes another sip of her drink and settles down alongside. Their noses and foreheads touch.

'It's been a weird day,' Sharon says.

'I keep having them at the moment.'

'I'm so glad we're still together, though. To be honest, I don't think I'd really mind sharing my space with you.'

'You wouldn't say that if I brought all my stuff over and dumped it here.'

'I suppose that's true. Maybe a fresh start would be best. No hers and hers. Do you think we'll get that far?'

'We've managed to get this far.'

'Can I ask you something, Rosie?'

'No law against asking.'

'How do you think Adam would feel?'

'About what?'

'About us, of course.'

'Adam always knew we were close. He wasn't the jealous type.'

'Yes, but we weren't, well, like this, were we?' She pauses. 'Do you feel that he's still around?'

'I haven't seen him for a while. Perhaps he's done a *Truly, Madly, Deeply* on us.'

'Call me old-fashioned, but that thought spooks me a bit.'

Rosemary grins. 'You'll be seeing archangels next.'

Their lips brush, and Rosemary remembers how bereft she felt when it seemed that Sharon was about to walk out of her life forever. She moves closer and slides her hand up the inside of Sharon's thigh.

She wakes to find the bedroom in darkness, even though Sharon always leaves a light on at night, and turns to see her friend's naked silhouette against the bedroom window. There has been no thunder, but a flash of lightning somewhere close illuminates the outline of Sharon's body. She does not flinch. Rosemary climbs out of bed and stands behind her. Sharon relaxes her body back into her and draws her hands around her waist.

'Look at that sky. It's a blast, isn't it?'

There is turmoil in the heavens, like a medieval depiction of the moments before the Last Judgement. Are the dense, restless clouds about to part to reveal a heavenly avenger? Is this the same scene which made such an impression on John Dee in Mortlake in 1582?

Rosemary looks down the street. 'How come only our house is in darkness?'

'Our house? You're getting the hang of this already. The switch must have tripped, I'll go and sort it.'

'Better put your dressing gown on. Just in case.'

'In case of what? It's pitch black. QED.'

Rosemary continues to watch the sky, remembering Adam's warning about Bonner, thinking of the strange white shapes in the trees. After a couple of minutes, Sharon returns with two candles which she has lit from the gas stove.

'The switch hasn't tripped. Things are getting weirder. I'll have to get someone out in the morning.'

They sit up in bed and finish their cognac while watching the dancing shadows from the candles which disappear every minute or so in the glare of an iridescent lightning flash.

'I haven't seen Mr Keats since we got back,' Sharon

says. 'I hope he's okay.'

'Cats are survivors. He'll have found somewhere to ride out the storm.'

'But if he's spooked he just takes to his heels. He could be anywhere by now.'

At length they succumb to the effects of alcohol and fatigue. Rosemary can hear from her breathing that Sharon is sleeping, but she lies awake imagining the sky descending while Richard Bonner rides on the clouds. Her watch warns that there are at least three more hours of darkness. After some deliberation she resolves to watch for the rest of the night and wait for dawn's rosy glow, like a medieval nun or a condemned criminal. Daylight will bring safety. If even these celestial pyrotechnics do not herald a cataclysm, then surely the worst must be over.

The danger of falling asleep becomes too great, so she creeps downstairs, takes a coat from the hooks by the door and sits outside on the front wall to watch the remainder of the show. Along the street, several other insomniacs are doing likewise. The violence of the storm seems to be diminishing; it has been several minutes since the last thunder, and the clouds resemble a fast-flowing river rather than a waterfall. Her eyes are heavy and her neck aches from staring upwards, but once this night is over she will feel secure. For the first time in many months, she will have a future worth anticipating.

A heavy weight presses down on the back of her left shoulder. She forces her eyes open, but all she can make out is a featureless grey canvas. With some effort she can twist her head just far enough to make out that Sharon, still fast asleep, has rolled onto her and is pinning her down, forcing her head against the pillow. She writhes to extricate herself and Sharon, rudely dumped onto her own side of the bed, begins to stir. The movement causes Mr Keats at the end of the bed to raise his head and widen his eyes in anticipation of a long-delayed breakfast. It is almost mid-day.

'Wake up sleepy head,' she says gently to Sharon. There is no response.

'Wake up, you lazy cow.'

Sharon's mumbled response vaguely resembles, 'Piss off, I'm tired.'

'I've got a surprise for you.'

'I'll have it later.'

'You'll want it now when you know what it is.'

Sharon screws up her face and slowly opens her eyes. Rosemary leans forward and brushes her lips against Sharon's while looking deeply into her eyes.

'Is that it? I thought it would at least be a fried egg sandwich.'

'I bet you still haven't got any eggs.'

'Bloody have too. Organic duck eggs. Feisty bastards.'

'It's a pity you haven't trained Mr Keats to take care of such domestic duties.'

'That might take another few million years of feline evolution. Or some genetic engineering. Imagine my little man tottering around on his back legs wearing a butler's uniform.'

The sun is shining and the tempestuous skies of the previous night have cleared. Rosemary feels lighter. They look at one another and smile. Sharon rolls on top of Rosemary again, but this time she is very alert.

Through the crackling from the frying pan she hears a muffled thud, but puts it from her mind as she continues buttering bread. Did Sharon say she wanted breakfast in bed or in the kitchen? She heads out into the hall to call up to her.

Sharon is in a crumpled heap at the turn of the stairs. She has somehow come to a halt half-kneeling, with her head against the wall and her legs folded beneath her. Rosemary rushes forward, but draws back from trying to rouse her when she sees how contorted her spine is. Blood is flowing from an already-swelling wound on her head, a wound suggesting she has struck the wall with more force

287

than seems feasible from the momentum gathered from falling down a dozen stairs. She is still breathing, but shallowly. After a few moments of paralysis, Rosemary dials 999 and tells the emergency operator in a quivering voice that her friend has had an accident. At that moment, she cannot bear to consider any alternative explanation. Waiting for the ambulance, she kneels beside Sharon and gently strokes her hair.

42

'I'm afraid Miss Turner is in no state to have visitors yet. Unless you're close family.'

Rosemary has heard these words every day for the last ten days. She considers for a moment. 'I'm her partner.'

Is this true? The nurse makes no attempt to conceal her surprise, but the conceit seems to be effective.

'Wait here a minute, I'll go and talk to the doctor.'

The minutes tick past. Just as Rosemary decides she may as well take the weight off her feet while she waits, the nurse returns.

'You can go in, just for a few minutes.'

She can only take it on trust that the patient she has been shown in to see is Sharon. The lower half of her body is protected from the weight of the bedclothes by some kind of frame. What is visible above the bedclothes wears a smock. Her head is wrapped in bandages, only her eyes, mouth and nose left visible, so that she resembles an effigy on a medieval tomb. But Sharon is not dead, although her voice sounds lifeless.

'Who's there?'

'Who do you think?'

'Rosie? What are you doing here?'

'Thanks for the welcome. Good to see you again too.'

'I told them not to let you in.'

'What? Why?'

'Rosie, do yourself a favour and go.'

Sharon has not so far opened her eyes. Rosemary leans forward and kisses her on the bridge of the nose, picking up as she does so the scent of dry skin and antiseptic.

'Rosie, please, just go. Get out, for Christ's sake.'

'No. It's taken over a week just to get them to let me see you.' She wants to take Sharon's hand, but both are buried under blankets. Sharon opens her eyes and turns them towards Rosemary. Her head does not move.

'Please, you haven't a clue. For your own sake, forget

289

all about us.'

'It's for my own sake that I'm here. Believe it or not, I've been going out of my mind worrying about you. I can see that you're badly injured.' Sharon closes her eyes once more. 'But I haven't forgotten what we talked about. And as far as I'm concerned, nothing has changed. We'll just wait till you're better.'

Sharon's voice is now little more than a whisper. 'I'm never going to be better. Look at me.'

'Don't say that. We'll get you better, together.'

'My skull's been fractured. And, just for good measure, my spine's been snapped.'

Rosemary cannot keep her eyes from scanning the bed in front of her, with its elaborate protective superstructure. 'I'm sure it's too soon to know. You never know what they can do these days.'

She has no idea why she is saying these ridiculous words when Sharon must wish that she had died. And, at this moment, Rosemary is equally helpless. Sharon's voice is suddenly strident.

'Nurse! Nurse! Help!'

The nurse strides into the room and wordlessly points Rosemary towards the door. Turning back as she leaves, she sees the nurse consoling Sharon as she sobs uncontrollably.

The Champion of the Thames does not offer the welcoming environment it formerly did. Even in her alcove seat, she stares down at her glass sniffing and rubbing her eyes.

'Penny for them.'

'Fuck off. You know I hate it when people say that.'

'At least I got a response. You don't seem very pleased to see me though.'

'I said goodbye to you weeks ago. Why are you still here?'

'Because you still need me. You know you do.'

'All right. Tell me what to do then. How do I salvage

anything from this train wreck of a life?'

She is conscious that a tense silence has fallen over the other occupants of the bar. As she surveys them one by one, they sip their drinks and slowly resume their conversations, though still glancing in her direction.

'They can't see or hear me, Rosie. Still, no matter. Do you really still want to be with Sharon, or do you just feel sorry for her? Or even worse, guilty?'

She considers the question. 'What drew me to Sharon must still be there. Her mind seems to be intact. As for her body, I'm sure it's still too soon to know.'

Adam raises his eyebrows, and Rosemary looks down.

'Okay, even if her body's trashed, she's going to need someone to look after her. And what else have I got to dedicate my life to? In twenty years time I could be a world-famous expert on the evolution of roman minuscule script, and inside I'll be washed-up, dried-up, lying awake on my own every night wondering why I ever thought the sacrifice would be worth it. How could the future be worse than that?'

'Then go and tell Sharon that. Tell her that you want to be with her from now on come what may, and that whatever difficulties the future holds it can't be worse than spending it without her.' Adam places his hand on her shoulder. 'Come on, Rosie, you used to have more fight than this. Since when did you take no for an answer? Remember when you first asked me out?'

'I was pissed.'

'No you weren't. You knew what you wanted, and decided that going for it and running the risk of not getting it would be preferable to never knowing if you could have had it. Is that English? That's the Rosie I fell in love with, and that's the Rosie who's sitting with me now.'

'You were still with Alice then. I was being a trollop.'

'Indeed, and I knew then that you were my kind of girl.' Adam's eyes briefly flare. 'You're still my kind of girl. So go and prove it.'

She realises that she is smiling to herself. A shadow

falls over the table.

'Look, don't mind me asking, but are you all right, love?'

'Yes, I'm fine. I've just been having a chat with my imaginary friend. It's a form of therapy, you know.'

The barmaid clearly has no intention of putting this to the test. Rosemary finishes her drink and leaves, still smiling.

43

The fading leaves along Hills Road signify the imminence of an early autumn. Is that supposed to mean that a hard winter is on the way? Rosemary is wearing a jumper for the first time in months and knows that, for meteorological reasons or otherwise, some kind of turning point is approaching. She is making slow progress, not because she is toiling against the wind, but because she is not sure she really wants to arrive. That the trees are preparing to shed their summer finery seems apt; now that the moment is here, she is no longer carefree and sure of the future. On the contrary, she faces the prospect of leaping across a chasm, without knowing in advance how far it may be to the other side. Still, as she vaguely remembers someone singing, better to burn out than fade away.

Before entering the hospital, she sits on a seat outside the main entrance to calm herself, leans forward and covers her face with her hands. She is not left in peace for long.

'Penny for them.'

'If you say that once more—'

'Then what? You'll kill me? That would be interesting.'

'I hope you're here for a reason.'

'I've just got one thing to say. Our mutual friend was responsible for Sharon's accident.'

'Who revealed that to you, Nostradamus? Anyway, do you think I don't already know?'

'Fair enough. I was just trying to help.'

Rosemary rubs her eyes. 'So, is the psychopathic time-travelling bastard still around?'

'Having wreaked havoc and caused suffering and misery, he's moved on to his next victim. It seems that's what he does.'

'So you're telling me that after all this, after what he's done to my life and Sharon's, he never really wanted me at all? He just wanders through the centuries screwing up people's lives for the fun of it?'

'Perhaps it's the only way he can escape the boredom of being immortal. Anyway, my point is, you can't ever let Sharon know what really happened. If she finds out, she'll assume that any gesture of affection and support from you is born from guilt.'

'Perhaps she'd be right. I'm struggling as it is to cope with having destroyed my best friend's life.'

'Never forget that Bonner pushed her down the stairs, not you. Well, I've said all I came here to say. The rest's up to you.'

'Look, Adam, I don't know what I'm going to find when I get in there and meet Sharon. Nor, I suspect, do you. I'm going to have to weigh it up and make my own decision.'

'Fair enough. It's your call. But you forgot Adam's last Principle of Life.'

Sighing, Rosemary trawls her memory banks. 'Is that the one that says, The *deus ex machina* is the devil in disguise?'

'Rosie, Rosie, how could you have forgotten so soon? Adam's final Principle is, Always trust Adam.'

She is shown into a day room with PVC-covered chairs and sliding doors which give access to a landscaped area outside with low shrubs and a single cherry tree. Only after a few moments does she notice the figure sitting in a wheelchair in shadow in the far corner. The figure is looking at her with no indication of interest, or even recognition. Sharon's head is free of bandages, but a patch of bare scalp where her lank hair has been cut away reveals a still-ugly scar. Rosemary feels her legs shaking, swallows to suppress an upwelling of nausea, then walks forward and sits on a chair next to the wheelchair. Sharon does not give her time to begin the conversation she has rehearsed a hundred times.

'I told you not to come here.'

Her voice does not convey anger or even displeasure,

as if simply stating an obvious fact, impassive and without emotion. Rosemary hears it as the voice of someone who has hardly spoken for a long time.

'Then why did you agree to see me?'

'Who said I did?'

'The nurses.'

'They just told me I was going to have a visitor. They didn't say who it was.'

'And you didn't ask?'

'I didn't care.'

Rosemary is tempted to accept that her mission is already doomed, and cut short the agony. She resolves to make one more effort.

'Look, now I'm here, why don't we go outside and get a breath of air? I don't suppose you've had the chance too often.' She tries to bite her tongue off. 'That is … '

'I've got a better idea. Why don't we just get this over with here and now? I don't want you to come and see me. I don't want you anywhere near me. Is that clear enough?'

'So what happened to all the plans we made?'

Sharon responds with a look of withering contempt, and angles her finger-tips down towards her thighs. 'For Christ's sake, this is what happened.'

'That doesn't mean we can't still have a life together.'

Sharon tilts her head back and closes her eyes. Rosemary notices for the first time that her legs are already shrinking as the muscles atrophy. She wants to cry, but whether from sorrow or anger is unclear. Perhaps both. Sharon opens her eyes.

'I need to go the toilet. In fact I need a shit. Can you come with me and wipe my arse?'

Rosemary replies even before she is aware what the words mean. 'Yes, of course I will. I'll do anything for you, Sharon.'

Sharon blinks hard, as if waking up. 'Let's go outside. Can you ask the nurse for a blanket?'

Rosemary sits on the end of a bench, the wheelchair

alongside and angled in slightly so that their knees are nearly touching.

'How's Mr Keats?' Sharon asks.

'He's settled in fine. You know what cats are like, they're survivors.'

'How's the therapy going?' Sharon's voice sounds as if she is reading a litany.

'Great fun, as long as you like long, awkward silences. God knows if it's doing me any good.'

Sharon watches a robin hop across a patch of grass, from time to time cocking its head to one side.

'I've been reading up,' Rosemary says, 'about people who've suffered spinal injuries. Some say it's like going through the stages of bereavement. One of those stages is that you feel angry and resentful, even towards people that you love.' She pauses, but Sharon does not respond. 'And just as in a bereavement, you have to get through that stage before you can reach the sunny plateau of acceptance.'

'Great, so it's just like fucking *Pilgrim's Progress.*'

Rosemary has nothing to add, no idea how to turn this situation around. The bottom of a chasm appears far below. Sharon's voice is suddenly tinged with sadness.

'Look, Rosie, I'm sorry it has to be like this. But there's not going to be a future. For me, anyway.'

'That's up to us, isn't it?'

'No it's not, it's up to me. And I've already made my decision. I'll leave you to work out the rest.'

Rosemary is not sure that she wants to. Sharon's eyes look cloudy. She speaks into the middle distance.

'They wanted me to go to some specialist rehab centre where they teach you how to live with no legs and no bladder or bowel control. At first I refused, but then decided that it would be the quickest way of getting back to the real world where I can end my life in a place and at a time of my own choosing. Within reason, of course. I can hardly throw myself off the top of a high mountain, obviously, but—'

'Sharon, stop it, I don't want to hear this.'

Sharon turns to her and, for the first time, smiles. 'Would it help if I tell you that I actually feel calmer since I made this decision? It may not have seemed like it earlier, but you should have seen me a few weeks ago. I can't bear the prospect of living like this. And if there's one thing I regret, it's that we never did get the chance to find out if we'd have been happy spending our lives together. But there it is. Too late now.'

'And I don't suppose it will make any difference if I tell you that my life's been empty without you? If I remind you that people with disabilities have still been able to have outstanding academic careers? Look at—'

'Rosie, I go through all that in my mind every night, and still wake up feeling the same. I'm taking a rational decision. I've weighed up the pros and cons, done all the equations. Sorry, that's just how it is.'

Rosemary sniffs and searches her pockets with increasing desperation for a tissue. Sharon hands her one from a stock which she evidently keeps concealed about her person.

'And what about me? What am I going to do without you?'

'You'll find someone else to settle down with. Probably a lovely man who'll give you beautiful children and a holiday home on the coast. And you'll be happy.'

'I won't. I don't want a lovely man and beautiful children and a fucking holiday home. I want you. I want you even if your legs don't work. It's not your legs I want, for Christ's sake, it's the rest of you.'

Sharon smiles again. 'Okay, you asked for it. There's one thing I haven't told you, but you may as well know. They think that just before I fell down the stairs I must have had some kind of seizure.'

Rosemary's mind is working too quickly to form words. Sharon takes this as an invitation to continue.

'All I remember is being at the top of the stairs preparing to go down when I felt something thump me in the back, like I'd been whacked with a hammer. Then I was bumping against the stair treads, and when I reached the turn I thought I'd come to a stop, but instead it was as if someone was picking me up like a rag doll and whacking my head against the wall. Well, that's what it felt like, but obviously there must be another explanation. They haven't been able to find anything on the scans, but I suspect my brain's still too bruised for it to show up.' She looks hard at Rosemary. 'So you see, I haven't reached rock bottom yet. There's still a long way to go.'

Surely now she has to tell the truth, despite Adam's warning. Even if Sharon dismisses the explanation as ridiculous and tells Rosemary that she is still delusional, that is a risk she has to take. Perhaps deep down Sharon even suspects the truth but cannot bring herself to voice it.

She delays too long.

'Look, would you mind wheeling me back inside? I've got a nasty feeling I've just pissed myself.'

44

It is early evening, and the clouds have just lifted to reveal the mountains of Snowdonia, only a short way to the south, for the first time that day. The temperature has risen by several degrees in the space of a few minutes to approach the warmth expected in this part of the world in early summer. The balmy effect is increased by the dying of the westerly wind from the Irish Sea which has been making its unwelcome presence felt all day. The pleasure boats moored in the harbour below are finally at rest.

Rosemary sits on a folding metal chair on a terrace at the back of the cottage. The framework is rusted from having been stored in a damp shed for months on end. The paving slabs from which the terrace is constructed are, in places, broken and uneven. Alongside her is a small folding table whose plywood surface is beginning to curl away from its base; it too has fallen victim to excessive humidity. Rosemary is unconcerned about any of these visible signs of entropy. She picks up a notepad and paper from the table and jots down the following lines:

To live my life in a single moment,
See the universe in a falling star,
The tears of the world in a wave on the ocean,
The face of death in the teeth of a storm.

Deciding that she still has some work to do before being celebrated alongside Sylvia Plath, she closes the notepad.

Another folding chair, identical to her own, is placed on the other side of the table, and Jayne sits down.

'I'm glad the day finally cleared. I was starting to despair of ever seeing the sun again.'

'Wales is like that, I'm afraid. When the sun shines it's glorious. Most of the time it doesn't. What's Mary doing?'

'Having a shower. She won't be long, she'll be gasping

for a g and t.'

'So you two have been up to your sordid activities again.'

'A woman has needs. Anyway, tell me if I'm wrong, but I got the impression you're happy to have some time to yourself.'

'No problem. I'm fine.'

They fall silent for several minutes, content to give their attention to the ridges and crevices on the side of the dark grey peaks as they are highlighted in sequence by the movement of the sun tracking across them. Their reverie is interrupted by the clattering of a third chair being shaken in an attempt to open it one-handed. In the other hand Mary holds a glass containing a large gin and tonic. Realising that the vigorous activity is causing her to spill her drink, she places the glass on the table and resorts to using both hands.

'Thanks,' Jayne says to Mary. 'I'll have one too.'

'I was just about to ask. Rosie, you going to join us?'

'I'm okay at the moment, thanks.'

While Mary is inside, Jayne says, 'You can talk to us, you know. If it helps. We're not going to curl up in horror or embarrassment.'

Rosemary turns to Jayne and forces a smile. 'I know you're not. To be honest, I feel that in some way Sharon's here. Don't get spooked. I suppose it's because this is the trip that she always wanted to make. It sounds stupid, but I have conversations in which I tell her what we've been doing, describe what I can see. I try to give her a flavour of the sights and sounds. And I tell her how I'm feeling too.'

'Do you get any response?'

'Oh yes, she talks back.'

'What about?'

'One large gin and tonic coming up,' Mary says as she places Jayne's drink on the table beside her. 'I brought you a glass of wine anyway, Rosie. I'm sure you'll manage it later.'

'No, no. Okay. Thanks.'

Mary nods towards the mountains. 'Jayne and I were thinking we'd get our walking boots on tomorrow and head up into them thar hills. You up for that, Rosie?'

'Sounds good to me. Apparently there's an old drovers' trail which cuts through the pass. There's even a waterfall, and a hostelry when you get to the other side. Hope you've brought some waterproofs though.'

'Dah, it'll be fine tomorrow, I can feel it in me bones.'

'Sorry to be the bearer of bad news, but the fact the sun's shining now means the chances of it shining tomorrow morning are, statistically speaking, zilch.'

'Is that an eagle?' Mary says, pointing upwards.

'Not unless it's got lost,' Jayne replies. 'Looks like a buzzard to me.'

'Wouldn't it be great to be able to see the world from up there,' Mary asks, rhetorically.

Jayne raises her eyebrows. 'Mary, that's the single most predictable thing anyone could say at the sight of a bird of prey.'

Rosemary takes a sip of wine, sits back in her chair and closes her eyes. Which vision of Sharon does she wish to conjure up? The one who smiles and waves as they spot one another from a distance in the library? The one who cares for her before and after mum's funeral and stops her world from disintegrating? Or the Sharon whose broken body slumps helpless in a wheelchair, who has calmly, so she says, decided to reject life if she cannot live it on her own terms? This is the Sharon she sees day after day as she struggles to rewrite history, to make their last conversation conclude in a different way. The result is always the same; the words are immutable, pre-ordained. They cannot be altered. This is how it was, and how it will always be.

After dark, they huddle around one end of the huge oak table in the farmhouse kitchen with its ancient, and very smoky, inglenook fireplace. The plates and pans are in the sink, and a cardboard box, the week's receptacle for empty wine bottles, sits alongside. Two days into the trip, it is clear that they will need more boxes. The Police perform *King of Pain* in the background.

'Do you ever get lonely?' Mary asks Rosemary.

'Sometimes. But I promised myself a while ago that I'd learn to enjoy my own company more. I felt I'd spent too long living my life through other people.'

'But it's hard not to, isn't it?' Jayne says. 'We're social animals, like chimpanzees, we need other people. We can't just demand that they be around when we want them, and piss off when we don't.'

Rosemary suspects that the answer to this is complex. Mary jumps in. 'Have you ever tried to get back in touch with your dad and your brother?'

'No, I haven't. I suppose I should feel guilty. On the other hand, it doesn't seem to have been a high priority for them either, so I don't feel inclined to beat myself up about it.'

'I'm sure you'll all get back together one day,' Jayne offers.

'At a wedding or a funeral, probably. More likely the latter.'

'Don't speak too soon,' Mary resumes. 'The senior who's just started in our department is really sweet and about the right age for you, Rosie. I'll introduce you if you like.' Jayne buries her head in her hands. 'What?'

Rosemary laughs. 'Have I just wandered into the pages of a Jane Austen novel? I'm in the happy position of having no desperate need for a permanent partner.'

Mary is unabashed. 'But if you were, would it be a man or a woman?'

Rosemary is taken aback; this is a direct line of enquiry even for Mary. 'That's a good question. Until last year, it never occurred to me that I'd ever want to be intimate with a woman. I mean, I know lots of people do while they're experimenting when they're young, but I'd never felt the slightest inclination even then. And when I was with Adam, everything felt perfectly right. It was only Sharon who ever made me feel comfortable in that way. But with Sharon it wasn't just about sex, it was as if we were one mind in two bodies. Oh God, I've just remembered Yoko Ono said that about her and John Lennon. But I know what she meant now.'

'What I find difficult to get my head around,' Jayne says, 'is that she was such a strong woman I'm sure in time she'd have come to terms with being in a wheelchair. Instead, it was that same strength of will that drove her to do what she did. And if even you couldn't talk her out of it, Rosie, I'm sure no-one could.'

'I tried. I offered her everything I had to offer, but it wasn't enough. It was as if someone had taken control – no, sorry, I don't really mean that. I think she was just so angry that she wanted to punish someone, and the only one she could punish was herself.'

'Except that she ended up punishing you as well,' Mary says.

The three fall silent. From the darkness outside, in their rural isolation, the sounds of the natural world filter into the cottage: owls moaning, moths vibrating their wings against the windows, a dog fox barking in the distance. Rosemary suddenly feels dislocated. Jayne and Mary are the best friends she has left, but she no longer knows them. Her surroundings are from another world. She imagines that, if she were to open the door and look outside, she would see that the cottage was adrift in space.

'Are you okay, Rosie? I'm sorry, I know I shouldn't have said that. My usual problem, foot in mouth disease.'

'It's okay. To be honest, I deserve to be punished. I was responsible for her death. I put her in danger. It was all my fault.'

Jayne gets up and stands behind Rosemary and drapes her arms around her neck. Rosemary begins to cry without really understanding why. 'It's okay, Rosie, let it go. It wasn't your fault. Don't ever think that.'

Rosemary takes hold of Jayne's hands and looks at Mary, who is also on the verge of tears, and knows that she will never be able to share with anyone the real cause of her guilt. Sharon rejected her life sentence, took the quick way out, but Rosemary will accept hers and perhaps, in the far distant future, find some way of making atonement. She owes Sharon that much. She squeezes Jayne's hands and allows her head to sink back into her chest.

'You know, Rosie,' Mary says, 'if you feel like you really don't want to be on your own, you're welcome to join us in our room. Just to be with other people, if you like. Whatever gets you through the night, and all that.'

'Thanks. I'll keep that in mind. But I've got a feeling I'm going to have to get used to surviving on my own.'

A few hours later, silence has taken control of the cottage. Rosemary tiptoes into the now-darkened kitchen en route to the fridge, and senses immediately another presence, a benign one.

'Where are you hiding?'

Fearing that to turn on the light would risk destroying the connection, she gropes her way along the back of the chairs until she reaches the far end of the table. The presence is close at hand. There is a stirring from the bed which Jayne and Mary occupy in the room above, then all is quiet once more.

'Lucky I got thirsty when I did.'

The fire has long since died and the night is cold, but even Rosemary's bare feet are protected by a warmth which is localised and, she knows, just for her. She stretches out her hand across the table and closes her eyes, and a tingling passes through her fingers.

Lightning Source UK Ltd.
Milton Keynes UK
UKOW04f0937210116

266845UK00006B/401/P